THE

DEFENSE

THE DEFENSE

STEVE CAVANAGH

FLATIRON BOOKS
NEW YORK

This is a work of fiction. All of the characters, organizations, and events portrayed in this novel are either products of the author's imagination or are used fictitiously.

www.flatironbooks.com

Designed by Steven Seighman

Originally published in paperback in Great Britain by Orion Books, an imprint of The Orion Publishing Group Ltd.

The Library of Congress Cataloging-in-Publication Data is available upon request.

ISBN 978-1-250-08225-1 (hardcover)
ISBN 978-1-250-09071-3 (e-book)

First U.S. Edition: May 2016

10 9 8 7 6 5 4 3 2 1

For Bridie and Sam

"Sentence first—verdict afterwards"
From *Alice's Adventures in Wonderland*, by Lewis Carroll

THE DEFENSE

CHAPTER ONE

I'd grown sloppy. That's what happens when you go straight.

"Do exactly as I tell you or I'll put a bullet in your spine."

The accent was male and Eastern European. I detected no tremors or hints of anxiety in his voice. The tone sounded even and measured. This wasn't a threat; it was a statement of fact. If I didn't cooperate, I would be shot.

I felt the unmistakable electric pressure from a handgun pressed into the small of my back. My first instinct was to lean in to the barrel and spin sharply to my left, turning the shot away from my body. The guy was probably right-handed, which meant he was naturally exposed on his left side. I could throw an elbow through that gap into the guy's face as I turned, giving me enough time to break his wrist and bury the weapon in his forehead. Old instincts, but the guy who could do all of those things wasn't around anymore. I'd buried him along with my past.

Without pressure on the faucet, the patter of water falling on porcelain faded. I felt my fingers shaking as I raised my wet hands in surrender.

"No need for that, Mr. Flynn."

He knew my name. Gripping the sink, I raised my head and looked in the mirror. Never saw this guy before. Tall and slim, he wore a brown overcoat over a charcoal suit. He sported a shaved head, and a facial scar ran vertically from below his left eye to the jawline. Pushing the gun hard into my back, he said, "I'll follow you out of the bathroom. You'll put on your coat. You'll pay for breakfast, and we'll leave together. We're going to talk. If you do as I tell you, you'll be fine. If you don't—you're dead."

Good eye contact. No blushing of the face or neck, no involuntary movement, no tells at all. I knew a hustler when I saw one. I knew the look. I'd worn it long enough. This guy was no hustler. He was a killer. But he was not the first killer to threaten me, and I remembered I got clear last time by thinking, not panicking.

"Let's go," he said.

He stepped back a pace and held up the gun, letting me see it in the mirror. It looked real: a snub-nosed, silver revolver. I knew from the first second the threat was genuine, but seeing the short, evil weapon in the mirror set my skin alive with fear. My chest began to tighten as my heart stepped on the gas. I'd been out of the game too long. I would have to make do with thinking *and* panicking. The revolver disappeared into his coat pocket and he gestured toward the door. The conversation appeared to be over.

"Okay," I said.

Two years of law school, two and a half years clerking for a judge, and almost nine years as a practicing attorney, and all I managed to say was *okay*. I wiped my soapy hands on the back of my pants and ran my fingers through my dirty-blond hair. He followed me out of the bathroom and across the floor of the now-empty diner, where I lifted my coat, put it on, slid five bucks under my coffee cup, and made for the door. The scarred man followed me at a short distance.

Ted's Diner was my favorite place to think. I don't know how many trial strategies I had worked through in those booths, covering the tables with medical records, gunshot wound photos, and coffee-stained legal briefs. In the old days, I wouldn't have eaten breakfast at the same place every day. Way too risky. In my new life, I enjoyed the routine of breakfast at Ted's. I'd relaxed and stopped looking over my shoulder. Too bad. I could've used being on edge that morning: I might have seen him coming.

Walking out of the diner into the heart of the city felt like stepping into a safe place. The sidewalk bustled with the Monday-morning commute, and the pavement felt reassuring under my feet. This guy wasn't going to shoot me in New York City, on Chambers Street, at eight fifteen in the morning in front of thirty witnesses. I stood to the left of the diner, outside an abandoned hardware store. I felt my face reddening with the pinch that November brings to the wind as I wondered what the man wanted. Had I lost a case for him years ago? I certainly couldn't remember him. The scarred man joined me at the boarded-up window of the old store. He stood close so we couldn't be separated by passersby. His face cracked into a long grin, bending the scar that bisected his cheek.

"Open your coat and look inside, Mr. Flynn."

My hands felt awkward and clumsy as I searched my pockets and found nothing. I opened the coat fully. On the inside I saw what looked like a rip, as if the silk lining was coming away from the stitching. It wasn't a rip. It took me a few moments to realize there was a thin black jacket inside my coat, like another layer of lining. I hadn't seen it before. This guy must have slipped the jacket sleeves into my coat when I was in the bathroom. Slipping my hands across my back, I found a Velcro seam for a pocket that sat low down, just above my waist. Pulling it around so I could get a look at it, I tore open the seam, put my hand inside, and felt a loose thread.

I pulled the thread from the hidden pocket. But it wasn't a thread.

It was a wire.

A red wire.

My hands followed it to what felt like a thin plastic box and more wiring, and then to two slim, rectangular bulges in the jacket that sat on either side of my back.

I couldn't breathe.

I was wearing a bomb.

He wasn't going to shoot me on Chambers Street in front of thirty witnesses. He was going to blow me up along with God knew how many victims.

"Don't run, or I detonate the device. Don't try to take it off. Don't attract attention. My name is Arturas." He pronounced it *Ar-toras* through his continuing smile.

I took in a sharp gulp of metallic air and forced myself to breathe it out slowly.

"Take it easy," said Arturas.

"What do you want?" I said.

"My employer hired your firm to represent him. We have unfinished business."

My fear subsided a little: This wasn't about me. It was about my old law firm, and I thought I could palm this guy off on Jack Halloran. "Sorry, pal. It's not my firm anymore. You're talking to the wrong guy. Who do you work for, exactly?"

"I think you know the name. Mr. Volchek."

Oh shit. He was right. I did know the name. Olek Volchek was head of the Russian mob. My former partner, Jack Halloran, had agreed to represent Volchek a month before Jack and I split. When Jack took on the case, Volchek awaited trial for murder—a gangland hit. I never got to look at the papers in the case or even meet Volchek. I'd devoted that entire month to defending Ted Berkley, a stockbroker, on an alleged attempted kidnapping charge—the case that broke me, completely. After the fallout from that case, I'd lost my family and then lost myself in a whiskey bottle. I got out of the law almost a year ago with what was left of my soul, and Jack had been only too happy to take my law firm. I hadn't set foot in a courtroom since the jury delivered their verdict in the Berkley case, and I hadn't planned on returning to the law anytime soon.

Jack was a different story. He had gambling problems. I'd heard recently he planned to sell the firm and leave town. He probably split and took Volchek's retainer with him. If the Russian mob couldn't find Jack, they would come looking for me—for a refund. Cue the strong-arm routine. With a bomb on my back, what does it matter that I'm bankrupt? I'll get him the damn money. It was going to be okay. I could pay this guy. He wasn't a terrorist. He was a mobster. Mobsters don't blow people up who owe them money. They just get paid.

"Look, you need Jack Halloran. I've never met Mr. Volchek. Jack and I are no longer partners. But it's okay; if you want your retainer refunded, I'll gladly write you a check right now."

Whether or not the check would cash was another issue. I had just over six hundred dollars in my account, my rent was overdue, and I had rehab bills I couldn't pay and no income. The rehab fees were the main problem, but with the amount of whiskey I was putting away, I would've died if I hadn't checked myself into a clinic and gotten help. In counseling, I'd realized that there was no amount of Jack Daniel's that could've burned away the memory of what happened in the Berkley case. In the end, I'd gotten clean of booze and I was two weeks away from securing a final agreement with my creditors. Two weeks away from starting all over again. If the Russian wanted more than a few hundred bucks, I was screwed—big-time.

"Mr. Volchek does not want his money. You can keep it. After all, you'll earn it," said Arturas.

"What do you mean *earn* it? Look, I'm not in practice anymore. I haven't practiced law for almost a year. I can't help you. I'll refund Mr. Volchek's retainer. Please just let me take this off," I said, gripping the jacket, ready to heave it off.

"No," he said. "You don't understand, lawyer. Mr. Volchek wants you to do something for him. You *will* be his lawyer and he will pay you. You'll do it. Or you will do no more in this life."

My throat tightened in panic as I tried to speak. This didn't make any sense. I felt sure that Jack would've told Volchek that I'd quit, that I couldn't hack it anymore. A white stretch limousine pulled up at the curb. The shining wax finish carried my distorted reflection. The rear passenger door opened from the inside, sweeping away my image. Arturas stood beside the open door and nodded at me to get in. I tried to settle myself; I deepened my breathing, slowed my heart, and tried desperately not to puke. The limo's heavily tinted windows spread an intense darkness over the interior, as if it were brimming with black water.

For a moment everything became remarkably still—it was just me and that open door. If I ran, I wouldn't get far—not an option. If I got into the car and stayed close to Arturas, I knew he couldn't detonate the device. At that moment, I cursed myself for not keeping my skills sharp. The same skills that had kept me alive on the streets for all those years, the same skills that helped me to con million-dollar-salary defense attorneys before I'd even been to law school, the same skills that would have spotted this guy before he got within ten feet of me.

I made my decision and climbed into the rabbit hole.

CHAPTER TWO

I felt the bomb pressing into my flesh as soon as I sat down.

There were four men in the back of the limo, including Arturas, who followed me inside, closed the door behind him, and sat on my left, still wearing that disconcerting smile. I could hear the engine purring, but we remained parked. The smell of cigar smoke and new leather filled my nose. More tinted glass separated the luxurious rear of the vehicle from the driver.

A white leather gym bag sat on the floor.

To my right, two men in dark overcoats filled a seat built for six people. They were freakishly large, like characters from a fairy tale. One had long blond hair tied up in a ponytail. The other had short brown hair and looked truly enormous. His head was the size of a basketball, and he easily dwarfed the big blond guy next to him, but it was his expression that frightened me the most. His face appeared to be bereft of all emotion, of all feeling, the cold, dreaded look of a half-dead soul. As a hustler, you rely on being able to spot a "tell." You rely on your ability to manipulate emotions and natural human responses, but there's one class of individual who's immune to the usual moves, and every hustler can spot them and knows to stay the hell away from them—psychopaths. The giant with the brown hair looked like a textbook psycho.

The guy opposite me was Olek Volchek. He wore a black suit over a white shirt, which lay open at the neck. Graying stubble covered his face, and the same coloring ran into his hair. He might've looked handsome if it weren't for a simmering malevolence in his eyes that seemed to temper his good looks. I recognized him from newspapers and TV; he was a mob boss, a killer, a drug dealer.

But he sure as hell wasn't going to be my client.

I'd dealt with people like Volchek my whole life, as friends, enemies, and even as clients. Didn't matter if they were from the Bronx, Compton, Miami, or Little Odessa. Men like this respected only one thing—strength. As shit scared as I was, I couldn't let him see it or I was a dead man.

"I don't work for people who threaten me," I said.

"You don't have choice, Mr. Flynn. I'm your new client," said Volchek. He spoke with a thick Russian accent in slightly broken English.

"Sometimes, as you Americans say, shit happens. You can blame Jack Halloran if you like," said Volchek.

"I blame him for most things these days. Why isn't he representing you? Where is he?"

Volchek glanced at Arturas, and for a second he mirrored Arturas's indelible smile before he looked back at me and said, "When Jack Halloran took on my case, he said it was impossible to defend. I knew this already. I had four different law firms look at the case before Jack. Still, Jack could do things other lawyers could not. So I paid him and I gave Jack a job. Unfortunately, Jack couldn't hold up his end of the bargain."

"Too bad. Nothing to do with me," I said, struggling to keep the nerves from my voice.

"That's where you're wrong," said Volchek. From a gold case beside him, he removed a small chocolate-colored cigar, bit it, lit it, and said, "Two years ago I ordered a hit on a man named Mario Geraldo. I asked Little Benny to do it for me. Benny did his job. Then he got caught and he talked to FBI. Benny will give evidence at my trial that I ordered the hit. All the lawyers I spoke to said that Benny would be the prosecution's star witness. His evidence will convict me. No doubt about it."

My jaw was clenched so tight it began to ache.

"Benny is in FBI custody. He's well protected and well hidden. Even my contacts can't find him. You're the only one who can get close to him because you are my lawyer."

He lowered his voice and said, "Before you cross-examine Benny, you will take off your jacket and, when the court is empty, we will tape the bomb underneath the chair in the witness box. Benny takes his seat, and we detonate the device. No more Benny, no more case, no more problem. *You* are the bomber, Mr. Flynn. You'll go to prison. The prosecutor won't have enough evidence for a retrial, and I will go free."

"You're one crazy son of a bitch," I said.

Volchek didn't react at first. He didn't fly into a rage or threaten me. He just sat there for a moment before tilting his head as if he were considering his options. There was no sound, other than my heart jackknifing in my chest, and I wondered if I'd just earned myself a bullet. I couldn't take my eyes from Volchek, but I could feel the others staring at me, almost quizzically, like I was a guy who'd just put his hand into a snake pit.

"Have a look at this before you decide," said Volchek, nodding to Arturas.

Arturas picked up the white gym bag and opened it.

Jack's head was inside.

My stomach cramped. My mouth filled with saliva. I retched, covered my mouth, and coughed. I spat and fought to hold on to my senses and gripped the seat beneath me until I could feel my fingernails scraping the leather. All traces of a calm facade left me completely.

"We thought Jack could do it. We were wrong. But we take no chances with you, Mr. Flynn," said Volchek, leaning forward. "We have your daughter."

Time, breath, blood, motion—everything stopped.

"If you so much as touch her . . ."

He took a cell phone from his pants pocket and flipped it around so that I could see the screen. Amy stood on a dark street corner in front of a newsstand. My little girl. She was only ten years old. I saw her standing somewhere in New York, hugging herself against the cold and staring warily at the camera. Behind her, the news banner carried the headline on the cargo ship that sank on the Hudson on Saturday night.

I hadn't realized how much I was sweating; my shirt was soaked, along with my face and hair, but I was no longer afraid. I no longer cared about the bomb, the gun, or the pair of mute giants staring at me with their dead eyes.

"Give her back to me and I'll let you live," I said.

This produced laughter from Volchek and his crew. They knew me as

Eddie Flynn, the lawyer; they didn't know the old Eddie Flynn: the hustler, the backstreet fighter, the con artist. In truth, I'd almost forgotten him myself.

Volchek inclined his head before speaking. He seemed to be considering each word carefully. "You are in no position to make threats. Be smart. Nothing will happen to your daughter if you do as I tell you," said Volchek.

"Let her go. I will do nothing until I know she's safe. Kill me if you want. In fact, you'd better kill me, because I'll go to my grave with my thumbs in your eyes if you don't let her go now."

Volchek took a pull from his cigar, opened his mouth, and for a moment, he let the smoke play over his fat lips, savoring the flavor.

"Your daughter is safe. We picked her up outside her school yesterday while she waited for the bus to take her on her field trip. She thinks the men looking after her are security guards, working for you. You've had death threats in the past, and she knows this. Your ex-wife thinks Amy is on the school trip, hiking in Long Island. The school believes she's with you. She won't be missed for a day or two. If you refuse to carry out your instructions, I will kill her. But that will be a relief. Your daughter will suffer if you don't cooperate. Some of my men . . ."

He trailed off deliberately, pretending to search for the right words, letting my imagination build me a nightmare. My whole body tensed, as if preparing to repel a physical attack. I felt adrenaline washing my system with rage.

"Well, some of my men have *unusual appetites* for pretty little girls."

I lunged at Volchek. Out of my seat before I knew what I was doing. Cramped, no purchase, ducking my head, but fired up, I still managed a decent right cross that connected sharply with Volchek's left cheek. The cigar went flying out of his filthy mouth. My left hand drew back, and I steadied myself before I punched him in the throat.

Before I could throw that second punch, a huge hand grabbed me and picked me clean off the floor. Turning, I saw the giant psycho had taken hold of me. He was about to put me on my ass like an errant child when my old habits took over. My right hand grabbed for his face, hard, driving my fingernails into his fleshy forehead. It was an automatic, unconscious response and distraction. My left hand slipped into the big guy's jacket, and I lifted his wallet. It took half a second. Fast and soft. I hadn't lost much speed over the years after all. It was a clean lift. The big guy hadn't noticed; he was too busy trying to take my head off. As I slipped the wallet into my pocket, a fist the size of a dinner plate appeared in front of my face. I turned away from the blow and felt the impact burn across the back of my skull. I fell, smacking my head on the limo floor.

I stayed on the deck and felt the pain roaring into my head. It was my first pocket dip in fifteen years. It was instinct; it just happened because that's who I was.

No—it's who I *am*.

The skills and techniques that I'd developed and used as a successful con artist—distraction, misdirection, persuasion, suggestion, the load, the switch, the drop—I'd used these methods just as much on the street all those years ago as I had for the past nine years in the courtroom. I hadn't really changed. I'd just changed the con.

My eyes and my mind closed as I gave in to the thickening dark.

CHAPTER THREE

I woke up on leather seats, the back of my head aching. One of the gorillas held a bag of ice on my neck. It was the big blond guy who looked as if he'd just lost his spot in a Swedish heavy metal band. The sweet, acrid smell from Volchek's cigar made me feel sick. I figured that I'd been picked up from the floor of the limo and dumped in the seat. My eyes burned a little from the smoke, but it took me only a second to realize the giant psycho who'd knocked me out was no longer in the car. I took the ice pack and dropped it to the floor.

"We're at the courthouse now," said Arturas.

I sat up.

"Why are we at the courthouse?" I said.

"Because Mr. Volchek's trial starts this morning," said Arturas.

"This morning?" I said. I summoned the image of my daughter on Volchek's phone and felt the anger building more pain behind my neck and iron tension in my muscles.

"Trial starts in an hour. Before you go, we need to know that you can do this. Otherwise we kill you now and your family later," said Arturas. He took out his revolver and placed it on his folded knee.

Arturas handed me an expensive-looking glass with a splash of urine-colored liquid swilling within. It smelled like bourbon. I downed it and felt that familiar, sour heat. It was my first drink since I'd checked out of rehab for alcohol addiction. For a second I thought about how much money I still owed the clinic, then dismissed the thought. There was a time and place for falling off the wagon, and right then seemed as good a time as any. I held my hand out for another, and Arturas spilled more of the liquor into my glass from a matching crystal decanter. I swallowed it fast and enjoyed the burn. A shudder ripped through my body from the strong alcohol, and I shook my head. I was trying to clear my mind, like shaking a Magic 8-Ball; I didn't come up with any answers.

"Where's my daughter?"

"Safe and happy for now," said Arturas. He poured me another drink. I tucked that shot away and started thinking.

"Why'd you kill Jack?" I asked.

Volchek nodded to Arturas; he was happy to let him fill in the details.

"All of the lawyers we saw said Benny's evidence would convict Volchek. So it made sense just to kill Benny; it's a simple solution, but we can't find him. We . . . *persuaded* Jack to wear the jacket, so we could kill Benny when he got to court. But he couldn't do it."

I wondered what kind of persuasion they'd tried on Jack. No doubt he would've been tortured. He was an asshole and a gambling addict, but he had been my partner, and my feelings toward him softened a little then. Whatever Jack used to be, he wasn't cut out to carry a bomb. Most days he was lucky if he could carry his briefcase without tripping over his own feet. They must have worked him pretty hard.

"Why Jack?" I asked.

"It had to be a certain kind of lawyer. We know you and Jack started that firm with loan-shark money. Jack had a bad reputation for lying and not paying his debts. He needed money; clients started leaving the firm after you quit, and we needed someone who could carry the bomb through security. Security at the courthouse is good. It will be better today. We couldn't smuggle a bomb in there; everybody's searched going in, body scanned and then searched again—everyone except you and Jack. We know this. We watched both of you walk into that court building every day for months. Neither of you were ever searched. The security guards let you two straight through—like old friends. We told Jack what we told you; plant the bomb and take the hit."

Arturas leaned back in his seat and shot a quick glance at Volchek. It was almost like they were a tag team; Arturas had laid out the facts, straight and clear. After that, he seemed happy to let his boss handle the intimidation.

"Jack sat where you are now, Mr. Flynn, just three days ago. He wore the same jacket as you, with the same bomb inside. We told him what we told you. I opened the door of this car and told him to go and do his job," said Volchek, lowering his eyes to the floor.

His head came up through the pall of smoke, framing his face in the gray mist as he continued. "Jack froze. He shook like a . . . what you call it? Epileptic? Like he was having a fit. He had piss running down his leg. We closed the door and took him to our place."

He sucked on the cigar again and watched the warm glow at the tip.

"I tied him to a chair. I tell him I will kill his sister if he doesn't do as I ask. Victor here"—he pointed at the blond guy—"brings the sister to us. I take my knife and I cut her face in front of him. '*Will you do it now?*' I ask him. Nothing. I go to work on her with my knife and he just sits there."

I could almost feel a clamp coming down on my chest. This monster had my little girl. A noise startled me slightly; my knuckle joints cracking with the tension in my fist. In my other hand I held the empty bourbon glass, and I thought about punching it into Volchek's eye before deciding against it. Given that my last attempt at taking him on had gone so badly, I didn't want to take another shot.

Not yet.

"I realize then that I could not rely on Jack. Before I kill him, I gave the sister some satisfaction. I hand her my knife. I helped her cut him, cut him bad."

A hellish fire kindled in his gaze, bathing his eyes in light. He appeared to find the memory delicious.

"Jack was in over his head, so I cut it off and gave it to his sister before I killed her, too. She was brave. Not like her brother."

I looked at the gym bag on the floor, now mercifully closed, and thought of Jack. My opinion swung back to hating him. If I could, I would have kicked his severed head into the Hudson. Just plain kicked the shit out of it. Jack deserved to lie at the bottom of the river next to that sunken ship.

"We don't have time for a dry run for you," continued Arturas. "You take the bomb in now, Mr. Flynn. Calm yourself. Remember your daughter. You get the bomb in—you are a step closer to her. If you get caught, you go to jail for trying to blow up a public building. You'd get life, no parole. What do you think?"

I thought he was right. People who try to blow up public buildings in this city don't usually fare too well in sentencing. I would be in the running for life imprisonment without doubt. The only saving grace would be that I'd planted the bomb because they'd threatened my daughter. Extreme duress isn't an absolute defense, but I might avoid life.

That sickening smile spread over Arturas's face once again. I almost got the impression that he could guess what I was thinking. Volchek stubbed out his cigar and peered at me through the dying smoke. I thought that they were both intelligent, ruthless men, but each had a different kind of intelligence. Arturas seemed to be an adviser, the man with the plan who thought through the eventualities and carefully weighed up the risks, a calculated thinker. His boss was way different. Volchek's movements were slow and graceful, like a big cat sitting in the long grass, stalking its prey; his intellect was primal, instinctual—almost feral. My instinct told me that these men weren't going to let me live to tell my tale, no matter what happened.

"I haven't set foot in that building in a long time. What makes you think I'm going to be able to just walk in today without being searched?"

"You know the security guards and, more important, they know you," said Arturas. His voice began rising, and he sat forward to hammer home his point. "We've been watching the courthouse for a long time, lawyer. I've spent nearly two years planning this to the last detail. Whoever carries the bomb has to be someone the guards trust, someone they least expect. There is no other way of getting a bomb into that building. I've watched you myself, running through the doors late for court, waving at the guard on the desk when you jog through the sensors and set off the alarm. They ignore it and wave you on. You talk to the guards. They know you. They even take your calls for you."

I didn't carry a cell phone. I never liked the thought of anyone being able to pin my location to the nearest cell phone tower. It was a hangover from the old days that I'd never shaken off despite Jack having bought me more than one cell phone. I lost them all. When I was practicing, I'd be in the courthouse most of the day. If anyone needed me urgently, they rang the pay phone in the lobby. Usually somebody in security had a good idea what court I'd be in and they'd come get me. A couple of bottles of whiskey for the security guys at Christmas and a basket each at Thanksgiving was a small price to pay for that kind of help.

My head began to clear a little.

"Why can't you kill this guy some other way? A sniper could take him out as he travels to court."

Arturas nodded. "I've thought about that. I've thought over every possibility. We don't know where he is or how he will get to court. This is the only way. We had lots of law firms look at the case. Those big firms practiced all over the city. You and Jack had nearly all of your cases here, in Chambers Street. You got to know the staff. Those other lawyers charge nine hundred dollars an hour. You think they have time to talk to a security guard? No. I knew this had to be the way the very first time I saw you and Jack run through security, setting off the alarm, and no one batted an eyelid. You showed me the way."

Arturas was the brains here. This was clearly his plan. He seemed somehow detached, coldly rational, and I imagined he'd be that way even when it came to pulling the trigger. The opposite could've been said for Volchek. Even though he appeared calm after I'd hit him, I could sense that a monster lay behind his restrained pose, pawing at the surface, ready to break free at any moment.

I put my head in my hands and breathed deeply and slowly.

"There is one more thing, Mr. Flynn," said Volchek. "You should know that we are fighters. We are proud. We are Bratva: This means *brotherhood*. I trust this man." He put his hand on Arturas's shoulder. "But much can go wrong. You must get the jacket inside. Your daughter's death is one phone call away. You will get in. I know this. I can see a fighter in you, too. Do not fight me."

He paused to light another cigar.

"Arturas and I came here twenty years ago with nothing. We spilled much blood to get where we are, and we will not run without a fight. But we are not stupid men. The trial is scheduled to last for three days. We are giving you two days. We cannot risk more. Two days to get Little Benny onto that seat so we can kill him. If he is not dead before four o'clock tomorrow, I have no choice. I will have to run. The longer the case goes on, the more likely the prosecutor will try to revoke my bail. A nine-hundred-dollar-an-hour lawyer told me that. You are smart enough to know he is right."

I'd seen that happen before. Most prosecutors don't have their most damaging piece of evidence at the arraignment when the accused applies for bail. DNA and expert evidence takes time to prepare. But by the time the case comes up for trial, the prosecution have all their ducks in a row, and if the prosecutor gets a good run on the evidence, they will make an application to the judge to revoke the defendant's bail. That usually seals the defendant's fate. All it takes is a small, yet deliberate, delay by the custody officer for the jury to see the defendant in handcuffs. A second's glance at those bracelets and it's all over—the jury will convict every time.

I nodded at Volchek. He knew that I was experienced enough to know prosecution tactics, so there was no point in denying it.

As Volchek delivered his ultimatum, he struggled to hide the brutality of his true nature from his voice.

"The court has my passport as part of my bail terms. I get merchandise flown in from Russia three times a year, by private plane to a commercial airstrip not far from here. That plane arrives tomorrow at three o'clock and leaves at six. If Benny is still alive at four—you've run out of time. I will need to leave the court at four to make the plane. That plane is my last chance to get out of the United States. I want to stay. I want to fight. Little Benny must die before four tomorrow, or I will kill you and your daughter. Know this as a solemn vow."

The whiskey glass shattered in my hand.

I felt like I was falling. My body slumped, my jaw trembled, and I shut my teeth tight to keep them from rattling. Blood dripped from a cut in my palm, but I couldn't feel the pain. I couldn't move. I couldn't think. My breath escaped in a short, low moan. If anything happened to Amy, the pain would kill me. I could feel my brain, my muscles, my heart, burning with the mere thought of that agony. My wife, Christine, had put up with a lot from me: the long hours in the office, the three a.m. phone calls from police precincts all over the city because the cops arrested one of my clients, the missed dinner dates and excuses I made for myself that I was doing it all for her and Amy. When I hit the bottle a year ago, she threw me out. I'd lost one of the best things I'd ever had. If I lost our daughter? I couldn't even begin to contemplate that horror.

From somewhere I heard the voice of my father, the man who'd taught me the grift, the man who'd told me what to do if I ever got made during a con—*hold it together no matter what.*

I closed my eyes and silently prayed, *Dear God, help me. Please help my little girl. I love her so much.*

I wiped my eyes before the tears came, sniffed, and scrolled though the menu on my digital watch, past my alarm call, and on to the timer. I set it to countdown.

"You need to make a decision, lawyer," said Arturas, fingering the revolver.

"I'll do it. Just don't hurt Amy. She's only ten," I said.

Volchek and Arturas looked at each other.

"Good," said Arturas. "Go now and wait for me in lobby after you get through security."

"You mean *if* I get through."

"Should I make your daughter pray for you?" said Volchek.

I didn't answer. I got out of the limo alone and saw Arturas looking up at me from the car as I stepped to the sidewalk.

"Remember. We are watching you, and men are watching your daughter," Arturas said.

I nodded and said, "I won't fight you."

I lied.

Just as they'd lied to me. No matter what they said, no matter what they promised me, come four o'clock tomorrow, even if Benny should be reduced to a stain on the courthouse ceiling by then, they weren't letting Amy go. They were going to kill me and my little girl.

I had thirty-one hours.

Thirty-one hours to double-cross the Russian Mafia and steal my daughter back. And I had no clue how to do it.

I folded my coat around me. Buttoned it, flipped the collar, and turned toward the courthouse. My father's voice still played softly in my ear—*hold it together.* My hand had stopped bleeding. It felt even colder now; my breath seemed to freeze and fall in front of me. As that cold mist cleared, I saw something that I'd never seen before in nine years of daily practice at that courthouse—a line of maybe forty people comprised of reporters, lawyers, witnesses, defendants, and TV crews—all of them waiting to get though security.

CHAPTER FOUR

There's a strange electric sensation at the beginning of a major trial. As I joined the back of the line, I felt the excitement rising off the crowd, like heat shimmering on a stretch of distant Texan blacktop. Some of the crowd carried the early edition of the *New York Times*. I could see the front page in the arms of the man in front. The paper led with Volchek's picture and the headline RUSSIAN MOB TRIAL BEGINS. The guy in front of me looked like a crime reporter. Probably freelance or attached to a rag. You could spot the type a mile away: bad suit, bad haircut, and nicotine stains on his fingers revealing him as a chain smoker. I ducked my head into the folds of my overcoat and tried not to look at him.

The New York Chambers Street Court building was an old Victorian Gothic-style courthouse on steroids. Twenty-one courts spread over nineteen floors.

I counted twenty people in the line ahead of me.

The courthouse greeted visitors with a fifty-foot-wide stone staircase leading up to a row of Corinthian columns that sheltered a run-down entrance hall last decorated in the sixties. More people came and stood behind me as we slowly shuffled up the steps. I chanced an upward glance at the building. Statues, busts of former presidents and the first justices of New York, sat along the ledges, but time and weather were taking their toll on the old place.

As I climbed the last step, I felt sweat running down my cheek. My shirt clung to my back and made me even more aware of the bomb, which felt warm and alien. I counted only twelve people in front of me.

Getting into the courthouse without being searched seemed to be even more of a remote possibility than it had first appeared in the limo. Without consciously removing it from my pocket, I suddenly became aware of my pen in my right hand. Trudging slowly toward the entrance, I rolled my pen around my fingers absently. I'd often found myself doing this without even realizing. Somehow it helped me think. The pen had been a gift from Amy.

At the time it had felt like a parting gift. When I'd been drinking, I'd rarely made it home. About a week before Father's Day, Christine decided I should move out and that Amy had a right to know. Christine told me that she didn't recognize me anymore and that it was better for Amy not to have to watch me decline any further.

Kids are smart, and Amy is smarter than most. She knew something bad was on the horizon when she saw both of us standing at her bedroom door. She'd tied up her long blond hair so that it wouldn't get in her eyes while she worked on her computer. As usual, she wore her favorite denim jacket over her jammies; if she wasn't sleeping or in school, she wore that jacket, covered in pins with smiley faces and rock band logos. She'd saved her weekly allowance for a whole month to buy it in a cheap clothing store, then set about decorating it in her own style. I stared at her for a while—we both did. Before we could say anything, she simply put aside her laptop and cried. We didn't need to tell her anything. She saw it coming a mile away. She asked the usual questions: How long would I be gone? Is it permanent? Why can't we just get along? I didn't have any answers. I just sat on the bed beside her, hugged her, and tried to be strong. Instead, I felt ashamed. Glancing at her laptop, I noticed she was looking at a website that sold engraved pens and had selected one with the inscription WORLD'S BEST DAD.

The pen stopped in my hand, the same pen Amy gave me just after I moved out of the house. I glanced down at the single word engraved on the polished aluminum shaft—DAD. She nearly broke my heart with that one. I stuffed the pen into my hip pocket and checked the line.

Ten people in front of me.

A whir from heavy machinery drew my attention skyward. The mayor had authorized extensive, external building restorations for the courthouse, and a huge suspended scaffold stage hung from the roof, cradling the stone workers about four floors from the top. It was difficult to make out the workmen from the ground, but even from this distance I could see the stage gently swaying in the wind. They were blasting the dirt from the masonry and restoring the broken ornamental work. Developers wanted to pull down the courthouse and move justice to cheaper accommodations. With the mayor being a former lawyer, it hadn't taken long for a petition to get the backing of influential councilmen. The courthouse could stay. They would restore the exterior and continue to let the interior rot away. New York was like that sometimes, content to let the polished veneer hide the rotting corpse in the basement. The reality was that Chambers Street Courthouse had historical value, as it was the first night court ever to be established in the United States. Night court is the most important court in the city. Every defendant has to be brought before a judge within twenty-four hours of being charged. With three hundred arrests per day in Manhattan alone, that meant an extra court sitting from five p.m. through to one a.m. When the recession really took hold, crime in the city went up. Now Chambers Street ran a criminal court twenty-four hours a day. Justice didn't sleep in this courthouse, and it hadn't closed its doors in the last two years.

As the line moved slowly forward, I began to hear the occasional *beep* from the security equipment. Luckily, I knew the security guards by name. One of the secrets to successful litigation was getting to know the court staff—all of them. You never know when you'll need a favor—an urgent fax picked up, a wayward client located, change for the coffee machine, or in my case, somebody to come get me when an urgent call came through to the pay phone in the lobby.

Eight people ahead of me.

I looked around the reporter's shoulder to get a better view of the entrance hall security. Barry and Edgar were handling the door. Security in most New York courts is handled by security officers who are really cops in all but name. They carry guns and wear a uniform. They can arrest you, restrain you, and if you are enough of a threat, they can put you down, permanently.

Barry stood behind the bag scanner, handling the trays, collecting cell phones, keys, wallets, and bags and putting them through the X-ray scanner while people stepped underneath the arch of the walk-through metal detector and hoped not to *beep*. Edgar patted down, removed forgotten offending items found on a person, and then resubmitted them through the gray arch until he was satisfied.

Beyond those guys, I saw a young, fair-haired guard I didn't recognize. Behind him I saw a fourth guard. He stood ten feet back from the security entrance with his hands resting on his gun belt, thumbs tucked behind the leather, his arms hanging over his bloated stomach. It wasn't unusual to have an extra security officer in the lobby as a backup. I couldn't place this guy; he had a mustache and small, piglike black eyes. Although I couldn't remember seeing him before, I decided that I must have met him because he clearly recognized me. Barry, Edgar, and the new kid were concentrating on checking those people at the head of the line. The fat guard never took his eyes off me.

Six people between me and the security check.

I brushed sweat out of my eyes.

If I waited in line, I would be put through the same procedure as everyone else. I tried to recall how I usually acted. For me, entering this building had been like brushing my teeth; I had done it every morning, but I couldn't remember a single thing about it. Did I just rock in past the security check? Did I wait like everyone else and then get waved through? As I stood in the line, with hands trembling and my mouth dry and bitter, I was close to panic. I couldn't remember any single occasion of having walked through those doors.

Only four in front.

The bomb felt bigger and heavier with every step. The fat guard was still staring at me. Maybe I was giving off all the warning signals that these guys were trained to look out for. Since 9/11, everyone who's even remotely involved in law enforcement gets trained on how to recognize a potential terrorist threat.

I thought of Amy wiping her tears on her jammies, begging me not to leave.

No. I was through letting down my daughter. I made up my mind instantly. Terrorists don't bump the line. They wait. They want to blend in and look inconspicuous. I decided to be a brash, arrogant dick and be as loud and obnoxious as possible in the hope the fat guard thought I was just a jerk, not a potential bomber.

People called after me as I moved past them. I heard the reporter mutter, "Asshole." My heart rate picked up its pace again, faster and faster the closer I got to the head of the line.

"Hey, Barry. Let me buzz in real quick. I'm late for my big comeback," I said as I moved through the metal detector, causing a really loud *beep*. It was probably just as loud for everyone, but it seemed deafening to me. I switched my gaze to the fat guard. He hadn't moved. He just stared. Edgar, on the other hand, was focused on searching a man at the head of the line.

"Eddie!" said Barry. He got up out of his seat at the scanner screen and shuffled around the machine. "I need to see you for a second."

I quickened my pace and moved for the hall, but the young, blond guard put his hands up to bar my way. He kept his hands there, in a crucifix position, and it took me a second to realize he wanted me to adopt the same position—so he could search me. I kept my hands low.

The fat guard started forward. Had I been made?

I thought about making a run for it. Push everyone out of the way and dart back out past the crowd. Behind me, a huge, bearded guy stood in the doorway, blocking out everything including most of the daylight. No way past him. I fought down the urge to run, and my legs started to shake.

"Hey, kid, usually you have to buy me dinner first," I said.

"Just hold up your hands, sir. I need to do a quick search."

"Look, kid, I have to go. I've never met you before, but trust me, I practically lived here for about ten years. I'm a lawyer. Ask Barry," I said as I tried to move past him.

His open palm hovered inches above the butt of his Beretta, and his fingers flexed like a bad actor in an old Western.

I stopped dead.

"What? You gonna ask me to draw, cowboy?"

I could feel people behind me getting out of the way. It was all going to be over in a heartbeat, thanks to a walking doughnut shop and one stupid kid who just wanted to do his job.

"Hank, let Eddie through," Barry said, coming to my rescue.

Hank dropped his arms, rolled his eyes, and stepped to the side. The fat guard stopped and folded his hands across his stomach.

Barry waved a finger at me, chuckled, and said, "That bastard Saint Christopher will end up earning you a cavity search one of these days."

How the hell had I forgotten that? I thought. Popping open an extra button on my shirt, I drew out the silver chain. I laughed nervously before I swung the white-gold Saint Christopher medal at Barry.

It all came back to me.

When I first started out in the law and began representing clients in this courthouse, I set off the alarm every day. Barry, Edgar, and others would search me, find nothing, and then send me through the scanner again, only to hear the same *beep*. That medal had been around my neck since I was a teenager. I never took it off; it was like an extra limb. I didn't think about it. While the guards asked me if I had a steel plate in my leg and I took off most of my clothes and they scratched their heads in disbelief at why I was still beeping, a line would begin to build up behind me. It was Barry, one wet Wednesday morning, who finally found the chain. He told all the security guards about it. Looking back, I couldn't remember being searched after that. If I beeped, I walked on, and if a guard bothered to get out of his seat to search me, I would take out my chain and wave it at him as I went by. Even after 9/11 I wasn't searched. By then I was a known face; I was there every day. Searching me would be like searching the judges. I'd even represented a couple of the guards. They began to see me as a fixture in the court, as a friend. There was no need to search a friend. It must have been the adrenaline, the shock of my situation hitting me, or the booze or the knock on the head from the big Russian, but for some reason, I hadn't remembered anything about the medal until Barry had mentioned it.

"Don't you know who this guy is?" said Barry. "This is Mr. Eddie Flynn. I forget you haven't been here that long. This guy's the best lawyer in New York. You look after him and he'll look after you. He needs anything, you call me."

Reluctantly, Hank nodded and turned to the person behind me to call them through the metal detector. Barry was probably busting this kid's balls every minute of every shift.

I watched the fat guard turn and walk away.

That was close, far too goddamn close.

"Barry, I really got to go, man. I'm so late. I'm in the mob trial starting this morning, and I don't even know what court I'm supposed to be in."

"I didn't know you were representing that scumbag. You're in luck anyways: Judge Pike is hearing that case, and she's still having breakfast. Edgar and I have to go get her in fifteen minutes. Sorry about the kid. Been trying to teach him something, but he's too stupid to learn. Come on, just over here. It won't take a sec."

Looking around, I couldn't see anyone from Volchek's crew in the line. But they could have other eyes I hadn't spotted yet. My ears rang with the sound of my pulse. I didn't know what Barry wanted. *What if he had a whiff of something from Jack? What if the Russians saw me in whispered conversation with Barry?*

I had to talk to him. He would know something was up if I didn't.

"Sure," I said, my head spinning in all directions as we walked to the corner of the lobby. Barry gestured for me to come in close.

"It's Terry," said Barry. "He meant to speak to you about his RSI case." I thanked God silently. Barry wanted to catch a freebie for his pal. I liked Barry. He was in his sixties and close to retirement, an ex-cop who just wanted to sit behind an X-ray machine until he finished his shift and then hit the bar.

"Terry's with Hollinger and Dunne, and they're costing him a fortune. I told him to go see you at the start of all this, but he wanted to go with the union lawyer. I couldn't talk him out of it. They've taken sixty grand already, and he's only seen one doctor. Could you take a look at his case file?"

At that moment I would have given Terry a kiss and a seven-course meal at the Ritz if it got me away from security, never mind a free ride on a repetitive strain injury case.

"Tell him I'll represent him for free," I said.

Barry smiled. "I'll tell him, all right. I'll call him right now. He's up on twelve."

"Look, I really gotta split, Barry."

"No problem. And thanks. I'm gonna tell him right now. He won't friggin' believe it."

I got out from under Barry's spell quicker than I'd hoped, and he sprang back to his seat behind the scanner.

I was *in*.

Turning, I put my back to the cool marble and felt the bomb clinging to my spine as I took in the line of people pouring through the entrance.

My watch read nine thirty. We had maybe a half hour before the trial began.

Arturas came through security and then hefted a large, Samsonite suitcase off the rollers after it had been through the X-ray scanner. He put it down on the floor and wheeled it behind him as he came over.

"Well done," he said.

I said nothing. He reached behind me and pressed the elevator button.

The elevator doors opened, and I pressed the button for the fourteenth floor, which housed court sixteen. Arturas pressed the top floor, floor nineteen.

"We're in court sixteen. It's on the fourteenth floor," I said.

"We have a room upstairs. You need to change for court," said Arturas.

The doors closed, and I heard the counterweight take off as we began to slowly ascend.

CHAPTER FIVE

As I rode the elevator to the top floor, I couldn't help but think about the old courthouse that had shaped so much of my life. The Chambers Street Courthouse had made me and broke me. Old-timers who hustled plea bargains in the lower courts called it the "Dracula Hotel," but no one was really sure why. Some said it was because of a long-serving judge who bore a striking resemblance to Bela Lugosi. For me, this courthouse had *actually* served as my hotel for the last six months of my law practice. Jack Halloran and I were trying desperately to fight off the recession and capitalize on the rising crime rate in the city. It could have been a gold mine for the right set of criminal attorneys. So we hit the criminal courts hard. We handled our cases during the day, then hung out and hustled the new arrests at night court. Most defendants didn't have a lawyer at night court because most law offices were closed, and there were only a limited number of reliable criminal law practices that carried a twenty-four-hour emergency service.

We worked our regular nine-to-five and then split the shifts; on Monday I would do the first court session of five thirty to one a.m.; then Jack took the graveyard shift. We'd swap shifts the next day and so on. By the time I wrapped up a case at, say, three a.m. or sometimes five a.m., there would be little point in me going home, so I'd put my head down in a conference room, or sometimes, if the other lawyers got there first to speak to their clients or get some shut-eye themselves, some of the clerks let me doze in their colleague's office. Or I might have had a drink with Judge Harry Ford before falling asleep on the couch in his chambers. The only good thing about the Dracula Hotel was that it was free.

The old courthouse was due a health check in the next six months. The money City Hall had spent on refurbishing the outer shell was being reported as wasteful by city management. Most of the upper floors were unoccupied apart from old filing cabinets and furniture that wasn't worth saving. A lot of the support staff had relocated to the new offices across the street, which was another blow for the campaign to save the building.

The elevator door opened on floor nineteen: a whole floor of unused offices. I'd been up there before in the early hours to sleep before my next hearing. I'd spent more nights sleeping in different parts of the courthouse than I cared to remember. There were few facilities in the building, and the main problem was the lack of conference rooms where you can talk privately with your client. I'd used some of the old offices up there to consult. But aside from the occasional lawyer whispering with a client, or a lawyer catching a power nap, nobody came up there.

A moldy smell seemed to permeate through the walls. No one had been up there to do any cleaning in some time. We turned right out of the elevator, walked along a wide corridor, and then stopped at the second door on the right. Arturas took a set of keys from his coat pocket and slipped one into the lock. The lock looked brand-new. Arturas had planned on bringing me here. He opened the door and went inside, dragging the suitcase behind him. He closed and locked the door after me. The room within served as a large reception area for a judge's chambers. The reception area contained a stained desk, three green leather, studded couches, and an ancient photocopier.

A yellowed, framed print of the *Mona Lisa* sat above the desk.

Beyond the couches, I saw an inner door to the chambers. I opened the door to the private quarters and saw, straight ahead of me, a long sash window. On the left, a bookcase ran the length of the room. It held law reports and out-of-date textbooks. A small desk and chair sat tight against the bookcase. On the other wall were two rather poor artworks depicting barren Irish countryside scenes set upon peeling, floral wallpaper. One couch sat sullenly below the paintings. The place smelled of old newspapers, and thick dust lay on every surface.

I walked back into the reception room and saw Arturas taking a suit bag from the Samsonite case. He opened it and handed me a neatly folded pair of black suit pants. The jacket he placed on the chair. He then produced a white shirt, still in its packaging, and a new red tie.

Apart from my overcoat, I wore light chinos and a navy blazer over a blue shirt.

"Take off the coat," said Arturas.

I removed my overcoat, and as I did so, the thin jacket that contained the bomb came off as well and slid out of my coat. As it fell to the floor, its deadly contents dragging it earthward, I dove into the judge's chambers and covered my head.

Nothing.

Then laughter.

Feeling foolish, I got up and came back into the room. The jacket lay crumpled on the floor, and Arturas was smiling.

"Don't worry. You need a charge to set off the bomb. You could bounce it off the walls and it would not detonate. You need this to set it off." He produced something small and black from the pocket of his brown overcoat. It looked like a central locking pad for a car: a little plastic oval about the same size as a matchbox. It had two buttons—one green, one red. "One button to arm it, one to set it off. The bomb is not very large. It has a kill zone of four or five feet, no more," said Arturas.

He picked up the thin jacket and laid it out flat on the reception desk.

Someone knocked. Arturas opened the door to the tall, blond Russian I'd met in the limo, the one Volchek called Victor. The big man closed the door and fixed his eyes upon me.

Arturas returned to the reception desk, opened the Velcro seam of the thin silk jacket, and removed the device that I'd felt through the material: two thin, rectangular blocks of hard putty with what looked to be a circuit board on top. Wires ran from the circuit board to something else. It could have been the inner workings of an old pager or something like that. More wires ran from this to the off-white plastic explosive. The whole thing looked to be around the same size as a pocket notepad. It was thin, and despite the damage it could do, it didn't weigh much. Arturas lifted the suit jacket that he'd left on the chair. He placed it inside out on the desk and began running his hands along the lining. He'd known that I would need a suit for court. This one looked as though it had been custom tailored to conceal the device in a hidden pocket in the back of the jacket. He closed the seam after he secured the bomb, then lifted the jacket. I couldn't tell there was something hidden in the back. It looked perfectly normal.

"Get changed," said Arturas.

Lifting the pants, the shirt, the tie, and my overcoat, I moved into the chambers office. "You don't mind?" I said.

He shook his head.

The pants were a good fit. The white shirt was way too big at the collar, but the blue button-down I was already wearing would do. I left the rest of my clothes and the tie in the chambers and went back into the reception room to try on the jacket. Arturas held it open for me, like a salesman. Turning, I held my arms out behind me and he slipped the sleeves onto my arms and threaded it up and over my shoulders. I thought it was a little big, like the shirt. Arturas strode around me, checking the angles, smoothing down the material, making sure it looked normal.

"It will do well. The white shirt was too big?" he said.

"Yeah. Too much room in the collar."

He nodded.

Without another word, I went back into the chambers and folded my collar up so I could put on the tie. The Russians were in my peripheral vision. Arturas was closing up the large suitcase, which still looked plenty full. Victor watched Arturas. Before they could notice, I picked up my overcoat and drew out the wallet that I'd lifted from the big Russian in the limo. If the jacket were a size or two smaller, it would have been a problem concealing the wallet in the inside pocket of my new suit. With the extra width, no one would notice. I couldn't risk taking a look at the wallet just yet; I would have to wait. It was likely that I would find nothing useful in the wallet. But I was damn glad that I had it. The mere fact that I'd been able to pocket it without being seen gave me some hope that the skills I'd learned so long ago had not deserted me completely. Opening and closing my fists and rolling my shoulders, I tried to calm myself and let my mind absorb the situation.

A dirty mirror sat in the corner of the bookcase. I wiped the layer of dust from it and made sure my tie was straight.

There was no denying it; every time I put on a suit and looked in the mirror, I didn't see a lawyer. I saw a con man.

A man just like my father.

Lifting a wallet unobserved is no easy task. It takes a long time to learn how to complete the perfect pocket dip. You need quick, easy hands, steady nerves, and the ability to either take off or take down the mark. I learned from one of the best cannons in the business, a true pickpocket artist—my dad, Pat Flynn. Most pickpockets don't like to be called "pickpockets," and always refer to themselves as cannons. My abiding memory of my father is him sitting in his armchair in front of the TV, eyes heavy, breathing slowly, looking almost dead or asleep, and all the while he would be running a quarter over his knuckles like droplets of mercury slipping over a fork.

For a big guy, he had dainty little hands, and each individual finger moved like a dancer: fast, fluid, clean. Much to my mother's disapproval, my dad ran an illegal gambling ring out of the back of McGonagall's Bar in Brooklyn. He'd been a con artist and a smuggler in Dublin until he'd saved enough to buy a ticket to America. When he got off the boat, he went straight to the nearest diner and ordered his first hamburger. He didn't tip his nineteen-year-old waitress, and she chased him for four blocks before finally catching him. He gave her a huge tip, used his God-given charm, and they started dating. The waitress was a second-generation Italian girl named Isabella. My parents, Pat and Isabella, married in secret a year later.

I would go down to the bar after school and drink a soda while I watched my dad run his crew. At the height of his little operation, he had maybe forty runners hustling the action on dogs, horses, boxing, and football. Once he'd dealt with his runners, we'd shoot a game of pool. Then he'd lift me up onto a barstool, plant his worn red book beside him, and teach me how to palm a card, a dime, a silver dollar, a watch, how to dip for leather while looking the mark in the eye, how to fold a ten-dollar bill and make it look like a hundred, how to signal your shill for the perfect distraction while you made the dip, how to hide money in your clothes so no one could find it, and more, much more. I still remember the taste of the Dr. Peppers, the citrus smell of his aftershave, the smoothness of the polished rosewood bar, and beneath it, my dad's pretty hands working their magic.

At first he had refused to teach me. Even then, at age eight, I could be persuasive, and eventually I wore him down. He agreed to teach me on two conditions. The first was that we kept the lessons secret; Mom was never to know. Second, if he was going to teach me, he knew that he wouldn't be able to stop me from honing my skills on the street, so the next best thing in his mind was to make sure that if I did make a slip, I would be able to defend myself. After an hour or so working on my form at the bar, he'd take me to the gym and watch me learn how to box. Mom didn't know about any of it. She worked late, waiting tables at a restaurant ten blocks away. It was our secret, me and my dad's. When Mom came home from her shift, my dad always had something hot waiting for her. Then she'd curl up on the couch with a romance novel, the trashier the better, and read until she fell asleep. By the time I'd turned fourteen, I'd beaten every decent fighter in the district, including kids two and three years older than me. I was fast, I hit hard, and I didn't go down easy. My dad wanted me to get better, so after our session in the bar, we'd take the E train to Lexington Avenue and I'd spar in Mickey Hooley's gym on 54th Street against the best young fighters that Hell's Kitchen had to offer. That's where I met most of the guys who ended up in my crew. And one particular guy, a squat little boy with a sledgehammer right cross, by the name of Jimmy Fellini, who quickly became my best pal. Jimmy would go on to be a promising amateur boxer, and I watched every one of his fights. We were brothers back then. But Jimmy missed out on his shot at turning pro.

He had family commitments.

Two years after I'd joined Mickey's gym, my dad got sick. We weren't poor, and my dad always paid the health insurance for the whole family, right on time, every month in life. The rare form of cancer that took him wasn't covered under the policy. My dad hired a lawyer, the cheapest one he could find. The insurance company hired a big-city law firm, and the case went to court. I watched my dad's lawyer get crucified. It wasn't his fault; he was hopelessly outmatched. We lost the case, and even with money from friends and Jimmy's family, we didn't have enough to pay the hospital fees. Without proper treatment, my dad was dead within six months.

I wasn't there when he died. In his hospital room, I'd held his frail, skeletal hand in mine for eleven hours and then got up and left to get a soda from the machine. When I got back, I saw my mom waiting for me at the door to his room. I knew he was dead. She didn't say anything. She just handed me his Saint Christopher medal and cried. After that, it was just me and my mom, and she looked after me as best she could. She even let me box as long as I got straight As. I kept my promise and graduated top of my class. I made sure to have mac and cheese or a plate of eggs waiting for her when she got home from the restaurant. Most nights she didn't eat it, but she never failed to thank me. I couldn't cook for shit, and she knew it, but she was thanking me for being the man of the house and keeping a little part of Dad alive. She'd stopped reading the romance novels. Instead she watched a little TV with me before turning in.

When I'd completed school, I hit the illegal fight circuit for a year and ran a few scams on the side. Before the year was out, I had enough money to stake my operation. I hit the street at eighteen, ready to set up: a perfect con, a surefire way to steal every last cent that I could from the people who killed my dad—insurance companies and the rich lawyers who protected them.

Looking back, they hadn't stood a chance.

"Lawyer," said Arturas, from the reception room. "Time's up. We have to go. The trial is about to start."

CHAPTER SIX

Leaving my coat and pants in the chambers office and sporting my new suit, I joined the Russians at the door. Arturas wheeled the suitcase behind him.

"What's in the case?" I asked.

"Volchek's files—all the papers that Jack prepared for the hearing."

"Is there a prosecution witness list?"

"Yes, and Benny's at the end of it."

I'd guessed about as much. The prosecution always saved their best witness till last.

We rode the elevator to the fourteenth floor and court sixteen. The elevators opened up to a wide hall. The white stone walls were bedecked with four huge plaques listing the names of lawyers and judges who fought and died in World War II. Bathrooms and vending machines were scattered around the corners. To the left of the elevators, the long marble staircase rose to the upper floor.

Directly ahead of us were the open, oak double doors that led to a packed courtroom.

Court sixteen was the grandest courtroom in the building. Four large arched windows on the left-hand wall revealed a familiar skyline. The marble floor seemed to sip at the pale morning sun. Newly installed pine benches made up the public gallery. Two judges had threatened to quit if they didn't get the new benches because the old theater-style seats had become infested with fleas over the years—no doubt due to the type of clientele that the criminal court attracted. When the infestation spread to the judges, replacement seating suddenly became a priority.

There were around twenty-five rows of benches, which were split into two sections on either side of the central aisle. A rail separated the gallery from the legal tables: prosecution table on the left and defense on the right. Both tables faced the judge. The prosecution table sat empty. A small clump of gallery seats behind the defense table had been saved for Volchek and his entourage. I heard my name being whispered by a few people as I made my way to the defense table. At the back of the court, the judge's leather seat waited behind a mahogany judicial bench. About fifteen feet in front of the prosecution table stood the witness box. Three steps led up to a small half door in the otherwise solid oak box that contained a single, straight-backed steel chair with a worn, upholstered seat. Directly opposite the witness box and ten feet to the right of the defense table was the jury stand with twelve empty chairs. The jury stand faced both the witness box and the windows behind it. A thought occurred to me as I took my seat.

"Is jury selection complete?" I asked Arturas.

"Yes, but . . ."

Before Arturas could answer, Miriam Sullivan, acting district attorney for New York County, walked into court sixteen flanked by an entourage of assistant DAs and paralegals, who were quickly followed by another three guys in dark suits. From the way they moved and looked, I guessed the stragglers were FBI.

I'd followed this case in the papers like every other New Yorker. A man in his forties with links to an Italian crime family had been found shot in his apartment two years ago. An unidentified man was arrested at the scene: the man I now knew to be Little Benny. Benny got caught red-handed with the murder weapon and the body. Filling in the blanks that Volchek had left, I guessed that the FBI had been watching Volchek for years and they stepped in to make a deal with Benny. They wanted to go light on the trigger man and get to the real boss. After Volchek got arrested, the *Times* reported that the judge set bail at five million dollars. Volchek paid that sum in cash within a half hour.

The murder didn't cross state lines and wasn't, as far as I could tell, drug related, so the NYPD and the district attorney's office held on to the case. The feds would hold the witness so they could keep an eye on proceedings. I remembered an unusual feature of the case, something that had grated on me from the first time I read the reports in the papers. There was only one charge—murder. Volchek hadn't been indicted for drug running or racketeering or any of the usual organized crime charges. He faced a single charge of first-degree murder.

The prosecution team heaved cardboard boxes full of files onto their table, grabbed extra seats, and built a fortress of paper on their desk. Psychological tactics for the jury—*look at all the evidence we have against this guy.* The state had an army of the top prosecutors, who'd had months to prepare a watertight case, and an unlimited budget.

Miriam looked cool and professional, every inch the seasoned litigator. She wore a black suit with a skirt. She wasn't classically beautiful, and I'd heard her described as having quite plain features. But her demeanor changed when she came to court; her eyes took on an intensity that was almost hypnotic. Throw in the legs, the shapely figure, and it was a good visual package for the jury. Not that she needed an advantage. She could've looked like Danny DeVito and it wouldn't have made any difference. Miriam was just a devastating lawyer—period. She'd made her name in vice before moving to sex crimes. During the five years that Miriam prosecuted sexual offenders, the conviction rate for rape almost doubled. She'd graduated to homicide, and so far, she was on track for the DA's job come election season.

Arturas placed the suitcase on the floor underneath the defense table and took his seat at the end of the row behind me. I heard a rumble of heavy footfalls and murmurs from the crowd, and I didn't need to turn around to know that Volchek was making his entrance. I opened the suitcase and looked inside at the seven files that contained probably six or seven thousand pages in total.

The rumble from the crowd became louder. I turned around to see Volchek walking down the central aisle, alone. Then a Hispanic male stood up in the middle of the crowd. He wore a red and blue bandana, a white shirt and track top. Tattoos spread from his neck up over his jaw and onto his face. It wasn't the mere fact that he'd stood up that caught my eye; it was what he was doing. He clapped his hands in a slow cadence. An Asian guy in a dark suit got up and began to join in with the applause just as somebody else stood to attention. The third man was also Hispanic. He wore a maroon T-shirt and he also sported black, wiry tattoos on his bare arms and neck.

Volchek nodded politely at each of the men as he passed them and sat down beside me at the defense table.

"Friends of yours?" I said.

"No. They are not friends. They are my enemies. They've come to watch me fall."

The slow, staccato applause for Volchek died down.

"So exactly who are these enemies?" I asked.

"The Puerto Ricans and the Mexicans run lines for the South American cartels here in New York. The other man is Yakuza. They are here to show me that if I go to prison, they are coming for me and my operation. They are in for a surprise," he said.

CHAPTER SEVEN

Jean Denver, one of the few female clerks, emerged from the entrance to the judge's chambers. She winked at me. I liked Jean; she was intelligent, fun, and kept the court running efficiently. She wheeled a heavy trolley. It contained five binders that were thick with paper. The judge's case files. Judge Pike must be ready to make her appearance. That meant I was about to get my first look at the jury. You can be the most knowledgeable lawyer in the world and be an amazing cross-examiner, but if you don't know how to talk to a jury, you're in big trouble. Before you talk to them, you have to understand them. Most jurors don't want to be jurors. The minority that actively want to be jurors should be avoided at all costs.

I could feel the muscles in my neck getting tighter and tighter each minute, as if the wiring from the bomb was sliding up my back to choke me.

Miriam walked over to my table and stood beside me. Staring into space, my head was running at a hundred miles an hour. I could feel the heat from Miriam's smile. She held a handwritten message on a yellow Post-it, which she waved at me before sticking it to the desk.

YOUR CLIENT'S GOING DOWN. I'LL HAVE HIS BAIL REVOKED BY 5 P.M.

My mouth was dry. That note was a death sentence for Amy. If Miriam was right, and she was successful in revoking Volchek's bail, then Amy and

I would be dead before the cuffs warmed up on Volchek's wrists. I was aware of my heels bouncing on the marble floor, and I swore silently and battled to calm down and think.

Miriam didn't normally get so personal. Like most good lawyers, Miriam usually stayed detached. We'd come up against each other a few times in the past and came out about even. In the first case I tried against Miriam, I'd underestimated her badly. She wiped the floor with me. My client was caught selling meth outside a school. No deals on a plea, so we fought it and my scumbag got heavy time. Her performance for the jury was flawless; she'd remained composed, restrained, and gave the impression to the jury that she was just recounting facts, not playing on their emotions. About a month after the trial, someone told me that Miriam's son went to that school and had been offered drugs by my client. She hadn't mentioned it to me and sailed through to an easy, dispassionate victory. Even though it was the right verdict, and an easy one for the jury, the way she secured that win impressed me.

The note she'd handed me was intended to rile the defense. That meant Miriam was worried. This was no ordinary murder. Miriam's career case started today. If she lost this open-and-shut wonder, she'd be out of a job. Prosecutors often experience more pressure on such a case because they're expected to win, and if she secured a verdict, with the feds holding the hand of her star witness, news of her victory would travel in the right circles. I handed the note to Volchek. First, so that he could see I wasn't swapping notes with the prosecutor about the bomb, and second, I needed him scared. People who're scared like options. If such things had existed, the hustler's bible, page one, would read exactly the same as the first page of the trial lawyer's manual: *Give the people what they want.*

"She's going for your bail straight off the bat," I said.

Arturas leaned over the rail to listen. I watched as Volchek grew pale and turned toward Arturas.

"You did not expect this," said Volchek.

"She can't do that yet. The other lawyers told us the prosecutor would try, but that they were confident she wouldn't get it," replied Arturas.

"You think they were maybe being optimistic because they wanted to get retained in your case?" I said. I watched Arturas's face tighten, his eyes narrow.

"She must think she has a great first witness: a game changer. A good trial attorney will always start a case with a strong witness. Miriam Sullivan is a great attorney. She thinks the first witness will be enough to put you in handcuffs."

Volchek bared his teeth and snarled, "Arturas, you told me you had thought of everything. You've had two years to plan. First Jack can't even get out of the limo with the bomb, never mind get through security. Now this . . ." His arm reached out as if to claw at Arturas's face, but he held back at the last moment. "If you fail me again . . ." He shook his head.

Arturas stroked the scar on his cheek. He saw me watching him and took his hand away from his face. Up close, I saw that the scar had not fully healed. A translucent liquid oozed from a red, puckered section of the wound just below his eye. Guys like Arturas don't go to the ER for that kind of treatment, and whoever had stitched his cut hadn't done a very good job. Backstreet doctors, high from their own prescription pads, aren't known for their care with hygiene, or their skill with a needle for that matter. The scar looked keloid and infected and would probably stay that way; damaged tissue sometimes never fully heals.

I began to wonder about that scar. Perhaps it was a punishment from Volchek for a past failure. Arturas focused his anger on me.

"You will not let her revoke bail. Your daughter's life depends on it. One phone call is all it takes to have her little throat cut," he said.

Rage stripped the anxiety from my voice. "Take it easy. I won't let it happen. She would need something incredible to get Volchek's bail revoked on the first day. Whatever it is, I'll deal with it," I said.

I heard the door to the judge's chambers opening. I was about to start a case that I knew nothing about. Whatever Miriam had up her sleeve that was so good, I would learn all about it from her opening statement to the jury. I straightened my tie, adjusted my jacket, and felt the weight of the bomb on my back.

"Silence in court! All stand for the honorable Justice Gabriella Pike, case docket number 552192, the People versus Olek Volchek on one count of murder in the first degree." With that announcement from the court officer, a small, unassuming brunette in dark robes jogged into the courtroom and sat down before the announcement finished and long before most people had lifted their ass off their seats. Judge Pike did everything at high speed. She spoke quickly, walked quickly, and ate quickly. As a defense attorney, she'd been a formidable lawyer because, just as she was with everything else, she could think on her feet with stunning rapidity. This made her a devastating cross-examiner. She could shift tactics at the drop of a hat, and her skills soon became noticed by the right people. Deeply ambitious, it didn't take long for Gabriella to become the youngest judge in the history of the state, and because she was a former defense attorney, she made a point of giving all defense attorneys a real hard time.

"Please be seated with Her Honor's permission," cried the officer, and people settled.

Judge Pike looked at me. "Mr. Flynn, I thought your partner was counsel in this case," she said. She spoke with a slightly diluted Brooklyn accent, but her speedball delivery hid the breadth of that accent well.

A throbbing pain began in my head.

"I'm stepping into my friend's shoes for the duration of the trial—unless Your Honor has any objection?" I said it more in hope than anything else. I knew she would have no objection, and she said so. Changing the counsel of record happened a lot. Criminal clients were always firing their attorneys and hiring new ones. Some defendants changed counsel five or six times during the life of their case—usually because they didn't like the advice they'd been given or because their attorney sent them a large legal bill.

"Can we have the jury, please?" said Judge Pike to no one in particular, but the jury officer heard his cue and departed through a side door to fetch them. I prayed for a little break to bring me some hope. The judge would watch the jury closely. If the prosecutor's opening witness was really strong and the jury was leaning against Volchek, this might give Judge Pike enough confidence to revoke Volchek's bail when the time came. The pain in my head worsened, and I began to feel nausea creeping into my gut. I had no choice at the moment but to deal with what was in front of me. Jack had been a good lawyer. Surely he would've picked a good jury.

The jury filed in and took their seats: six in the first row and six in the elevated row behind.

I doubted if I would've picked any of them.

The first juror was a white guy in his early forties. He wore a plaid shirt and spectacles. He looked considerate, moderately intelligent, and probably ranked as the worst choice of all. The rest were not a jury of Volchek's peers—five small black women in their late fifties to early sixties, wearing floral dresses, strong ladies with a certain charming appearance but no friends of the Russian mob. Then another four women in their thirties and forties: two white, one Hispanic, and one Chinese. I saw a black guy wearing a white shirt and a red bow tie. Bow ties spell danger to trial lawyers; no one is more strident in their views than a man in a bow tie. The last guy was Hispanic, and his shirt looked well ironed with sharp creases down both arms. He looked clean, well presented, and something about him spoke of a quiet intelligence. He didn't rank as a good choice either, but he was probably the best of a bad bunch. At least he would listen. It's so vital to have a jury member who is willing to listen. Their face can be your barometer for success: As long as that face is computing and occasionally smiling and nodding at your points, you've got a chance. Other jurors might listen to him and be led by him.

"Ms. Sullivan, your opening statement, please," said the judge.

An expectant silence fell on the room. Arturas reached into the case, produced a legal pad and a pencil for me to take notes. He'd thought about everything. I opened the pad, pushed the pencil away, took out my DAD pen, and readied myself to take notes.

My first note is usually the name of the case and the name of the judge and prosecutor. When I looked at my pad, I'd written only one thing—*Amy.* Until a year ago, I'd cherished Sundays. That was our day. No matter what case I'd been involved in, or how overworked I was, on Sunday I made pancakes for breakfast and Amy and I would hit Prospect Park for the afternoon. It was our time. She'd learned to ride her bike on the footpath leading up to the Nethermead Arches Bridge and couldn't wait to get home to tell Christine; she'd fallen asleep on my shoulders on the way back from the zoo and dribbled all over my shirt; and we'd eaten ice cream cones beside the lake as we watched the geese flying over the boathouse and talked about her best friends and the kids that gave her a hard time for being a little different. Amy didn't listen to the latest boy bands or hip-hop artists, and she didn't watch much TV. She liked reading and listening to old rock bands, like The Who, the Stones, and the Beatles. If it was raining, we'd buy too much popcorn and go watch an old movie. I'd always looked forward to Sundays. But it was no longer our day; since the breakup,

Christine wanted Amy to be settled for going back to school, so we'd switched to Saturdays. At the end of every Saturday afternoon, I dropped her off, kissed her goodbye, and left to drive home to my empty apartment.

I looked around the courtroom and saw that everyone was waiting for the prosecutor to begin.

Miriam rested her elbows on the desk and held her hands delicately below her face. I'd seen her do this before. All eyes were upon her. She drew you in, framing that trustworthy face with those fragile hands. Rising from her seat, she approached the jury and began, confidently, to look at each one of them in turn, holding their eyes in her forensic gaze. Her way of connecting with them, each of them, and they connected all right. If she'd told the jury right then that Volchek was guilty, they would've convicted on her word—that instant.

"Ladies and gentlemen of the jury, my name is Miriam Sullivan. I'm responsible for prosecuting Mr. Volchek for murder. In a moment I'll give you an outline of the evidence. I'll give you a route map to the truth about this murder. This map will show you the path that we have to take before you can say that Mr. Volchek is guilty. You've seen the TV coverage of this trial; Mr. Volchek is regarded by many to be the head of the Russian Mafia. Our main witness will tell you about life inside the Bratva, the Russian name that's given to these criminal organizations. Indeed, ladies and gentlemen, you will see that the defendant faces a mountain of evidence against him." As expected, she threw a manicured hand at her team's table as an illustration. They probably had two or three copies of the evidence on that table and probably not that much of it proved Volchek was a murderer. However, it was the impression that counted.

She continued. "And that is what you have to evaluate—the evidence. Not the press coverage. I'm going to tell you a little bit about our case now and about the expert witness who will tell you that Mr. Volchek ordered Mario Geraldo to be killed."

I had no clue what expert witness Miriam was talking about, but I had an inkling that this was her opening witness, her shot at revoking Volchek's bail.

"But more important than the expert in this case is the man who actually pulled the trigger. That man will tell you that his boss, the head of the

Russian Mafia, Olek Volchek, ordered him to kill Mr. Geraldo. That man, the man who shot Mr. Geraldo, is under FBI protection. His old and new identity will be protected in these proceedings because as a former member of the Bratva, this man is living under a death threat. In this trial, this man will be known as Witness X."

Miriam paused for effect, allowing me time to read over the notes I'd just written. I reread the phrase *This man is living under a death threat* and underlined it. Twice.

CHAPTER EIGHT

Miriam talked for an hour about the burden of proof. She explained to the jury that they must be satisfied of Volchek's guilt beyond a reasonable doubt. The jury nodded throughout this portion of the speech, and Miriam went on to explain what pieces of evidence would satisfy that burden.

"Ladies and gentlemen of the jury, the first witness you will hear from the prosecution will be Dr. Irving Goldstein, the eminent forensic document examiner. He is a man who examines pieces of handwriting to determine who created them. Dr. Goldstein knows the defendant's handwriting from public documents that we, the prosecution, have obtained. He can then look at another sample of handwriting and determine with scientific accuracy if the defendant wrote it or not."

Those expensive high-heeled shoes of Miriam's clicked over to the prosecution table, where she picked up what looked like some form of currency in a sealed plastic evidence bag.

"This is prosecution exhibit twelve. This is an old, one-ruble bill that has been torn in half. One half is unmarked; one half has a name written on it in marker pen. That name is *Mario Geraldo*, the victim in this case. Witness X will tell you that he was given one half of this note—the unmarked half—by his boss, the defendant, Olek Volchek, and when he was subsequently given the other half of the note with the victim's name on it by an unknown messenger, that was his order to kill the victim. Witness

X will tell you that this was the MO for the Russian mob; this was how the orders to kill were handed down by the defendant. How do we know the defendant wrote the victim's name on the bill? Well, that's where Dr. Goldstein comes in. Dr. Goldstein will tell you that the handwriting on this note matches exactly with the defendant's handwriting."

Miriam paused, the note still held aloft in her hand. This was the game changer. This evidence would blow his bail for sure. Several of the jury members fixed Volchek with a stern look.

I rocked back in my chair and folded my arms before whispering to Volchek in the seat beside me, "Lean back. Smile. The jury is looking at you. Pretend that you're relaxed. The jury will think we're not in the least concerned about this evidence and that we've got it completely covered."

We both smiled.

"You're shitting me, right? How the hell did you get bail in the first place?"

"The prosecution didn't have this evidence for the arraignment. They only produced the handwriting report at the beginning of the year," said Volchek.

I thought for a moment. "Why the hell would you write down an order for a hit? That's the stupidest thing I've ever heard. Tell me she's lying and we've got something to challenge this," I said.

Volchek's smile disappeared. His brow furrowed, and his voice deepened. "Do not presume to know anything about me or how I run my business. This is the old way. Back in Soviet Union, the gangs ran wild, but there was always loyalty to the boss. That loyalty did not always extend below, to the *vor*—what you would call the soldiers. If a soldier wants to move up in the Bratva ranks, the easiest way is to kill his biggest rival. But he cannot do this himself. Instead he uses other soldiers. He tells them that the boss, the *pakhan*, has ordered the rival to be killed. The other soldiers obey absolutely, and the *pakhan* knows nothing until it's too late. I've seen entire Bratva kill one another in this way. I use the old way to make sure this does not happen. The old way is this," he said, pointing to the exhibit just as Miriam lowered her hand and slowly walked back to the prosecution table.

He continued. "The only man who can order a hit in my organization is me. I control all kills. This way I do not start wars with other gangs, and

I make sure my men do not kill each other. To do this, I have one man who is my torpedo." He pronounced it *tor-pedd-o*. "It is old Soviet name for hit man. This man comes to me and me alone. In front of him, I tear an old, one-ruble bill in half. I give him one half of the bill. In this way, he becomes torpedo. When I need a man killed, I write down that man's name on my half of the bill and it is sent to torpedo. He will check if his half of the bill matches the one he has been sent. If they are a match, he knows the order is real and that it comes directly from me. In this way, the old way, my men have trust from me and I have total loyalty from them."

"And this Witness X, Little Benny, he was your torpedo, right? So why the hell did he keep the note?" I said.

"In Soviet Union we called a one-ruble bill *tselkovy*, meaning *the whole one*. It means that the torpedo has my whole heart in trust and loyalty forever. The torpedo is supposed to burn the bill after the job. Most do not. They keep their rubles. Old ruble bills can be hard to find these days. They are like a badge of honor. Some even have the one-ruble bill tattooed on their backs. I do not allow tattoos. We wear our pride in our eyes, not on our skin."

I couldn't react in case the jury saw me, but I wanted to put my hands over my head and scream. The courtroom no longer felt huge. It felt small and public and dangerous. I wondered where Amy was being held. Was she, too, feeling enclosed, trapped, and afraid? If I let myself wonder what was happening to her, I would go crazy.

Instead I started thinking. "Pass me the case files," I said.

Volchek looked into the suitcase. He seemed to be looking for a particular file. He found one and handed it over. It said DOCUMENT EXAMINERS on the spine of the folder. I began flicking through it. Volchek had gone to nearly every major criminal defense firm in the state and gotten reports from several forensic document examiners. The index to this file said there were eleven such expert reports. Volchek must have been desperate. I flicked through to the concluding summary of each one of the reports. They all said the same thing—in their opinion, Volchek wrote that name on the ruble bill.

Miriam continued her opening statement.

"Ladies and gentlemen of the jury, you will also hear from the victim's family. You will hear from Tony Geraldo, the victim's cousin. He'll tell you about his cousin's dispute with the defendant. He'll tell you about the threats that the defendant made to Mario Geraldo's life. He'll tell you he feared the defendant would kill his cousin or arrange for his murder."

That name, Tony Geraldo, seemed to stir some memory for me, but I was so wired that I couldn't trace the thought. Miriam stepped into a nice rhythm.

"You'll hear from the police officer who arrested and interviewed the defendant. You'll hear this officer describe his investigation . . ."

My interest trailed off. I'd found the witness list in the file of papers. In all, we would hear from five witnesses. A small, tight, well-prepared group. Miriam avoided the usual machine-gun approach to prosecution, which relied on the hit-and-miss tactics of *just keeping going* with witness after witness after witness and something somewhere is bound to stick. She knew better than that. The forensic document examiner, Dr. Irving Goldstein, was the first witness. A good strategy, I thought. Get the boring bit out of the way and put a smoking gun in the hand of the defendant on day one. But I saw this as my biggest chance. Volchek must have spent a fortune getting all those reports and paying all those lawyers only to get back the same result every time—*It's your handwriting.* As far as he was concerned, this witness was a lost cause. He couldn't find another expert to challenge Goldstein's evidence. Every single lawyer that Volchek retained had told him that Goldstein was watertight.

I had no choice. If Dr. Goldstein was as good a witness as Miriam hoped, Volchek could have his bail terminated within a few hours, and Amy would pay for that with her life. I had to destroy Goldstein's evidence. If I could do that, I accomplished two things. One, I would get my remaining twenty-eight hours to figure my way out of this, and two, the Russians would begin to trust me. If Volchek thought I was busting a gut to keep him out of jail long enough to kill Benny, then he wouldn't notice me cramming that bomb up his ass first chance I got. But before the con, I needed to gain his trust.

In the confidence game, we called it a *persuader.*

Miriam wrapped up her speech. "And, ladies and gentlemen, if you consider this simple proposition to be correct, then you *must* find the defendant guilty. We will show you his guilt and you *must* convict him."

Miriam sat down. The jury looked tired.

Judge Pike said, "Mr. Flynn, will you be addressing the jury now or at the conclusion of the prosecution's evidence?" I slowly rose from my chair and said, "Your Honor, the jury will want time to absorb Ms. Sullivan's speech. Might it be preferable to give them a break and allow them some time for refreshments? I will need to take some instructions from my client before I address the jury."

This was my usual tactic and one that most defense attorneys employed. I always liked to speak to my client after I'd heard the prosecutor's opening. It was usually only then that the defense got to hear what kind of spin the prosecution was putting on the evidence. That meant checking with the defendant again, to see if any of what the prosecutor said was true. I also wanted the jury to like me. They'd sat for almost two hours listening to Miriam. I wanted to be the savior. I wanted them to see me stand up, say something quick, and get them coffee and pastries. I'm concerned they might need a break; I'm caring, connecting, and listening to them. Pretty soon I would be the only show in town.

Miriam saw my shot at wrestling the jury from her spell and tried to take back their favor. "Your Honor, I fear I may have gone on too long this morning. Perhaps instead of coffee, we could break for lunch?"

"Back here in one hour," said Judge Pike.

The courtroom began to empty, and I felt a strong hand on my shoulder. Arturas said, "We'll go upstairs to talk."

I didn't have time to talk. I had one hour to read eight thousand pages and prepare the greatest opening speech and the greatest cross-examination of my life. I shifted around in my seat and looked at him straight. "We can talk later. I have to work. And I need your help."

CHAPTER NINE

Victor closed and locked the door of the reception room that we'd occupied earlier, up on the nineteenth floor. Arturas stood with his arms folded and tapped his foot. He was nervous and angry. His boss simply folded himself into the couch and watched.

"I need a laptop or a smartphone with Internet access," I said.

"What for?" asked Arturas.

I ignored Arturas and spoke directly to Volchek—he was the client; he needed the answers, and he called the shots. "Your other lawyers tried to get expert testimony to challenge Dr. Goldstein directly. They wanted another handwriting expert to say that the murder note couldn't have been written by you. I saw the bundle of reports in the case file; they couldn't get anyone to offer that opinion. That's because that opinion doesn't exist. Not legitimately, anyway. You could probably get an expert to say that the handwriting *may* not be yours, but those guys don't have Goldstein's credentials, and when it comes to a Mexican standoff with expert witnesses, the one with the best résumé usually wins."

Volchek nodded. He seemed to be buying it, but Arturas wasn't. "What can you do? The other firms had months to challenge this evidence. What can you do in one hour?" said Arturas.

"Well, I have to do something. If we let this evidence go unchallenged, Miriam Sullivan will have your bail canceled, and you'll be in handcuffs before Goldstein gets his ass out of the witness box. That means you don't get the luxury of being able to jump on a plane tomorrow if this all goes to shit."

I could hear Arturas grinding his teeth. His lips curled up in a grimace as he began shifting his weight from foot to foot. He'd been planning this caper for a long time, and he didn't like intangibles. But that was trial law. Stepping into a courtroom is just like going to Vegas and rolling the dice—anything can happen. Volchek continued to listen. It was his liberty at stake.

"You don't need me to tell you what the outcome will be if an accused goes into custody and something happens to a state's witness. There is no way you will get out on bail until a full investigation has been done and you've been cleared. How long is that going to take? Two, maybe three years? Anything can happen on the inside. The state might not be able to link the bomb directly to you, but that doesn't mean they won't put you in a cell with a four-hundred-pound cannibal. And that's if you can avoid the cartels' soldiers. Yeah, your buddies in the courtroom will get to you on the inside real easy. I can take the fall if it means Amy is safe. I can live with that. Better that than the alternative. But if you go to prison—you lose."

Volchek exchanged glances with Arturas. He smoothed his pants and tried to swallow down a knowing grin. Despite what I'd just said to Volchek, I knew they weren't going to leave me or Amy alive at the end of this. They didn't want me telling the FBI about my daughter being kidnapped and my being forced to plant a bomb in the courtroom. But I needed to let Volchek and Arturas think that I had bought their bullshit story.

"I still want to know what you can do that the other lawyers couldn't," said Arturas. A fair question, and I gave him a simple answer. "The other firms were trying to counter the evidence. That's the wrong approach. It's like football; say you're a small, broke football team and you come up against a rich team with a great quarterback. You can't win in a straight contest. Me, I don't hesitate. If there's some gifted, lightning-quick man mountain that I can't compete with, it's real simple—I take him out of the game. I cripple him. I tackle him so hard and so fast he isn't going to wake up until the season's over. It's an old saying—sometimes you have to play the man instead of the ball. Litigation is the same; if I can't destroy the evidence, I have to destroy the witness giving the evidence. If the jury don't think Goldstein's credible, it really doesn't matter what he says. I need the Internet to dig on him. Look, it's not like we've got a choice. Either help me, or I'll hold your coat while the court security officer puts you in handcuffs. It's that simple."

Volchek and Arturas nodded in agreement.

"What will you find in an hour?" said Arturas.

"I won't know it until I see it." I really didn't know. But I had an idea where to look. I could see a smile attempting to force its way through Volchek's lips. He looked intrigued.

"Okay," said Arturas, taking out his iPhone. "You tell me what to look for."

"He's from the University of Wisconsin. Start with his university bio and then a list of his work. Let me see his published articles for 2000, 2004, and 2008."

"Why?" asked Arturas.

"If you're cross-examining any academic witness, you have to look at their publications for those years. Those years were the ARAE: the American Research Assessment Exercise. The more articles published by academic staff in the ARAE, the more funding comes to their university and the more money those nerds take home. During those years, everyone writes articles like crazy, and perfectly reasonable academics write crap that they wouldn't dream of writing ordinarily. Writing for volume does not promote good theories, and pretty soon they're writing papers on fairies and UFOs. Back then articles meant cash. So if there's anything out there that will give us something on Goldstein, that's where we'll find it."

I'd cross-examined a few academics and I'd learned all about the ARAE some years ago. It never failed to give me ammunition. It's just like everything else in life—you follow the money and it always takes you to where you need to go.

While Arturas looked online, I read through Goldstein's expert report. I'd once represented Archie Mailor on a check fraud indictment, so I had read reports like this before. Archie had been my counterfeit guy when I was running my insurance scams. He had talent. IDs I got from Archie were usually pretty good. During his case, I had to cross-examine a forensic document examiner who testified about Archie's handwriting and the fraudulent checks. I had a little knowledge of what these guys looked for, but I hadn't thought about it for a long time. What I remembered was that they tended to look at the capital letters at the beginning of words. From scanning Goldstein's report, I saw that he had indeed focused on the capital "G" at the start of "Geraldo," which Volchek had written on the bill in marker pen. Behind Goldstein's report, I found a statement from a CSI. He had analyzed the one-ruble bill for fingerprints. Apparently, Little Benny's fingerprints and those of the custody officer at the precinct who handled Benny's property had either obscured or wiped out all other identifiable prints.

Arturas took seven minutes to find the right page on the university's website—*List of Publications 2008*—nothing. We checked 2004 and nothing leaped off the page.

We hit 2000 and there it was, staring at me like gold in a panhandle. Goldstein, like most academics, wanted the greenbacks while they were hot. He'd written half a dozen stupid articles to boost his volume, standing, and pay.

And he'd written one particularly bad one. That gave me a great idea.

"I need this article printed out. I need a photocopier, paper, hot coffee, and to be left the hell alone," I said. With Arturas listening in, I called the judge's clerk, Jean, on Arturas's iPhone, and I sweet-talked her into printing the article for me. I told her I owed her a box of doughnuts and told her where to find the article online. I thought that Miriam probably didn't even know Jean's name. Most hotshot lawyers ignore court staff that they would call the "little people." They did so at their peril and at their cost. Most of the time, the little people were, in fact, the best people.

I had peace in the chambers at last. Victor was in the outer reception, trying to turn on the photocopier. Once he got it working, I would just need to photocopy a couple of pages and blow them up so the jury could take a better look. I spread out some papers on the desk and stared into space, letting the plan come to me. My head still hurt from the punch I'd taken to the back of the head in the limo. If I was to even attempt to double-cross the Russians, I had to put them at their ease, get them to trust me—so they would stop looking over my shoulder. My dad told me you can't con an honest man, but the hard part was getting the dishonest mark to trust you. Good fraud was all about trust.

"Volchek," I said. He gestured for me to sit next to him on one of the couches. "Your former lawyers were all excellent, talented professionals. You don't need me to tell you that, right? You know these guys are at the top of their game. They told you the handwriting expert would kill your defense."

Volchek's every action seemed halting, considered, planned. It was almost as if he'd taught himself restraint in order to mask his true nature. He lit a cigar and let it burn down while he thought about his answer. Finally, he said, "They told me that, on its own, it's not enough to convict me."

"Right, but they didn't tell you it might be enough to blow your bail and get the prosecution a retrial, even if Benny's dead."

He said nothing. I pressed on.

"And your old lawyers had months to work on this guy's evidence, right?"

"Right."

"They couldn't challenge him, right?"

Volchek sighed. "Right. What're you getting at?"

"I'm going to obliterate the expert's evidence, and you're going to give me a chance to win this case without making Little Benny into soup."

I told Arturas to let Volchek read Goldstein's paper. He flicked through the article on Arturas's iPhone, and cigar ash fell over the screen.

"This is nothing. How does this help?"

"Leave that to me. If I wipe the floor with this guy, you've got to give me a shot at Benny. I'll do whatever it takes to save my daughter. She's my world, my life, and I'll go to jail to protect her. But I'm not relishing spending the rest of my life in an eight-by-six. Give me a shot at Benny. Let me cross-examine him, and if it doesn't go well, I'll press that button and blow him to hell myself."

The first rule of the hustler's bible—give the people what they want.

Before he whipped his head around to Arturas, I saw fire in Volchek's eyes. He didn't want to have to blow up a witness in live court. The risk was huge. Running was just as big a risk. He'd given up all hope of winning this case a long time ago. And I was giving that hope back to him.

"There is no chance you can win this case, lawyer. Better, smarter lawyers looked at all of this before," said Arturas.

"It doesn't cost you anything to let me try. At least with Goldstein, I have no choice. I've got to work on his evidence or your boss loses his bail."

The room became silent. I could hear Victor's heavy breathing. The hum from the photocopier fans. A car horn outside. Volchek wanted this, I could tell. I was the answer to his prayers.

"There's one more thing," I said.

"What?" barked Arturas.

"You haven't brought me my coffee yet," I said.

Tipping the ash from his cigar onto the floor, Volchek said, "Victor, get Mr. Flynn some coffee."

CHAPTER TEN

Lunch had taken an hour and fifteen already.

I checked my watch and saw twenty-six hours left on my clock. The watch was a twenty-dollar digital with an LCD display. Cheap, nasty, and I loved it more than any other watch that I'd ever owned. Amy and I shared the same birthday—September first. I had picked her up on the morning of our last birthday and taken her shopping. Christine and I had been separated since late June. I'd felt awkward going to the house in Queens that I'd once shared with my family, and Amy and I went out instead. I'd had no idea what to buy for a ten-year-old, so I thought she should pick something out. As we passed a little jewelry store off Broadway, I felt Amy tugging at my sleeve. In the store window she saw digital watches for sale. We went in and she said she wanted two exactly the same—one for me and one for her. I told her I already had a watch, a gift from her mom. She put her mane of white-blond hair on the glass counter and studied the watch she'd chosen. Christine often worried about how serious our daughter could be; I hadn't listened. I thought Amy was just more mature than most girls her age and that she had an adult's intelligent curiosity.

Amy curled her little fingers around the watch and said, "Daddy, you're going to stay with the doctors to get better, right?" She was talking about the residential alcohol clinic that I'd tentatively signed up for, at Christine's insistence. The store clerk walked in back, giving us some room.

She whispered the rest of her plan, like it was our secret. "Well, I thought if we both got these watches, we could set the alarms for eight o'clock. Then you would remember to call me and we could like, talk, or you could, like, read me a story, or something."

She was so sincere, so earnest. And although she was tall for her age, and impossibly cute and even mischievous at times, the beauty in her heart shone out of her in everything that she did. Her kindness saved my life that day; if we hadn't bought those watches on our last birthday, I wouldn't have made it through rehab. Every night, our alarms went off simultaneously at eight, and I called her. I had called her from the clinic, and I had read *Alice's Adventures in Wonderland* to her over the phone. She was much better at being a daughter than I was at being a parent.

Sitting at the defense table, I tried not to play with my pen; it made me look nervous. Jean had left Goldstein's ARAE paper on my chair.

This judge took her sweet time because she could. The courtroom largely consisted of reporters. Due to the perceived threat on the life of Witness X, there would be no televised coverage of this trial, just print reporting. Judges were always sensitive when it came to cameras in the courtroom. Most didn't like being filmed and would happily rely on any old reason to exclude the cameras. There wasn't even any CCTV in the courtrooms. No judge wants to be recorded saying something stupid when they're off their guard.

I could sense the anticipation in the room. Everyone who'd heard Miriam's opening knew this was a no-hoper of a defense case. The Asian gang leader that I'd seen earlier was already shaking his head, wondering what the delay was. Surely Volchek should have been found guilty by now.

I couldn't think about Amy any longer. If I did, I'd go crazy. Volchek sat beside me in the defendant's seat. Arturas and Victor were behind us.

I swallowed back my emotions, my fear, my doubts, and I turned to look at the menacing face of my client.

"Where's my daughter?"

"She's close by, and she is well. I check in from time to time. She's eating potato chips and watching TV. You keep doing okay, maybe I let you see another photo," said Volchek.

Another few minutes passed and there was still no sign of the judge. My opening speech would be simple, but my cross-examination of

Dr. Goldstein worried me. I played the cross-examination in my mind—question, answer, question, answer, over and over, trying to perfect my style.

"You," said Volchek. "I hope this delay is not down to you." He wore an accusatory look. Running a persuader on this guy would be tougher than I'd imagined.

"You know, my father was a war hero," continued Volchek. He looked at the ornate ceiling of the courtroom as he recalled his parent. "He killed a whole sniper team single-handed in battle of Stalingrad. Stalin decorated him personally. My mother was a Polish Jew, liberated from the camps, and she fell in love with my father—the hero." His features softened as he thought of his mother, and his voice seemed to drop and drift in tandem with his recollections. "She gave me the name 'Olek.' It means *protector*. She didn't live long after the war."

"Too bad. Tough in Russia, huh?" I said. I wanted to tell him that once I'd gotten my daughter back, he wouldn't live long either.

"My father drank after my mother died and lost both legs to diabetes. I would wheel him around the bars in east Moscow with his medals shining proudly on his chest while he sipped at a bottle of vodka. I was only twelve, not much older than your daughter. I was proud of my father."

His eyes took on that bitter, almost predatory aspect as he said, "That pride faded when he got really drunk. Then he wanted to fight. The lion in him didn't remember that his legs had gone. He would start trouble; then he would realize he couldn't stand, and he would say, *My son will fight for me,* and I would have to fight whatever drunk or pimp he'd insulted. Maybe he wanted me to live up to the name my mother gave me; maybe it kept a piece of her alive for him. When I turned sixteen, I killed him, sold his medals, and bought my first gun. But I loved him. I always loved him. If I lost a fight, the beatings he gave me were bad; his disappointment was worse. If you disappoint me, lawyer, your daughter can fight for you."

I wanted to take his head off. I focused my anger, locked my eyes to his, and said, "You know a lot about me from watching my movements. You probably know where I live and what I've been doing for the last few months, but you have no idea what I'm capable of in a courtroom. All those other lawyers you saw, they don't know how to work over a witness like me. They don't know how to get the prosecution to make mistakes, and they don't know how to marry a jury to your cause. I do." I stood up now, unable to contain myself, and I bent over him to ram this home. "This witness is more than enough to kill your case and your bail. I'm going to stop him, and you're going to give me a shot at Little Benny. You need to understand something. You don't need a bomb to win this case. You've already got one—*I'm* the bomb."

As I spat those words at Volchek, I could feel the hairs on my neck prickling; I could feel my shoulders tightening, a feeling I'd had before, a feeling that had eluded me in the bathroom that morning when Arturas put the revolver to my back. Hustling for a living is no joke. You develop an instinct for danger, a sixth sense that keeps you one step in front of the mark and the cops. If you don't listen to that voice in your head, you either die or you go to jail. Everyone has that instinct but not many embrace it. We've all had that feeling of being watched, of sitting at a bar and knowing that behind you, someone was boring their eyes into the back of your head. It's those instincts that con men tap into. They hone those feelings and learn to trust them. My alarm bell rang loud at that moment. My early-warning system usually let me know when I was being watched, when I'd been made, and when it was time to run.

In that second I knew I had eyes on me other than Volchek's.

My head came up instantly to scan the room. The crowd was talking and laughing in nervous anticipation of the battle that was to come, like a ravenous mob eager for the first sight of blood in the bear pit. I focused on the back wall, letting my peripheral vision pick up inconsistencies in my view. That's when I saw him. A man unlike the others; he wasn't nervous; he wasn't talking. He was perfectly still—a statue in a sea of movement.

As soon as I saw him, I knew instantly why I'd felt his singular presence in the mass of people. Out of the hundred or so people in the benches, he alone sat motionless, staring at me intently.

And I knew why.

His name was Arnold Novoselic. I'd come across him about four years ago and I'd never forgotten him. This in itself was not to be expected, as Arnold had a rare and undervalued quality; he was inconspicuous, a nobody among nobodies, an innocuous man in a city of isolated souls. His hairline receded almost to the top of his fat neck. He wore the same brown suit, ivory shirt, and big, black-rimmed glasses that he'd worn when I'd first met him, but it wasn't his appearance that made him memorable. In fact, Arnold took great pains in crafting his appearance with the deliberate intention of being as unmemorable as possible. His appearance and the indifference it inspired in others was his hiding place, his armor.

I knew that Arnold's gifts lay in observation. As a natural voyeur, he always looked out, paying little attention to himself, and maybe because of that, no one paid attention to him. A gift well suited to one of the best jury consultants in the business. He could tell what way a particular juror would vote, how social dynamics worked within a jury, who were the leaders of the group, and who would follow what vote. He did this through personal study, statistical analysis, racial profiling, and one particular skill that Arnold liked to keep secret.

I'd met Arnold four years ago, when he'd interviewed to be a jury consultant in a case that I was preparing against a pharmaceutical company. I remembered that I'd been unimpressed and a little creeped out by Arnold Novoselic in person. On paper, Arnold clearly had the best results in his profession. He never missed a call. In every case he'd ever done, he had predicted the jury's verdict precisely. That worried me, but what made me even more suspicious was the fact that in four cases in which he'd consulted, he'd been able to accurately predict each juror's verdict *before* they were polled. That meant he'd achieved one hundred percent accuracy four times out of four. I knew that in the jury business, there was no such thing as perfect predictions. So I'd asked him there and then, in my office, what his secret was.

Arnold knew he couldn't hide anything from me, and for once, he told the truth. He told me his secret. While other jury consultants merely wondered what the jury was saying, Arnold knew precisely what they talked about because Arnold was a gifted lip-reader.

Juries aren't supposed to talk about the case anywhere except in the locked, and very private, jury room. In reality, they talked to one another almost constantly. They whispered their comments on witnesses to one another and even swore at crucial points of the case. Arnold saw and read all of that. And used it.

Looking past Volchek, my eyes focused on Arnold as he sat twenty-five feet away. As much as he liked to hide himself away from the public eye, he couldn't hide either himself or his expression from me. Fear almost dripped from his fat little nose. I knew then that Arnold had lip-read my conversation with Volchek. Arnold knew about the bomb for sure. But I didn't know why Arnold was there, or what he might do with that information.

I looked back at Volchek and said, "Give me a minute. There's somebody I have to talk—" But I couldn't finish my sentence; everyone in the courtroom stood up for Judge Pike as she made her return to the bear pit.

CHAPTER ELEVEN

Mr. Flynn, if you'd like to give your opening statement, please," said Judge Pike.

Pikey was in a fine mood today. She had a big media-hungry case and a chance to advance her career by putting away a known Russian gangster.

The opening statement is always important. It's your chance to frame the case for the jury. Miriam had hit the jury with a lot of information. She told them there was more than enough evidence to convict. She sounded like a real person, not a lawyer. I had to change that. I stood up and immediately began fidgeting with my jacket. The bomb felt awkward and heavy and somehow hot. My back was sweating even though I felt quite cool. My hands shook a little as I tilted the jug to pour myself a glass of water. After a long, cold drink, I felt ready. Miriam sat poised to take copious notes of the defense case. Her expert witness, Dr. Goldstein, sat three rows behind Miriam. He wasn't expecting to give evidence until later this afternoon or tomorrow morning. I recognized him from his photo on the university website. If possible, he looked like even more of a super-nerd in person than in his terrible photograph.

I turned to the jury and gave them a smile.

"Members of the jury, it's a pleasure to be here with you all. Ms. Sullivan spoke today for around two hours. I will speak now for around two minutes." A ripple of laughter from the jury. "This case involves a terrible crime. It's for the prosecution to prove to you that Olek Volchek committed this crime. If, at the conclusion of this case, you have reasonable doubts about whether Olek Volchek committed this crime, then it's your solemn duty to acquit. But it's your choice. Ms. Sullivan *told* you to find Mr. Volchek guilty. We won't *tell* you to do anything. We will *ask* you to consider the evidence, we will *invite* you to consider our view of the case, and we will leave it to *you* and *your* good judgment. And that's all I have to say at this point."

I sat down.

In a criminal case, there are two doors for a jury to walk through: guilty or not guilty. Miriam tried to push the jury through her door. I wanted to hold my door open for them and welcome them in. Juries behave just like every other person on the street—they don't like being pushed into anything; they like having a choice.

Dr. Goldstein looked nervously at his papers. The more surprised and off balance he became, the better it was for me. At that point I had a choice before me—I could play it safe or set a trap for Miriam. The trap was a risk that could easily backfire. On the other hand, if it worked, it could win me favor with the jury.

I took my chances.

I leaned over to Miriam, and Arturas strained to hear what I said. I'd told him to look out for it, that I might do it if it felt right. I didn't want to give the impression I was letting Miriam in on the bomb.

"Goldstein—he's a graphologist. Don't call him, or you'll regret it," I said.

"What the hell is a graphologist?" asked Miriam, as I'd expected. I had my answer already lined up for her.

"Goldstein is a forensic document examiner. His job is to determine authorship from a sample of handwriting; it's a scientific analysis. Graphology tries to interpret the author's personality from his handwriting; it's a bunch of shit. It's like a Christian archaeologist who digs up dinosaur bones testifying that the world is only five thousand years old. You can't be in both schools at once; it's hypocritical. Don't call him."

I sat down.

She would call him.

A look of anger spread over her proud features. The judge looked at her.

I'd finished my opening. It was time for the prosecution to begin their evidence. I'd thrown Miriam off guard. Goldstein looked to be the only prosecution witness in court. She stood up.

"Your Honor, I call Dr. Irving Goldstein."

Surprised at hearing his name so soon, Dr. Goldstein quickly folded his papers, buttoned his jacket, and moved forward. The smirk spreading across his face failed to mask his nerves. After all, this was the biggest case of his career. If my work paid off, it would be the last case of his career. He tripped over the leg of a chair on the way to the witness stand and held tightly to his papers. The report was his rock, and he clung to it. He had every right to feel confident, as his report was accurate, well written, and true. I couldn't challenge a single word of it.

Without anyone knowing it, I'd relied on Miriam being predictably brilliant. I thought of her as a great trial lawyer. She would do the same thing that I would do in her situation. I would take my opponent's best point and I would use it. I would ask the doc about graphology. I could control the question, make it sound normal, ordinary, even boring. I could give him all the time in the world to explain his answer fully, throwing out my opponent's best point like a dirty rag. Miriam would do the same thing.

I counted on it.

CHAPTER TWELVE

Goldstein was in his fifties, and it looked to me like he'd been fifty for around thirty years. His suit looked older than him, and to top it all, he wore a bow tie.

He stood for the oath. Adjusting his glasses as he read the card, he carefully recited the words that put him in my domain. Pouring himself two glasses of water, he settled down for a marathon session on the stand. Miriam would be quick with Goldstein. A good lawyer should be fast with all expert witnesses because, more often than not, they're just boring as hell. Their evidence is vital, but they're just pretty awful at explaining it so you have to keep it brief: *Who are you? Why are you smarter than any other guy in your field? Tell us what we need to know and then shut the hell up.* Miriam probably told him he would be in the box for a day. He didn't know he'd be in and out in an hour or two.

Miriam held Goldstein's report before her as if the paper itself were steering her toward the truth and Volchek's conviction.

"Dr. Goldstein, please outline for the jury your particular expertise and any relevant qualifications you hold," said Miriam. Her question was designed to settle the doc. *Tell these people on the jury why you're so smart.* It gets the doc talking, eases him in.

"I'm a forensic document examiner. I analyze handwriting to determine the identity of the author. I have studied at . . ." And away we go for five minutes on the doc's brilliance. I let this go. The more he told the jury how smart he was, the more he would look like an idiot when I tore into him. The doc started to look a little nervous, probably thinking that he'd been talking for too long. He began playing with his bow tie. Miriam read the signs and stepped in to save him.

"Thank you, Doctor. That's an impressive résumé. Please explain to the jury why you were engaged by the prosecution in this case."

"Of course. If the jury would turn to bundle D, page 287, you will see a copy of the murder note. These are the two halves of a one-ruble note with the victim's name written on one half. I am instructed that this note was found in the car driven by Witness X. I was instructed that Witness X will testify as to what the note means and its significance to the victim's murder. I can't comment on that. I was engaged by the prosecution to determine whether or not the handwriting on the note belonged to the defendant."

Miriam paused to let the jury find the page. Let them see the note. See the handwriting.

Mario Geraldo.

"Doctor, tell us how you examined this note." Miriam was careful to use the word "doctor" as often as possible without annoying the judge. The repetition of an expert's official title helped build confidence with the jury.

"This is the disputed handwriting. The defendant does not concede that this is his handwriting. To determine if this disputed handwriting belongs to the defendant, I conducted a scientific analysis of the defendant's known sources of handwriting for the purposes of forensic comparison."

"Where did you obtain this evidence of the defendant's known handwriting, Doctor?" asked Miriam.

"From tax returns, social security records, passport applications, citizenship applications, and other publicly filed documents bearing the defendant's signature and or handwriting."

"And what did you discover from your *forensic examination*?"

"I determined that there were distinct and unique characters or, as you might call it, letter formations present in all samples, including the disputed sample. In other words, the way he formed the letters and the particular and distinct manner in which he moved the pen to create the individual letters was enough to identify a definitive pattern of handwriting. From this I am able to say with a considerable degree of certainty that the defendant is the author of the note you see before you."

The big point. Like a good lawyer should, Miriam paused and looked at the jury, letting it sink in.

"Give us an example, Doctor, would you please?" said Miriam.

"Sure," said Goldstein, who fetched a blowup of the letter "G," which he explained was the letter "G" at the start of "Geraldo" from the disputed handwriting source. He also produced several slightly smaller copies of similar-looking letter "Gs," which he explained were from known sources of the defendant's handwriting. He placed all of the enlargements on the wide A-frame easel for the jury to consider.

"When one looks at the construction of the letter 'G' from 'Geraldo,' one can see there is a pronounced tail on the 'G,' which is formed with a continuous unbroken line descending from the top curve of the character. The character or letter is then finished with a horizontal dash beginning inside the curve of the 'G' and moving from left to right and slightly ascending. This letter or character is constructed identically in all the samples I examined, including known samples of the defendant's handwriting. Therefore I'm able to say, with a large degree of certainty, that it was the defendant who wrote the name of the victim on this one-ruble bill."

"To what degree are you certain, Doctor?"

"Ninety-five to ninety-eight percent certain."

"How can you be so certain?"

"This character has such a unique and consistent construction throughout all of the handwriting I examined. The note could only have been written by the defendant."

"Doctor, what is graphology?" she asked.

Miriam could have played out Goldstein's evidence for the rest of the day, but she couldn't afford that luxury because she'd taken up too much time in her opening statement. She had to keep things moving for this jury. Besides, Miriam no doubt believed I would take hours with the witness. Taking a long time cross-examining the expert is believed, by some lawyers, to be the best way to disable an expert witness. Trot out every theory; confuse, obfuscate, and argue with the expert about everything until the evidence becomes meaningless and dull. I didn't have that kind of time. Neither did Amy.

Dr. Goldstein appeared to be a little taken aback by Miriam's question, but he did manage a smile despite the obvious discomfort it caused him.

He shifted in his seat, crossed his legs, and wetted his lips. Graphology must have been close to his heart, and he obviously knew it was a possible line of attack.

"What is graphology? Well, it's a term used to describe an examination of handwriting and what it reveals about the author in relation to personality or sickness or psychosis. It's not concerned with determining who wrote a particular document. It's more about interpreting the personality of the author."

Go on, Miriam. Ask him. You know you want to, I thought.

"Doctor, some would say a single individual who practices both forensic document examination and graphology would be like having an archaeologist who's a born-again Christian testify that the world is only five thousand years old. In other words, it's a contradiction."

Bingo.

"Objection, Your Honor." I jumped to my feet, and despite my joy at hooking Miriam, I did my very best to look pissed as all hell.

"On what grounds?" asked the judge.

"On the grounds of religious belief, Your Honor: I believe in God, and I don't want my beliefs questioned by the prosecutor; nor do I think it's right that the Lord Jesus Christ, our Lord, should be dragged into a legal argument by the prosecution. It's a discriminatory statement against Christians; it implies an atheist belief on behalf of the prosecutor, and it's against the constitutional right to religious freedom. No matter what the prosecutor might believe, it's wrong to impose those beliefs on others or ridicule my beliefs to prove a point."

Miriam looked like she wanted to kill me. I didn't blame her. It was nasty, and she'd fallen for it.

The jury looked like they would happily carry me home on their shoulders. I'd banked on a Christian jury in this part of town, and I was right. Four jurors wore crucifixes. Finding a juror's idol and holding it before them is the surest way of getting them on your side. You just need to find the right idol. If I were in Vegas, it would have been Elvis, or Sammy Davis, Jr.; in football-crazy Texas—Sammy Baugh; in Oklahoma—Mickey Mantle. In this part of New York, something liberal and Christian works every time. Most of the jury smiled at me, but the ones who weren't were too busy giving Miriam dirty looks.

Big score.

But the judge was not at all impressed. She saw that coming a mile away.

"Ms. Sullivan, perhaps you could consider rephrasing your last question," said the judge.

Miriam was done.

"Nothing further, Your Honor."

CHAPTER THIRTEEN

On my feet, behind the defense table with my props ready, tucked underneath the desk like a cheap magician, I suddenly became conscious that I hadn't prepared, that I could fall flat on my ass at any second. I told myself to take it slow. My eyes closed for a moment. Just enough time to take in a deep breath, and yet I knew I would see her in the dark. Hanna Tublowski. I saw her most nights before I fell asleep. That same image woke me every morning. I'd tried to wash away that vision with bourbon and cold beer. I knew when I first saw her that my heart would forever bear a scar, and I hadn't practiced law since. The path of my life seemed to be broken in two, a life seen in terms of what happened before I took on the Berkley case and what happened after.

When my eyes opened and my head cleared, I looked at Goldstein and I could again see the questions in my mind.

"Dr. Goldstein," I heard myself say, "would I be right in saying that if you're comparing handwriting samples, it's best practice to compare like for like documents? So, for example, two résumés, two passport applications, two driver's license applications."

"Yes, but that's not always possible. Not unless your client wrote two different orders to have people killed and I could examine them both," said Goldstein, looking at me over the rim of his glasses. A nervous round of laughter made its way across the audience. The doc looked rather too pleased with himself and his answer. I needed to take more care.

"You said that you formed the opinion that the unknown author of the note and the known author of the sample documents, my client, were in fact the same person. And you came to that conclusion based upon your examination of the letter formation and construction?"

"Yes," said Goldstein. He'd obviously been told to keep it tight with me, to make his answers short and snappy. The idiot's guide to surviving cross-examination—don't say too much and you can't do too much damage.

"Isn't that what graphology does? It's an interpretation of letter and word formation?"

"Yes."

"So there's a strong similarity in the analysis?"

"To a degree."

"So there's a strong similarity in the analysis?" I repeated, very slowly, like talking to a naughty child and making sure he understood the question. He had to give a more definitive answer now or risk looking like a liar or a moron in front of the jury. My method of repeating the question already made him look evasive.

"Yes. There is a strong similarity in the analysis."

Excellent, I thought.

"The prosecutor tried to ask you about graphology. I think she was trying to ask you if it's a legitimate system of analysis. So, is it legitimate?"

"Yes. Of course it is."

"Isn't it true that a graphologist interpreted a blot on John Wayne's signature to be his unconscious mind telling him that he had lung cancer? That's correct, isn't it?"

I gave the jury an incredulous look, like this was the craziest thing I'd ever heard, but I put my back to the witness so that he couldn't see my expression. I had, in fact, asked him if a graphologist had made that interpretation about John Wayne, and of course, he would know that to be correct. But because I gave the jury a strong visual aid, the jury heard an answer to a different question.

"Yes," he said. He answered correctly, that a graphologist had indeed made this interpretation, but because of my face pulling, the jury heard him say that he agreed with the crazy theory, not the mere fact that the theory existed.

"So it's more like fortune-telling?"

"No. It is a legitimate interpretational method of analysis."

"I don't know what that means, Doctor." I turned to the jury and put my hands in the air to let them know that even the high-paid lawyer didn't know what this guy was talking about. They smiled.

"Let's see if we can have a practical demonstration."

It was time to load up the base without the doc seeing. I pulled out my blowup of a letter "G" that I'd made in the photocopier upstairs and held it up for the jury. I turned it so the doc could see it and then placed it on the easel next to the "G" from the one-ruble note. With both the blowups side by side, they looked identical. Most prosecutors would object at this point, and we'd have an argument on whether I could test the expert's findings. Normally the judge gives a little leeway to cross-examine. Miriam didn't object because she knew I'd get my way and that it might appear to the jury that she was shielding her witness. When she could, Miriam liked to let witnesses stand on their own feet.

"Doctor this 'G' is constructed in a similar way to the letter 'G' in the disputed note and the known samples of my client's signature, correct?" I hoped he would agree. It seemed like a minute had gone by with just him and the jury staring at the large letters in front of them. Goldstein screwed up his face as he carefully examined the letters.

I had to give him a nudge. "The 'G' on this blowup does appear to be similar to the letter 'G' in the note, doesn't it?"

"It could be, yes."

"It is similar, isn't it?"

"Yes."

"And this one?" I pulled up another big sheet of paper. The "G" looked similar, but it was a different sample; part of another letter was visible on this copy. A long laborious stare from Goldstein, but not as long as the last.

"Yes. It's very similar."

"Graphologists make judgments about people based on the way a person might construct the letter 'G,' correct?"

"Correct."

"And isn't it correct that a graphologist would say that the person who wrote this letter 'G' is a *sexual deviant*?" I let the last two words dominate the sentence by increasing my volume and letting those words boom and echo around the courtroom—a great way to wake everybody up. Handwriting is dull. Sex is interesting. Sexual deviancy is damn interesting.

"Yes," he said. "The author, or whoever wrote those letter 'Gs,' would have tendencies toward deviancy in their sex life."

I paused. I wanted the jury's mind working, questioning this statement.

"You have met the acting district attorney for this part of the world, Miriam Sullivan?"

He was suddenly nervous. "Yes. Of course I have."

"Is Miriam Sullivan a sexual deviant?"

"What? Of course not!"

"Your Honor . . ." Miriam cried.

"Yes. It's okay, Ms. Sullivan," said Judge Pike. "Mr. Flynn, please behave yourself."

"My apologies, Your Honor, but might I just ask if Your Honor indulges in any sexually deviant practices?" Now, this was totally outrageous. I was in danger of losing all my jury points and ending up in the cells below the court for contempt.

Judge Pike dragged her glasses to the end of her cosmetically corrected nose and looked at me over those rims, like a serial killer surveying her prey over the hood of a hot Chevy before running over the little maggot. "Mr. Flynn, you've got ten seconds before I throw your ass in jail." The jury looked physically shocked.

I felt two blasts of vibration across the small of my back. Arturas had triggered the device. I remembered what he'd said earlier about the remote detonator: two buttons, one to arm, one to detonate. I figured the bomb was now armed and live.

CHAPTER FOURTEEN

Arturas looked at me like I held a knife to his mother's throat. I was certain that arming the bomb was a warning—if I got sent to custody, Arturas would trigger the device.

Judge Pike seemed to rise from her chair as if the fury boiling in her cheeks was enough to physically levitate her from her seat.

"Your Honor, members of the jury, please turn to bundle B, page seven," I said.

I'd never seen pages turned more furiously. Judge Pike opened her file to the correct page and returned her outraged stare to me. The jury looked perplexed.

I placed myself beside the easel to emphasize my point.

"Your Honor, the first character I have blown up here is the first 'G' from your signature on the certificate of listing on page seven—Gabriella Pike. Correct?"

"Yes," she said, still angry but now a little curious.

"Dr. Goldstein, according to your findings, the judge could have written the disputed note."

"No."

I took a yellow Post-it note out of my pants pocket and handed it to the well-dressed Hispanic juror.

"This note was handed to me by the prosecutor this morning. Please pass it around to your fellow jurors."

YOUR CLIENT'S GOING DOWN. I'LL HAVE HIS BAIL REVOKED BY 5 P.M.

"The jury will see the 'G' at the beginning of 'going' is in fact the same letter that I've blown up here, in this poster. It's the same method of construction used by the author of the disputed handwriting. Isn't that right, Doctor?"

"I already said it was similar."

"On your evidence, the murder note could have been written by the defendant or the judge or the prosecutor?"

"No. You're twisting everything."

"Let's allow the jury to look at the note. They can decide."

The note passed around the jury. One by one they looked at the note. Looked at the blown-up "G" from "going" and looked at Miriam. The look was the same; Miriam was a kid with her hand in the candy jar. She put her head in her hands. The jury would think her presumptuous, cocky, not one of them.

"Let's be clear about this, Doctor. Some graphologists say that a person who puts a pronounced tail on their letter 'G' has sexually deviant tendencies, but not all graphologists have the same opinion, right?" He thought I was throwing him a rope, and he grabbed it.

"That's right."

"Doctor, isn't it correct that we construct letters of the alphabet according to how we were initially taught to write them, either at home or in school?"

"That's a big factor, but not the only one. Some people alter their handwriting as they get older, but not substantially; I grant you that."

"So, the nuns who taught me to write in Catholic school. If they put a tail on the letter 'G' when they wrote it up on the blackboard to allow me to copy it, that wouldn't mean they were sexually deviant, now, would it?"

The members of the jury who wore crucifixes seemed to sit up a little straighter.

"No. It wouldn't."

"And it doesn't mean that the judge or the prosecutor have deviant inclinations either, or indeed, whoever wrote on this one-ruble note. It's more than likely to do with the way they were taught to write, and lots of perfectly normal people construct that letter in exactly the same way, correct?"

"You're right."

"It's a fairly common way of constructing that letter?"

"Yes."

"There's maybe two hundred people in this court. How many would construct that letter of the alphabet in the same way? A quarter? A third of them?"

"A good many would construct it that way," he said. He was backpedaling rapidly. His hands shook as he took a sip of water. I'd taken him to a place he really didn't want to go, and Goldstein wanted to get out as quickly as possible and move on.

The jury finished handing around Miriam's note, and the court officer handed it to the judge. If possible, she looked angrier with Miriam than with me. I'd almost finished with Goldstein; the lid was on the coffin, and I just had to nail it down.

"It's impossible to tell if someone is sexually abnormal just from their handwriting, isn't it?"

"I would have to say yes. On reflection, it's impossible," he said, quick to divorce himself finally from graphology. Unfortunately, that was the end for Dr. Goldstein.

"You now say it's impossible, yet in the year 2000, you wrote a paper entitled, *Identifying Repeat Sexual Offenders through their Handwriting.* In this paper you say you can identify rapists, pedophiles, and deviants from nothing more than their tax returns. You did write this paper, didn't you?" I held it aloft for the jury.

Goldstein stared straight ahead. His jaw and mouth worked soundlessly until he nodded.

"I take it that's a 'yes.' So, Doctor, given that your sworn testimony today is that it's impossible to identify sexual practices from handwriting, but in the year 2000, you wrote a paper claiming that not only can you identify sexual predators from their handwriting but that you can discern what kind of predator they are . . ." I paused. I hadn't actually asked a question yet, but the pause served to let me look at the jury as if I were taking my question from them. "The question this jury will want an answer to is this: Doctor, were you lying in your paper in 2000, or are you lying now? Which is the lie?"

An unanswerable question is clearly the best kind. It didn't matter what he said; no one would believe a word. Indeed, he said nothing. He simply hung his head. Two of the black women on the jury physically recoiled from Dr. Goldstein with a healthy look of disgust on their faces. The rest of the jury looked angry at the doc or just couldn't look at him at all and stared at their shoes instead.

No re-examination from Miriam. Her note had given me the idea. The "G" in her note had been written in a similar way to the letter "G" that Goldstein focused on in his report, and it didn't take long to find another similar letter in the trial bundle. Lucky it was from the judge. Doc Goldstein walked sheepishly from the witness stand to take his place at the back of the court.

"I can't stand any more of this today," said Judge Pike. The armed guard came back into court to escort the jury to their room before they left for the day.

"All rise," said the security officer. Pike slammed the door of her chambers closed on her way out. The court began to empty. It was four thirty. Miriam went into a huddle with her team. The jacket felt heavy on my shoulders. I'd run my persuader as best I could; if it worked, then Volchek should have been dancing a jig. When my gaze fell across him, I saw him smiling, but Arturas, curiously, was not.

As the reporters rushed out, I saw one man standing against the exiting tide: Arnold Novoselic. He buttoned his coat and slipped along the benches as he made his way toward the prosecution table, his gaze permanently fixed upon me.

I shook my head, but his stare never faltered and his look seemed to be one of determination. At least I knew Arnold wasn't just here to observe: He was batting for the prosecution.

Miriam ignored her team once she registered Arnold's approach. She met him before he could reach her table, and they sat down on an empty bench together. I glanced at Volchek and saw that he'd remained seated with his arms folded. As I looked back at the benches, I saw both Miriam and Arnold turning their eyes away from me: Arnold had told Miriam about the bomb.

They got up together and made for the door. Miriam's team saw their leader leaving and quickly packed away their files and followed her. Before Miriam reached the door, she turned back and looked at me with a puzzled expression. I thought that could only be bad news. After the pounding she'd just taken, she should've been looking at me like I'd just keyed her car. Averting her gaze, she scanned the emptying room, and her eyes found the three men in crisp suits whom I took to be feds. Arnold and Miriam waited at the door, and I saw Miriam introduce the jury consultant to the FBI before they left together.

I hung my head and swore under my breath. I'd run the perfect persuader and hopefully bought enough trust from the Bratva, but all that was about to change. From the look on Miriam's face as she left the court, I knew I had a fifty-fifty chance of being arrested the second I stepped out of that courtroom and Amy wouldn't live a moment longer.

CHAPTER FIFTEEN

I felt more and more uncomfortable as the courtroom emptied. The Russians didn't move from their seats. Within a minute, I was alone with them in the courtroom.

"Victor, get the door," said Volchek.

Big Victor looked like he could eat his way through any door. He had a huge set of shoulders and a neck like a Michelin tire. Victor put his hands on the rail as he got up, and I noticed that his knuckles were misshapen and scarred. His nose looked like it had been set improperly after a bad break, and I figured him for a fighter. I'd been the toughest kid on my block and quickly grew to be the best young boxing talent in Brooklyn. But when I started training in Mickey Hooley's, I quickly realized I didn't have what it took to be a pro fighter. I still liked the training, though. Until I was eighteen, if I wasn't hustling in the street, I was in the gym, pounding the shit out of something. That was a long time ago, and even though I had a little talent, I didn't rate my chances against Victor.

Victor walked slowly toward the exit. He put his wide back to the double doors, barring entry. It looked like we were going to have a little talk.

"I want to talk to my daughter," I said.

"I will rape and kill your daughter if you ask that question again," said Arturas.

I didn't know what the hell had gotten into him. He should've been pleased things had gone so well. I shut up and silently vowed that if I got out of this, Arturas would suffer. Volchek, on the other hand, seemed much happier.

"You did well, lawyer. If you do as I ask, your daughter will be returned to you unharmed," said Volchek, now trying to take up Arturas's trademark smile.

"We're not risking the security checks again. The courthouse stays open all night, and there are people all over the building for night court. You will stay in the little office upstairs. Don't worry. Gregor will be back soon. You will have plenty of company. Victor and Arturas will also stay to keep an eye on you," said Volchek.

I thought then that Gregor must have been the monster who put my lights out in the limo. When I'd woken up on the limo seats, he was gone.

I'd spent more than one night in this courtroom, and in hindsight, I regretted every single one of them.

Christine once told me that she felt alone in our marriage. In the last year of our relationship, I hadn't actually slept in our house that often. Jack and I were killing ourselves to cover the courts twenty-four hours a day, and I'd missed my family. I had told myself I was doing it for them, so they could have a better life. But Christine and Amy really just wanted to see me. Even with all the extra work, the money still wasn't coming in too fast. Christine asked me if I was really working or if I was having an affair. She didn't really think I was having an affair; she was just angry. This wasn't the kind of life she'd expected. In the aftermath of the Berkley case and my law license being suspended for six months, instead of staying home, I headed out to the bar and spent more time away from the people I loved the most. I came to realize that I didn't want to face Christine and tell her that I'd thrown away all those nights spent in the Dracula Hotel; that I'd missed Amy's school plays and sports days to duke it out in court with a judge; that I'd sacrificed our marriage for nothing. Up until last year, Christine and I'd had a pretty good marriage. We had a good house in Queens, a smart daughter, and even though I didn't make that much money and worked impossible hours, we had been reasonably happy. Or so I had thought.

I'd met Christine in law school. I didn't speak to her for the first month of school. I just couldn't summon up the courage. There were plenty of pretty, rich girls in my class and not too many guys like me, who turned up to lectures with ripped jeans, oil on their T-shirt, and the stink of last night's beer still on their breath. Back then I wasn't a bad-looking guy, and I didn't lack attention from the girls who wanted to slum it for a night. But I wanted Christine. We had met for the first time on the day after Saint Patrick's. I stumbled out of Flannery's at nine a.m., still drunk, and jumped in a cab to take me to class. Before the cabdriver took off, a girl opened the passenger door and hopped in beside me; it was Christine.

"You're going my way, right?" she said.

"Right," I said.

The cab pulled away, and she began stripping down to her underwear. She took off her top and her jeans and dumped them on the floor of the cab, reached into her bag, put on some deodorant and a fresh pair of pants and a top. She had been on an all-night drinking session, too. Throughout this performance, she didn't say a word. The cabbie and I just stared, open-mouthed. We pulled up outside the entrance to the law school, and she paid the fare, got out, tucked her long brown hair behind her ear, and said to me, "Sorry. Are you shocked?"

"No," I replied. "I'm delighted."

That was the start of it. We met again that same evening and fell in love over a pitcher of beer and a bucket of shrimp that I hadn't paid for.

She was free. That was what I loved about her. I loved her even more after we got married and she gave me Amy to hold for the first time. Amy had the same free spirit as her mom.

I felt that vibration at the base of my spine again, the same vibration that I'd felt earlier in court, and I guessed that was Arturas deactivating the device.

"Do you know what pleased me most of all today?" said Volchek. "You didn't flinch when you felt the bomb arming. I saw Arturas arm it. You understand what you have to do now to get your daughter and get out of this." He gestured to the witness box. "If I gave you a chance at cross-examining Benny, what would you ask him?"

"I don't know yet. The obvious questions spring to mind, that he's trying to implicate you to save himself. That he made a deal with the prosecution to avoid a life sentence and that he's no more credible than your average jailhouse snitch." My train of thought led me into a question, something that had bothered me about this case since I'd first read about it in the paper. Volchek was on trial for a single murder, the murder of Mario Geraldo. Volchek was the head of a vast, multimillion-dollar criminal organization. If Benny got caught in the middle of a hit, why didn't he make a good deal? Why didn't he spill his guts to the FBI about Volchek's entire operation and walk into witness protection instead of giving him up for one murder and having to do serious prison time when all of this was over?

"You see, the problem with attacking Little Benny because he's a snitch is a little flawed because he only dropped the dime on you for this murder. He didn't tell the feds about the rest of your operation. That gives him some credibility as a witness. He could have told them, couldn't he?" I said.

Both Volchek and Arturas remained silent. I took that to be a *yes*.

"He's been sentenced already, hasn't he? I read in the *Times* that an anonymous witness in an upcoming Russian Mafia trial got time. Everyone reading that knew it was your case. How long did he get? Ten years?"

"Twelve," said Arturas.

"So what stopped him giving up the good stuff? It doesn't make any sense. Why didn't he give up your whole operation and walk away a free man with a new identity, courtesy of the FBI?"

Volchek spat on the floor, and although his face was turned toward me, his eyes sought out Arturas as he said, "Perhaps Little Benny still has some loyalties." His bleak, ferocious gaze returned to me.

"No matter. I do not think you can win this case, Mr. Flynn. You can try. I will allow you that. But come tomorrow, we plant the bomb under the seat. We won't risk planting it tonight in case a cleaner finds it. Tomorrow we plant the bomb, just as Arturas planned," said Volchek, and as he spoke the name of his lieutenant, I saw again some form of dark, bloody desire in his expression, as if the murders that went before and the deaths still to come were a source of sadistic pleasure for Volchek. This man was the head of his organization and yet he'd taken the time to torture Jack and his sister. Arturas was all business, whereas Volchek enjoyed the wet work.

For all of Volchek's talk of the Bratva, of loyalty and trust, it didn't change the fact that when his man got caught, he pointed the finger straight at the boss, at the *pakhan*, at the very man who, in giving him that ruble bill, had given him his *tselkovy*, his *whole heart*. In large criminal organizations you have to have a certain level of trust. You demand loyalty or you don't stay in business too long. I guessed Volchek was in his early fifties. Not many gangsters live to that age, never mind stay out of jail, and this fact was testament to the loyalty that existed in the Bratva's ranks. Loyalty clearly came with high expectations, and if they were not met, the consequences were inevitable. The scar on Arturas's cheek was probably some form of testament to that demand. Volchek despised Little Benny. Blowing someone up sends a message to everyone in the Bratva ranks. It sends a message to every law-enforcement agency in the world. It sends a message to every rival gang: We can get you—anywhere. Betray the Russian Mafia and die.

Darkness fell on the building as a huge rain cloud moved overhead, muting the dying light.

I heard a noise, loud and urgent. Someone pounding on the courtroom door.

CHAPTER SIXTEEN

I watched Victor and Arturas drop to their knees and remove something from their shoes. A hidden compartment in each of their boot heels stored short, wickedly curved blades. They were made of the same material; no bulky handles, just slim, gray, single-piece knives. I guessed them to be ceramic. That material wouldn't show up on the metal detectors. The blades probably cost a lot of money. You can buy a decent knife for seventy-five dollars. These knives probably cost seventy-five hundred each.

This was their backup. If it all goes to shit, they pull out knives. No guns. Whatever Arturas had on me, I knew then he didn't have that big revolver with him. If they couldn't get the bomb in there, then he sure as hell couldn't smuggle a gun through security, either.

Victor listened at the door, his knife in his left hand held down by his side, the tip of the blade held upward, toward the ceiling. Arturas appeared more accomplished with the knife. He drew it, reversed it, and held it blade to ground in the ideal fighting grip: allowing him to cut, stab, and run. The reverse grip keeps the knife discreet and avoids creating an easy target for your opponent to knock the weapon out of your hand. In addition, striking down allows a lot more force to be generated, and it's a lot faster than driving a blade upward. I'd had occasion to use a knife in the past—for protection.

Arturas joined Victor at the door.

They listened.

Nothing.

BANG! BANG!

Arturas gestured me forward and said, "We'll open the door. You speak to whoever is there and deal with it."

Victor took the left-hand door. Arturas moved to the right, holding the detonator in his left hand. The bomb vibrated again, and for the first time I noticed a red dot of light on the detonator, which I guessed meant that it was armed and ready.

The courtroom echoed softly with our breath.

"What if it's the feds?" I said.

Arturas said, "Why would the feds want to speak to you?"

"The prosecutor hired a jury consultant. I saw him in court today. His name is Arnold Novoselic. Arnold is a renowned lip-reader. I'm concerned he may have read me or one of you guys talking about the bomb."

Volchek shook his head and said, "Impossible. See who's at the door."

Arturas and Victor gripped the door handles and looked at each other.

They opened the doors to a tumultuous river of light.

They were lined up like a firing squad, but instead of muzzle flash, I drowned in rapid fire from a dozen cameras. I instinctively put my hands up to my face, shielding my eyes from the sudden fluorescent onslaught.

When we started our law firm, Jack had insisted on publicity shots for advertising. I had to sit in a bright room next to a large plant and smile for forty minutes while a photographer got overpaid to make me look half decent on a poster or a coffee mug. In hindsight, the coffee mugs were a mistake. No client likes to have their attorney's face on their mug. Only reminds them of their car accident, rape, divorce, murder rap, or—worst of all—their bill. The memory of that day at the photographer's made me smile. I'd been bored. I'd taken out a pack of cards and hit the photographer and his assistant for fifteen hundred each. I'd had to. In those days, Jack and I didn't have the money to pay for gas, never mind photo shoots. I felt my teeth grinding at the thought of Jack and what he'd gotten me into.

With my hands in front of my face, I started forward. The photographers weren't expecting it. A tall guy who shined a permanent beam of light in my face from his TV camera almost fell when I started toward him. I'm sure every one of them had shot me before with a big stupid grin on my face and my arm around some lowlife. Like it or not, I operated a scale; the more horrific the crime the client was alleged to have committed, the closer I would be to them when we were photographed. According to that ratio, I should have been standing beside Volchek with my hand on his ass. If you are any kind of a decent criminal lawyer, you will get your picture in the paper and you will get to know some reporters.

Behind the cameramen lay the real sharks—the reporters. The camera guys gave way, and instantly, I was surrounded by microphones, voice recorders, and pleading hands. Apart from the ship that sank on the Hudson a few days ago, this was the big story in town. Every reporter wanted a piece. Volchek was one of the biggest organized crime bosses ever to face a modern trial, and since no cameras were allowed in court, they had all waited for him to leave the courtroom so they could get their shots and sound bites before he ducked into an elevator.

"Eddie, how are you going to defend Volchek?"

"Eddie, great show today. What's in store for tomorrow?"

"Mr. Flynn, will your client testify?"

A dozen other questions were flung at me all at once. I made it across the hall to the elevators and turned to the crowd of reporters. They hadn't noticed Volchek. He stood behind Victor, which was much the same as standing behind a moving wall. The elevator doors chimed and opened. Victor dragged the suitcase of files and moved behind the reporters and around their left flank as they continued to focus on me. Sneaking in front of them and then ducking behind me into the elevator, Victor beckoned me inside. Volchek moved into the corner of the elevator while Arturas and Victor stood in front. The reporters now realized who was being protected and called the photographers forward. But it was too late.

The doors started to close. Arturas and Victor were both on edge, breathing heavily. They kept their hands in their coat pockets, no doubt clutching their knives. Their eyes were wide and watchful for any threat. These guys were dangerous like this. Adrenaline and fear were a powerful combination in anyone, but in men like Arturas—deadly. A hand stretched out and caught the closing doors, arresting their path and forcing them open. It wasn't an overenthusiastic reporter, as I'd hoped.

It was Barry, the security guard. He had the look of a man who'd been searching for me all day. As the doors opened again, he joined me in the elevator.

"Eddie, I got to thank you again for what you're doing for Terry. I told him you would represent him for free, and he nearly hit the ceiling he's so happy. He called his wife; they want you over for dinner."

Barry stood around a lot. When you do that long enough, you develop a pose. A way of standing that eases your body and causes you the least pain. Barry shifted his weight onto his right leg. He waited for an answer from me with his right hand resting casually on the butt of his .45 Beretta.

Victor hit the button for the top floor again.

I looked over Barry's shoulder and saw Miriam standing about twenty feet away, talking to one of the feds, the tallest one. He wore a sharp navy suit, white shirt, and blue tie. His hair was so black that I thought it had been dyed. Miriam pointed at me. The fed looked straight at me and then glanced upward as he began to walk toward the elevator. He must have known he wouldn't reach me before the doors closed, and he was checking the electronic floor display above the elevator doors. He would wait and check which floor we stopped on before following us up.

The elevator doors closed.

Jesus Christ, Barry. What the hell are you doing? I'm wearing a bomb, was what I wanted to say.

I didn't, of course.

Barry waited for me to accept his friend's invitation for meat loaf and beer, but I couldn't look at him. It was because of me that he was in this elevator. If I hadn't said anything about Terry's case, if I'd politely declined, he wouldn't be here. Arturas set his lips tight.

I picked up Barry's face only in my peripheral vision. He chewed gum. I could see his jaw muscle flexing and relaxing at the side of his head. A faint wet chewing sound as Barry rolled the gum around in his mouth. The elevator slowed at the nineteenth floor.

"Nineteenth floor?" said Barry, clocking the illuminated floor number on the elevator panel. "You pulling an all-nighter?"

"Yeah. Big case. It's quiet up there, and we can use the space. The conference rooms downstairs are too small. I'll be here with my clients most of the night. If I get a chance, I might slide down to night court later. Which judge is taking the graveyard shift?"

"Judge Ford," said Barry.

"You'll have to tell Terry I need a rain check on dinner. Say, it's still okay to work up here, right? I haven't been in this courthouse in a while."

"Sure. Happens all the time. I found a pillow, a toothbrush, and a shaving kit in the conference room on the tenth floor yesterday. As long as you don't move in permanently, it's all good. This is a public building, after all, and we never close, so yeah, be my guest. I'm pulling a double shift myself, so I'll make sure you're not disturbed. Say, some of the guys are ordering pizza later. You want I could send you up a couple slices?"

"No, thanks, Barry. Appreciate it."

The elevator opened on the nineteenth floor. Barry moved to the side so we could squeeze past him.

"Tell you the truth, judging by the state of this place, I don't think even the cleaners come up here no more," said Barry with a derisory laugh.

Barry stayed in the elevator for the ride down. We moved back to the reception room and the chambers that we'd occupied earlier. Arturas unlocked the door and we filed in. He closed it and was about to insert his key into the lock.

"Don't lock it. The FBI are on their way up here."

Arturas and Volchek crowded around me.

"What are you talking about?" said Volchek.

"I just saw the prosecutor pointing me out to the fed in the blue suit. The jury consultant I spoke to you about, he must have told her about the bomb, and now she's told the feds. They're on their way. I saw one of them before the elevator closed on the fourteenth floor. He was looking up at the floor-level indicator above the elevator. He was checking which floor we were headed to."

"Victor, go watch the elevator. Tell me where it stops and where it's headed," said Volchek.

We stood in the reception, silently waiting for Victor.

"Moving past the seventeenth floor on its way down," cried Victor from the hallway.

"If it stops on fourteen, they're coming straight up," I said.

"Moving past sixteen."

Volchek and Arturas stared at me, but I couldn't look at them. I kept my gaze on the floor and prayed the elevator made it past the fourteenth.

"It's stopped on fourteen," said Victor.

Arturas put his knife to my cheek.

Volchek took out his cell phone and dialed a number.

My legs began shaking, and I could feel my pulse thumping in my temples.

Volchek's call was answered quickly. "It's Olek. We may need to kill the girl. Stay on the line and wait for my order." He dropped his arm, holding the phone by his side, listening, waiting to hear from Victor whether the elevator was headed this way.

The tremors began to crawl over my whole body and I shook my hands, set my jaw, and waited.

CHAPTER SEVENTEEN

My mind raced as I fought to control my panic. Arturas pressed the knife harder into my cheek.

"Wait," I said. "Just relax. The feds aren't going to arrest me. They're not going to risk blowing the trial. The jury consultant spoke to the prosecutor, and it was the prosecutor who spoke to the fed. Miriam is trying her dream case against the head of the Russian mob. There's no way she would allow the feds to pick me up because that leaves you without a lawyer. That puts the trial in jeopardy. If they do come up, it doesn't mean anything. It's just a shakedown. I'll bullshit them and send them on their way. Don't hurt Amy, please." The last word caught in my throat.

"Elevator's passing the fifteenth floor; they're coming up," said Victor from the hall.

"It's over," said Volchek. "Arturas, kill him. We have to run."

My heart stopped as Volchek began to raise the phone to his ear.

"No! You can't. The feds will be here any second. You're out of time. Let me talk. I'll get rid of them. I can do it!" I yelled.

"Olek, we can't run. He's right. We have no time," said Arturas, his face pale with fear; his plan was collapsing around him.

"Sixteenth floor," Victor called.

"Let me go. Let me do it. I'm your only play here," I said.

Volchek hesitated and hung his head. He whirled around, ready to lash out, but stopped. He swore. I readied myself, arms wide, feet set. It would take half a second to grab Arturas's wrist with my right hand, drag it to my chest, and hold it firm with the knife close to my skin and another half a second for my other hand to grab his elbow and push for the sky, breaking his arm and dislocating his shoulder. That still wouldn't give me enough time to grab the phone from Volchek before he ordered my daughter murdered.

"Seventeen," said Victor, marching back into reception.

"Everyone sit down. Arturas, give me a file. We're in this room to work on your case. Everyone calm down—I can do this," I said, my voice almost giving out.

Arturas removed the knife from my skin and reversed it, hiding the blade from sight.

"If you try anything or if I even see you get off your chair, I will have the girl's throat cut. Do you hear me?" said Volchek.

"I hear you," I said.

He was back on the phone. "I'm hanging up. If you get a text from me in the next few minutes, you kill the girl."

I watched him typing something onto the keypad of the cell phone before he held it up toward me. It was a text message.

Kill her, it read, and below the message were two options: send and delete.

"My phone will be on that table. If I push one button, she dies. Remember that," said Volchek.

I heard a chime and the clatter from the elevator doors opening. We scrambled for the chairs. Volchek and I sat at the desk. Arturas threw a file to me from the suitcase, and I opened it to a random page. Arturas and Victor sat on the couch.

Just for a second, I saw a man in a suit walk briskly past the door. He turned and signaled to someone behind him, then quickly moved past the office. Behind him came a tall man wearing a white shirt and navy suit—the same man with the dark, slicked-back hair whom I'd seen talking to Miriam just moments before. He stopped at the door, made a circling motion to the first man, then stepped into the office.

"I'm Bill Kennedy, FBI," said the tall man in the navy suit, flashing ID. I was right; I can spot a fed a mile away. "Are you Eddie Flynn?" he asked.

"I'm Eddie Flynn. If you don't mind, I'm in the middle of a meeting with my client. He's on trial for murder, in case you hadn't noticed, so if you'll excuse us."

I turned away from Kennedy and met Volchek's eyes. His phone lay on the reception desk. The text message still there, waiting either to be sent or deleted. I hid my hands. In these situations, when you can, you hide your hands. They give you away. They shake, or you hold your fists too tightly, revealing bone-white knuckles, or they become variously colored, depending on which hand you've been squeezing to hide your anxiety.

"I'm afraid you're going to have to come with me," said Kennedy.

"I'm afraid I don't have time for the FBI's little games. Close the door on your way out."

Kennedy said, "Mr. Flynn, if you don't come with me, I'll have no choice but to place you under arrest."

"The DA put you up to this?" I asked.

"I've been informed of a possible bomb threat. My protocols are clear, but I'm hoping we can clear this up and avoid an arrest. If you step out, we can talk. I'll just need a few moments."

A small, almost imperceptible shake of the head from Volchek and he placed his fingers on top of his cell phone.

"I'm not going anywhere," I said.

"Mr. Flynn, I want you to stand up."

"No," I said firmly. My hands began moving nervously under the table.

Kennedy reached into his jacket, drew his Glock 19, and held it against his thigh.

"Mr. Flynn, this is your final warn—"

I cut him off. "You have to be the dumbest FBI agent I ever met," I said.

"Let me spell it out for you—if you're not on your feet in ten seconds, I will arrest you," said Kennedy, his voice rising, his tone more aggressive.

Two men arrived in the hall behind Kennedy; one came from his left-hand side, one from his right. The other agents I'd seen earlier. They must have come up in the elevator together and swept the whole floor while Kennedy kept me talking. These men wore dark suits and white shirts. The man on the left looked Italian. He had good skin and clear, youthful eyes.

The other man was squat and powerful, with red hair and an untidy mustache.

I don't know if I saw Volchek move or if I just sensed his movement. It didn't matter really. I reached for his phone, to stop him, but he had taken his hand away and placed it on the desk beside the phone. Inclining my neck, I saw that the draft text message remained on the phone, the options to send or delete still available. I couldn't read Volchek's expression, but I heard him exhale before he folded his arms.

"Floor is secure," said the young, tall agent.

Both of the agents registered that Kennedy's gun was drawn.

"What's going on, Bill?" said the red-haired agent.

Kennedy ignored his colleague.

"Mr. Flynn, time's up." He took the Glock two-handed and held it before him, aiming it at the floor.

The smaller agent with the red hair said, "Bill, take it easy. He's just a lawyer."

Kennedy ignored him. I took a moment to survey Agent Kennedy. He held the Glock in a two-handed grip: his right hand around the butt of the weapon, his left cupping his right, stabilizing the aim. The skin surrounding his left-hand thumbnail looked raw and swollen, as if he'd been worrying the nail. I took this as a sure sign of a nervous and cautious man. The FBI held Little Benny in protective custody somewhere, and Kennedy was obviously worried as hell about losing his prize witness. He had every right to be nervous.

In moments like this, I was usually cool. I'd been in tight spots before, but never with my daughter's life hanging in the balance. It was that thought that brought my anger. Just like in the limo. I needed that anger. It cleared my head, and I remembered Arnold Novoselic, downstairs, talking to Miriam, and I saw my way out.

"I want to know your probable cause," I said.

Kennedy didn't answer. He didn't retaliate with another threat, either. He just stood there. Then I realized that if Kennedy had felt solid about arresting me, I would have been facedown on the floor with his knee on the back of my neck two minutes ago. Kennedy was unsure about this whole thing. I pressed harder.

"So what's the probable cause, Agent Kennedy? I have a right to know the probable cause for any action by the state affecting my constitutional rights. What's your cause?"

The gun wobbled a little in his grip before he said, "We have information from a source that you discussed explosives with another individual in court," said Kennedy.

"I think there's been a misunderstanding here. This can all be straightened out after the trial. I wouldn't want anything to jeopardize it."

I let this sink in for a moment. I wanted to get him thinking, doubting.

"Agent Kennedy, this conversation I supposedly had in court about explosives. By any chance was I having this conversation with Mr. Volchek?"

"I believe so," said Kennedy.

I breathed slowly, calming myself before I made my play.

"So who did Miriam Sullivan hire to spy on the jury? Wouldn't be Arnie Novoselic, by any chance?" I said.

Kennedy looked surprised but tried desperately not to show it.

"We can debate this later. On your feet, Flynn."

He'd dropped the "Mr.," and I knew I was getting somewhere. I formed the impression that I'd touched a nerve. Kennedy shifted his feet, growing anxious, probably wondering if he'd just made the biggest mistake of his life. I leaned back in the chair and gave him my best shot.

"Agent Kennedy, if you arrest me, I'll sue the federal government for ten million dollars. And I'll win. I'll take your job and your director's job. But the cherry on the cake for me will be the mistrial. If you arrest me, my client will be guaranteed a mistrial. The prosecution will have to adjourn the case to allow my client to seek new representation, and Judge Pike won't let a jury sit on a mob trial that's going to adjourn for a year while Volchek's new lawyer gets up to speed. No way. She'll declare a mistrial and swear a new jury next year when Volchek's new lawyer is ready."

Kennedy suddenly became very still. Any nervous movement stopped. I felt like I'd made an impact.

"Prosecutors operate on a strict budget in this town. How's it going to look if it comes out that the DA paid a huge sum of money to dirty little Arnold? Agent Kennedy, your prosecutor's jury consultant is illegally spying on the jury. Now, I don't know if Miriam was fully aware of how Arnold operates when she hired him, but she knows now that Arnold professes to be able to lip-read. He probably told you he lip-read *me*. I can assure you I didn't mention a bomb. He didn't tell you that he *heard* me say that, right? If he is lip-reading me, or trying to, he's also lip-reading the jury. That's contempt of court. That's jury tampering. That's five to ten, real time. That man spied on me when I was talking to my client. Anything I say to Mr. Volchek in court is about his case. You won't be able to persuade a judge otherwise. Everything we discussed is confidential, protected by attorney-client privilege, and it's illegal to violate that privilege without a court order that's seen the inside of the Supreme Court." I leaned forward to hammer my closing home. "So let me get this right. You're going to rely on the evidence of an unscrupulous man, engaged in illegal activity in a courtroom, who violates my client's attorney-client privilege and reports some bullshit story to you so he can look good and maybe get on the federal expert witness panel? You arrest me now, on that, and you're a fool, and I don't mind taking your job and the government's money. So go right ahead; arrest me. Win my case for me and make me a rich man."

I held out my wrists for his cuffs. I looked confident and assured. Secretly, my guts were churning and my heart beat so fast I felt like I was about to go into cardiac arrest.

Kennedy didn't move.

"Bill, don't do this," said the red-haired agent behind him.

Kennedy's lips curled into a snarl. He couldn't make up his mind, and it was killing him. I didn't know if it was the crippling indecision or the rant from me, but he stood down.

"This isn't over, Mr. Flynn," he said, holstering his pistol. In spite of my efforts to hide my anxiety, I couldn't help but let out a sigh.

His hands fell to his thighs, and I saw him scratch at his thumb.

He turned to leave. As I dropped my hands down, he stopped suddenly and looked me over.

Anger and indecision seemed to leave him. He noticeably relaxed and said, "We'll talk again."

And then, as quickly as they'd arrived, they were gone. I could hear the hushed voices of the agents in the corridor and then a dull metallic clang as one of them kicked the elevator doors. Sweat rolled down my brow. I wiped my face and felt a sting from my cheek. In my hands, I saw glistening sweat and a dark smear of blood. Arturas must have cut me when he held the knife to my face. Dried blood had stained the cuff of my shirt. It must have been the blood from my palm when I'd crushed the bourbon glass.

None of this mattered. I'd gotten through it. That was all. My right arm came across my chest to still my heart. The tips of my fingers brushed against the small bulge from the wallet that I'd taken off the big guy in the limo, the monster who'd almost taken my head off. I needed to get a look at that wallet. I needed to know exactly who I was up against. I couldn't risk a look until I was sure that I was alone and unobserved. Not yet, but soon.

CHAPTER EIGHTEEN

Tension headaches had plagued me for most of my life until I'd learned how to cure them. What was the cure? A six-foot-tall hooker named Boo, who posed as a fake physiotherapist in an insurance fraud I ran before I became a lawyer. She stopped turning tricks when we started to make real money from the insurance companies on the whiplash scam. Then she really got into her role. She took a night class, stopped wearing short skirts and plunging necklines beneath her white coat, and began wearing the proper uniform.

I would be up most of the night, repairing the hit cars for the next sting with my neck burning from the strain of working under the old wrecks. Boo stayed in the office and studied anatomy. She taught me all about posture: holding the neck up, relaxing the muscles, straightening the back and breathing correctly. Her technique never failed—a snap of the head, hold it back for two seconds if you can stand the pain, then relax. I later adapted her posture advice for my stance in court; it made me more relaxed and natural. Rolling my shoulders, I performed her stretch. I heard the elevator gather the feds with the clank of the old doors as they closed.

Arturas's grin returned. Volchek laughed.

"You did well," said Volchek as he picked up his phone and deleted the text message.

A successful con artist relies on a number of different skills. None of these skills is worth a damn if you can't get people to trust you. Building trust with a potential mark is no different from building trust with a jury—the same shit applies. My persuader ran perfectly by destroying Goldstein; now I'd shown the FBI the door. I felt like I'd earned Volchek's trust. The only thing left to do was exploit it.

"How do I know my daughter's still alive?" I said.

The grin that Arturas wore slipped slowly away, and he set his lips firmly together.

"You can talk to her. You've earned it. Do not try to give her any signals. She is calm. Remember, she thinks the men with her are private security that you arranged because of a threat."

Arturas dialed a number and pressed speaker on his cell phone. I couldn't understand the conversation; he'd reverted to his native Russian. It sounded as if everything was cool. No raised voices on either side of the line. The voice on the other end was female, and Arturas's features softened as he spoke. I thought the woman was likely to be his girlfriend. Arturas stopped talking and handed me the phone. I held it about three inches in front of my face.

"Amy, are you there?" I said.

Nothing.

"Dad?"

I tried desperately to keep the emotion from my voice.

"Yeah, it's me. Are you okay?"

"I'm okay. What's happening? Where are you and Mom? Elanya says I can't . . . I . . . that I can't go outside."

Her voice sounded shaky. The speaker buzzed with Amy's quick, full breaths. She was frightened. I guessed Elanya to be the woman Arturas had spoken to, maybe his girl. It made sense for the Bratva to have a female on hand to look after a girl of that age. A woman would have sounded more convincing to the school.

"Best do as the lady says, honey."

1-646-695-8875.

"Why aren't you here with me? I mean . . . we should be together, right?" said Amy, her voice rising tremulously at the final word.

That was Amy—smart, inquisitive, and recently equipped with a finely calibrated bullshit meter that all kids seem to develop at that age. She knew. She knew something wasn't right, and it terrified her.

I cleared my throat, put my hand over the speaker, and blew out my cheeks. I couldn't let Amy detect any fear in my voice, so I swallowed down that clawing, sour tightness in my throat.

"I love you so much, sweetie. I'm going to see you real soon. Don't be scared. I won't let anything happen to you. You're my angel, remember?"

"Dad?"

1-646-695-8875.

"Yeah?"

"Is Mom there with you? Can I . . . please . . . I want to talk to her. I want you . . . I want you and Mom to come get me, please. I love you. Please come get me, Daddy . . . please . . ." She broke down completely, each shrill cry bringing her closer to hysterics. Her sobs grew fainter as the phone was taken from her.

Blinking away a single tear, I tried to call out to her, but the words were strangled. Arturas made a cutting motion across his neck. I'd had all the time he was prepared to give me, and he put his hand on the phone.

1-646-695-8875.

"Honey, it's okay. Don't cry. I love you, too," I said, raising my voice, which had become thick with fear and anger.

Arturas hung up.

I wanted to kill them all. Right then, right there. It took every last reserve of willpower that I had left to stop myself. I couldn't allow that to happen. Not yet. There were three of them. Even with my speed, at least one of them would have time to make that call. The call that would end Amy's life. I tried to think of something else.

"Where's my wife?"

"She doesn't know Amy is missing, so far as we know," said Volchek. "The school thinks we have her in protective custody. A fake security firm ID brought no questions from the school. Your wife is not expecting Amy home until tomorrow night. Your wife will not trouble you. Or me. If she does—she joins your daughter."

I gently moved my neck from side to side to ease the pain that spread from my shoulders into my brain. Amy knew something bad was happening. She didn't trust her captors. She didn't buy their story. I had never known her to be so frightened. Last time she was scared was around eighteen months ago. Her English class had to do a public speaking event.

Amy, being smart and funny, had been chosen to do a three-minute speech in front of the whole school. She sat in the dining room of our house, quietly sobbing over her speech. I read it; it was fine. The problem was standing up in front of hundreds of kids and delivering it. After a lot of encouragement, she read her speech to me and couldn't even finish it; she froze, stumbled over her words, and then cried.

"I can't do it. I'll have to leave school. There's, like, just no way."

So I told her that I would give her the secret to becoming a great public speaker—I was a lawyer after all.

"Wiggle your toes."

"That's it?" she said.

"That's it. Our brains somehow perform best when our bodies are occupied. That's why so many people come up with a solution to a problem or have a great idea when they're driving, or cooking, or just plain old sitting on the can. Nobody will be looking at your feet, and you won't be thinking about how nervous you are—you'll be thinking about your toes."

She wiggled her toes and read her speech again, perfectly.

Funny thing about sitting at the dining table that night. I couldn't remember the last time she had hugged me. I missed her speech the next day. Clean forgot about it; Jack and I had picked up an armed robbery case. When I got home late that night, Christine told me Amy's delivery had been great, but she had cried all the way home from school because I hadn't been there to see it.

I was through letting down my little girl.

1-646-695-8875 repeated over and over. I let it resound inside my head.

I would not forget that number. I saw it brightly lit in white, on the screen in front of me during the call. What could I do with it? I didn't know at that moment.

But I had it.

That's where Amy was, at an apartment or house or office at the other end of that cell phone number. I didn't own a cell phone, hated them, so I memorized whatever phone numbers I needed. I knew that 646 was an area code. Specifically, an area code that covered Manhattan. That narrowed Amy's location down. The island of Manhattan is more than thirteen miles long and less than two and a half miles wide. Around two million people live on the island and maybe another two to three million commute in and out every day. So yeah, I'd narrowed it down, all right.

I needed help to trace that cell number to a location, to find Amy, to get her out. There were two men I trusted with my life; the first was my best friend from childhood, Jimmy Fellini, who was now someone to be feared. The other person was a judge, Harry Ford—a man who had held my fate in his hands twice before and on both occasions had changed my life. In my thirty-six years on this planet, I had occupied two different worlds—the world of the hustler and the world of the lawyer—and the skills that my dad had taught me allowed me to flourish in both realms, because, in reality, they weren't so very different after all.

I needed help from both men. I hadn't yet figured out how to contact them or how much I would tell them.

My watch told me there were twenty-two hours left. Twenty-two hours to get Amy and double-cross the mob. The LCD display read six o'clock. The first session of night court was already under way. Barry had told me Judge Ford would preside over the graveyard shift, the second sitting of night court. That meant Harry was probably already in the building, reading the case files, readying himself for his night's work. So much of my life had been changed by unforeseen circumstances, by chance, by luck. Was that fate? All I knew then was that I had seven hours to get to Harry before he went into court. If I didn't get to him before one a.m., I wouldn't get to him at all.

CHAPTER NINETEEN

The files sat open in front of me in the chambers office. I'd told Volchek I needed to read the case files to make sure there were no more surprises that could threaten his bail. Outside the chambers, in the reception room, Arturas and Volchek were whispering. I tried listening to their conversation, but I couldn't really make it out. It was past seven, full dark outside and raining hard. Victor lay on the green couches in the outer office, relaxed. I thought of Harry—there was a huge risk in roping him into this. Harry was, after all, a judge. But to me he was more than that; he was a friend. If it weren't for Harry, I would've stayed in the con game my whole life.

Hustling seemed like a cocaine rush for the first few years, and if the kick wasn't addictive enough, the money sure got you hooked real fast. My targets were mostly insurance companies. Companies just like the one that had taken my dad's health insurance premium every month and then let him die instead of paying out on the policy. Health care fraud played a small part in my operation; I mainly focused on motor accident fraud: a high-risk, high-reward game against some of the most devious minds you could imagine. Hustling an insurance company was like playing poker with Satan—his house, his rules. But I'd always won. By the time I'd quit, I had almost perfected the art of the whipper.

Pulling off a fraudulent claim was no mean feat. The trick was letting the insurance company think that they'd hustled you.

You start off with a fake law firm. Some might think that's pretty difficult to set up, but that was the easy part. I kept an eye on the obituary columns and death notices, and I usually got a hit on a dead small-time lawyer once a month. Those kind of lawyers are usually high-cholesterol, high-alcohol, and highly stressed chain smokers. Every lawyer whose identity I'd stolen died from a heart attack. Lucky for me that booze and stress kills hundreds of lawyers every year. So I'd find a likely dead candidate and pay the grieving widow a visit. Flowers and a check were my weapons. I'd tell the widow that her husband represented me and won me a fortune in a case and because he was such a gentleman, he would never accept any gifts. I'd like to give the widow a few thousand bucks as a thank-you. After I handed over the cash, I would ask for a memento of my great legal hero—usually his practicing license, which I would have framed and put on my wall as a permanent reminder of the dearly departed.

The license was really all I needed. The New York State Bar Association is usually the last to know that one of their number had passed away. Lawyers don't go to other lawyers' funerals. If they did, they wouldn't have time to go to court. So, one fake ID later, I would set up as the deceased lawyer and start my practice.

The practice involved more mechanical and auto-body repair work than legal enterprise. It all started with a crash. A cheap and easy-to-repair car would approach a stoplight just as it was about to turn red, and instead of going through it, the driver slammed on the brakes at just the right moment, causing the vehicle behind to ram into the back of the car. It's not an easy task, and at the height of my career, I employed two precision drivers who masqueraded as various injured plaintiffs.

The rules of the road say you have to drive within a safe stopping distance, and by the time the vehicles hit, the light would be red. A no-brainer for an insurance claims handler. They would want the case settled quickly and cheaply. Enter the stupid plaintiff's lawyer. My bogus firm would send a letter of claim to the driver at fault, who, in turn, would send it on to his insurer. Once communication was established, the insurance company needed to see bait. The bait was another letter to the insurance company or their defense lawyers about the accident, but this time there would be another letter in the envelope. This extra letter would be neatly crumpled and ink stained, as if it had jammed coming out of the printer and shouldn't have been attached to the letter to the insurance company. The crumpled letter was from the bogus law firm to the bogus client, telling him that despite his mother's operation/kid's accident/burst water pipe, etc., on no account was he to settle early, as his preliminary medical report indicated his case was worth maybe two hundred grand.

The fake medical would be enclosed. This was the expensive part, as we had to rent a unit and set up a whole fake medical practice. That's where Boo, ex-hooker turned massage therapist, came in. She would man a fake medical practice for a few weeks, answer the phones and let me know when the insurance investigators had done their due diligence by checking out the medical center. This was real easy to tell, as the only people who came to the medical center were investigators, the center not having any real patients at all. The lower the blouse that Boo wore, the quicker the due diligence happened. I'd met Boo on the street just after my nineteenth birthday. I came out of McGonagall's Bar around midnight to find two fierce-looking guys bearing down on a tall, beautiful woman in a white dress and ketchup-red lipstick. She stood her ground in ten-inch pencil heels. One of the men held a pipe; the other swung his belt. I stepped in, drunk, of course, and managed to land a sloppy punch on the guy with the belt before his pal drove the pipe into the side of my head. When my vision cleared, Boo was standing over me, wearing flats and smoking a cigarette. The two guys lay on the ground beside me. One of them, the one who was screaming, had his belt around his neck and the heel of a stiletto buried in his knee. The other guy didn't make a sound, and I saw the pipe sitting beside him with one end bent out of shape, wet and bloodied. Boo didn't have a mark on her. She took me back to her apartment, cleaned me up, and put me to sleep on her couch.

Usually, within a week of either the insurance company or their law firm receiving the bogus letters, an investigator paid a visit to Boo's fake medical practice to check it out. A couple of days after that, offers would arrive for amounts between twenty and fifty thousand dollars on the condition that the offer of settlement was accepted within fourteen days.

Needless to say, all my fake clients accepted the offers. The check came made out to the firm, for deduction of legal expenses, and the banks were only too happy to cash up for the young lawyer trying to resurrect his mentor's old law firm. And that was my life. I was happy hitting back at the defense lawyers and the insurers that robbed my dad of his dignity and his life. But fate or luck, or whatever you want to call it, intervened when a nine-pound hammer and a split second's misjudgment changed my life forever.

CHAPTER TWENTY

I tried concentrating on the files. This case had brought me here, and I had to learn everything I could about it. Part of my plan required me to find some kind of leverage with the Russians, and I felt confident I could find it in the files. My skin felt hot, and my eyes couldn't seem to focus on anything for long. If I wasn't fidgeting with the pages, I seemed to stare into nothing. I was panicking. At least I was aware that I was panicking. I controlled my breathing and concentrated on that single task of inhaling and exhaling.

Three files were of no use at all. Expert reports compiled by four different law firms: legal opinions and expert summaries on the case—none of which helped. Some experts said Volchek would be the worst witness they'd seen in their careers. I thought that to be a fairly reasonable assessment. All of the reports and expert opinions came to the same conclusion—Volchek was guilty.

The other four files contained the trial bundle. File one contained the charges and a transcript of Volchek's interviews with NYPD. Volchek hadn't answered a single question in any interview. The only other document of interest was a photocopy of the front page of the *New York Times* from April fifth, two years ago. A mug shot of Mario Geraldo, probably from an early arrest, and below the fold, a picture of Volchek being led from the court. The article focused on the murder and subsequent arrest of the leading light of the Russian Mafia.

File two largely consisted of photographs and maps. Mainly photos of the crime scene. The photos revealed an untidy apartment with a fat man on the floor. The fat man had a bullet hole in his face, an inch below the left eye and a quarter inch from the nose. A pretty central shot. There was bound to be a medical examiner's report somewhere in the papers, but I hadn't found it yet. I didn't need to read the report. This guy had the cause of death written all over his face. Momentarily, the pain in my neck eased, and I stretched my shoulders again to prolong the relief.

The fat man in the photos wore a grubby white vest and dark pants. He was barefoot. Mario Geraldo, the victim. His appearance didn't give the impression of him being a typical victim. He looked like he came straight from the casting couch of the best Scorsese movies. There were four Italian crime families in New York. I couldn't think of anyone by the name of Geraldo, but the name had some resonance that I couldn't quite define yet.

I held the photo under the desk lamp in the chambers and peered closely at the fat man lying in the middle of the room. I tried to make out his tattoos in case they were old gang tats. None of the ink was territorial. I saw powder-burn marks around the entry wound. He'd been shot close; the gun almost at his face but not touching the skin. If the gun had been touching his head when it went off, the powder wouldn't have burned such a wide area of skin and there would be a smaller, but more profound, circular burn from the hot mouth of the gun barrel.

I emptied all the photos from the file onto the desk and started piecing together the scene. There was a report from the CSI and a statement from the IO, a guy named Martinez. I didn't want to read either one of these documents before I'd examined the photos and made up my own mind. If I read their reports, it might infect my interpretation of the scene. Not that there was a lot to interpret. The cops caught Little Benny in the apartment with the gun still hot on the floor. He confessed to the murder a day after he signed his plea bargain. He got twelve years, would be out in seven.

I could see no blood spatter on the floor behind the victim's head. I picked up three more photos: close-ups of the head from different angles. Mario got shot either when he was sitting or kneeling down, but definitely not lying down, as there was no evidence of spatter on the carpet. The blood on the carpet was clearly postmortem leakage.

I could still hear Volchek and Arturas in conversation in the next room as I pored over the shots of the apartment.

The walls of the victim's apartment were cream. The spatter showed up easy. A closer inspection of the photos revealed red spots in the center of the wall directly behind Mario's body. In the middle of the staining I saw a small hole, the bullet's final resting place and, an inch above that hole, a picture nail. From this I felt fairly certain that Little Benny had sat at the small dining table when he'd fired the fatal shot. The table lay just in front of Mario's body, and an upturned chair wasn't far away. Little Benny and his victim had sat at the table together before Benny fired the shot.

Volchek hadn't mentioned the reason for the hit, but it became clearer when I saw photo fifty-two. Glass covered the dining table. On the floor I saw a broken picture frame. A close-up shot revealed the photo in the frame to be a black-and-white professional photograph of a good-looking man holding a baby. It must have been the photo that came with the frame.

The victim didn't take pride in his appearance: He hadn't shaved in days and there were food stains on his vest. His apartment seemed filthy, but even a slob would sweep up broken glass and there were no cuts on his feet. I couldn't see any wounds on Mario other than the gunshot, so he probably hadn't been hit with the photo frame. The rest of the furniture remained intact: no open drawers, no signs that the apartment had been ransacked or even searched. I guessed the picture frame had originally hung on the nail that I'd seen just above the blood spatter. There didn't appear to be any blood on the picture frame and no bullet holes in the photo. It appeared that Mario had taken the picture off the wall for some reason before he was shot.

I spread out the rest of the photos on the desk, and my attention was drawn to shots of the kitchen sink in Mario's studio apartment. The first crime-scene photo wasn't so clear, but it appeared to show a mixture of black sludge and paper in the sink. The last photo in the set was a close-up. It wasn't sludge in the sink. It was the remnants of one or maybe two Polaroids that looked as though they had been burned before somebody ran the faucet and tried to mash up what was left. Only one corner of a single photo was still visible. I could just make out an arm and a hand. That was it.

Easing my back into the chair and squirming when I felt the bomb jab into my skin, I tried to piece together what had happened in that apartment. Mario had not been shot at his front door. Little Benny had gotten into the apartment, and I figured he even sat down across the dining table from his victim. Why not sit on the couch? Why sit at the table? Mario had taken the picture frame off the wall; the bullet hole and the blood spatter were framed in the clean rectangle of wall where the picture had saved the paint beneath it from the accumulating dust and grime. The frame was on the floor, beside the table, the broken glass spread across the tabletop. The picture itself was a generic photo that came with the new frame. Then the burned photographs in the sink. My best guess was that this was a business transaction gone wrong. Little Benny had arrived at the apartment on some pretense of doing business. That's why they sat at the table. Mario took the picture frame off the wall. They broke it open because something was hidden in that frame, and my only thought was that the photos in the sink were once hidden behind that stock image of the father and child.

It was a leap, a thin, treacherous leap.

But it made sense.

The short statement from the arresting officer, a female cop named Tasketh, confirmed that they'd received a call about a disturbance in Mario's apartment from one of his neighbors. The NYPD patrol car was only a block away, and the cops got into Mario's apartment building just as the shot was fired. They broke down the door to find Mario dead and Benny sitting patiently at the table, his gun on the floor. Tasketh stated that a smoke alarm began whirring as they were breaking down the front door. I noticed that this cop's statement bore a mark saying it had been agreed by the defense so Tasketh wouldn't have to give evidence.

My theory was that Little Benny was sent to Mario's to kill him and get back the photos, but Little Benny got coldcocked by the cops and he probably figured he had to get rid of them. So he burned the photos in the sink. I had no way to be sure. Surely Miriam must have thought about this, and I thought it likely that Miriam came to the same conclusion I did but rejected it as motive because of lack of evidence. For me, it was just a hunch, a gut feeling.

My survival on the street for the first part of my life had largely been based on listening to my gut. The prosecutor couldn't present her gut to the jury; she needed evidence for a motive.

In her opening statement, Miriam hadn't talked a lot about the motive behind Mario's murder. Prosecutors love motive because juries love motive. Only reason she didn't hammer it into the jurors was because she didn't *have* a strong motive. If Little Benny had told her why he'd been ordered to kill Mario—that would have been the first thing Miriam told the jury. Instead, she would let the jury come up with their own motive. This was a powerful and risky play for any prosecutor.

What did those burned photographs show?

Why did Mario have them? Why was he killed?

Something didn't add up. Not yet. But this felt important. The murder of Mario Geraldo served as the spark to ignite this whole situation. Little Benny had given his boss up for murder and kept quiet about the rest of the operation, but why? Was it out of loyalty to his fellow *vor*? Something about Little Benny's motives didn't make sense.

I felt like I'd just dipped my fingers into a black pool, that there was a good deal more about this murder and this whole situation hidden below the surface. What I didn't realize then was how deep those waters ran.

CHAPTER TWENTY-ONE

Turning my attention to a new file, I found the depositions and statements. There were no depositions or statements from Little Benny. That made sense. In order for the prosecutor to depose a witness, they had to let the defense know when and where the deposition would happen. That meant revealing Little Benny's location to Volchek's lawyers. The FBI had probably spent a fortune keeping Little Benny hidden, so they weren't going to send an open invitation to every hit man in the Russian Mafia by naming a date, time, and location for Benny to appear. Even if they didn't hit Benny at the deposition, they would make sure to follow him afterward. The rules often went out the window when the witness's life was at risk.

The investigating officer's statement read well. Raphael Martinez could be a star in the making. He stuck to the facts, didn't pose theories of the crime like he was taught in the academy, didn't infer anything from the crime scene, and didn't embellish the facts. He'd basically ignored everything he'd been taught, and that made him a great witness. This guy would be almost impossible to cross-examine.

I closed the files for a moment. My eyes felt raw, my throat dry.

"Arturas, do you have anything to drink?" I called.

"It's coming."

If I was going to be up all night working, I needed something to keep me going.

An image of Amy flooded my mind, the thought of her shivering and whimpering, scared out of her mind. She was a smart girl, did well in class, and loved reading. When she was younger, her mother liked to read her princess stories and fairy tales. The alarm had sounded on my watch at eight on my first night in alcohol rehab, and knowing that she had that same alarm call made me feel connected. We talked, and I read her a chapter a night from *Alice's Adventures in Wonderland*. She could read just fine on her own. She said she liked my voice; it was soothing. At the beginning of my treatment, I'd felt a lot like Alice: that I'd been tumbling around in a strange world, drinking everything in sight to get out of it, to get out of the law, to change what had happened. By the end of my time in rehab, I'd come to realize that disappearing into a bottle didn't solve anything. When I'd left rehab, I had been sure that I would never practice law again. Christine and Amy picked me up after I checked out of the addiction center, and we ate hamburgers and fries at a little joint around the corner. That felt good. Felt like old times. My wife was always there for me when I needed her, even though I hadn't been there for her. There was tension between us, but I felt that was easing because of Amy. My daughter and I were slowly reconnecting through reading and talking about books, although I made sure not to tell Christine about the kind of books that Amy really loved. In my apartment I kept a small library on sleight-of-hand techniques, magic tricks, poker, and lots of books on my hero—Harry Houdini.

During Amy's second overnight stay at my apartment, I came out of the kitchen, having fixed dinner, to find Amy reading a biography of Houdini. Christine knew all about my past, and she would not have approved of Amy reading that stuff; she thought it was a bad influence. I didn't tell Christine about Amy's appetite for Houdini. Just as I didn't tell her that I had taught Amy a few coin tricks to wow her friends. At ten years of age, Amy was in that magic time of her youth when I was still the most important man in her life. My pal, Judge Harry Ford, had told me to enjoy it because in a year or two I would turn into a nobody who ran a free car service.

My lips began to tremor. Amy had her whole life ahead of her.

I coughed, rubbed my face hard, and reopened the files.

Apart from the cop, and the inevitable Benny, there were two other witnesses. The first was a girl, Nikki Blundell, a twenty-six-year-old nightclub dancer. She saw Volchek and Mario having a fight in the Sirocco Club on

East Seventh Street, the night before he was killed. Miriam knew, just as well as I did, that a bar fight wasn't enough motive for a professional hit, but it was still pretty damning evidence.

The only other witness was the vic's cousin, Tony Geraldo. And suddenly I remembered. I knew a Tony G who worked for Jimmy "the Hat" Fellini, my boyhood pal. Jimmy's amateur boxing career came to an end when he went into the family business; that business was organized crime. Tony G and I had met once, a long time ago, at Jimmy's place. He collected for Jimmy. I couldn't quite picture Tony, but I would know if it was the same guy just by looking at his shoes. Bagmen cover a lot of miles in the car. They wait around a lot; they spend a long time collecting, protecting, and being there for the money. Being an employee in a high position of trust, they tended to be older guys. After spending a week in their car, a couple more days collecting, and a day beating somebody half to death, these guys didn't care to look after their appearance. Hence the one important thing—they wore expensive, soft, light, old-fashioned shoes that your granddaddy would wear. No Italian leather, pointy-toed shoes for these guys; they'd be in agony before they got through their first pickup. Octogenarians and serious Mafia men—they kept the manufacturers of comfortable American shoes in business.

Tony's statement focused on his cousin Mario and his animosity with Volchek. It started well, talking about Mario's time in juvie, then his graduation to federal lock up, Mario turning over a new leaf, Mario having a long-running disagreement with Volchek over a debt, then Tony's recollection of the nightclub altercation with Volchek. This could be the same argument that had been independently witnessed by Nikki Blundell. Tony's statement was bad for Volchek. It helped set up more of a motive. It established a timeline to the murder, and it corroborated Nikki Blundell's story. Not good.

I ran through the witness list again.

The IO could be a big problem, but his evidence wasn't too controversial. The female cop who had arrested Little Benny at the scene wasn't giving evidence because it didn't establish anything toward Volchek's guilt.

The nightclub girl I could deal with.

The vic's family member—he was trouble. Miriam probably had an ace in Tony Geraldo. Something I hadn't seen yet.

Then there was the last witness—the star man, Witness X. The anonymous moniker served only to protect whatever new identity he would be given from being discovered by the press. Volchek knew, as sure as he knew his own face, the identity of the man who'd betrayed him.

Tony Geraldo and Little Benny sank Volchek. Both of them were devastating. I felt sure I had enough to cause problems for the prosecution, enough to keep Volchek occupied so he wouldn't worry about me.

If Tony G was Tony Geraldo, then I'd found my leverage.

I turned slightly in my chair. Arturas and Volchek were whispering. I made a soft noise and moved a little. Volchek saw me. He closed the door separating my judge's room from his reception room. He wanted privacy and didn't want me trying to listen in on the conversation. I couldn't hear a thing, but I wanted him to see me listening so he would close the door. I could then watch them unobserved.

Below the handle on the old, paneled oak door, I saw a keyhole.

I looked through it, but the key must have been in the lock. The key narrowed my vision even further. I could just about make out Volchek talking to Victor. Volchek turned and embraced Arturas, then left. Arturas sat down and struck up a conversation in Russian with Victor. I had some privacy now. Kneeling down, I felt the bomb components jabbing into my side. I'd almost forgotten the damn thing was there.

I reached into my coat pocket and took out the wallet that I'd lifted from the big guy who'd put my lights out in the limo. Inside the leather foldable, I found around six hundred dollars in loose hundred-dollar bills, together with two brass money clips holding a thousand dollars each, again, in hundred-dollar bills. Among the credit cards for "Gregor Oblowskon," I found something that took my mind into a blizzard of questions: a business card with a telephone number scrawled on the back. The number was written in blue ink. A cell phone number. I couldn't find a name on the card, but it was the printing on the card itself that worried me the most. The card gave the address and the title of an organization. I didn't need to read the name of the organization; the address—"26 Federal Plaza, 23rd Floor, New York, NY"—was well known to me. It's on Broadway, south of Canal Street, north of City Hall, and home to the Federal Bureau of Investigation.

I knew then I could trust no one, not cops and certainly not the feds.

My watch chimed—eight o'clock. Amy's watch would be chiming, too. Our time. I couldn't let myself think of her. I had to stay sharp, focused, and angry. Sending myself crazy with worry wouldn't help my daughter.

Five hours to get to Harry before he began court duty. There was only one way I could get to his office without the Russians knowing, and the thought of it terrified me.

CHAPTER TWENTY-TWO

I heard a footstep outside the door and plunged the wallet back into my pocket, sat on my chair, lifted one of the open files, and buried my head in it.

The door opened and Arturas stood over me. He tossed a bottle of water into the corner.

"Olek has gone home for the night, so I'm locking you in here. Victor and I need some rest. You get some sleep, too. If you try to escape . . ."

"Where am I going to go?" I said. "Can't I at least take the jacket off?"

"No. Try to get some sleep anyway. I'll be back to check on you at daybreak."

"Please." I stood and grabbed his right forearm and gave him a pleading look. He began to pull away, and I turned, quickly, catching his retreating body with my hip. As he fell, my right hand moved swiftly into his coat—my second pocket dip of the day. He landed on his ass and swore. Digging his heels beneath his thighs, he sprang up at me. I kept hold of his wrist and pulled him back up.

"Jesus. I'm so sorry, man. It was an accident," I said. I put my hands up defensively. My hands open, palms toward Arturas with my fingers splayed, cradling my prize in the fold of my right wrist, in between the back of my hand and my forearm. A tricky hide, but I'd practiced it for years. I could hide a silver dollar in the crook of my wrist unobserved and still play a round of poker. I pretended to look scared—when really my limbs were tense with anger. Arturas feigned a right hook. I flinched and exaggerated it. He smiled and closed the door. Victor let out a big laugh from the next room.

"Pussy," said Victor.

I listened to the key turning in the lock, gave it a few seconds, then snapped the back of my wrist toward the ceiling, sending the little black device tumbling into the air. Catching the detonator in my right hand, I wondered how long I had before Arturas discovered it was missing. I needed the detonator. I didn't want Arturas triggering the device if he just happened to open the door and find me gone. I was going to see Harry, and I needed to bring the bomb with me because if any man knew how to disable it, it was Superior Judge and former Captain, United States Army, Harry Ford.

CHAPTER TWENTY-THREE

Before I did anything, I had to be sure my babysitters wouldn't come looking for me anytime soon. Volchek had already left. I heard a whispered conversation, then the door to the hall opening and footsteps walking toward the elevator. The door to the corridor closed. I heard the rattle of keys locking it, and through the keyhole I saw Victor lie down on the couch and close his eyes. Arturas had just left.

Victor was on his own.

I watched Victor carefully for a little over an hour. I could hear him breathing heavily as he lay on the couch. His eyes were closed, and his hands rested on his stomach. Apart from a small lamp, the only light in my room came from digital billboards across the street. Rhythmic dances of red, blue, and white slipped in and out of the room every few seconds and threw strangely shaped creatures around the walls.

I thought I could hear Victor snoring again, louder than before.

Turning over the FBI card in my fingers, I thought about my conversation with Volchek that morning in the limo.

Benny is well protected and well hidden. Even my contacts can't find him.

The phrase "my contacts" made sense to me now.

Volchek had a rogue FBI agent in his pocket, someone on the inside. And whoever that agent was, he couldn't locate Benny. I couldn't trust anyone. If the mob could buy a federal agent, they could buy a hundred New York cops. Peering through the keyhole again, I made sure Victor remained asleep on the couch. It didn't look like Arturas would return tonight; he said he would come get me in the morning. I put my coat on.

It was 9:10 p.m.

Time to escape.

I moved quietly to the sash window. The windowpane misted with my breath as I opened the latch locking the lower pane. I put my hands on the frame, shifted my body underneath, and pushed.

The window didn't move.

Not even an inch.

I checked and made sure all latches and locks were open. I tried again. It didn't budge. The poor light didn't help, so I felt around the frame with my fingertips. I couldn't feel the join. The window must have been painted shut about twenty years ago, and nobody had dared open it since. Patting my pockets, I listened for the jingle of my keys and heard nothing. I was going to use the sharp edge of my key to cut the paint. Checking my pockets, I realized my keys were gone. At that moment I didn't know if I'd dropped the keys somewhere or if Arturas had taken them, but I didn't have time to think about it. Instead I took out my pen and ran the point around the frame. When it had run its course, a ball of hard paint covered the tip, and dried, rubbery ribbons of the stuff fell around the window ledge like streamers.

I got up onto the large windowsill and started to push. It was noisy. I couldn't help it. A tearing, cracking sound came from the paint, and a dry, satisfying groan escaped from the frame as it separated from its mate and the window opened to a cacophony of traffic, music, and the hum of New York City. It had stopped raining. Night court was in full swing, and I could see, below me, a line of taxis stretching from my side of the building and then turning right toward the front entrance. Monday nights can be slow, but there's always business around the arraignment court. Anybody who posts bail after nine invariably needs a ride.

I closed the window a little to drown out the worst of the noise. I didn't want Victor to hear. Hunkering down on the balls of my feet, I took four steps sideways and began edging myself out onto the ledge, tucking my head into my chest to get below the windowpane. My head came up on the outside of the window, and my eyes shut of their own volition. I forced my eyes open and then immediately regretted it. I knelt on a three-foot-wide ledge, nineteen floors up. An old stink came off the thick green moss and the ancient bird droppings that covered the masonry. It felt slippery. To my right—a dead end: an impassable outcrop for the elevator. Left was my only option. I had to move down a floor, get to the right window, and just hope Harry remained a creature of habit.

Closing my eyes again, I pictured an internal map of the building and tried to plot a route from the outside. The courthouse stood alone, surrounded on the south and west sides by a small park. I stood on the east side of the building. Below me was Little Portland Street, which led to Chambers Street and the front entrance of the courthouse at the north side of the building. Harry's room was on this side of the building, the east side, but not on this floor, and there was an even bigger problem. There was something on this side of the building that blocked my way; something that was probably around thirty feet tall. The top third of the obstacle came onto my level. The head, the arms, the sword—they would be difficult to get around, but not impossible.

Before I got to my destination, I had to climb down the gray lady.

Slowly, both hands gripping either side of the brick slab window arch, I levered myself to a standing position and started freaking out. I'd always experienced the same weird sensation with heights; didn't matter if I was fifty or five hundred feet from the ground, it always felt worse when my head was close to a ceiling. If I was ten feet off the ground on a balcony where I could see a ceiling in my horizon view, I would freak. Give me a limitless sky and I'd be fine. I could never work out why.

Standing in the arch, my head inches from the roof of the granite recess, I felt like I was about to lose it. I clung to the wall, my fingernails biting and breaking for grip as I fought for air. The piercing cold wasn't helping, and the wind whipped my coat around me. Every breath felt fierce. The car horns and engines, bus air brakes and cab doors closing beneath me were a constant reminder that life existed nineteen floors below me and that I was nowhere close to being safe.

I blew out all my disabling nerves in a series of quick exhalations and took a step forward. Even as I did it, my brain screamed at me—*What the hell are you doing?* I didn't care. I held to an image of Amy in my mind's eye, *my* image of *my* Amy, her hair in my hand as she blew out all those birthday candles before we compared our new watches. The ledge narrowed beyond the window's recess. It was maybe two and a half feet wide. I stared with amazement at my right foot as it moved forward and steadied, ready for my left to join it.

I'd never tried to hold on to something with my face before. I hugged the side of the building as my left foot shimmied farther and my fingers began shaking from the death grip on the brickwork gaps. I moved again.

Ten minutes later, I stood five feet from the Lady.

The Lady was familiar. Most people would recognize her figure. A woman blindfolded, wrapped in a toga, sword in one hand and scales in the other. Both arms raised parallel to the floor, balancing mercy with retribution just as she balances her hands. She is blindfolded to symbolize her indifference, her blindness, to race, color, or creed.

Yeah, right.

The Lady is known as Justitia: a bastardized version of Greek and Roman gods of justice. She's not always blindfolded. The Lady that sits on top of the Old Bailey in London wears no blindfold. Scholars say the blindfold is superfluous because the figure is female and therefore must be impartial. They obviously never tried a case in front of Judge Pike.

My feet shuffled forward again, but almost imperceptibly this time. It felt agonizingly slow. My brows furrowed, and I felt a quickening heat in my brain and chest. *Welcome anger; welcome fresh adrenaline.* The rush took me another two feet, and I stretched out a hand to grasp the sword hilt. I wasn't able to reach it. I couldn't move any farther—no more ledge. Everything in my mind and body screamed at me to hold on to the wall, but I had to reach for the sword, for Amy. My right foot took my weight, and I raised my other foot for balance.

A dull, rumbling crack came from beneath me. My weight shifted, dropped, and I jumped.

CHAPTER TWENTY-FOUR

My right hand caught the sword. My left slipped over her arm and I swung my legs onto the granite folds of the toga, both feet scrambling wildly for purchase.

"I'm okay. I'm okay," I repeated.

My arms shook violently. Looking over the statue's shoulder, I saw a wide alcove behind the Lady on the lower floor. I could go over the arms or try to slide underneath. Letting my feet find a firm hold, I then adjusted my grip to my left hand, ready to take the weight. Against all my natural instincts, I let my body swing out before sweeping my legs underneath the arms of the Lady. As soon as my feet hit the apex of the swing, I let go.

I landed on the alcove ledge on the eighteenth floor. A violent beating of wings and squawking welcomed me, and I grabbed the statue again and pulled my face close to the granite as the city crows protested at my invasion of their resting place.

Adrenaline surges usually don't bother me. I'm trained to use them. When you stand up in a room in front of hundreds of people and all eyes are upon you, you feel a huge adrenaline surge. You're not human if you don't. Everything slows. A second's pause feels like a three-minute nightmare when the juice is flowing through your system. That's what it's supposed to do. A slow-motion moment that allows you time to fight or flee. It quickens your reactions and completely distorts your sense of time and space.

Every sense stands on high alert, and every reaction becomes sharpened to a razor's edge.

I forced my system down a few gears. Let my engine cool and looked up at the path I'd taken to the statue. The ledge I'd leaped from was almost gone. The brick had all but disintegrated. I checked the street. There was nobody lying on the ground, looking back at me. The rubble had hit the pavement. No one got hurt. Thankfully, I was in New York and real New Yorkers never look up. I leaned against the cold brick and looked up at the back of the Lady. She was part of the game. Lawyers are often asked how they can represent someone they know to be guilty. I'd been asked that question many times, and I'd always given the same answer—we don't. In reality, we operated just like the US military operated for years in relation to gay personnel—don't ask, don't tell. I never represented anyone I knew to be guilty because I never asked any of my clients if they were guilty. I never asked because there was always the terrible possibility that they might just tell you the truth. The truth has no place in a courtroom. The only thing that matters is what the prosecution can prove. If I met a client facing criminal charges, I told them what the cops or the prosecution thought they could prove and asked them what they thought about that. This leads them into their own little performance. If they wanted to say the cops were right, they fessed up. If they wanted to dance, they told me they were innocent. What they all understood was that if they told me they were guilty but that they wanted to fight the case anyway, I could no longer represent them. That was the game.

Don't ask, don't tell.

Eleven months ago, I found out that playing the game costs lives, and I'd decided that I never wanted to play the game again.

My heartbeat came back under control, and I looked at the route I was about to take: another ledge—just as narrow, just as treacherous.

The sounds of the city still pulled at me, and just at that moment I heard something familiar. I checked the street below and saw a few cars moving swiftly along. I didn't see many people. I moved closer to the exposed ledge and tested it with a tentative foot, putting more and more weight on it until I was reasonably sure it was safe. I stepped out and heard it again—a drumbeat, a voice; I knew both as well as I knew my own name. The band were the Rolling Stones; the song was "Satisfaction." It was distant and muted but unmistakable.

I knew the song, I knew the band, and I knew the record owner. The music gave me the final boost I desperately needed, and holding to the side of the building, I moved out and kept moving. Keith Richards's guitar sounded better and better the farther I got out. It didn't take me long to see a welcoming glow from a window maybe five feet away.

My pace quickened.

Reaching for the window, I hunkered down again and tried to pry it open. Locked. The scene inside the room looked almost cozy. A record player in the corner belted out my siren. A lamp on the desk sent a warm pillar of light through a neighboring whiskey bottle, which in turn threw bright golden sprites onto the floorboards. An elderly black man wearing a red pullover sat at a desk, drunk or asleep or both, his chin resting on his chest. His white hair stood to attention, as if straining to catch the bass lines from the music before transferring their magic directly into his brain.

I knocked on the window.

Nothing.

I knocked again, loudly this time.

He was definitely drunk and asleep.

I knocked a third time. The window almost fell in, and His Honor, Superior Judge Harry Ford, woke up, looked around the room nervously for a second, then put his head back down for another snooze. I hit the window yet again, and this time he could orient the direction of sound. He looked straight at me, his mouth open, and I heard a muffled scream before his legs lifted and he tumbled backward off his chair, ass over tit. He got up in a rage, his face contorted in fury. He must have thought I was on a drunken escapade. The window opened.

"I have a damn good mind to call the cops or push you off this goddamn building, you crazy son of a bitch."

My mood changed because I had to tell him. My amusement at his drunken shenanigans passed, and I felt the weight of my predicament and the plastic explosive on my back.

"Harry, I'm in trouble. Big trouble. They've got Amy."

"Who's got Amy?"

"The Russian mob."

CHAPTER TWENTY-FIVE

I pulled the window shut to keep out the freezing wind. Harry knocked the needle on the record player, abruptly cutting off Mick in full flow. Turning from the window to look at Harry, I still felt jacked up on adrenaline. His anger seemed to be subsiding into a thoughtful stare.

"I need a drink," we said simultaneously.

He poured three fingers into a dirty glass and held it out to me. It was my glass. It hadn't been used since the last time I was here, the night before I went into rehab. The liquor felt warm and soothing. I told myself that I needed it. That I wasn't starting back down that road, that this was just a fix to calm my system. Harry found his own glass under his chair. He poured a big one and sipped at it with both hands, then righted his old swivel chair and sat down with a practiced sigh.

"What the hell's going on, Eddie?"

Another sip of bourbon and I laid it all out. Everything that had happened that day from the moment Arturas put a gun to my back in the bathroom of Ted's Diner.

Harry just listened. He didn't interrupt; he knew better. Get the full story out, then pick at it later.

When I finished, he looked at me like I was an idiot.

"What in God's name are you doing here? Call the cops."

He picked up the phone and pressed nine for an outside line. I hung up his call.

"I can't go to the cops. These guys have a fed on their payroll, and that means they sure as hell have a few cops, too. If I call, I can't be sure that I won't get one of their men."

"But I know cops—I'll call Phil Jefferson."

"This is my daughter's life we're talking about. I'm not gambling it on the honesty of a cop. And I don't care who he knows—not even you. The system doesn't work; you know that. And I have no proof. I'm the one holding the bomb; even if I found an honest cop, they'd probably arrest me instead of the Russians. Even if the cops or the FBI believed me, which I doubt, it only takes a second for Volchek to make a call and my daughter is dead. One thing I've learned today: I shouldn't ignore my instincts. My gut tells me that I have to handle this my way—at least for now."

Harry put the phone down. His eyes darted around the room, and I saw the skin on his face pull tight; his chest rose and fell quickly.

"Is Amy okay?"

"They told her that they were a security team, working for me, that I got sent a death threat and that I'm being cautious. I think she bought that initially. When I talked to her, I was pretty sure that she didn't believe that story anymore. She knows, Harry. She knows she's been kidnapped. I have to get her out."

Harry drained his glass and winced with the hit. The wooden legs of his old swivel chair creaked as he reached for the bottle.

"What about Christine?" said Harry.

"She thinks Amy is in Long Island on a three-day field trip. As far as I know, she is oblivious to all of this. But you know Christine. I don't want her melting down and calling the cops. So I'm not going to tell her anything."

"You *have* to call the police."

"If I call the cops, they'll kill Amy. I told you I can't go to the police; they've bought a fed. If they can do that, they can buy an entire precinct."

"How do you know they've got a fed on their payroll?"

"I told you I found a card in one of their wallets. I lifted a wallet from one of them in the limousine. It's an FBI card. It looks genuine. There's a phone number on the back."

"You stole a wallet?"

"Don't tell me you're surprised. You know where I'm from."

"What I'm wondering is if you ever left."

He bowed his head and sighed. He was probably right; I hadn't left my old self behind. I was still on a con, but instead of insurance companies, I'd been hustling juries.

I took another drink and stretched my neck and back. The ledge maneuvers had finally put my cervical spine into a chronic spasm. The alcohol would help, but just for now.

"Is there a name on the card?"

"No."

"Could be the Russian flipped, too. Maybe he's got the card to call the FBI."

"No. This guy hasn't been flipped. He looks like one of the meanest sons of bitches I ever saw. Picked me up like a doll. No. Doesn't make sense for him to have the card if he's a snitch. Not unless he's the stupidest informant on the planet, who carries around his handlers' contact number on an FBI business card. Somehow I don't think so. He made no attempt to hide it. The number on the card is for an employee. That employee is probably in the FBI. I can't see another reason for a number to be on the card, but I'm open to suggestions."

He had none.

"I need you take a look at the device, see if you can disarm it."

"I haven't done anything like that in a long time, Eddie," he said. As he spoke, I thought I could see a shadow move across his features, but maybe it was just his movement in the half-light. Harry had been among the first African Americans in Vietnam to reach the rank of captain. He'd led a team of tunnel rats, guys who fought the VC underground, in the dark. He did three tours, never talked about his experiences, and had a bunch of medals that he never showed anyone. That was Harry.

I slipped off the jacket, reversed it, set it on Harry's desk, and opened the seam. My knowledge of explosives was zero.

Harry approached the device warily, his hands on his hips. Then he bent over. For a moment I thought he was taking a closer look, but then I noticed he was sniffing the thing.

"That's C4. Two blasting caps dug in and a complete circuit rig," he said.

"You can tell all that from the smell?"

"Don't be stupid, I can tell it's C4 by the smell. Take a whiff."

There was an odor from the plastic explosives, but at first I couldn't quite discern what it reminded me of.

"Gasoline?" I asked.

"Close. Motor oil. C4 is a composition explosive made up of lots of different chemicals and compounds. For some reason, they cut it with motor oil. That's why it came in handy in Vietnam. We carried a lot of it because we had to block up the VC tunnels. But we mostly used C4 for cooking our rations."

"Cooking?"

"Yeah. Gave off a stink, but it burned real good in the rain. Even having that stink in your nose was better than eating cold rations. See, you need a small explosive charge for this sucker to go off. You can burn it, or even hammer it, but without some kind of primary explosion to set it off, it's as safe as Play-Doh. These cylinders, the ones that look like little pens, they're blasting caps. But there is more circuitry involved here. I couldn't even begin to tamper with it in case it's booby-trapped. You said you lifted the remote detonator?"

"Yeah." I took it from my pocket and laid it on Harry's chair.

"Easiest thing to do would be to take the battery out of the detonator. I've got a screwdriver somewhere . . ." And off he went.

Harry spent a minute or two riffling in cardboard boxes and searching a bookcase in the corner that held more tools, shot glasses, and whiskey bottles than law books. He came back with a screwdriver set. The remote detonator looked like an ordinary remote control that operated a garage door or vehicle central locking. It was about two inches long, an inch wide, and half an inch deep. There were two buttons on one side. On the reverse, there were three countersunk screws to hold the two halves of the remote together. I selected the smallest flathead screwdriver on the set, removed it from its sheath, and tried to fit it into the screwhead on the detonator. It didn't fit. The head was too big.

Harry began opening and closing drawers, banging cupboard doors, and muttering. After a few minutes, he came back with a box cutter. The tip of the blade just fitted the screwhead and no more. I had to be careful with the thin blade; if it snapped, I was done.

I held the remote in my left hand, careful not to touch any of the buttons, and began, slowly and carefully, to loosen the first screw. My eyes were having difficulty shifting from the darkness of the room to the intense brightness from the desk lamp. Harry leaned over my shoulder. I could feel his impatient scrutiny.

The room grew colder despite the warm glow from the lamp and heater. Harry turned up the heat and helped himself to a whiskey. He poured me another. My head began to spin from too much alcohol and no food.

I tipped the first screw into my palm and carefully placed it on the desk.

Harry bent over and began rubbing his head—running alternate hands from the back of his neck to his white dome of unruly hair. We'd been friends long enough for me to know his little tells. When he was worried or he was thinking through a problem, he rubbed his head. A surprising number of people do the same. It's as if they're trying to coax the thought out physically.

"Spit it out," I said.

"Did Volchek give you the case files?"

"Yes. I've read most of it, whatever's worth reading anyway."

"Anything in there about the witness, the kind of deal he made?"

I knew where Harry was going with this.

"You mean why he only gave up Volchek for Mario's murder? I know. I've had the same thought myself. I tried asking Volchek about it. He said something about Little Benny still having some loyalty. I got the impression Little Benny didn't want to implicate his fellow soldiers, that he was still loyal to his comrades even though he was putting his boss in the frame. Doesn't make much sense to me, either. Little Benny told the FBI enough to get himself killed, but not enough to buy his way out of jail."

He nodded and sucked down the last finger of whiskey. Put the bottle back in a drawer and began fixing coffee. Somehow the physical routine of making coffee allowed him to think better. I knew not to interrupt him, to let him work it through in his mind. He would tell me when he was ready.

"You ever heard of the Penditi?" asked Harry.

My mother was Italian; my oldest friend was head of the New York Mafia. Of course I'd heard of them.

"Sure, the *repenters*. That's what the Sicilian police called them. They were hit men and bagmen. They got caught and they testified against the Mafia. Every one of them. What's your point, Harry?"

"As far as I know, the Penditi were some of the toughest men in the world. Ruthless killers. Even *they* gave up their organizations. I guess what I'm saying is there has to be a damn good reason why Little Benny is keeping his mouth shut about the rest of his gang."

The coffee machine began gurgling its fanfare, and Harry poured us both a big mug each. I thought then how lucky I was to have befriended Harry and how lucky the men were who served under him in Vietnam. The man was smart, a leader, and even now, in his sixties, nothing seemed to frighten him.

"So are you going to tell me what you've got planned?" said Harry.

"I've got a friend who can help me find her and get her out. It's probably best if you don't know anything about that. I'll need to contact him before we meet face-to-face. This might get messy, so I don't want anything traced back to you. This is the kinda guy who has his phones tapped. I can't call him from here. But there is something I need you to do for me. I need a few pieces of equipment. All I need is for you to pick them up and drop them somewhere in the building. Maybe the disabled john on this floor. Hide them somewhere no one will look. There's no bathroom on the nineteenth. I'll go down a floor and use the one on this level. It's just one big room, no stalls. It's perfect. It's the closest bathroom, and the Russians will wait outside. They won't follow me in if there are no stalls. I'll write you up a list of what I need and where you can get it. It's best if you keep your involvement limited, Harry. Whoever is holding Amy isn't likely to hand her over without a struggle."

Harry rubbed his head. "So this guy who's going to help you, how are you going to meet him without Volchek finding out?" said Harry.

"I can't," I said, "but I think I've found a way to convince the Russians to take me to *him*."

CHAPTER TWENTY-SIX

The window rattled in its frame, shaken by the rising wind. Harry sat down in his favorite chair, an old wooden-framed swivel chair. The chair reminded me of Harry: old, worn, solid.

The second screw landed on Harry's desk and danced around before rolling to a stop.

Harry took off his glasses and pinched the top of his nose. That was Harry's other tell.

"I just don't like it. Something stinks," said Harry.

He sighed and said, "No matter what you do, they're going to kill you and Amy. This bullshit about letting you take the fall for blowing up a witness—if you play their game, they'll make sure you don't survive to tell anyone what really happened. They can't risk it."

I concentrated on the last screw.

"But you already thought of that," said Harry.

Nodding, I tilted the last screwhead into the tip of the blade and lifted it clear of the housing.

Harry pulled up a chair next to mine. We hunched over the lamp light and waited nervously. I gripped the detonator casing gently and took my time prying it apart.

It separated.

My fingers trembled, but I didn't drop the thing. I placed the two pieces of plastic casing open-end up beside each other on the desk.

At that moment, I had a plan. I'd been thinking it over for hours.

I knew I couldn't trust the cops or the FBI, but once I had Amy back, Volchek no longer had a hold on me. I could take her and go, and I'd somehow figured out a way to do it—how I would con the Bratva into taking me to see Jimmy, who could track the cell number that I'd seen on Volchek's phone so I could find Amy. Once she was safe, I could contact the FBI and tell them everything, help them nail Volchek and his whole crew, work out a deal.

That was the plan.

Everything changed when I saw the inside of that remote detonator.

Inside, there were no workings, no chip, no circuitry, no battery, nothing.

It was an empty plastic shell.

"A fake?" said Harry.

"This doesn't make any sense. Arturas armed the bomb a few times. I've seen the red light flash on the detonator when the signal is activated. It's this bulb on the tip of the control," I said and pointed out the small bulb to Harry. That bulb would never light; it had no power source.

"When Arturas armed the bomb, I felt something vibrate."

I folded my arms and swore.

"What the hell is this?" I said.

At that moment, more questions swirled around my mind: Why would Arturas carry two detonators—a dummy detonator and a real one?

"Something else is going on here. There's another game being played. What do you think this means?" said Harry.

"This means two things," I said. "First, there's a real bomb and I'm wearing it. Second, there's a real detonator; but I don't have it. I didn't know Arturas was carrying two detonators. If I'd known that, I would've lifted the real one," I said, picking up the two empty halves of plastic casing.

I stopped, frozen.

Harry gasped as the same realization hit him, too.

"Move," said Harry. "If they find that room empty, all they have to do is press a button . . ."

CHAPTER TWENTY-SEVEN

My fingers trembled as I slid the two halves of the casing together. The screws seemed to have shrunk since I'd removed them because I couldn't manage to pick them up.

"Calm down. They haven't discovered you're missing yet," said Harry.

"How do you know?"

He looked at me as if I was being stupid. I didn't need Harry to spell it out. I was just making conversation, anything to take my mind off the situation so my fingers would begin to obey me again.

"I know, Harry. I know," I said.

The first screw tinkled back into its housing, and I started to wind it back into place.

Harry paced the floor, mumbling again.

"So I get the gear and do the drop. What is it that you need and where am I going to get it?"

For a moment I held my breath and prayed as I watched the screw I'd just dropped hit the wooden floor and roll toward the vent. I lunged at the screw and just caught it before it fell into the abyss.

Breathing heavily, I managed to slot the screw home and began working it with the head of the blade.

"Write this down," I said.

Harry picked up a pencil and began taking my dictation.

"I'll need to make calls. So I can set things up with Jimmy and keep in touch with you. You'll need to get me a pirate cell."

"A what?"

"It's a special kind of disposable cell phone. Don't worry about this. You can get everything in one store. It's a little place on Baker Street called AMPM Securities. Ask for Paul. When you get there, the store will look closed. It isn't. Keep knocking until somebody opens the door and sticks a gun in your face. Tell Paul I sent you. He knows what this stuff is. I'll need a secure property marker. Either SEDNA or Security Water. I don't mind what brand. And I'll need a small black light to read the trace."

He looked confused.

"Don't worry. Paul understands this. He'll make sure I get the right stuff."

Paul Greenbaugh ran AMPM Securities as a legit business by day and sold a lot of illegal items at night. For Paul, the night shift was the most profitable, and I'd bought equipment, most of it illegal, from Paul for a long time. Sometimes a hustler is only as good as his tools.

"Is that it? Come on, Eddie. Move it," said Harry.

Harry paced to the window, opened it, and looked out over the city. Another rain shower was just dying out.

With the last screw in place, I checked the fake detonator and felt satisfied that Arturas wouldn't know that I'd opened it. I'd hoped to disable the bomb or the detonator. But I hadn't reckoned on lifting a fake detonator from Arturas. That gave me an idea.

"Harry, you got a camera on your phone?"

"Yeah," he said, fetching his flip-top cell.

"Take a picture of the detonator. Tell Paul I need an exact match."

Holding the remote between thumb and forefinger, Harry photographed the detonator from all angles, added it to his list, and read over it.

"You'll have to go and get this stuff now. I'll be making my move soon, and I'll need that equipment. Baker Street isn't too far. Do you think you can make it back in an hour?"

"I'll do my best, but I don't even know what half of this stuff is. I'm not even sure that I want to know," said Harry.

Folding away the bomb and putting the jacket back on, I said, "Trust me, Harry. You *don't*."

CHAPTER TWENTY-EIGHT

There are times when you really need to listen to your instincts and times when you need to do whatever is necessary to get the job done. As I stood on the ledge again, outside Harry's window, every instinct I possessed told me not to go out on that ledge, that I should go back inside and find another way because I couldn't possibly make it this time.

I ignored my fear and thought again of Amy. Harry seemed to sense my thoughts.

"She's one tough little girl, Eddie. They'll keep her alive, and we're going to get her back. I'm supposed to be taking a civil court tomorrow. It might take me a while, but I'll get out and I'll watch your back. I'll be sitting alongside Judge Pike so I can keep an eye on you."

Any words of gratitude that formed in my throat were choked before I could speak. I was so relieved, so glad, so very grateful that I had a friend like Harry.

"How—how are you going to do that?"

"I'll tell Gabriella I'm evaluating her for an appellate judgeship. Never mind about that. I'm worried. There is so much that can go wrong here. I'm not leaving you alone in that court. I'll be there."

I nodded and took his hand again, remembering the first time I'd taken that big, soft hand in mine all those years ago.

When I shook Harry's hand on that first occasion, I'd put my hustling days behind me—well, almost.

Harry released his grip and closed the window. As I moved farther out onto the ledge, I wondered if I would ever get to shake that big hand again. Harry was risking a lot for me. I thought part of it was Harry's moral code, his honor and his loyalty to his friends. Somehow, though, I knew that Harry felt responsible for me. He was that type of man.

Thankfully, the rain had stopped, although it had put a fine, fresh sheen on the already slippery ledge. As I shuffled forward, my foot slipped and my left leg shot toward the ground.

In a split second, my body felt like it weighed a thousand pounds. I grabbed for the brickwork, but my fingers couldn't catch hold. Sliding my other leg underneath me, I let myself drop, trying desperately to alter the angle of my fall. My chest gratefully slammed into the ledge, punching the air from my lungs. My hands scrabbled for grip as I felt myself slipping on the wet surface. My left leg swung out. My right hand caught an exposed brick, and I quickly twisted my torso, my back screaming with the effort as I managed to keep both legs from sweeping over the precipice.

I was pretty sure I'd torn some muscles in my lower back, but I'd clung on.

My breath came back just as my body shut down and refused to move. Lying facedown on the narrow ledge, I could see New York below me. The street seemed to have quieted. The cab line that caught the night court business no longer stretched to this side of the building. There was little traffic and no people except . . . except one. Even from my vantage point, I could see a thin, bald man standing under a streetlight, the orange glow catching his dome. He wore a dark overcoat, and he seemed to be waiting for something. I saw a white limo pull up on the other side of the street, the same limo that had picked me up earlier that morning. The man under the streetlight had to be Arturas. The rear passenger door of the limo opened and an enormous guy got out—Gregor. I thought about his wallet burning a hole in my pocket as I saw Gregor carrying a large suitcase. It looked identical to the suitcase upstairs in the reception room that had held the case files. I'd left that case with Victor and taken the files into the chambers office beside the reception room.

Under the streetlight I saw Gregor unlock the case and lift the lid just a little. Arturas quickly checked the contents before Gregor closed the case. Both men were then joined by a third man. He wore a navy blue uniform, and I could see a badge on his fat chest catching the streetlight. The fat guard that I'd seen in the lobby that morning.

The three of them waited. The surrounding buildings were largely office blocks that remained still and silent at this time of night. Two white vans turned into the street and parked behind the limo. Gregor gestured to the drivers, and the first van disappeared into the basement parking lot of the courthouse. The second stopped, and the driver opened the passenger door. Gregor wheeled the case around the van; then, two-handed, he lifted and heaved it onto the passenger seat. This was the man who had picked me up like a rag doll that morning. Whatever was in that case was damn heavy. He closed the door, and the van drove into the basement lot of the courthouse. Then Gregor, Arturas, and the fat guard stepped close to the wall, out of the glare of the streetlights. They were waiting for something. The limo remained parked. After a few minutes, two men came out of the basement lot on foot. I guessed they had been the van drivers. Both men sallied up to Gregor.

For a second my breath froze.

Gregor put his hand into his coat. Then he checked his other coat pockets. He patted his pants, repeated the process, and finally used his huge fingers to feel his coat before throwing his hands into the air, mystified. He knew his wallet was gone. Arturas produced his own wallet and handed over a clutch of bills to each of the van drivers. Both men then got into the back of the limo, which pulled away. I guessed that the money in the clips, which I'd found in his wallet earlier, had been destined as payment for the drivers. Some kind of joke seemed to pass between Arturas and Gregor, and I saw the big man hold up his big paws in a display of innocence. Maybe the big man lost his wallet or failed to produce his wallet on a regular basis. There's no way they would've suspected I'd taken Gregor's leather. To them I was just a lawyer; they didn't know my past. And lawyers don't lift wallets. The Russians and the fat guard then walked up the street and turned right, out of my line of vision, toward the courthouse entrance.

Arturas and Gregor would enter the building the same way I had entered that morning, walk past the security station, through the lobby, and make their way to the elevators. My best estimate was that it would take around ninety seconds to make that journey. If they took the elevator, I could add another sixty seconds to that time before they reached the nineteenth floor and maybe ten seconds before they walked back into the chambers office. They would wake up Victor and then they would check on me—maybe another ten to fifteen seconds. For safety, I guessed I had two and a half minutes to get back to my room before they found it empty, made a call that would end Amy's life, and then hit the real detonator.

I'd gotten used to timing my cross-examinations, and I thought I enjoyed a pretty accurate internal clock. I drew my legs beneath me, stood up, and started moving. By the time I'd reached the statue, around forty-five seconds of my time had gone. The gray lady wasn't as slippery as the ledge, and it took me twenty seconds to lever myself to her shoulders, my feet planted on her back and my hands gripping the sides of her head. Part of the brickwork that had fallen away on my outward journey created a four-foot gap between the statue and the safety of the ledge.

Five seconds passed with my motionless form clinging to the Lady. I put one foot on the top of her right shoulder, stood up, and grabbed the sword for balance.

Everything Arturas had told me earlier that day had been a lie. Arturas could have moved a grand piano into the courthouse if he wanted; he just got two vans and a suitcase inside without a security check. The bomb that lay across my lower back could easily have been placed in the case that Gregor had put in the van. They didn't need me, or Jack, to smuggle anything into court. I cursed myself for being so stupid; if the Russians could afford an FBI agent, they could damn well afford to bribe a security guard to allow them to swing a bag past security. In fact, they probably had enough money to make every guard in the courthouse millionaires. In my mind, I replayed my entrance into the courthouse that morning. Barry had hollered my name; the blond guard named Hank had wanted to search me. Even before I got to the X-ray scanner, the fat guard had his eyes on me. At the time I had thought that the fat guard knew me, but I hadn't recognized him. Watching him help the Russians to smuggle the vans into the basement, I reevaluated his presence in the lobby that morning. When Hank asked me to assume the position, the fat man strolled toward us. I had thought he was backup for Hank—now I knew he'd been eyeballing me to ensure I got through security in one piece, without Hank or anyone else finding the bomb.

They would kill Amy as soon as they had no further use for me. What I couldn't figure out was why. Why involve me at all?

My dad once told me that you can't run a con unless you know all the angles. Nothing about this situation made any sense. I got the feeling that I was nothing more than a pawn in a much larger game. At least I was beginning to realize who the players were. That meant I would have to start a whole new game of my own.

I let go of the sword, breathed out, and jumped.

CHAPTER TWENTY-NINE

My body landed flat on the ledge and my legs kicked loose some more bricks. I hugged the wall and shuffled along as quickly as I could to the window that I'd left open. Two minutes twenty seconds had elapsed as I fell into the chambers room, sprang to my feet, and closed the window. I took off my coat and began brushing it with my palm. It was damp, along with my pants. The radiator in the corner was off, and I cranked it up full, put my coat on it, and leaned up against it to dry the damp patches on my knees while I caught my breath. In between gasps, I heard footfalls from the corridor. Leaving the heat from the old rad, I peered through the keyhole and was grateful to see Victor asleep on the couch, in the reception, in much the same position as I'd left him. The Samsonite case that had contained the case files remained open and empty on the floor, just where I'd left it. The files themselves were still on my desk in the chambers.

The silence was broken by a faint, metallic rattle: the elevator doors opening in the hall. Sweat dripped onto my jacket, and I wiped my forehead. Along with one set of footsteps, I heard a much heavier man's feet coming behind. Arturas quietly strolled back into the outer office and folded himself softly into a chair. Gregor came in behind him and kicked Victor, waking him up. Gregor asked Victor to move over, and the two huge men leaned back into the couch and closed their eyes. Soft lighting from a lamp, identical to the one in my room, made the outer reception look almost serene. I tested the handle of the door and found it locked. No one had checked on me. If they had opened the door and found me gone, they wouldn't have relocked it.

As quietly as I could, I went back to the radiator and let the growing heat dry my pants. My next step was already planned out. I needed to contact Jimmy before I made my move with the Russians. To do that I required the phone on Harry's list. Even without traffic, it would take Harry at least an hour to get the gear and make the drop. There was nothing I could do but wait. Stretching out my legs and putting my back to the wall, I could still see through the keyhole.

They were resting.

After a half hour, I caught my head falling into my chest. I'd almost dozed off. My coat and knees were dry, and thankfully, the dark color hid any stains. The little room felt hot and I turned off the radiator and settled back down with my thoughts.

I already owed Harry Ford so much. Without him I'd either be in jail or dead. That's the inevitability of life as a hustler. There's no retirement plan. And no health care. Toward the end of my life in insurance fraud, the evil of complacency had crept in. Either that, or I had wanted to get caught. It certainly didn't feel like that at the time. When it was happening, I blamed myself for a split-second bad decision, and I blamed a nine-pound hammer. Well, it wasn't the hammer's fault; nor was it the fault of the man who had wielded it. It was really my driver's fault for sleeping with somebody else's wife.

I had scouted my mark, and we were all set up for a Friday-morning fender bender. My precision driver, a washed-out NASCAR racer called Perry Lake, got himself all busted up by a jealous husband on the Thursday night. The husband tied Perry to a chair, went to his tool bag, and showed Perry a brand-new nine-pound hammer. He went to work on Perry: broke his knees, his hands, his elbows, and his teeth. I should've called off the job. I didn't. I'd forgotten the rules of the game: Get the money and get out. During those last few years as a hustler, I'd stashed away close to two hundred grand. I wasn't in it for the money anymore. I was in it for the scam, for the rush of conning a big insurer and their legal team out of thousands of dollars and then toasting my dad in a bar before cashing each damages check. So I took Perry's place that day. I might have done better if I had strapped Perry to the driver's seat and left him to it. I messed up; I hit the brakes too hard, too soon. The Mercedes hit me from behind, well short of the intersection. My fault, not his. Instead of me threatening to take the driver of the Mercedes to court, he sued *me* for personal injuries. In fact, he brought me to the civil court in Chambers Street. The judge that eventually heard the case was Harry Ford.

Ordinarily, an accident like this wouldn't see the inside of the courtroom. The accident was my fault, but I lied and said that a pedestrian ran out in front of me and that's why I'd had to break hard. A cop said he had been across the street and had witnessed the accident. He said he didn't see a pedestrian running in front of me. If not for the cop coming on the scene of the accident, I would just have taken off immediately afterward. Instead the cop took my details. The only ID I had on me was my own, another mistake.

I turned up in court that day to offer the guy ten grand to walk away. His lawyer told him not to take it and just run the case in court. The car I had driven in the accident wasn't insured, and hiring a lawyer would've sent the signal to the Mercedes driver that I had enough money to get a lawyer, so I just showed up to defend myself. When the case began, the judge, Harry Ford, seemed to be profoundly bored. If not for the cop, the case would have been my word against the word of the Mercedes driver. It wasn't until I began asking questions that I noticed Harry taking more of an interest. The mark gave evidence that he didn't see any pedestrian before I had put on the brakes. I asked him one question: "You say you didn't see me braking until it was too late and you ran your car into me. So if you weren't paying attention to what I was doing, you wouldn't have seen the pedestrian either, right?" He didn't answer.

The cop said he had a clear view of me, a perfect recollection of how the accident happened, and he sure didn't see any pedestrian running across my path. I knew if I could shake the cop, then I had a pretty good chance, so I tried to test him on what he really remembered.

"Officer, you say you have a perfect recollection of that day, events that happened more than six months ago?"

"Correct."

I held a page in front of me: a letter from the mark's lawyer threatening to sue me if I didn't pay his client one hundred thousand dollars. The cop saw me looking at a piece of paper but couldn't see what it was.

"Officer, what was the next call that you attended after witnessing the accident?"

He was about to lie, to make something up. He hesitated as he saw me looking at the document while I waited for his answer. The cop thought that I already had information about what call he'd attended after the accident and that information was on the paper in front of me.

"I don't remember," was his safe response.

A similar setup for the next question about the nature of the call he attended immediately before the accident. Same response—all of a sudden he didn't remember.

As a young boy, I'd watched my dad perform the exact same routine with his runners if they were light on a payment. He'd hold up his little red book as he questioned them, as if to say that he knew exactly what had gone on and he had the evidence to prove it. He didn't, of course. He was bluffing.

After a few more questions, I heard Harry laughing.

He addressed me for the first time. "You don't need to ask anything more. I'm dismissing this case."

I had kept my bankroll. Only just. The mark stormed out of court, shouting obscenities at his lawyer. The feeling that little victory gave me was astonishing. It was just as sweet as any con I'd ever pulled. There is a little tapas bar across the street from the courthouse. I headed there, feeling elated and suddenly hungry. As I waited for a table, I heard a deep voice behind me. "You did well today, son. Pity you're not a real lawyer." It was Harry.

We ate together. Harry told me he'd never seen an unrepresented litigant perform so well and that I'd done a better job than most of the lawyers who appear before him. I'd never met anyone like Harry before. He was straight, successful, with a wicked sense of humor, and well, I suppose he had something dangerous about him. He asked me what I did for a living and I told him I had a little money put aside from my parents but that I hadn't decided upon a career.

He licked sauce off his fingers and said, "You know, you have a rare gift. You should think about law school. I like the way you asked questions. It shows real talent and aptitude for the job. Particularly with the cop. You blew him away."

"To be honest, I didn't have a clue what calls he'd attended on the day of the accident. I suppose I was kind of conning him. Don't think they teach that in law school."

He laughed.

"You ever heard of Clarence Darrow?" said Harry. "He was a trial attorney a long time ago. You remind me of him. Before Clarence began a trial, he would thread a long hat pin through the center of one of the big Cuban cigars that he liked to smoke in court. When his opponent's case began, Clarence lit up his cigar. As his opponent presented their case, Clarence's cigar burned down, but because of the hat pin, the ash held together and didn't fall. The pin worked like a sort of central support beam. That column of ash got longer and longer until the entire jury were ignoring Clarence's opponent and the witness. Instead, the jury were watching the ash on Clarence's cigar, waiting for it to crumble and fall all over his white linen suit. The ash never fell, and Clarence never lost a case. You think there's much difference between Darrow and the stunt you pulled today with the cop?"

"Never thought about it that way."

"That proves you have talent. If you ever decide to try law school, give me a call. A recommendation from me should help. When you're done studying I could always use a clerk," he said. And that was that. Although Harry planted the idea of being a lawyer in my head, it was my mom who made me take the final leap.

The snoring coming from the reception area got cut off abruptly before beginning again.

Midnight.

Sixteen hours left on my clock.

Harry surely had had enough time to get the equipment and make it back to the courthouse before twelve.

It was time to find out.

In a confidence game, the moment just before you play your hand is the most nerve-racking. It's the point of no return, and it's always in your mind right until the second when you actually do it. Once you're making that move, somehow the nerves disappear.

Standing and stretching my back and neck, I gave my clothes and my coat a final check. Some mud on the bottom of my coat came off with just a little water from the bottle that Arturas had thrown me earlier. After rinsing my hands from the same bottle, I rubbed them together until they were dry. Having decided that I was okay and that I didn't immediately look like a guy who had been climbing over a dirty building, I watched the tremors disappear from my hands as I knocked on the door firmly and said, "Hey, open up. I need to talk to you. Your boss needs to eliminate another witness if he wants to avoid a retrial."

Returning my eye to the keyhole, I saw movement. Victor stood, and as he did so, he obscured my view of the *Mona Lisa* print that I'd seen when I first walked into the office that morning. Somehow, his body standing in front of the picture created the germ of an idea, a spark, something that related to the dummy detonator and the case that I'd seen Gregor heave into the van, but at the moment, that train of thought was clouded in mist.

CHAPTER THIRTY

I heard the key scraping the lock open, and the door swung inward. All three men stood before me.

"Even if I kill Little Benny, the prosecution could still get a retrial with Tony Geraldo's evidence. Your scheme won't work without taking him out. Trouble is, you can't shoot Tony Geraldo without risking an all-out war with the Italians. Lucky for you guys that you don't need to kill him. If he's the kind of man I think he is—money will buy his silence."

Arturas looked at me and nodded his head.

"Yes. The other firms mentioned the greaseball's evidence. They said it did real damage but would not be enough to convict Volchek on its own," said Arturas.

"And they were right, but it *will* be enough for the DA to get a new trial. You can buy your way out of that now, but I need real money to do it. I think Tony Geraldo also goes by the name of Tony G. If it is the same Tony, then I know the head of his family. I represented him a long time ago. I can broker the deal. But I need four million dollars to do it: two for the brokerage fee for his boss and two for Tony."

Arturas didn't react to the figure. No overt expressions of shock. Four million didn't appear to be big bucks for these guys. They could get it in a few hours. I recalled an article in the newspaper reporting that Volchek paid five million in cash for bail. Four million would be no problem. I bet my daughter's life on it.

"Tony G is Tony Geraldo. And you're right, we can't talk to those men. Maybe you can; maybe you can't. It doesn't matter. After we kill Benny, no one will be willing to give evidence against Volchek even if there is a retrial. Forget about it," said Arturas.

"I can't do that. Your boss is giving me a shot at Benny—a shot at winning this thing without killing anyone. But I don't have anything to throw at Tony Geraldo. You need to buy him off."

"I told you to forget about it," said Arturas, this time with steel in his voice.

"You want me to *forget* about a damaging prosecution witness in your boss's murder trial?"

His shock registered immediately. I saw the skin tightening around his eyes before that terrifying smile emerged again.

"This is my plan, lawyer. You are not in charge here."

"It may be your plan, but it's my case. Volchek is *my* client. I'm playing for my daughter's life. If you don't tell him about this, I will. And I'll tell him you tried to shoot me down. How will that make you look?"

Blue neon flashed across the room from the billboard on the adjacent building. The sudden pulse of color illuminated a wet glimmer on Arturas's cheek: his scar—weeping again. Behind his fake grin, his brain was running the calculations, weighing up his options.

"Remember who has your daughter," he said, as he dialed a number on his cell.

In not so many words, we understood each other. If I pushed him, he'd push back at me through Amy.

I listened to him talking to Volchek in Russian. Occasionally, Arturas would glance at me while he listened to his boss.

After a few minutes, Arturas hung up the phone and dropped himself back onto the couch. Assuming he was waiting for a decision, I took my place at the desk in the next room and waited. Tony Geraldo's evidence might get the prosecution their retrial; it didn't quite hit a home run on motive, but it was strong circumstantial evidence of animosity almost immediately prior to Mario Geraldo's death. Miriam would paint a picture of a murdered family member, the terrible loss of such a promising young man on the say so of a cruel Russian mobster, but that was bullshit. If Arturas was right and Tony Geraldo was in fact Tony G, he probably didn't give a shit about his cousin. From the crime-scene photographs I'd seen of Mario and his apartment, he'd looked to me like a low-life drug dealer. Tony was a big player in the family and the community. He had status. Volchek had probably done Tony Geraldo a favor. Tony was climbing high within the family, and his bottom-feeder cousin always had the propensity to drag him back down. He didn't need that. He needed respect. And that started at home. After all, if he couldn't keep his own cousin in check, who in their right mind would trust Tony to run a crew?

All the same, Mario was family. His murder was an insult that would have to be dealt with. You don't just knock off a member of the family and get away with it—no matter what. Tony Geraldo needed a way to save face. He didn't want to start a war—not for his shit-bird cousin anyway—and this probably caused him a dilemma. Perhaps Tony giving evidence against Volchek was the payback for Mario. Whatever his reasons, Tony's evidence was my ticket to see my old friend Jimmy "the Hat"—the head of the family.

My right arm and my back ached following my escapades on the ledge. I thought about asking Arturas for painkillers, then dismissed the notion.

Arturas's cell phone signaled a call coming in.

He answered the call and looked at me. He didn't speak for a time. After about thirty seconds, he ended the call, stood up, and said something in Russian to Victor. Victor looked at me fiercely.

"You lie," said Victor as he took a knife from his pocket.

CHAPTER THIRTY-ONE

Eight feet of nothing separated me and Victor. I sat at my desk in the judges' chambers. Victor stood very still in front of the couch, staring at me. He held the knife in his left hand. I couldn't begin to match the intensity of that stare. My eyes rolled nervously around Victor and the knife.

He began walking toward me.

He said nothing.

My brain ran a spectrum of scenarios before my mind's eye, each more elaborate and detailed. I couldn't fathom how I could have been found out. My eyes began darting more erratically, pawns to the theories that were vibrating around my head. My fingers reached for my mouth. If I'd been found out, it should be obvious by now.

Then my head put on the brakes.

My dad's training—*keep it together.*

What if I hadn't been discovered?

"You know what, Victor? I've been sitting here trying to think of a way that Volchek could've misinterpreted my actions." Victor slowed his advance and listened.

"I'm a pretty smart guy. I have to tell you that in case you're too stupid to realize it on your own. I'm acting in good faith toward your boss. There's no way that Volchek can reasonably think otherwise. So I figure he doesn't believe that I'm lying. He's being cautious, overly cautious in my opinion. How the hell did he ever make any money without taking some chances?

Anyway, I'm not a liar. You are. You're trying to scare me into giving something away, trying to find out if I'm double-crossing your boss. Let's save some time. I don't have an ulterior motive. What? I'm going to take his money and leave my daughter with him? Is he crazy?"

Victor stopped around three feet from me, the knife still in his hand.

"Well?" I asked.

"Do it," said Arturas, urging Victor on.

"This is bullshit," I said. "You guys have nothing on me. You're just seeing how I'm reacting to the situation. You're wondering if I'll crack and do something stupid or reveal a plan. Don't worry. Where the hell could I go? I've been with you assholes all day. I want my daughter. I want her safe. I have to win. I *will* win this case to save my daughter."

Victor didn't move. For a moment, nothing happened.

He moved toward me quickly, the knife by his side. I planted my feet and gripped my seat. When he took his next step forward, I planned to dive to my left and start swinging the chair.

His foot stopped in midair, he flashed the knife, and then laughed as he stepped backward and turned to Arturas.

"He's not liar. He nearly took crap in his pants. What a pussy," said Victor, with a heavy Slav accent before taking a long belly laugh.

I relaxed a little. I'd passed a test and an important one at that.

Arturas made a call and again reverted to his native language. He was probably talking to Volchek. The call ended and he pointed at me.

"You had better be good, lawyer. Four million is a lot of money. Not for us, but it's still a lot of money. We would be upset if it went missing."

"When?"

"We will have to go and get the money. It will take a few hours to have it ready, no more. Where are we going with it?"

"I'm going to Jimmy's restaurant for breakfast. That's where you're taking me, and that's where I'll meet Jimmy. You won't meet him. He sees you and you're a dead man, understand? Your boss needs this. I'm the only one who can make it happen."

Arturas said nothing.

"You do know who Jimmy is? Right?" I said.

"He is a fat Italian son of a bitch," said Arturas.

"Correct, but he's also head of one of the biggest crime families in

New York. And he doesn't like anyone messing with the family, no matter how distant the relation. What I don't understand is why you guys aren't dead already."

"Because he doesn't want to start a war over a little junkie like Mario, and trust me, it would be war. In the end, Jimmy would probably win. But he would lose many men and much money in the process. Is it worth it for one junkie? No. He marks our cards. So we lay off dealers in his area for a month. Let him think business is too good to lose. He soon forgot."

The press had reported Mario's death as a gang hit—a territorial dispute. Tony corroborated the fight in the nightclub between Volchek and Mario Geraldo and said the killing was over a debt. What I didn't know now seemed very important. My best guess was that Mario had been killed for the photographs that were hidden behind the broken picture frame in the crime-scene photos and subsequently burned by Little Benny when the cops started hammering down the door. What was in those photos? And why was Mario killed to obtain them? Without knowing anything about the photographs, I couldn't be sure.

"Okay, so Jimmy saw dollars instead of blood this time. Or maybe that's just what he wants you guys to think. Depends how personal it was to Jimmy. So how personal was it? Why was Mario killed?"

"He died because he was a stupid junkie who started a fight with Volchek."

"But Tony Geraldo talks about a debt."

"Everyone owes Volchek," said Arturas, and his eyes momentarily strayed into the distance.

"So was it a debt or a drunken bar fight? Or did Little Benny kill him for the photographs that the cops found burned in Mario's sink?"

Arturas looked me over, surprised.

"It was fate. That's all you need to know. Do not ask too many questions, lawyer. One of those questions might just get your daughter killed," said Arturas, as his hand tracked the scar on his cheek.

That was the second time that I'd seen him finger that scar. He probably wasn't even aware that he was doing it—like most people that unknowingly reveal their tells. The scar appeared to be relatively recent: pink and angry—perhaps no more than eighteen months old. My guess was that Arturas suffered that scar around the same time that Volchek found out Little Benny would testify against him.

CHAPTER THIRTY-TWO

I couldn't sleep.

The small couch in the old chambers felt lumpy and sunken in places. Broken springs and broken supports dug into my legs, but even if I'd been lying on a king-sized bed in the Waldorf, I would've had the same problem trying to sleep. I couldn't stop turning everything over in my mind. In a way, it helped. Thinking through the problems helped keep my mind off Amy. My head raced with theories, most of them probably crazy, some close to home, one or two could be right on the money.

I'd never heard of a mobster turning state's evidence for anything less than full immunity bought by the witness providing a sworn statement on every last detail of the organization: These are the suppliers; this is our distribution network; this is who launders our money, who killed who, when, and where. Usually all of this would be accompanied by a heavily pinned map showing exactly where the bodies were buried. Just like the Penditi.

We were very far from that situation here. Little Benny coughed to one murder, that's it, and he wasn't going into the witness protection program after this trial. He still had time to serve. So far he'd been serving that time in FBI protective custody.

I couldn't understand why Little Benny would be stupid enough to do any time at all. Why didn't he give up everybody, get himself an immunity agreement, then get the government to set him up for life in witness protection?

There had to be good reasons. First among my theories was family. The statements were silent on this, but if Little Benny did have a family, I was pretty sure they were in Mother Russia. Not even the feds would be stupid enough to try to offer protection there. No, Benny wasn't worried about family in Russia; if he had family there, he wouldn't have opened his mouth about Volchek at all, as there would be no way to protect his loved ones back home. If he had family in the United States, he would spill his guts for the whole operation and get his family into witness protection—or he would say absolutely nothing. Family considerations didn't fit my theory.

What would be his primary motivation? I wondered.

Staying out of jail had to be his only motivation.

Again this didn't sit well with the facts. Little Benny had another eleven or so years on his sentence. Why not give up Volchek for a payday and no time? Why give up enough to put a price on your head but not enough to get you paid or out of prison?

Of course, I was ignoring the ultimate game changer—stupidity.

As an intelligent, rational human being, you can always see another angle when in fact there is no angle. I was just rationalizing what I would do when the situation might have been that the person was just plain stupid and you can't rationalize their kind of decisions.

But was Benny that stupid?

He got caught red-handed.

The answer that Volchek gave me seemed closest to the truth, that Little Benny was still loyal to some—Arturas. That was the key; I needed to find the connection between Arturas and Little Benny.

I got up slowly. My back sang with pain in protest at my movements.

I ran over the evidence again, the photographs, the witnesses, and the officers' statements.

Something wasn't right.

When I thought of the fat guard downstairs, the identical suitcase that Gregor put into the passenger seat of the first van before it had been driven into the parking lot, the FBI card, it all just swam in front of my eyes. My head thumped with the effort of trying to contain it all. Then one image came floating to the surface of my consciousness and stayed there—Amy. I examined every corner of her features in my mind and imagined myself holding her, telling her everything was okay, that she was safe, Daddy came for her. My body shook. I gritted my teeth, holding back the tears, and collapsed into the chair.

I must have passed out over the files. I didn't know how long I'd been asleep, but I woke up fast when the chambers door opened.

"We leave now," said Arturas.

Victor and Gregor said something to Arturas in their own language, and he responded to both of them angrily. I couldn't understand what they were saying, although it sounded a lot like an argument. Threading my arms through the sleeves of my overcoat, I hefted it onto my back and folded down the collar over my suit.

"Wait," said Arturas before launching into a full-blown argument with Victor. The blond man pointed at me.

"If you two don't keep it down, security will come up here to see what all the fuss is about," I said.

"Shut up and take off the—" said Arturas, before Victor cut him off.

They were arguing about whether I should leave the bomb in the chambers office or wear it out and risk having to smuggle the bomb into the courthouse a second time. I didn't want to do that again. Their dilemma was a difficult one. If they left the bomb in the office, there was always a small chance, even with a new lock on the outer door, that security or the FBI might find it. Plus, without the bomb on my back, I had more freedom. Making me wear the bomb out gave them more security; if I didn't come back after I'd met Jimmy, they could just press the button. That's if they assumed I'd keep the bomb on me, which, of course, I wouldn't.

"Do you want me to leave the jacket here?" I asked.

They stopped arguing.

"Take it off," said Arturas. "I'm not risking you getting searched on the way back in."

I took off my coat and the jacket. Delicately, I hung the jacket over the back of the chair in the chambers office and put my overcoat back on.

"Call Jimmy," said Arturas, offering me his phone.

"After. I have to go to the bathroom first," I said, and I prayed that Harry had returned from his impromptu shopping trip at AMPM Security and managed to hide my equipment in the john.

CHAPTER THIRTY-THREE

I had to go sometime, and Arturas appeared to have expected it.

He said, "Use the bathroom downstairs. Victor will go with you."

"I've been using the bathroom on my own for some years now," I said.

"You'll be shitting in a bag for the rest of your life if you keep that up," said Arturas.

Victor led the way to the staircase and down to the next level. The stairs were precarious in the dark. They turned most of the lights out in the courthouse after nine p.m., keeping only a few floors lit for night court.

We took our time on the stairs. I found the bathroom and ducked inside quickly before Victor could protest. The bathroom consisted of one large room directly off the corridor. The lock moved slowly and silently until it turned a full one hundred and eighty degrees and secured me. It would not save me. Victor could have that door off in seconds.

I dropped the toilet seat down loudly and imagined Victor listening suspiciously at the door, but I told myself that it just was my imagination playing tricks on me.

Where did Harry put it? I thought as I looked around the bathroom.

My search began badly. I lifted the porcelain cistern cover and almost dropped it, creating a loud scraping noise in the process.

I waited and held my breath.

No calls or questions from Victor.

The cupboards below the basins wouldn't open. I checked the ceiling for loose or out-of-place tiles. Then I saw a drop point beside the paper towels.

It was perfect: a disused paper towel dispenser affixed to the wall. I opened the protective cover and felt inside. I touched a paper bag. The bag came out of the casing easily. The towel holder had been broken for some time, so the cleaners wouldn't have gone near it. I opened the bag as slowly and as quietly as I could. The items were all there. One by one I removed them.

The spray was called SEDNA. It came in a small, black spray bottle like a perfume tester, easy to hide. Then I found the flashlight, or what appeared to be a flashlight. It was in fact a black light that illuminated traces of the SEDNA, which was visible only under ultraviolet light.

The cell phone felt incredibly small, but I didn't want it for its size—I wanted it for its features. The main feature being that the phone operated through an illegal pirate network that allowed untraceable calls and signal capture. That too would be easy to hide. The dummy detonator looked to be an exact match. I took out the detonator I had stolen from Arturas and compared the two. They were identical.

I heard a phone ringing and almost dropped the cell phone in panic. The ringtone ceased and I heard Victor talking outside the door. His phone—not mine. His voice trailed off a little, as if he paced the floor while taking the call.

Harry had done well. I turned on the cell phone, made sure that it was on silent in case anyone called me, dialed a number, and waited for a good ten seconds before the call was answered.

"Who's this?"

"I need to speak to Jimmy urgently; it's Eddie Flynn."

"Hang on."

I could hear conversation on the other end of the line.

"Call me back on this number," said Jimmy.

I redialed to a secure line.

"What the hell's going on?" said Jimmy "the Hat" Fellini, in a soft Italian accent.

Keeping my voice low, I said, "I'm in deep trouble. Some people have taken Amy. I'll call you in a few minutes. Pretend we haven't spoken. I have a deal and you *will* see me right away. The kidnappers will be listening. Don't let me down."

"Eddie, do you need money?" asked Jimmy.

"No. I'm coming to the restaurant to give *you* money. I'm buying a hit team."

CHAPTER THIRTY-FOUR

After ten seconds of silence, I felt pretty sure I'd gotten away with my hushed call with Jimmy. Victor's booming voice came through every few seconds, sometimes closer to me, sometimes farther away as he walked around outside the bathroom. I let out my breath. I hadn't even realized that I'd been holding it.

That left me with two more calls to make.

I called Harry and left him a message. It was just coming up to four a.m. and he was probably still in night court. I told him I got the bag, thanked him, and said that if I needed anything else, I would send him a text message.

The last call I had to make made me nervous beyond belief.

The keypad on the phone was small and I made lots of mistakes dialing the number, but it probably had more to do with my body coping with stress than the size of the keys. After all, I'd managed to make the other calls without any problems. My hands were shaking, not for the first time that day. It took me a good ten seconds to make sure I'd typed the correct number into the phone, rereading the handwritten number on the back of the FBI card and checking it against the number I'd typed. Satisfied, I hit dial.

I could have been making a mistake with this call, but I had to do it, and I had the phone to do it—a heavily modified Nokia with a special SIM card. The phone was very expensive and for good reason. The cell captured the network of the mobile phone it was calling. Technically, whoever I called was in fact calling themselves. For landlines, it threw out a random wireless search and hit the nearest landline connected to broadband and the call would be registered from that landline number. The same line is never captured twice.

Somebody answered my call.

"Yeah?" said a male voice with an American accent.

"Hello. Can I speak to the operator, please?" I said.

"What? Operator? You must have a wrong number," said the voice. He sounded like a smoker. I heard the low breath and baritone drawl of a nicotine fan.

"I'm sorry. I was using technical jargon again. I'm new at this, and they tell you not to do that. I meant can I please speak to the handset owner?"

"Speaking. Who is this?"

"This is your telephone company, sir. I'm afraid I'm calling with a sixty-second warning—your phone is about to be cut off. If you have an emergency call to make, I suggest you do it now, sir. Do you have an emergency or do you anticipate an emergency arising?" I sounded like I was reading some bullshit from a prepared script, not really understanding what I was saying. Like a real telephone company employee.

"You're not cutting me off. Why would you cut me off?"

"Your bill is outstanding, sir."

"This is a scam. This is a group package phone—it's paid for by the Federal Bureau of Investigations, buddy." He gave me the full title.

"I'm afraid it hasn't been paid, sir. Unless you can pay me sixty-six eighty in the next few minutes, I have to cut off your service."

"You can't do that. I already told you the FBI pays for this phone."

"Not for a while, I'm afraid, sir. Can you pay the amount now?"

"No. It's already been paid."

"Then I have to cut you off."

"You can't do that. I mean, how could you do it?"

"I already have, sir, just now. If you don't believe me, just try making a call after you hang up this one."

He hung up immediately. I didn't. I'd captured and was using his cell network. If he did try to make a call, which I was sure he would do, he wouldn't be able to get a dial tone.

I waited thirty seconds, listened to Victor laughing on the phone, then called again.

"See?" I said.

"How did you do that?" he said.

"I just pressed a button here, sir. That's all. Can you pay the overdue amount, please?"

He let out a sigh and paused. I thought for a moment that I'd blown it. This call was too risky; I shouldn't have made it. I put my thumb over the disconnect button and waited. I prayed he wouldn't take the gamble of losing his cell today, when the Russians might need him most.

"Do you take credit cards?" he said.

I almost punched the air.

"Sure, but before I take the number, can I have the name as it appears on the card, please?"

A moment's silence followed; then he said, "No way. This is a scam."

"Would a low-life con man be able to do that to your phone?" I asked.

"No, but . . ."

"Okay, so what's the name?"

"How come you don't know my name? I mean, you called me. I'm a customer, right? What do you need my name for?"

"I just need to verify the name on the card, sir. This is not Al Qaeda."

It was the big weakness with the idea, which of course came to pass. I expected it.

"Sir, I have all your customer details here, but of course I don't know if I'm speaking to the customer right now. Anyone could answer your phone, so I just need your identification details from your card."

Another agonizing pause came.

"You said you were calling from my telephone company. What company am I with?"

I checked my signal indicator at the top of the screen; I'd captured AP&K.

"AP&K, sir. Do you want me to ask you what color pants you're wearing?"

"Wha—" He stopped and sucked air through his teeth. This could've blown up in my face at any time, but I was relying on this guy being gullible. Thankfully, he was in the FBI and not the DEA. Cops and FBI agents get stung all the time. I know hustlers who exclusively target cops and feds because they're more trusting of what they believe to be authority. Little old ladies and beat cops, ripe for the picking.

"The name as it appears on the card is Thomas P. Levine," he said.

"Thank you, Mr. Levine. Can you tell me the type of card and confirm the first line of your address?"

Victor banged on the door. I already had what I needed.

I pretended to take a payment, then disconnected the call.

CHAPTER THIRTY-FIVE

Creeping up the dimly lit stairs with Victor following behind me, I couldn't help but wonder what Thomas P. Levine looked like. Back in the chambers office, I chewed this over as I made the call from Arturas's phone.

"Could I speak to Jimmy please?" I said.

"Who is this?" said a voice.

"Tell him it's his lawyer."

Jimmy came on the phone. "You know what time it is?" he said.

"It's Eddie," I said.

Silence. I didn't say anything. I just waited.

"Been a long time. Call me back on this number," said Jimmy.

I memorized the number for a cell and dialed it right back.

He answered quickly. "You're good. Nobody is listening. What's up?"

"I have four million with your name on it. Got a job for you, and it's easy money. Somebody needs to keep their mouth shut," I said.

"We're usually pretty good at keeping people's mouths shut. When you coming in?"

"Got to pick up the cash first; shouldn't take long."

"Come at six a.m. I'll throw in breakfast. There's a shift change around that time. Got a lot of bird watchers in the area, all different kinds of agencies. So you gotta take the long way around. Side entrance, knock three times. Smile for your picture. See you soon, bub."

The call ended.

Jimmy and I had gone our separate ways when I went straight. We more or less agreed upon it. The feds, NYPD, the Justice Department, the IRS, and God knows who else all had their eyes on the Mafia. It would make straight life difficult for me and possibly put a target on my back if we were seen together. We'd called each other occasionally, but that hadn't lasted too long. I'd forgotten that meeting Jimmy in secret could be tough. Taking four million dollars to him without any one of those agencies clocking me would be just about impossible. Just as I thought I was beginning to climb out of this hole, I suddenly had a whole new set of problems. I was about as tired as I'd ever felt in my whole life. I swore and kicked the empty suitcase on the floor, sending it across the room and into the door.

"There's a problem," I said.

"What? He wants more money?" said Arturas.

"No. He has company. FBI, ATF, DEA, take your pick. Somebody's camped out at his place. We need to approach carefully. If I'm seen hauling a huge bag of cash in there, I'll be arrested within seconds, along with most of the New York Mafia."

"So leave it. There is already too much risk. We take our chances with Benny. I'll call Olek and tell him it's off," said Arturas.

"Wait. I said it would be tough. Not impossible. I'll figure something out. Don't you think I want to get out of this without killing a witness? Don't you think I want my daughter back? I'll do whatever it takes to get Volchek off without killing Little Benny. I can do this. Your boss needs it to happen this way."

This set off another argument between the Russians. Except this time I thought I recognized a few words here and there; I heard "Benny" a few times. That was what sparked my interest. Arturas was wild with anger; his neck and chest flushed red, and spittle hung from his lips as he bellowed at Victor and I caught, "Benny" then "*nyet, nyet, nyet.*" I was pretty sure "*nyet*" meant "no." Then "Benedikta," and something I couldn't quite pick up before Arturas bellowed, "*Moy brat.*" This last phrase echoed around the room. They were talking about Little Benny, but I couldn't understand them.

Victor became quiet. Arturas seemed to have won the argument.

"All right. We'll go pick up the money. You will come, too. Then we will go straight to Jimmy's," said Arturas.

Four a.m. Two hours to get the cash and get to the restaurant.

CHAPTER THIRTY-SIX

Getting out of the courthouse was a lot easier than getting in. The lobby was pretty busy with the families and friends of those who'd been arrested and were trying for bail. A bunch of cops were blowing the steam off their coffees at the bottom of the staircase while they shared a joke. I didn't recognize any of the security guards on night duty. Not that it mattered—you don't get searched leaving the courthouse.

Outside, the wind was picking up, and I was glad of it. I was wired on adrenaline, but it was beginning to wear off. The cold air felt invigorating. Gregor had stayed in the room upstairs. It was just me, Arturas, and Victor who were headed for the limo across the street. I got in first. Victor came afterward and sat opposite me. When Arturas got in and sat down, I leaned toward him, banging shoulders, pretending to drag the bottom of my overcoat out from under my legs.

Arturas grumbled.

He hadn't felt the lift or the plant.

I'd taken the detonator, the real one, from his coat pocket and dropped in the fake that I'd lifted from him earlier and the new fake that Harry got for me from Paul. Arturas now had two detonators, like he'd had earlier that day, except that both of the detonators were now fakes. The real detonator felt a little heavier to me as I held it in my pocket, but then I'd become adept at sleight of hand twenty years ago. I could judge the half-a-gram difference in a phony dime just by holding it. Arturas wouldn't notice the difference in weight between the detonators. At least I hoped he wouldn't. I'd noticed that he kept the real detonator in his left pocket, and the fake in his right, to make sure he didn't mix them up.

As the limo pulled out, I saw that it had been parked outside the little tapas place where Harry and I had first met and had lunch. In that meeting, Harry had basically offered me a job. I'd never had a straight job before. Didn't need one or want one. My mom, on the other hand, thought I was working as a paralegal. The day after I'd met Harry for the first time, I visited her in the hospital. In the years since my dad passed away, Mom had experienced a steady decline. I gave her money every week so she didn't have to work, but that seemed to make her even worse. She rarely got out of bed before midday and had stopped socializing with her friends. She'd even stopped reading.

That day, that last day, she looked so tired. The skin on her face seemed so thin I thought that it might tear at any moment. Her lips were dry and broken, and her hair was damp and clung to her pallid skin. The doctors said they weren't sure what was causing her weight loss, her pains, and her cough. They had gone from diagnosing MS to cancer and back again.

Deep down I knew exactly what was killing her.

Loss.

When my dad passed, she kept going, for me. She hadn't cried much; she didn't want me to see her pain. For all her efforts, I knew. I knew she had already died inside. As soon as I started making money and she believed I was in a good job, she just kind of stopped. It was almost as if she had done her job. She had raised me, and now she wanted to let go. So that she could be with my dad. She was slowly dying of a broken heart.

Her eyes brightened when I brought her the flowers. She loved flowers.

She held my hand, and I saw a tear glisten on her cheek.

"Are you feeling okay? Is there much pain today?"

"No. There's no pain. I'm happy. I've got my big son, and he's going to be a lawyer someday."

Her smile hit me like a punch. I couldn't tell her. No matter how many times I'd told her, she couldn't understand that being a paralegal didn't necessarily mean I would eventually become a lawyer. She didn't listen. She wanted to dream for her son, and in the end I let her. If I'd told her that I wasn't a paralegal, that I was a con artist pretending to be a lawyer so I could con insurance companies, what little she had left would've faded away. In some way, that lie made me feel responsible for her death. If she had known that I wasn't really a paralegal, but a con artist, would she have given up on life? If I had told her the truth, she would have cried and wailed and ordered me to get out of that life, that my father had wanted better things for his son. Sitting by her bed, watching her slip away, I made a decision that I would be true to her memory of me. That I would give her a real reason to be proud.

Her hand fell in mine. I knew she wasn't asleep. The heart monitor sounded its alarm. No one came for a while. Then, slowly, a nurse opened the door, turned off the monitor, stroked my mom's head, and said, "She's gone."

I buried her with my father, paid off my crew, called Harry, who set up a place for me in law school, and until Arturas pulled that gun on me in Ted's, I had never looked back. I had put my life as a hustler behind me. Now I was glad. Glad that I still possessed those skills.

Harry had saved me that day when he offered me a job. He had held my fate in his hand and changed my life. Somehow, I thought Harry felt responsible for me.

A blast from a car horn brought me back to my ride in the limo. The windows were so densely tinted that I had trouble seeing where we were.

After a few minutes, I figured we were headed south, toward Brooklyn, and it wasn't long before we took the exit for the Brooklyn-Battery Tunnel. I still call that tunnel the Battery even though it has been renamed as the Hugh L. Carey Tunnel in honor of the former governor of New York. My dad often spoke about Carey as a good Catholic man; that had to be true—Carey had fourteen children.

"Where are we headed?" I asked.

"Sheepshead Bay," said Arturas.

I knew the Bay well. It wasn't too far from where I grew up. The Bay separated Brooklyn from Coney Island and stretched back into quiet neighborhoods from the rowdy Soviet bars that had opened up along the shoreline. We drove for around thirty minutes before pulling into a lot behind an auto-repair shop at the corner of Gravesend Neck Road and East 18th Street. The lot fronted for an old warehouse.

"Come with me," said Arturas.

We got out, and I looked around. The area was a mix of apartment buildings and businesses that mostly closed after five p.m. A quiet street at that time of the morning. The ground was slippery with frost, and we made our way to the steel door that served as a pedestrian entrance to the warehouse. The door led to a large furnished office. Two couches sat against the eastern wall facing a TV planted high on the opposite wall. The TV was on, fixed to a news channel. A news anchor talked over an image of the Hudson River. The banner headlines scrolling across the bottom of the screen said that the harbor patrol had begun to bring up bodies from the cargo ship, the *Sacha*, which had sunk with all its crew on Saturday night. The headline said they had found the ship and some of the crew, but so far only dead bodies. According to the news anchor, the fact that they had found the ship was good news for commuters, as debris from the sunken ship ceased to be an issue and the Holland Tunnel could reopen. The anchor seemed more concerned with traffic than the families of the dead. He obviously wasn't a New Yorker; we care about our own.

Two men silently entered the office from an adjoining room, each carrying a large duffel bag. They dumped the bags on the floor and left. I thought they might have been the van drivers that I'd spotted earlier from the ledge, but I couldn't tell.

"Four million. Pick it up and let's go," said Arturas.

"I'm not going anywhere. If I walk in there and that four million turns out to be a dollar short, I'm dead. I'm not going anywhere until I've counted the money. I've told Jimmy I'm bringing four million dollars, and I'm going to make sure that's exactly what I've got," I said.

Kneeling down, I unzipped both bags and began to count out the six-inch-thick tightly wrapped bundles of cash within.

As I knelt, I kept an eye on Arturas and Victor while I handled the money.

After a few minutes, I had a pretty big pile of cash on the floor. Arturas gestured for Victor to follow him into the hall. Shuffling around on my knees, I could make out both men. Arturas stood with his back to me. Victor's view of the office was blocked by Arturas.

The small black vial of liquid was easy to conceal and hard to find in a large pocket. The cap came off silently, and I hit the spray nozzle four times, sending what appeared to be a cloud of water vapor over the top piles of cash. Replacing the cap, I slid the little black bottle into my coat pocket.

Forty-five minutes later, I'd finished pretending to count the money. I stood, stretched my aching neck, swore in pain, and called Arturas.

"Say, does this guy Victor actually do anything?" I asked. "Ask him to give me a hand repacking the bags."

Victor knelt down beside me. I made sure to keep the pile I'd marked close to Victor. Each time Victor picked up a wad of cash, he touched the vapor residue. That left a trace, a unique chemical signature that linked Victor to the money.

CHAPTER THIRTY-SEVEN

The limo ride from the warehouse to Jimmy's restaurant took about thirty-five minutes in light New York traffic. Easily one of the worst journeys I'd ever experienced. I sat in the limo with millions of dollars at my feet, ready to pay the toughest man I'd ever met to go find my daughter.

As we sped through lower Manhattan, I saw the burrito vendors getting their carts set up on the corners and bundles of newspapers being opened as the city woke up to a new day. The sun threatened to crack through the buildings at any moment. I felt exhausted. Adrenaline carried me only so far. I hadn't slept properly in twenty-four hours, and almost as soon as I realized it, a yawn grabbed me.

Jimmy's was a great restaurant, one of the finest, set in the heart of Little Italy on Mulberry Street. I had an idea about how I could get into the restaurant without being photographed by every law-enforcement agency in the city.

"Take a right onto Mott Street," I said.

"Why?" said Arturas.

"I need to distract whatever surveillance teams are watching the restaurant. I can't just walk into Jimmy's with the money. There's a fish market in Mott Street. Stop there. I'll talk to a few guys who can help us out."

Arturas didn't speak for a time. He exchanged quick glances with Victor before telling the driver to turn onto Mott Street.

"Listen to me, lawyer. If you are thinking about running, I want you to know that it is pointless. For a start, I will kill your daughter, very slowly. She will suffer. Then I will find you and I will kill you. You know the name Kruchkurr?"

"No. Should I?"

"Former Soviet commander. After the fall of the Soviet Union, I came here with Olek to start our business. Kruchkurr supplied us with transportation lines for weapons and drugs. During the purge of the old Soviets, he got arrested and he fled, along with most of our money and our shipment."

He shifted in his seat and straightened his back so that he was now leaning over me.

"I found him in Brazil a year later. His wife and son died first. I made him watch. I tell you this so you know that there is nowhere on this earth that you can hide from me. Remember this."

There was no embellishment to this story. Again, it was a simple statement of fact, clear and unemotional.

"I won't run. I won't give up my daughter. But I need you to understand that I'm playing your game because I want her back. She means everything to me—so you don't need to worry about me running."

The limo slowly progressed up Mott Street. I'd told Arturas that I didn't feel the side doors of the restaurant would be safe either. In truth, I didn't know, but I did know that I needed to impress Jimmy. I needed a monumental favor from him, and the money, and whatever value our old friendship held for him, probably didn't warrant the risk. I couldn't ask him to put his faith in me if I skulked in through the back door; he needed to know the *real* Eddie Flynn was back, and to do that, I needed to make an entrance: I needed to walk in through the front door without the cops seeing me.

"Stop here," I said. "I need five hundred dollars, and I can't dip into the four million. I know a couple of guys who can help me get into the restaurant without being spotted."

Victor gave me five hundred in a roll. I stepped out of the limo and into the fish market.

Ten minutes later, I put my back to a corner half a block from Jimmy's. The limo waited up the street. I began my approach and scanned the area for surveillance crews. A year before Jimmy opened his restaurant, there had been two diners across the street. One served pretty decent food. The other turned out pretty special food. Then Jimmy's opened, and he didn't need the evening competition. So the diners closed at seven p.m. They still made good, though. No charge for protection and a monthly sub on the profits from Jimmy's. Some months, the cafés made more money being closed than open. Jimmy eventually bought out both premises. He used them for storage. That created a problem for the FBI and the ATF and the other agencies that categorized Jimmy as a person of interest—there were no diner booths for agents anymore. They could no longer hold up a table with a cup of coffee and watch Jimmy's restaurant from across the street. Instead they had to get creative with their surveillance methods.

I slowed my walk, and within a minute I made the agents—a brown van with tinted windows; cigarette butts gathered on the pavement outside the passenger window—this was Control.

This mobile monitoring unit controlled the rest of the surveillance operatives. Given the street layout, I guessed a three-man team: one with ready vehicle access, one to cover the traffic going into Jimmy's, and one with a high view, to monitor who came out. I saw a black Honda motorcycle on the sidewalk. The rider seemed to be taking a long time over takeout coffee—rover one. The other two were split for optimum POV. They would have one in the Laundromat with a view of the goods vehicles and the route to the subway station—rover two. The other would have a high position. I glanced up and saw a few people at their windows. Nothing stood out. Then I saw a man at a window in a crumpled shirt, like he'd slept in it. He was the top view. The eye in the sky would pose the most problems for me, unless I was across the street from the restaurant, out of sight. I made for that position, and once I got there, I parked my ass on a bus bench, whistled, and watched everything unfold.

I'd first represented Pete Tulisi about two years ago. Pete worked all hours in the fish market on Mott Street, and when Friday came, he took his wages to a bar, blew every cent on vodka, and started a fight—an average Friday night for Pete. His record showed a lot of assaults, disorderly conducts, and not much else. When the court fines began to rack up, Pete stopped paying his legal bills. We came to an arrangement. When he couldn't pay cash—he paid me in fresh fish. I had never insisted on being paid if it meant that the client couldn't make their fine payments because if they fell short on the fine, they would do time. I had called at Mott Street earlier, paid Pete the five hundred bucks Victor had given me, and now he was ready to give me my show.

Pete's pal, a delivery truck driver from the docks, stopped to tie his shoelaces outside Jimmy's. He pointed at Pete, who had just walked around the corner, having heard my signal. Both men eyeballed each other before stripping off their coats and shirts. A second later, Pete and his pal began killing each other. They were both big men: baseball-mitt fists and football shoulders, each weighing well over two fifty, and they weren't pulling their punches, what my old man would have called a real *slobberknocker* of a fight.

Soon they were rolling around on the sidewalk, throwing garbage at each other. Then a real piece of luck. NYPD showed up but refused to go near the men. The fight grew wilder as they moved down Mulberry Street, away from the restaurant, with Pete and his pal throwing each other into parked cars, setting off the alarms, and generally making as much noise and mayhem as possible. As long as each man gave as good as he got, PD would hang back and let the monsters tire each other out. When the police deal with guys this big, there's no guarantee that Tasers will have any effect.

Five hundred dollars was a small price to pay for the perfect distraction.

I checked both rovers and then the high-view agent—they couldn't take their eyes off the fight. The limo pulled up beside me, and the passenger door opened.

"It should take no longer than a half hour to count the cash, bill for bill. If you're not standing here in an hour, I will make that phone call and your daughter's blood will be on your hands," said Arturas.

"You forgot I have to brief Tony on what he's going to say in court today. I need two hours," I said.

"I'll give you one hour, no more."

An hour gave me problems. I would have to work fast.

My watch read 6:01 a.m. Less than ten hours to go before my deadline.

I took two bags full of cash from Arturas and headed for Jimmy's. Pushing my way through the front door, unobserved, I walked straight into the barrel of a .45 Colt automatic.

CHAPTER THIRTY-EIGHT

I was met at the door by muscle. Two of Jimmy's guys, dressed in black leather jackets and tailored pants. The smaller of the two men held the Colt at his side, pointing it at my chest. The weight of all that money pulled at my shoulders.

"Jimmy's expecting me. My name's Eddie Flynn."

"Hands against the wall," said the guy with the Colt. He didn't look as ugly as his pal. The man with the Colt had pools of black below his dull brown eyes, which were only barely visible beneath his caveman brow. His friend was taller and presumably had been born with a nose before somebody decided to bite it clean off. A red mound of scar tissue sat in the middle of his face, underlined with two black slashes, which must have passed for nostrils.

I didn't move.

"I don't give a shit who you are. You're not gettin' in here without me pattin' you down," said the gunman.

"You're not touching me and you're not touching these bags. I got four million reasons in here to hurt you and your boyfriend here, Rudolph. And if I walk out, Jimmy's going to want to know which asshole made me walk. I'll tell him it was the cute one. Now let me through, gorgeous, or I'll give you a kiss you won't wake up from."

Both guys looked at each other.

"You put a foot wrong and we'll blow you away."

They each pointed a gun at the back of my head and followed me to the dining area. The restaurant only seated one table at this time of the day: Jimmy's breakfast meeting. It was basically a small riot, but with catering.

Despite what people are told in the movies and the media, there were no real ranks or titles in the mob. Not these days, anyway. There was a counselor, an adviser, but no Mafia captains, no boss of bosses; leave that to Scorsese and Coppola.

Of course, the mob didn't operate like some kind of communist collective either. There was *a* boss. That was Jimmy, but the other families all worked together and elected a speaker for the committee. Out of the ten guys at the table, probably all of them had killed at least once. Jimmy probably more than most and usually up close and personal. Very personal. That was the job. Generally and wherever possible, their individual roles would be suited to their particular skills. For example, Cousin Albie, who was everybody's cousin no matter where you were from, had been through high school, graduated to college, and was a qualified accountant. He handled the moves; the large deposits and withdrawals of currency were Cousin Albie's affair, along with the "dirty thirty runs." Albie said that there were thirty foolproof ways to launder money, but you had to use all thirty at once. If you simply used one method, you'd get caught. Thirty processes cut down the risk to the overall cash sum and helped keep things relatively on the lowdown. Albie dressed well, looked young and professional and not at all like a gangster.

Cousin Albie was eating a bowl of cereal. He sat on Jimmy's left. On Jimmy's right, I saw the polar opposite of Cousin Albie—Frankie. Frankie qualified as one of the more hands-on type of operators. The skin on Frankie's hands shared a similar consistency to grade-three sandpaper. I remembered the story about Frankie's new knuckle: a large piece of hard skin on his middle-finger knuckle had built up over the course of three days, while Frankie beat on a Polish informer. By the time Frankie finished with him, the poor guy had no teeth left and his face had swelled to twice its normal size and bled constantly. Frankie's hands were so bad he couldn't drive for a week. He stayed home with his purple, broken hands in bowls of iced water. Frankie's face didn't look at all dissimilar from his hands. He was in his late fifties and it showed. At the table that morning,

Frankie's old, dangerous hands were safely wrapped around a breakfast sandwich.

The restaurant's heating must have been turned up full. I could feel sweat beginning to bead on my forehead. The restaurant could seat around a hundred people with its fifty or so tables. A thick carpet, which was a mix of grays and lilacs, set off the retro decor. In contrast to this decorative style, twelve large chandeliers lit the place like an old movie theater.

Jimmy looked ordinary, like he always did. He usually wore sweaters with black pants, and he never went anywhere without his hat, hence the name. The hat was his grandfather's, bought in Sicily in the sixties. That hat was a flat, gray cap. Ever since Jimmy's grandfather had been cut down in Chicago by the cops, Jimmy wore his granddaddy's hat every day. Some said he even slept in that hat. It was about respect. Short black hair escaped from the sides of the hat. Jimmy was small and built like a fighter: thick arms and lots of muscle on the chest and neck. We'd built our bodies together in Mickey Hooley's gym, pounding the heavy bags and running up and down the old stairs. When my dad first brought me to that place, I didn't know any of the other kids. They were all first- and second-generation Irish. There was one kid nobody went near, and that kid was Jimmy Fellini. Because I was half Italian, Jimmy and I got on well together, and we were soon tearing up our knuckles doing push-ups on Mickey's painted concrete floor. In truth, Jimmy had been my best friend for the better part of fifteen years. He'd put on quite a few pounds since I'd last seen him. I still kept my weight to an even one eighty-five, which was by no means lean but nowhere near overweight.

As the doormen brought me close, all activity on the table stopped and everybody looked at me.

"What the hell's going on, Eddie?" said Jimmy.

"I'm here to buy some help," I said.

"What's in the bag?"

"Four million dollars. Olek Volchek has my daughter. I'm in the market for a contractor."

"Are you sure? Haven't seen you in years, con man. How do I know you're not working for the Russians?"

"Because if I wanted to kill all of you guys, I could, in a heartbeat." I removed the detonator from my coat. "You want a couple of million dollars and a job? Or do you want me to redecorate?"

Silence bellowed around the table. Nobody moved. All eyes were on Jimmy. Waiting. One word from him and these men would tear me apart.

A smile broke through his lips. I was yanking his chain.

Then Jimmy got up and wiped his mouth with a silk handkerchief before bursting into deep laughter.

"Eddie Fly, I missed you, bub," he said as he embraced me. *Eddie Fly.* I hadn't heard that name in a long time.

Jimmy wrapped his hands around my back and patted me. It was a friendly gesture, but he was also checking for wires, guns. I felt relieved that I'd left the bomb in the courthouse. Coming back to Jimmy's felt like going home. That feeling lasted no more than a second when I realized that I'd gambled my daughter's life coming here. I loved my little girl and I wanted her to be back so bad I could feel it in my teeth.

I gripped Jimmy in a bear hug as I fought back the rising emotion in my voice.

"Jimmy, they have my little girl."

"Not for much longer," he said.

CHAPTER THIRTY-NINE

It didn't take me long to recount the events of yesterday, from Ted's Diner to my trip to the restaurant. There were a few open mouths around the table. I noticed a couple of suspicious looks as well, along with the stone-faced silence of the two men on either side of Jimmy.

Jimmy didn't give anything away, as usual. He didn't react to anything I'd told him. He just sat there, occasionally drinking his coffee but alert and paying close attention to every word. Sometimes his eyes would flit to his men, to gauge their reaction. I finished my tale and he lowered his eyes to his half-eaten breakfast.

"So let me get this right," he said. "You're supposed to plant a bomb in the witness stand and take out the informer, Benny. Amy's been kidnapped and is being held somewhere. You don't know where, but somewhere in Manhattan. You can't go to the cops or the feds. And you don't want Tony to testify in Volchek's trial. Have I got that pretty good?"

"Pretty perfect," I said, "but I left out Harry. Superior Judge Ford, that is. Harry got some stuff for me—like the phone I called you from."

Jimmy looked as if he were rolling the possibilities around in his head.

"I can hand you a dirty fed on a plate as well as the two million."

"I'm not interested in dirty feds. Can't trust them. And it was four million a few minutes ago," said Jimmy.

"Sorry. One bag is UV coded with DNA water, an invisible liquid with a unique chemical signature. It's registered on all the main databases. I need you to hold that bag for now and hand it over to the feds once this is over. I've marked the bribe money so they can trace it straight back to the Russians. The big guy who helped me pack the cash has the spray all over his hands. I'm going to tell the feds that the bribe was one million, and they've got all of it. That leaves a little extra for us."

Jimmy lifted a cigarette from an open pack on the table and lit it from a match offered by Cousin Albie. The cigarette burned down a half inch with the first long drag. With the smoke quickly blown at the ceiling, Jimmy gave me his full attention again.

"So that leaves three million, Edward," he said, like we were still kids. He used to call me Edward after my mom had scolded me for something or other. She called me Edward and so he called me that, too, around my mom or when he was ragging on me. The nickname "Eddie Fly" didn't materialize until I started my own crew.

I was hoping not to have to deal with this now, but there appeared to be no way around it.

"I need to borrow a million. Call it a debt. Help me get Amy back and I'll make sure you get three million: two million now and I'm good for the rest."

"Why can't I take three million now?"

"You just can't. I have to take care of something. You know I've never let you down."

He considered this. As a good businessman, he liked risk. I thought he secretly wanted some kind of war with the Russians. He wanted a chance to rip into them. Mario's murder wasn't enough because nobody gave a shit. Now he had an incentive.

"So can I count on you, Jimmy? There's no con here. This is my daughter. I'm putting her life in your hands," I said.

A long minute passed with Jimmy's eyes on me.

"I believe you, Eddie," he said. "The way I look at it, we're family, you and me. We grew up hitting the same people. That makes Amy family, too."

I let the doormen take the bags to the back of the room.

"So what do you want us to do?" he said.

I pulled up a chair and sat down, breaking in between two bagmen.

I fished in my coat, heard a murmur, turned, and saw that the guns were back on me again, but only momentarily. Jimmy waved them away. Slowly, I removed Gregor's wallet from my pocket.

"I need you to find Amy and get her safe. There's another team holding her. This is Gregor's wallet," I said, laying it on the table.

"Inside is his driver's license and last-known address. I doubt if she's there, but it's a start. Before I came here, we picked up the cash from a warehouse in Sheepshead Bay. There were two guys there. If you sweat them for the address, they might give it up. But they have to be taken without giving them a chance to alert Volchek or Arturas. The only other thing I have is the cell number that Volchek called. Amy mentioned a girl, Elanya. I don't know if it was her cell, but I have that number."

As soon as I said this, I looked closely at Jimmy. He hadn't disappointed me. He looked straight at Albie, a fleeting glance but a glance nonetheless. Albie was the guy who had contacts in the unions, the man who could get access to anything.

I continued. "I think you can trace the property through the phone or through this guy Gregor."

"You said it was a cell number. You don't know what kind of phone it is?" asked Albie.

"No. Arturas has an iPhone. Volchek has a little black phone with a good camera on it and a big screen. That's all I know. Can you trace an address with a number?"

"If it's registered, then sure. But it's likely these phones were bought on the black market. That means there's no paper. On the other hand, if they're new phones, then there might be a way of tracing them."

"They looked pretty new. I don't know if Elanya's is similar."

"If the phone was manufactured after 2005, then it has a GPS tracker built-in. Every new phone manufactured in America has that chip. Something to do with 9/11. We won't be able to find an address, or listen to their calls, but we can track the GPS chip. I've got a guy that can do that. I'll call him," said Albie.

"Okay. Get working on that number. All you guys start calling your people. We need to find out where this little girl's being stashed. I've got a couple of guys in Brooklyn that can get to the Bay pretty quick. Frankie, give our pals a call," said Jimmy.

I gave Frankie the warehouse address.

A pleasant waitress brought hot coffee, and I gratefully accepted a cup. She had long dark hair and wide, engaging eyes. One of Jimmy's many girls. Jimmy brought his cup to his lips and stopped as if something had just occurred to him.

"What time did you speak to Amy yesterday?" said Jimmy.

"The afternoon. Maybe around four or five o'clock. Why?"

He brought the cup closer and halted again, the steam close enough to warm his face.

"What if they're moving her?"

He was right. There was no guarantee that she wasn't being dragged around half a dozen safe houses. But I thought it unlikely. Hauling a ten-year-old girl around with them would make them stand out even more. They might have been thinking it was best to stay in one place.

"I doubt it. They probably want to lie low and stay put. If we're going to hit them, it might be an idea to spread our bets, hit the likely locations simultaneously. If we can track the GPS chip in the phone, then I'd say that's where Amy is being held," I said.

Jimmy seemed satisfied.

"Don't forget Tony," I said. "He has to go back on everything he said to the cops. Otherwise the Russians will think they didn't buy anything with their four million, and I'll probably get killed."

"Mickey, get Tony G down here," said Jimmy.

Jimmy's face softened and I thought of the tough little kid I'd first met in the gym. His gaze seemed to drift through me, catch my recollections, and ride on them, beyond the smoke from his cigarette, to happy days tearing up the neighborhood together and wild celebrations for every four-dollar hustle we got away with.

He smiled and then stopped and frowned as if it was somehow inappropriate.

"I heard what happened to you last year. I'm sorry," he said.

It took me by surprise. I didn't think he knew.

"That must have been tough, bub," he said.

"It was. It is. I dream of her sometimes, when I sleep at all. I think maybe she's telling me that she forgives me. Maybe that's what I want to believe."

Jimmy, despite his professional activities, also managed to be a father with a big heart.

"What do you know about the Bratva?" I asked.

"Not that much. They came here at the start of the nineties, after the Soviet Union collapsed. Lots of them did. Volchek and his crew were probably the best of the bunch, considering they've survived this long. Somebody told me they were ex-military. They did pretty good at the beginning, selling AKs to the gangs; then they got into drugs, hookers, people trafficking, and the usual. When the cartels moved in, they cut off a lot of the Russians' supply chains. They just bought 'em up. You can't compete with the kind of dough the cartel throws around. From what I hear, they're under a lot of pressure from their competitors. They're holding on to what they have by the skin of their teeth."

"Some of their competition appeared in court yesterday. Volchek said they were there to watch him go down."

"Probably. Most organizations work with the cartels because they don't have the numbers to fight them. Volchek has held out this long, but that can't last. Sooner or later they'll try to put his lights out. Maybe they think if he gets sent up the river they can make their move."

A lot of that made sense to me. There certainly was an air of desperation about Volchek and Arturas.

"How long do we have?" asked Jimmy.

"Forty-nine minutes. We need to move."

"Anthony, call Wong's and tell them we need two Ninjas ready to go in five. And call the Lizard; tell him to get into Manhattan and keep moving until we get him a location."

Anthony, a tall, good-looking kid in his twenties and a nephew of Jimmy's, started making calls. I couldn't help but notice the look of distaste on Frankie's face when Jimmy mentioned the Lizard.

"Who the hell is the Lizard?" I said.

"He's a friend. My guys will need to travel light if they're going to make it in time. The Lizard is all the backup we ever need," said Jimmy.

CHAPTER FORTY

I waited for Tony G to appear and marveled at how the occupants of Jimmy's restaurant took on a busy, military type of industry. Dealers and junkies who would know where the Bratva might have a stash house were called and questioned. Everyone around the table held a phone in their hand, shouting, dialing, on hold. Waitresses cleared away the breakfast items, and soon the tablecloth was covered in little scraps of paper, pens, and cigarette ash. Albie worked the telephone number. He had a union contact who was employed by the telephone company. He waited for his pal to answer his call.

One of Jimmy's men put on a set of latex gloves and held the money under a UV light. I saw some of the notes I'd marked show bright, purple patches. Whatever cash was not contaminated would be separated. It would be foolish not to.

Pretty soon the breakfast party started to get results.

"My guy says they run meatpacking out on the harbor."

"I got a stash house in Queens."

"We got two of their dealers; they don't know shit, no addresses, just car work."

"I got two whorehouses, a crack house, and a sandwich place."

"Get your best three locations, guys. Decide on the best shot you got. You've got five minutes. Come and see me when you've decided. Anthony and Frankie are hitting the phone address no matter what. You guys gotta go pick and hit. If you strike out, you hit again until we run out of addresses. If you find her, dead or alive, you call me," said Jimmy; then he stopped. He realized what he had said.

That crushing pressure of panic, guilt, and fear fell on my chest again. For a second it knocked the air clean out of me.

He turned and said, "Sorry, bub. Force of habit. Usually the people I have to track down end up as corpses. She's alive. I'm sure."

Albie got through to his man in the phone company, and his right hand began to move swiftly across the page, the pen making large bold sweeps as he wrote down an address.

"We got it," said Albie.

Jimmy read the address.

"That's six blocks from the courthouse. Call the Lizard and tell him to meet Anthony and Frankie there," said Jimmy.

"And me. I'm going, too," I said.

"No, Eddie, you're not. Look, I know you can handle yourself, but you're not a shooter," said Jimmy.

"Call Wong's. Tell him you need three Ninjas. I'm going with them. I need to see my daughter."

Jimmy sighed, shook his head, and told Anthony to make the call to Wong's.

At that moment, a man wearing a shiny gray suit walked in. His black hair stood up as if he had a full can of hair spray bolstering each strand. I remembered Tony G, the man I now knew to be Tony Geraldo, the man I hoped would answer a lot of my questions. I looked at Tony's shoes, and while they were highly polished, they looked soft and wide and extremely comfortable: a bagman.

"Tony, you remember Eddie, right?" said Jimmy.

"Sure, Eddie Fly, the hustler, the lawyer, the shit-bird that used to cream your ass at stickball when yous was kids," said Tony as he jabbed jokingly at Jimmy's ribs.

"How you doin', Eddie?" said Tony, sitting opposite me.

"Not so good. I don't have much time, Tony. Tell me why Olek Volchek wasted your cousin Mario."

"You don't mess around. Okay, it's like this. Mario was an embarrassment. He was stupid and he got pinched a couple of times when he was a teenager, but what can I do? He's family. So I took him under my wing. He worked for me on the construction angles because I thought even Mario couldn't mess that up. Guess what? He made a shit pile out of it. He leaned too heavy on a straight guy and the feds pinched him, but at least he kept his mouth shut. He did a nickel in Rikers and got out a couple years ago. After the shit he pulled I told him he was out of the business. Guess what? He got even more stupid."

"What did he do?"

"He got too ambitious. He did a photography class in Rikers. Seems he got pretty good at it. When he came out, he carried a camera everywhere. Now, I didn't know what he'd done at first. Me and him and a few guys were in the Sirocco one night. Mario goes to the bar. Next thing you know, Volchek's people are all up in his face until they spotted me, and then they backed down. Next day Mario was dead."

"That's what it says in your statement, Tony, but you didn't mention the photography part. What started the fight with Volchek?"

Tony wiped his mouth and looked at Jimmy, who nodded back at him.

I thought Tony needed a little push, so I laid out my theory. "I've seen the crime-scene photographs. There's a broken photo frame on the floor and what looks like burned photos in the sink. I'm guessing Mario took a photograph that Volchek didn't want taken, and Mario tried to sell it back to Volchek. If he was as stupid as you say, he could do that."

"Yeah, he was that stupid."

"So why didn't you tell this to the cops?" I asked.

"Mario got killed trying to sell those photos. I didn't want anyone to know that I got a copy."

"You have a copy?"

"Sure. I wanted a set of those photos in case we were going to war with the commies. Might be good leverage."

"Why does Volchek want those photographs so bad? What did Mario see?"

"I've seen 'em and I can't tell. I don't know why he wanted 'em."

"Where are they now?"

"I got 'em stashed at home. By the way, I hear I'm supposed to keep my mouth shut today; trouble is, I can't. I've got to give the same evidence that's in my statement, see, and there's no amount of money can persuade me otherwise."

CHAPTER FORTY-ONE

"Eddie, you have to move if you're gonna make it in time," said Jimmy.

I held up my hand. "Give me a second. There's no point unless your man here is going to play ball."

Tony leaned back in his seat and folded his arms. He wasn't going to say another word. I guessed correctly at the reason for his silence.

"Let me see if I've got this straight. You got busted and the DA offered you a deal, right? Guys like you don't testify for the cops. I knew there had to be a reason why you agreed to be a witness. Tell me—how much coke did they bust you with?"

The lights from the chandeliers seemed to soak into Tony's suit. He rocked back and forth in his chair.

"Not much, half a kilo. If I don't cooperate and give evidence like a good citizen, I go down. I got no choice."

I hadn't foreseen this. Four million dollars didn't matter to Tony G. You can't be rich in prison, and even if I'd brought double that amount, it wouldn't have changed his mind. I thought about his situation and came up with a solution. I took some paper and wrote down a few lines before flipping the page around and pushing it under the aura of Tony's suit.

"You say *that* in court whenever you're asked a question and you'll be fine. Your plea bargain deal is normally a standard agreement. I know it by heart. Say this and only this and you can't be prosecuted."

Tony read over the lines.

"This all I gotta say?"

"That's all. I give you my word this will work."

Jimmy's hand appeared on Tony's shoulder.

"Do it, Tony. I'll see you get a good split from the cash Eddie brought in. And if it all goes wrong, I'll take care of your family. But it won't. If Eddie says something will work—that's it. It'll work. Eddie's like my brother; his word is my word."

Tony nodded and got up. "Okay, Eddie, but if it don't work, I'll kill you. You know that, right?"

I stood and shook hands with Tony. "If that happens, you'll have to get in line. Look, I need to see the photos. Something else is going down, and I can't figure it out. The photos might help."

"They're at home. It's an hour-and-a-half drive each way."

"I need them, but I don't have time to wait. You'll need to bring them to court later."

"How am I going to give 'em to you, then?"

"You a religious man, Tony? I'm not. Why don't you give me some religion?"

Tony got the message.

Jimmy looked confused. "Hang on a second. If we get Amy out in time, you don't have to go back to court, Eddie."

My shoulders dropped. If I got Amy out, I would make that call then.

CHAPTER FORTY-TWO

I followed Anthony and Frankie to the back of the restaurant and through the swinging doors to the kitchen. The kitchen looked big enough to serve a restaurant twice the size of Jimmy's. A long, central stainless-steel work surface separated the pass from the four industrial-sized stoves. I'd met Anthony before, when he was just a kid sitting on his mother's knee. If Jimmy trusted him on a job like this, then the kid must have been talented. Anthony opened the door to the walk-in freezer and I followed him and Frankie inside. Our breath came in long white gasps of frosted air. Frankie began moving boxes of packaged meat from the far right-hand corner and soon revealed a secret door. We found ourselves in a small storeroom. The shelves on either side of the room were filled to the ceiling with guns of all sizes, bags of coke, and bundles of cash wrapped in cellophane.

Anthony and Frankie lifted a long steel bar each. The bars had a hook at one end. They placed the hooks into recessed holes on either side of an iron sewer cover that sat in the middle of the room. With effort, they lifted the cover to reveal a steel ladder leading into the sewer.

"You got to be kidding me," I said.

"It's the only way to travel," said Frankie, lifting a flashlight from the shelf.

Anthony lifted a bag from the floor, handed me a flashlight, and together we climbed into the dark, stinking tunnel, which was unexpectedly dry. I hit the flashlight, but the beam penetrated only about fifty feet into the gloom.

We turned left, then right at two crossroads, and then, after a minute of following the tunnel straight, Anthony stopped at another steel ladder on the wall. Frankie climbed up and knocked on the cover. Within seconds, the tunnel became flooded with light from above as an Asian man removed the cover and offered Frankie a hand up.

We stood in another storeroom of another kitchen. From the Chinese characters printed on the boxes, and the smell of garlic, ginger, and lemongrass, I guessed we were in an Asian restaurant. The man who had helped us from the sewer gestured that we should follow him, and we walked through a narrow corridor to a loading bay and an alley beyond. In the loading bay were the three Ninjas Jimmy had asked for: three black, Kawasaki Ninja 650 motorcycles with riders revving the engines. We were each given a helmet, and I watched Anthony climb onto the back of the first bike.

"This is the quickest way to travel, Eddie. A car can't make it there and back in the time you got. Sammy Wong is our courier. We sometimes move around the city this way. It's discreet and fast," said Anthony.

"Not to mention dangerous," I said.

"Relax, will ya? These guys are pros. Just do what they tell you and you'll be fine."

I squeezed the helmet over my head, climbed onto the back of the last motorcycle, and tapped the driver on the shoulder.

"It's my first time riding a motorcycle," I shouted.

"Me too," said the driver.

Everyone laughed apart from me.

"My name's Eddie. Don't kill me," I said.

"I'm Tao. No promises, man."

I wrapped my hands tightly around Tao's waist. He gunned the engine, and we burst down the loading bay ramp and turned right into the alley.

The alley was maybe four hundred feet long, but we seemed to cover that distance in around three seconds as I felt my stomach slam into my back and I heard myself screaming into my helmet.

Anthony's bike took point, and I wondered when it was going to brake as it rapidly approached the end of the alley. It didn't slow down at all. The bike continued to accelerate toward the main street. I didn't have to wonder what the driver was doing for very long. Instead of braking, the bike sped up, skipped through the traffic lanes, and disappeared into the early-morning shadows of the alley on the other side of the street.

"Holy shit," I said.

The street ahead looked busy; cars and bicycles darted from left to right across our intended path and beyond them, right to left. I heard Tao's excited scream as our bike fired out of the alley like a four-hundred-pound missile straight into four lanes of New York traffic. The bike weaved and braked and accelerated as the traffic swirled around us from both sides.

I shut my eyes and prayed to God I made it through this.

My chest pushed into Tao's back as he hit the brakes hard, and my nose filled with the smell of the brake discs smoking with the effort. I opened my eyes and saw a black Ford Taurus skidding toward us from the left, its driver thumping the horn in panic. We were about to be T-boned.

"Lean back," I heard Tao shout, and our helmets crashed together. My back burned with pain as I used every muscle I had to force my torso backward against our terrible momentum. Then I realized what Tao was trying to do—he let go of one brake, the back brake, and the motorcycle tipped forward onto the front wheel. Tao leaned to his right and the whole bike spun around ninety degrees before the back wheel smacked into the side of the Taurus, stopping the bike dead and keeping us upright and alive.

The back wheel rebounded off the side of the Ford and was already spinning with vicious acceleration as it hit the street and we shot forward, spun around the Taurus in a cloud of tire smoke, and were then quickly swallowed by the thick shadows of the alley.

CHAPTER FORTY-THREE

From Wong's loading bay, it took only nine minutes of hell for us to pass the courthouse. The bikes must have hit upward of one hundred miles an hour at times. We powered through the streets and ducked into the alleys, avoiding both traffic cameras and the cops.

Anthony's bike slowed up ahead as we reached our destination—Severn Towers, a new apartment building only a few blocks from the courthouse. We pulled up beside a blue Transit van in the underground parking lot. I must have been holding on too tightly. I felt as though somebody had worked on my thighs with a blow torch as I struggled to get my legs to move enough to let me get off the bike.

Twenty-seven minutes left until I had to meet the Russians outside Jimmy's restaurant.

"We'll wait around the corner," said Tao as the bikes moved quietly out of the lot. Even for a workday, the lot looked particularly empty with only a half dozen cars dotted around the basement. I called Jimmy from my disposable cell.

"We're here. What's the exact location?"

"Give me a sec. Okay, Albie says the best his guy can do is tell you the current location of the cell phone. That's Severn Towers. The GPS isn't too good when the cell phone is way above ground level. Best guess is that the phone is more than five floors up."

"Jimmy, this building is pretty big, maybe thirty stories. I'm going to need more."

"You'll have to wait for the guys to call in from Sheepshead Bay. I'll call you as soon as I have a solid."

He hung up.

A tall, wolf-lean man in a black T-shirt and black pants got out of the blue van and shook Anthony's hand. He then offered a hand to Frankie, who merely nodded. The man nodded back. He kept his hair in a military buzz cut. Veins stood out on his thick arms, and I guessed he could snap a thick neck pretty easily.

"What took you so long? The Lizard's been waiting," said the man.

Anthony laughed and introduced me.

"Eddie, this here is the Lizard. It's his show now."

I shook hands with him. He had a grip like a boa constrictor. Despite his heavily muscled physique, he moved gracefully, almost like a dancer.

"We got access all the way up to the twenty-fifth floor. After that, we're in difficulty. The stairs only go up to a barred steel gate on the twenty-fifth. The gate is key-code entry only. The elevator over here is also key-coded for the top floors. If your daughter is up there, then we can't do anything without that code. If I blow the door, they'll hear it and they could kill her. Just pray she's on one of the lower floors. Frankie, there's an art gallery across the street. You think you can get on the roof and give the Lizard some eyes on this place?" said Lizard, and I smiled as he referred to himself again in third person.

"Sure," said Frankie.

The Lizard handed Frankie a pair of binoculars and a cell phone.

"Conference call is marked on the phone. I'll put you on speaker. Be quick, Frankie," said the Lizard as Frankie jogged out of the lot and across the street.

Anthony dumped his bag on the ground, unzipped it, and removed a twelve-gauge sawed-off shotgun and a box of shells.

"You don't need to go in there, you know. We can handle it," he said.

"I'm coming with you," I said. "Give me a piece."

"Bad idea," said the Lizard as he opened the back doors of the van and unlocked a steel box that lay on the floor. He removed an assault rifle from the box and began checking it. The weapon was short and black with the magazine protruding from the shoulder stock.

"That looks new," I said.

"Oh, it's new," said the Lizard, nodding and smiling.

I moved around the van so I could talk to Anthony quietly.

"Who is this guy?" I said.

"He's an ex-marine. His cousin worked for Jimmy. When the Lizard came back from Iraq and started looking for work, his cousin set up a meeting. Believe me. This guy we can trust. He's a one-man army. If anybody can get your little girl out of that apartment, it's Billy over here."

"Billy," I repeated. "So how come he's called the Lizard? And how come Frankie wouldn't go near him?"

Anthony slipped red shells into the sawed-off and hung his head for a moment.

"Truth is, lot of the guys are afraid of him. Billy likes lizards. He's got a big tattoo of a lizard on his back, and he keeps all sorts of snakes and shit at his house in Queens; he's even got a pair of Komodo dragons in his yard. But that ain't the only reason. When we need something from a guy who won't give it up, we call the Lizard. You know how some of those reptile things shed their skin when they grow bigger? Well, that's Billy's specialty. If the guy won't talk, Billy starts peeling the guy like a friggin' banana and then he feeds the skin to his pets—scares the shit out of everybody. Personally, I like him. I just make sure I stay the hell away from his freakin' house in Queens."

CHAPTER FORTY-FOUR

A vibration came from the Lizard's phone. He answered and put the call on speaker, but I didn't listen. Jimmy was calling me.

"We got the address from one of the guys in the warehouse," said Jimmy. "It's the top floor. Penthouse. You're in the right place. Don't worry. Those guys in the Bay didn't get a chance to call anybody, and they won't be making any calls anytime soon. My guys will clean up real good. Professional. So even if the Russians do go back to that warehouse, they won't know their guys got creamed in there. You better head back here soon. You only got twenty minutes before you meet the Russians. I'll be waiting outside Wong's for you, bub," he said, then hung up.

My legs gave way, and I fell to my knees. Amy was on the top floor, behind the security gate that we couldn't bypass. I swore and clenched my fists. My hand felt wet. I'd opened up the cut on my palm.

"She's in the penthouse," I said.

"Frankie? Did you get that? Penthouse," said the Lizard.

Frankie's voice came over the speaker:

"Got it. I'm looking at it right now. Blinds are open in the living room. I got four guys in the apartment. Two on the couch to the right of the front door, one in the kitchen, and one lyin' on a chair with a newspaper. There's a rifle leaning against the left-hand wall. I see a girl in the kitchen, she's blond, maybe thirties. She's tossing a butterfly knife around. I don't see nobody else. There are three bedrooms on the right. Two of 'em got their doors open; one bedroom door is closed. Bathroom looks like it's just off the kitchen. That's it. I don't see no little girl."

My heart sank, nothing was going my way. I just wanted to know she was still alive.

"She must be in one of the bedrooms. There's a rifle there. Why would they have heavy artillery in an apartment? Amy told you a woman was looking after her, Elanya. That has to be the chick with the knife," said Anthony.

I stood and nodded in agreement. This had to be the place. I was so close to getting her back. I just wanted it to be over, then I could hold her and lock her up in a safe so that nobody else could ever take her again.

"Frankie, it's the Lizard. You see anything else in the apartment? We could use a little help with the door. You don't see a note pinned anywhere with a code?"

"Lemme look."

We looked at each other silently.

"No, nothin' pinned up."

"What else can you see, Frankie?" I asked.

"Pictures on the wall—some kind of modern art. Not really my taste. The furniture looks modern, too, kind of uncomfortable-lookin', leather, white. There's a stack of pizza boxes on the kitchen table—looks like the broad ain't the cookin' type. TV is on . . ."

"What's the name on the boxes? Can you make it out?" I said.

"Sure. It's Big Joe's Pizza. They ain't far from here. I hear they do a good slice."

"Are all the boxes from Big Joe's?" I asked.

"Yeah, 'bout six of 'em."

"They must be ordering out," I said.

I took out my phone and said, "Frankie, can you make out the number for Big Joe's?"

I dialed as Frankie called out the telephone number. They picked up after the third ring.

"Big Joe's Pizza, can I take your order?"

"Hi. I need a delivery to the penthouse in Severn Towers, my usual. But look, I need it in a half hour this time. You guys were late yesterday."

"Sorry about that. Who's calling?"

"It's Elanya's boyfriend. I think your guy forgot the code or something on the last delivery. I had to go down in the elevator in my shorts to let him in. I'll let it go this once, but just read me out the code you're giving your delivery guy. I'm not running down in my bare ass this time."

"I'm real sorry, sir. Please tell Elanya we won't let it happen again. I'm just checking your details here . . . Okay, we've got 4789 here. Is that right?"

"That's it. Thanks, man."

"That'll be thirty-nine fifty, sir. Be with you in twenty minutes."

"Don't rush it, kid," I said and hung up.

The Lizard smiled, slapped a fresh magazine into a Glock, stuffed the handgun into his pants, and slung the automatic rifle over his shoulder.

"The Lizard likes you, Mr. Flynn," said the Lizard.

"Let's go," I said.

Anthony patted me on the back. "Eddie, you're not coming. You don't have time. Tao's waiting around the corner."

"I've got time—"

The Lizard interrupted. "Even if you do have time, there's no guarantee your daughter is up there. If she's not there and you don't make it back . . . we've blown it and they'll kill her. Besides, the Lizard don't need you, Eddie. If you see her in the apartment and make a move, you might get caught in the crossfire. Or worse, Amy might get shot. Don't worry. If she's there, we'll take her back to Jimmy's."

He held out a hand. I took it. He was right. I had to let them do this alone. There was too much risk; I had to go back.

"Don't let anything happen to her. Get Jimmy to text me when you've got her."

Turning, I punched the panel of the blue van and ran out of the lot toward Tao.

CHAPTER FORTY-FIVE

Tao pulled up in Wong's loading bay. Jimmy kicked off the wall, flicked away his cigarette, and checked his cell phone.

"Nothin' yet," he said.

Six minutes left.

"Text me when you know. I've got to go meet them."

"They'll get her back, Eddie. I'm sure of it. I'll text you; then you run, and we'll take care of you."

My shoulders sagged. I closed my eyes and shook my head. "It's not as simple as that, Jimmy."

"Why not? We get Amy. You get the hell out of there and call the cops. What's complicated?"

"No. I still can't trust the cops or the FBI or anyone else but you and Harry. And besides, I've no proof of anything at the moment. Even if I found a straight cop or a straight fed, they wouldn't believe me. I've got to finish this."

"Why? If you want to finish it, we can open up the Lizard's rifle on the limo as soon as it turns the corner. They won't stand a chance."

"True, but that's only a few of them, and we would be doing that in full view of the FBI, the ATF, the DEA, and whoever else you got parked outside your door. And if Amy isn't in that apartment, then we may never find her. I can't risk it. Besides, I don't have the full picture yet. I'm not really sure what they have planned, but I know that everyone in that court building is at risk, including Harry. Think about it; the two vans parked in the courthouse basement, the suitcase Gregor put in the van, the fake detonator I lifted from Arturas, the inside man in courthouse security—something's going down and I have to figure it out. Tony G will bring me Mario's photographs this morning; that's a start. I'll figure it out somehow. I have to. The Russians know where I live. They know where my family lives. They know what school my daughter goes to. They know everything about me."

The story Arturas told me about tracking down a former Soviet in Brazil played over and over again in my mind.

"Jimmy, these guys can reach me anywhere. If I run—they find me and they kill my family. You know as well as I do that I can't run. I have to finish it."

For a second I was sitting with my dad on the tall stools in the back of McGonagall's Bar, where we had made our little agreement.

"So, this is the deal. I teach you my tricks; you learn how to handle yourself right. I know you're gonna try to use one of the scams for real someday. Remember what I told you—you get in a tight spot, keep it together. If that doesn't work, you run, like I told you. If you can't run—you fight and you put your man down, hard."

My father's Saint Christopher medal felt heavy around my neck. It was the only personal item that he'd brought with him from Dublin when he first came to the States. I knew what he would do. He would fight—he would do whatever it took to protect his family. This wasn't about revenge. It was about survival. If I didn't finish this, Amy would never be safe again.

"Eddie, don't do it. There has to be another way," said Jimmy.

Two minutes of my hour left and I began bouncing on the soles of my feet, ready to take off.

"I've been over this in my head a thousand times. There's no other way. I'm going to find out what's going on and then, if I have enough, I'll take it to the feds. People who double-cross the Russian mob don't walk away. Unless I put them down permanently, all I've done is put a price on my head and made sure every high-ticket hit man in the world will be looking for me and my family for the rest of our lives. Either I finish it or it finishes me. Text me as soon as you have her. Give her this."

Handing my engraved pen to Jimmy, I said, "Tell her she asked her mom to buy it for me for Father's Day. I don't want her worrying about your men; I want her to know that she's with family, that I sent you guys to get her."

"Sure thing, bub," said Jimmy.

I turned and sprinted for the restaurant, my shoes slipping on the asphalt, my breath almost gone through stress and fatigue. The pain in my back and neck felt like it had melted into lead, weighing me down, making me slow. I pushed the pain aside. If I didn't make it back to the restaurant in time, Arturas would call Elanya. If she didn't answer, he would go looking for her. I needed an edge. I needed the Bratva to believe they still held all the cards. Tearing around the corner at full speed, I pumped my arms and prayed that I would make it in time.

I pulled up fast, just as a PD patrol car sped past me, sirens blaring.

A white limo came into view.

CHAPTER FORTY-SIX

The rear passenger door opened, and I folded myself into the dark leather.

"Where did you come from?" said Arturas.

It took me some time to catch my breath before I could answer.

"Around back. I had to move quickly and do a circuit of the block to make sure I wasn't tailed. I'm clean, but I had to make sure—even the feds aren't stupid enough to fall for two distractions in one day. I know it was a lot of money, but it was worth it. Tony Geraldo is our man now, and you guys just bought a lot of grace from the Italians."

"I hope so," said Arturas.

"So do I," said Volchek.

I hadn't realized he was in the dark limo. They must've picked him up while they were waiting for me. If I'd known Volchek was in the car, I might have thought twice about Jimmy's idea of breaking out the heavy artillery.

"Don't worry. The prosecutor is about to have the day from hell," I said.

And so are you, Olek, I thought.

"Put this on. This should be a better fit," said Arturas, handing me a white shirt still in its packaging. Even the knot in my tie felt wet through with sweat. I changed in the limo. The fresh shirt felt good, and this time the collar was a good fit. Arturas gave me another tie, blue this time, and an electric razor. The detailed thought that he had put into this plan continued to surprise me; he didn't want me going into court looking like a guy who'd slept in his clothes.

The conversation dried up, for which I was thankful. I put my head back and closed my eyes, but no sleep came; my brain worked overtime. From the first moment I'd met Arturas, I'd sensed he was a killer, but a very different killer from Volchek. While Arturas seemed methodical and cold-blooded, Volchek indulged his passion for suffering. In my time as a con man and a lawyer, I'd met both types before. The men like Arturas were few and far between. Men like Volchek were more common. When I thought about it, Volchek had a lot in common with Ted Berkley—the man who finished my legal career almost a year ago.

Berkley tried to grab seventeen-year-old Hanna Tublowski as she got off the subway late one evening. Before she got to the exit, she felt strong arms grab her around her waist, lift her, and carry her toward the cold, black tunnel. There were no commuters at her stop at that time of night. The man who grabbed her timed it so that he made the grab while she was midpoint between security camera views. When she tried to scream, he put his hand over her mouth and whispered that if she made a sound, he would kill her.

A homeless man heard her cry out and he raised the alarm. The attacker fled. Subway cops arrived and managed to calm the young woman. They had found a monthly subway ticket on the ground, in the area where she had been grabbed. One cop bagged the card out of routine more than any genuine insight. It turned out the subway had been cleaned ten minutes beforehand. That meant the card was more than likely from the attacker. The subway pass had been bought on a credit card—Ted Berkley's card. I picked up Berkley in night court as he didn't have a criminal lawyer, and I even managed to get him bail.

At the trial, it was the card and the girl's evidence that she recognized Berkley in a lineup that formed the basis of the prosecution's case. NYPD raided Berkley's office, his apartment, and his summer house and had found nothing. Ted Berkley was in his early thirties, rich, had a great-looking girlfriend and a house in the Hamptons. Not your typical kidnapper. As a client, he couldn't have been better; he was polite, paid his retainer in full, and trusted me to save him. I thought, like him, that the girl just got it wrong, mistaken identity. Berkley said he lost his wallet, which included the subway card, about twenty-four hours before the attack happened.

Hanna Tublowski was a music student who had been taking the subway home from a recital. A talented cellist, she had been working toward a scholarship. She had long brown hair, pale skin, and as she sat in the witness box at trial, I saw her fear. Appearing as a witness in any trial is scary, and there is no more nerve-racking a situation than a young woman facing her attacker in court.

Deciding to remain seated, and therefore less threatening when I cross-examined Hanna, I cleared my throat and gave her a reassuring smile before I asked my first question. Just before I opened my mouth, Berkley had whispered to me, "Destroy the bitch." In all our meetings leading up to trial, he had never spoken like this before or shown any hostility toward the victim.

Ignoring him, I decided instead to take a different approach. The jury had liked the girl. I risked everything if I went in aggressively. Instead I approached it like a father, teasing out her answers and quietly, but maturely, displaying the inconsistencies in her evidence in order to show that she wasn't a liar; instead she was the victim of an attack but she had mistakenly and understandably confused her real attacker with my client.

Give the people what they want.

Juries like empathizing with victims. This way—my way—they got to empathize with her and with the nice young man in the Brooks Brothers suit whom I represented.

When I had finished cross-examining her, even though I'd gone softly, Hanna cried and looked desperately at the jury. I had felt like shit, and as I turned to my client, I saw the look on Berkley's face was one of disgust and something else. At that moment I took it to be nerves or fear. But when I looked more closely, I could see the true nature of that feeling—excitement. Seeing a seventeen-year-old describe the all-consuming panic of being grabbed and hauled away toward the dark had produced profound excitement in Ted Berkley. The jury were sent away to consider their verdict. After I saw Berkley's reaction to Hanna, I knew Berkley was guilty. In the months afterward, as I plowed through the bars of Manhattan, drunk, I'd told myself that there was nothing I could have done before the verdict came in.

The jury unanimously acquitted Berkley. Hanna, although a victim, had not properly identified her attacker.

An hour after the verdict, the IO called me and told me that Hanna had gone missing and would Berkley consent to another property search. He agreed. They found no trace of Hanna.

The following day, a Saturday, I paid a visit to Berkley's home. The IO had given me Berkley's laptop, which they had seized in the initial search. NYPD techs had found zero evidence on the laptop and were now giving it back. I told the cop I'd return it personally; I wanted Berkley out of my life ASAP because at that time I was not convinced that the jury had brought in the right verdict. My instincts told me Berkley was dangerous, that he was hiding something behind his perfect life.

He wasn't at his apartment, and I took the liberty of driving to his summer house, which he visited on weekends.

I knocked and waited. His Porsche was parked in the driveway. I heard the shower. After two or three minutes, he opened the front door, his hair and chest wet, a towel wrapped around his waist. Just below his navel, the towel bore fresh, reddish brown stains.

"Something wrong, Eddie?" said Berkley, breathing hard.

"The cops gave me your laptop. I'm just returning it."

"You didn't need to come all the way out here. I could have picked it up from your office."

I didn't want Berkley near me or my office.

"It's okay, I . . ." Before I could give a lame excuse for driving out there, I heard a cry.

Berkley smiled and said, "I left the TV on."

"I didn't ask you anything," I said, as I put my foot in the doorjamb.

He tried slamming the door. I pushed back, threw my shoulder into the door, and it caught Berkley square on the head, busting open a cut above his eye and sending him to the floor.

The cry became a scream.

I ran into the hall and kicked Berkley in the face as I passed by.

The scream seemed to echo around the house. Downstairs was empty. On the first floor, I saw a bedroom door open. On the edge of the bed I saw a foot, bright red, tied to the corner post.

I opened that door. I had done it many times since; almost every night I opened that door in my dreams and saw her again.

Hanna Tublowski's hands and feet had been tied to each corner of the bed with wire that bit deeply into her flesh. A ball gag had slipped from her broken jaw and hung loosely below her neck. My guess was that Berkley had tried to knock her out when he heard me at the door. He hit her too hard. With her jaw broken and dislocated, the gag had fallen from her mouth, allowing her to scream. Droplets of blood stood on her blue lips.

She was naked.

Dried blood covered her crotch and belly. Bite marks blossomed over her breasts and neck. Each mark surrounded by purple and black bruising and blood where Berkley's teeth had broken the skin. Her left eye was completely closed; her right eye was wide and wild in panic.

I couldn't untie her. The wire would need to be cut. Instead, I knelt beside her and told her she was safe and that the police were on their way.

Dialing 911 from the phone in the kitchen, I guessed that the police response time in this area would be superfast, maybe five minutes. Turned out to be less. The cops arrived at the house in less than three minutes. If they had arrived any later, I had little doubt that Berkley would have been dead by then.

He still lay in the hall, although he was starting to come around. Straddling him, pinning his arms down with my knees, I began pounding his face. When I felt my left hand break, I started using my elbows, throwing my body forward with each blow and crushing his skull between my elbow and the tiled floor. At the time, I couldn't feel the pain from my broken hand. I could only feel the wisps of hot blood that splashed my face after every blow. I don't remember the cops dragging me off of him. I don't remember being arrested. But I remembered seeing Christine's face when she bailed me out. The DA's office didn't prosecute me; the only reason Hanna had survived was because I'd saved her. But in my mind, I'd let her be tortured and raped because I had not acted on my instincts about Berkley.

The state bar was ready to pull my license and disbar me for beating a client half to death. Harry represented me at the hearing before the disciplinary committee. Instead of telling them how good a lawyer I was, he read out the list of injuries that Hanna had suffered. She lost an eye; her jaw, despite having been rebroken and reset a number of times, would never properly heal, leaving her face permanently disfigured. She was scarred for life both physically and mentally.

Berkley had caused so much internal damage that Hanna would never be able to have kids.

Although Harry was saving me, for the second time, I could feel my world slipping away; I was just as responsible for those injuries as Berkley.

Berkley got twenty years. I got six months' suspension.

I had to live with the fact that he had been able to do that to Hanna because I had gotten him off. It was my fault. No amount of booze would ever change that.

Before the jury acquitted Berkley, I knew in my heart that he was guilty and that he could do this again. I tried putting my faith in the fact that he would be unlikely to try to grab a young girl a second time, considering his last attempt failed so badly. My gut told me otherwise, and that same feeling brought me to his house on that blood-red day.

I would not make the same mistake again. Guys like Berkley, Volchek, and Arturas had to be stopped or they would go on destroying lives.

Sitting in the limo with my eyes closed as we raced toward the courthouse, I knew that I had made the right move; taking down the Russians was the only way to keep my family safe. I'd set my phone to vibrate, and even though I felt sure that I hadn't felt it go off, with the movement from the car and the sound of tires rolling on rippled streets, I couldn't be certain. I opened my eyes to see Volchek cross his legs, close his eyes. Was he thinking about the day ahead? I wasn't sure. The scarred one looked out of the window, unable to fix his gaze on his boss. My hand almost reached for my phone. Just to check. Just to make sure. Adjusting my tie, I cleared my throat and forced myself to look at the street and think about my next move. Arturas was playing his own game, and I felt that it was about time I found out what it was.

The closer we got to Chambers Street, the more I was convinced that my answers lay inside those vans in the basement parking lot.

CHAPTER FORTY-SEVEN

We arrived at Chambers Street just after seven thirty. The sun had already begun to warm the cold courthouse steps.

I had less than eight hours left before Volchek fled the country. I had to get whatever I could on Volchek and find a fed I could trust before four o'clock.

Volchek, Arturas, and Victor all got out of the limo with me, and together we headed toward the entrance.

"After you," said Arturas, and I walked in front, skipping up the steps to security.

As I got higher, I was able to see the lobby entrance. I didn't recognize a single security guard. They all looked new to me. I didn't have a briefcase, or the usual lawyer trappings. This time I wasn't concerned about security discovering the bomb. I didn't have it on me, but I had an illegal secure-water spray, what I believed to be the actual detonator for the bomb, the UV flashlight, and a cell phone. If the Russians saw any of those items, it was all over.

Once I got within twenty feet of the entrance, I did recognize a guard. He was blond, young, and eager—Hank, the same kid who'd tried to search me yesterday morning before Barry called him off.

Hank saw me coming. He stood in front of the security door, cracking his knuckles. If he could, he would've given me a cavity search.

Just then I heard quick footsteps coming up the stairs behind us.

I turned and saw Special Agent Bill Kennedy jogging toward me, accompanied by the two agents I'd seen yesterday.

"Glad I caught you, Mr. Flynn. I wanted to apologize for yesterday. But I do need to have a talk in private. Let's take a ride. It won't take long. I promise."

Volchek looked at the agents and then looked at me.

"All right, Mr. Flynn. You can go with the agent. We will wait for you in the upstairs office," said Volchek. "Just don't be late for court. You wouldn't want me to have to make a call, now, would you?" said Volchek. He leaned close and whispered, "*If you try anything, I will cut your little girl.*"

"Don't worry. I won't be long," I said.

As I walked away from Volchek, I could feel his eyes upon me.

The other agents didn't speak at all. The short, squat agent with red hair walked ahead of Kennedy and the tall agent with the athletic frame fell in behind me.

"Are we going anywhere nice?"

"We're going to the river, Pier 40. By the way," he said pointing to the tall, elegant agent behind us, "this is Special Agent Coulson."

"Pleased to meet you," I said. We shook hands.

Kennedy pointed at the red-haired man ahead of us and said, "This is Special Agent Tom Levine."

Levine didn't extend a hand; he just nodded. I nodded back, more in knowing than anything else. Now I knew why all of a sudden Volchek was happy for me to take a ride with the FBI: I was also taking a ride with Volchek's dirty fed, and everything I said would go straight back to him.

"Why are we going to Pier 40, Agent Kennedy?" I asked.

"You'll see, Mr. Flynn . . . You'll see."

CHAPTER FORTY-EIGHT

There was little conversation on the way to the pier. Levine drove and didn't say a word. Coulson sat up front, and I lounged in the back beside Kennedy.

"So what's at the pier that's so important?"

"You seen the *Times* this morning?" he asked.

"Haven't had the chance yet," I said.

He handed me a copy of the *New York Times*. My picture was on the front with the headline Russian Mafia Trial Continues.

"Look at the story below the fold."

I turned over the paper and saw the picture I'd seen on Sunday—a cargo boat called the *Sacha* moored along the riverbank. The same boat that sank on the Hudson on Saturday night with all her crew. The article in the paper thanked all the crewmen from neighboring boats for their help trying to locate the lost crew and the ship.

"We found a crewman who saw the *Sacha* go down near Pier 40. The Hudson is a big river, but we found the ship last night and some of the crew. We're here now. You can see for yourself."

We pulled up at a set of tall, iron gates. A cop waved us through, and we parked behind an NYPD patrol vehicle. Coulson and Levine got out and waited at the pedestrian entrance to the pier. In the distance, beyond the gates, sunlight glimmered on the river. The muscular Hudson looked choppy. Kennedy came close to me before we reached his colleagues and kept his voice low as he spoke.

"If there's anything you need to tell me, now's the time."

"I don't have anything to tell you," I said, looking over his shoulder at Levine, who was pretending to exchange small talk with Coulson but secretly keeping an eye on me.

"Fair enough," said Kennedy with a sigh.

A single question ricocheted around in my mind; why hadn't I heard from Jimmy? Something must have gone wrong. Maybe Amy wasn't in the apartment. What if the Russians took down Jimmy's guys? I gripped the phone in my pocket, squeezing it, willing it to vibrate. Stress often hit me physically, like a python twisting itself around my spine, and at the first spike of pain, I breathed and stretched to help loosen my neck and tried to organize my thoughts. I was exhausted. I hadn't slept, and my body was ready to quit.

Kennedy's stiff-soled shoes crunched on the gravel that led to the boat house on Pier 40. I kept my head down and let my feet follow Kennedy's. When I heard his footsteps come to a rest, I lifted my head just in time to duck underneath a length of yellow crime-scene tape that stretched across my path.

A low murmur, my cell phone vibrating.

A text. Either Amy was alive or still missing—or dead.

Blood rose to my face and I struggled for breath. I had an answer, but I couldn't risk taking a look with Levine around.

Ahead, Coulson and Levine put their backs to the boat house and Kennedy spoke to two CSIs in white plastic coveralls. I saw a coast guard boat anchored to the pier and divers in the water. Kennedy called me over to a tent, and I knew what kind of tent it was and what was likely to be inside. It was the same kind of tent that the police use all over the world, to keep the elements from interfering with the bodies they've found.

Inside the tent, two body bags lay on the ground. I pulled the door zipper all the way to the ground. Just me, Kennedy, and two body bags.

Kennedy put his back to me, knelt down beside the bodies.

The phone was in my hand immediately—*We got her. Clean. Four men and the woman down. Amy shaken but okay.*

My legs gave way. My knees dove into the gravel, and I covered my face in my hands. I mouthed *thank you* over and over. The pain in my neck seemed to vanish. It felt like a dark, poisonous lead weight that had threatened to crush my heart had suddenly evaporated. Taking a huge lungful of air, I felt suddenly ready.

Ready to take Volchek down.

"They had these guys in the meat van a half hour ago. I had them brought back in here so you could see them," said Kennedy.

"Thanks—that's exactly what I needed to see before breakfast. What the hell has this got to do with me?" I said.

"You tell me."

Kennedy knelt and put a hand on one bag, and as he did so, I saw water trickling from the zipper. I knew that bodies found in lakes or rivers were usually bagged in the water, to preserve whatever evidence was around them. Sometimes that evidence helped with the cause or time of death.

The zipper stood brightly against the dull, death gray of the bag, and the metal teeth parted as Kennedy worked the zipper around. He flipped open one bag, then the next. Inside each bag was the body of a male. Both wore navy blue coveralls; both were white; both looked to have been in the water more than twenty-four hours; and clearly both had been murdered. I saw two bullet wounds in the chest of the first victim. There were identical wounds on victim two. Whoever murdered them knew how to handle a gun and group their shots, but the third bullet hole in each body gave a strong hint at a professional hit. The third wound was clearly an insurance shot; both took a bullet in the head at close range.

"I take it you're not hoping to find foam in the lungs," I said.

"Drowning doesn't seem likely; these men were executed, Mr. Flynn. Dead before they hit the water. We don't get a lot of piracy on the river these days, and we've certainly never seen anything like this."

"You find any of the cargo?" I said.

"Not one little bit."

"What was the *Sacha* carrying?"

Kennedy didn't answer. Instead he grabbed the body closest to him and turned it over onto its chest. I read the company logo on the back of the coveralls—McLaughlin Demolition.

"So, let's recap, Mr. Flynn—a couple of nights before this trial starts, the *Sacha*'s crew are murdered and the cargo goes missing. Yesterday I get information about a possible bomb threat. There might be a link here; there might not. I wanted you to come see this because I don't believe in coincidences. I don't think you do, either. I wanted you to see firsthand what kind of people you're representing . . ."

I couldn't focus on a word Kennedy said. I'd tuned out completely. An image forced everything else from my mind—the vans that had driven into the basement lot of the courthouse.

"How much did they get?" I said.

"They got enough to give most buildings in New York a serious problem."

Kennedy leaned back a little and looked at me, waiting for me to come clean.

In the end, I didn't say anything. I heard a rustle from the tent plastic behind me and saw a silhouette framed in the morning sunlight. It was Levine, sucking on a surreptitious cigarette.

"Look, I'm going to be honest with you, Mr. Flynn. Yesterday we get information that you were discussing a bomb with your client. Today we discover there's a boatload of explosives stolen and the crew executed. Now, I don't think you killed these guys, but I'm sure you know a lot more than you're telling me. Then there's the blood."

"What blood?" I asked.

"The blood I saw on your shirtsleeve yesterday. Maybe that blood came from one of these guys?"

I'd forgotten all about that spot of blood—from my hand. Last evening I'd held out my hands for the cuffs in a last-ditch effort to intimidate Kennedy into leaving me alone. I remembered him looking at my hands.

"I cut myself yesterday. A glass broke in my hand. That was my blood. Look. Here's the cut," I said.

Kennedy examined my hand. "I think that's probably the first time you've told me the truth," he said. "So cut the bullshit and tell me the rest."

"There's nothing more to tell."

"Look, I know you're just nervous. You're protecting your client and all. But right now it's you who needs protecting. I want to rule you out so I can concentrate on your client. So, I'd like you to consent to a search of your apartment."

He unfolded a piece of paper from his coat pocket and put it in front of me. It was a standard form of consent for a property search. I remembered that moment the night before, standing in front of the window frame that had been painted shut and patting my pockets for my keys. Either the keys fell out of my pocket when I got knocked out in the limo the previous morning or . . . The terrible thought hit me like a punch; Arturas needed to set me up as the bomber. He took my keys to plant something incriminating in my apartment, something that linked me to the bomb. I couldn't tell Kennedy a thing, not yet, not with Levine listening and not until I had proof, proof enough to hand him Levine and the Russians on a plate, and that proof had to be good enough to trump whatever the hell they might have planted in my apartment.

Levine must have felt me watching him. He moved to the front of the tent and unzipped the flap.

"We'd better make a move if we're going to get back in time," said Levine, smiling.

Kennedy closed the bags, got to his feet, and removed his cell phone from the inner pocket of his jacket, right-hand side.

"Sign the consent and we can rule you out of the investigation and concentrate on the real bad guys. Last chance," he said, holding aloft the phone.

"I got nothing to say to you," I said.

Flipping open his cell, he dialed.

"It's Kennedy. I'm here with Flynn. He refused to consent to a search. Amend the last paragraph of the affidavit to read, *Eddie Flynn, attorney and officer of the court, refused to cooperate with a reasonable request from a federal law-enforcement agency to conduct a search of his property in order to rule out his involvement in suspected offenses.*" He paused to let whoever was on the end of the line take this down. As he spoke, his eyes never left mine. "*His lack of cooperation is unreasonable and is likely to obstruct and impede the progress of a federal investigation. We humbly request that the court reconsider the warrant to seize and preserve vital evidence.* You got that? Good. Get it over to Gimenez ASAP."

Closing his cell phone with a snap, Kennedy couldn't keep the satisfied smirk off his face. I thought over his phone call. It told me a lot. It told me that the FBI had already tried and failed to get a warrant to search my apartment because Kennedy was asking for the issue to be *reconsidered.*

If the FBI need a search warrant urgently, they can call an on-duty federal judge and apply for the warrant over the phone. I guessed Kennedy had tried for the telephonic warrant last night and failed, for good reason. First, his probable cause sounded weak; a lip-reading of the word "bomb," a federal witness under death threat, and the theft of demolition material, with no link to me, probably wasn't enough. Second, Congress has put special protections in place for certain classes of people—lawyers being at the top of the list.

Searching a lawyer's business or home is dangerous, due to the risk of the search team finding material protected under attorney-client privilege. A federal magistrate might be happy to suspend my Fourth Amendment rights, but because of the danger of violating my client's rights, it would be unlikely that a warrant would be issued without a hearing. Most warrants are obtained not on the phone, but on paper, without a hearing. An agent will draw up an affidavit, setting out the reasons for the search and what they're looking for, and nine times out of ten it's granted. If there is a difficult issue involved, like searching a lawyer's apartment, the federal prosecutor will need to argue the application in a hearing. That takes time. Some warrants get issued within a day or, if the feds are lucky, half a day. Some take weeks of preparation before the FBI even apply for the warrant.

Kennedy let that smirk grow into a full-blown self-satisfied smile.

He knew his application for a warrant would be granted, and I'd helped him do it. As a lawyer, I have a duty to cooperate with the court. By refusing to consent to the search, I'd pretty much handed the warrant to Kennedy. No judge would take the risk of refusing the warrant application because they wouldn't want to give the impression of protecting a dirty lawyer.

"Which judge is hearing the application?" I asked.

"Potter. We're scheduled for noon."

It was 8:05 a.m.

My timetable just went out the window. At noon, Assistant United States Attorney Gimenez would get the FBI their warrant. The feds had probably frozen my apartment already by having an agent on the door, making sure nobody removed evidence and patiently waiting for the paper with Potter's signature. After Potter granted the application, it would probably take ten, maybe fifteen minutes, to get the warrant signed and stamped by the clerk, then maybe forty minutes to get the original document to my apartment in order to legally commence the search. I thought I would have until four o'clock to figure this out. Now I had less than five hours, tops.

As we moved outside the tent, Kennedy took my arm. In his other hand he held his card. "This is my contact information. Think this over very carefully. You're in over your head."

I saw Levine take out his cell phone.

"No, thanks. You can keep your card," I said.

Kennedy returned his card to his jacket.

Bill Kennedy struck me as a nervous but diligent agent. He gave a shit and that was hard to fake. At that time I felt pretty sure that Kennedy was on the level. I would have to come clean to him eventually, but I needed to have the whole story before I went to him and I didn't want the Russians to know I'd taken Kennedy's card. I would have to think of another way to contact him.

One that the Russians wouldn't expect.

CHAPTER FORTY-NINE

The feds gave me a ride back to the courthouse. There was no conversation on the way back. I felt grateful for that, as it allowed me a little time to think.

I told myself that everything I would need to nail the Russians would be in that suitcase. The suitcase on the passenger seat of one of the vans that carried the *Sacha*'s payload of explosives.

During the return journey, Levine kept his eyes on me from the rearview mirror. Kennedy and the other agent, Coulson, didn't seem to have any inkling that Levine was dirty. Kennedy would take a lot of convincing about one of his own. One thing didn't make sense to me, though: If Levine was on the inside, how come he couldn't find out where the feds were hiding Benny?

"So, are you guys bringing Witness X to court this morning?" I said.

At this question, both Coulson and Levine appeared to prick up their ears as if they were awaiting Kennedy's answer with interest.

"That's on a need-to-know basis, right, guys?" said Kennedy.

"Right," said Levine and Coulson simultaneously.

"In actual fact, he *is* coming to court today. I have a special team from out of town looking after Witness X—guys from the protection program. Even I don't know where they're holding the witness. Better that way. Accountability begins and ends with the protection team until they get him to court. After that, I handle the security."

That explained it perfectly. Levine was definitely Volchek's man, and nobody in that car knew where Benny was being held. I thought that was pretty smart. Kennedy went up in my estimation.

"Mr. Flynn, I'll be keeping a close eye on you today," said Kennedy. "If we find something in your home, I want to be the one to make the arrest."

Shaking my head, I forced a false laugh that failed to convince Kennedy of my confidence.

"It doesn't have to be this way. If you know there's a bomb on its way to the courthouse, you have to tell me," he said.

"How do you know it's not already in there?"

"We searched the place from top to bottom. It's clean," said Kennedy.

Before I asked myself how the FBI missed the vans, the answer came to me. If there was a vehicle in the basement parking lot and that vehicle was authorized on the watchman's log, the FBI couldn't legally search it. Fourth Amendment precluded it. Arturas had planned this down to the last detail, and I would've bet my shirt that those vans were authorized on the security entry log. The parking lot construction had taken place in the seventies, moving the old basement cells up a floor and demolishing the execution chamber. This vast underground space now held maybe two hundred vehicles. It would probably take the feds a week to trace the owners for every vehicle in the lot, and they would need to because their warrant application required them to notify the registered owner. To legally search each vehicle would take too long. Instead the search party would give a car a once-over, from the outside, and leave it at that. Busting open a window was too risky; the car might belong to a lawyer or a judge.

The FBI car pulled up outside the courthouse and Kennedy let me out.

"Remember what we talked about," said Kennedy.

I ignored Kennedy and moved briskly up the steps. The workmen who were restoring the outer shell of the courthouse were already on their high moveable platform above me. The platform was suspended from the roof on thick steel cables and sat a couple of floors from the top of the building while the workmen blasted the masonry with jets to clean away a century of grime. A fine, brown snow descended onto the shoulders of everyone waiting in line to get through security. The fat guard with the mustache stood behind Hank to make sure I came back. The Russians weren't worried about me getting back in, as the bomb was already upstairs. However, I still had my phone, the spray, the flashlight, and the real detonator, and I didn't want the fat guard to see any of those. This time I didn't wait to get close to security before I jumped the line; this time I walked past everyone, straight toward the fat guard; this time I wasn't as nervous. I'd worked out a way to get in without much attention.

The security scanner beeped as I went through it, and I ignored Hank's call, went straight up to Arturas's inside man, and whispered, "Get rid of your buddy, Hank. I have money on me that I don't want them to find. The money's yours—Arturas told me I should give you your bonus now."

"It's okay, Hank. This guy's with me," said the fat guard. His name badge read ALVIN MARTIN.

Before Hank could protest a second time about not searching me as I entered the building, I nodded to Alvin that he should follow me and said, "Let's go somewhere quiet. There are cameras in the lobby. I know a place in the basement."

I'd remembered Edgar's little store in the basement—a hidden room where Edgar, former chief of security, had secretly brewed moonshine for sale and distribution to discerning clientele, like me and some of my other lawyer friends and even a few judges. I recalled that Harry had grown particularly fond of Edgar's "Root Juice."

Alvin followed me through the double doors on the west side of the lobby that led to the stairwell and the basement.

We entered the basement lot and turned left, down a long, unlit corridor. In a recess, a hidden door heralded the entrance to Edgar's old brewery. Thankfully, the door remained unlocked. The store appeared to be empty of home-brewing equipment. It had once been the boiler room, but now it merely held stacks of dusty folding chairs and a few tables. Edgar had got caught but didn't end up getting canned. I remembered that Harry put in a good word for him at his disciplinary hearing. With a judge backing him, Edgar didn't get fired. He got demoted and lost a lot of responsibility but he kept his job. In return, Harry kept the rest of his stock.

I held the door open for Alvin.

"I'm supposed to pay you now, but I want to make sure you understand what's expected of you," I said.

Alvin looked a little surprised and confused. Nevertheless, with the promise of money, he walked into the dark room. I flicked the lights on, and as he moved by me, my right hand reached for his gun. I popped the catch and lifted the Beretta clear, but he heard the click of the catch opening and the sound of metal clearing leather and grabbed my forearm. A straight left, hammered into the back of Alvin's neck, sent him down onto his knees and released his grip on my arm.

"Take it easy and you just might live through this," I said, pointing his own gun at the back of his head. "Have a seat."

For a man in his position, he appeared calm.

He picked a metal chair off a stack in the corner and sat facing me about five feet away. I closed the door.

"So, you let the Russian Mafia into the courthouse with the vans. Why'd you do it, Alvin?"

"Same as you—money. I get shit pay in this job, and I got alimony to meet. Don't try and tell me you're above taking a bribe."

"Maybe not, but I'm not going to kill anybody to get paid. What's in the vans?"

"They told me they needed the vans to make a clean exit. If Volchek's convicted, he's going to make a run for it. If I get asked about it later, then all I did was let in a couple of vans and add them to the log—how am I supposed to know who they belonged to? Even if I lose my job, I got a hundred grand in my apartment. I can't make that kind of money working this shit detail."

"Where's Volchek now?"

"They're all up on nineteen, waiting for you."

"You got keys for the vans?"

"No. Look, I told you everything. Lemme go, and we'll forget about this."

"I can't take that chance. You got handcuffs?" I said.

"Sure."

"Go get acquainted with that radiator in the corner."

Alvin got up and turned to his right to look at the radiator before whipping his body around. He spun toward me, sending the steel chair tumbling through the air toward my head. I put my arms in front of my face and felt the chair legs crack into my elbow and wrist. Alvin's gun fell from my grip. He was already moving toward the tumbling Beretta. He dove to the floor and grabbed the gun by the barrel. I skipped onto my left foot and curled my right leg behind me before heaving it forward into Alvin's face. It was easily a forty-yard field goal—his head rocked back on his shoulders before his face smacked back down into the concrete. His body became instantly limp and lifeless.

Retrieving the Beretta from the ground, I put my fingers to Alvin's throat and found a strong pulse. He was out cold, but at least he was still alive. I dragged him to the radiator and cuffed him to the pipe, careful to take his radio, cell phone, and the spare magazine for the Beretta from his belt. The radio and cell phone, I smashed against the wall. With the lights cut and the door closed, I felt confident Alvin wouldn't be discovered for a while. I slipped the Beretta and the spare mag into my coat.

The first van I found sat in the northwest corner of the lot. It had been driven straight into the space, and the passenger side sat maybe three feet out from the wall. An additional steel padlock secured the back doors. The van's suspension seemed to be sitting lower than normal, as if it was fully loaded, but it was difficult to tell for sure. I couldn't see the interior because of the tinted windows. If these vans were decked out with alarms and immobilizers, a red light should flash intermittently from the dash. I would be able to see it even through the heavily tinted glass. After a minute of careful inspection, I couldn't see any light and felt satisfied that I could use the old-fashioned method of opening the doors. Before I made my move, I checked the lot again and found it empty. The guard's hut wasn't visible from my position. If there was security in the hut, they would be doing exactly what security guards do best—watching cable TV and ignoring the CCTV monitors. Returning to the van, I smashed the butt of the Beretta into the passenger window twice. My second swing shattered the glass. Unless a cop or security guard took the time to walk to the end of the lot and check the passenger side of this vehicle, they wouldn't find any evidence of a break-in. I waited a minute to see if anyone heard me. Nothing moved in the lot.

The rear of the van was packed floor to ceiling. A tarp covered the load. I threw the tarp down and saw what appeared to be stacks of barrels wrapped in bright blue plastic. At first I didn't know what I was looking at—then my breath caught when I saw wiring running from the left-hand corner of the barrels. I followed the wiring to a large black plastic box, which seemed to be some sort of junction for multiple wires. A single wire ran from the box to a circuit board. Attached to the circuit board was a digital timer with a readout of 00:20:00:00, which I guessed to read twenty minutes, the other values representing hours, seconds, and tenths of a second. There didn't appear to be anything that looked like a radio receiver, so I thought they probably had to start the timer running manually, although there was no way to be sure about this. One thing appeared certain—this was not an escape vehicle.

The other van was located at the opposite end of the parking lot at the southeast corner. Both vans rested beneath the supporting walls of each side of the courthouse, with the passenger side closest to the wall. The tint on the second van's windows wasn't as dark, and I was able to see a similar huge load in the rear. Its suspension also looked low, so I guessed they carried identical loads. The suitcase that I'd watched Gregor haul into the van the night before sat on the passenger seat. The case was a silver hardtop Samsonite, identical to the case that sat upstairs, the case that Arturas had used yesterday morning to bring the case files to court. I forced the window, opened the van, and when I picked up the case to set it down on the floor, I noticed that it felt unexpectedly light. The big man, Gregor, had picked up the same case last night, two-handed.

This didn't feel right.

Before I opened the case, I considered running up the stairs, grabbing Kennedy by the hand, and leading him to the vans. Two things stopped me. First, Alvin the security guard. My DNA would be all over him, together with a solid imprint of my shoe on his face. Second, I had opened both vehicles. My fingerprints would be on the door handles, and I had nothing to tie the Russians to the vans.

It all depended on what was in the case. I slid my thumbs along the catch release and as the lid rose, I thought that I would find another detonator inside, or a clue about what Arturas planned to do with the vans or something that would give me clarity on this whole thing. When I saw what was inside, I couldn't help burying my head in my hands. My eyes closed, and I slapped my head twice.

For the second time in twenty-four hours, I felt completely dumbfounded.

The case was empty.

Then a thought hit me and stayed in my head. The case was empty—just like the first detonator that I'd taken from Arturas.

There was only one theory that fit. One idea that made even partial sense of all of this. I found the elevator and hit the button for floor nineteen. I took me a few seconds to hide the Beretta in the trash can before I got into the elevator and traveled up to the top floor to meet Volchek.

CHAPTER FIFTY

Volchek, Arturas, Victor, and Gregor sat in the small office on the nineteenth floor, eating take-out breakfast.

"Anything for me?" I said.

Gregor handed me a take-out box with the remains of a pancake stack.

"What did the feds want?" asked Volchek.

"They tried to convince me you were a threat to their witness and that if I knew anything, it would be in my best interest to let them know about it. I told them you were an innocent man, a paragon of virtue, and it was my pleasure to represent you."

Volchek laughed.

In the corner of the reception area, I saw the suitcase. A hardtop Samsonite identical to the empty case I'd found in the van. The case lay open on the floor.

Just like its twin in the basement, the case was empty.

Or at least, it *looked* empty.

The pancakes were greasy, but they gave me a boost and stopped the gnawing reminder from my stomach that I hadn't eaten in twenty-four hours. As I ate, I thought it through again.

The case in the basement appeared to be around four feet long, two feet wide, and about a foot and a half deep. Although the case that sat on the floor shared the same dimensions on the outside, with the lid open I could see that this case was only around a foot deep on the inside. That could mean only one thing: The extra half a foot of depth was still there; it was just covered with a false bottom. As I'd expected. Before I got into the elevator, I had carefully checked the case I'd found in the basement and there were no hidden compartments.

Since the early days of Prohibition, America has led the way in smuggling techniques. The false-bottomed case was a classic. The great trick with false-bottomed suitcases is that whoever is searching your case is only ever interested with what is *inside* the damn thing. No one is interested in looking at the outside of a case, and that really is the only way of telling if there is a false bottom. Often the patterns on the material lining can serve as a type of optical illusion, telling the eye that this is the entirety of the case. What had helped me spot the false bottom was that I'd just seen an identical Samsonite, so I already had a strong visual clue as to the true volume of the case.

The only drawback to a false-bottomed case was that it usually didn't stand too much scrutiny if you knew what you were looking for. I decided to test my theory so far.

Throwing down my empty take-out box, I knelt down at the suitcase, closed the lid, picked it up, felt the extra weight, compared to the case downstairs, and was about to walk into the chambers with it when the test paid off.

"What are you doing?" asked Arturas.

"I'm packing the files into the case. I'll need them for court."

"Put the case down. Victor will do that for you."

"No. It's okay. I can—"

"Put the case down!"

Arturas lost his cool. He didn't want me poking around in the suitcase. He was worried I might find the hidden compartment. Volchek seemed a little puzzled.

"Arturas, calm down. The lawyer is trying here. He might pull this off, and we won't have to . . . well, you know. Give him a break, for now," said Volchek.

I put down the suitcase and sat on the couch. My attention fell on the print of the *Mona Lisa* that sat above the reception desk, and suddenly, what was just a theory took shape and solid form in my mind.

The false detonator, Alvin the fat security guard, and the false-bottomed suitcase: The functions and roles of all these things now became clear to me as I stared at the portrait.

The key to understanding all of it was the *Mona Lisa*. From a con man's point of view, the *Mona Lisa* had its attractions. It was the most copied painting in the world, and historically, copies had hung in famous galleries and museums all over the planet. Every couple of years, I read in the paper about some new scientific discovery that claimed a copy of the painting was in fact the original masterpiece. I maintained an interest because to me, the only reason somebody would make a copy of anything was to make a switch, to make somebody believe the original was still in place when, in fact, they were looking at a copy. The forger is the con man's best friend.

I figured the suitcase that Arturas brought through security the morning before, which contained the case files, was in fact the case that I'd just seen in the basement. Gregor had remained in the courthouse overnight while Arturas, Victor, and I had gone out to get the money and pay off Jimmy. During this time, Gregor must have gone to the basement and switched cases, so the case that Arturas had used to carry the case files into court yesterday now sat in the basement and the case that Gregor put into the van last night sat on the floor in front of me. That meant whatever was in the false-bottomed case would have set off the alarm if Arturas had tried to bring it through security yesterday morning and, most important, the X-ray scanner would have seen through the false bottom.

Volchek was not in the least interested in the case. He didn't have a clue that the cases had been switched. If he didn't know about the cases, I was pretty sure he didn't know about the vans or Alvin, or that Arturas had brought along two detonators, a real one and a fake.

Why have a fake detonator and a real detonator? Why have two identical suitcases? Why make a copy of the *Mona Lisa*?

So you can switch them without your mark noticing.

All along I'd thought I was running a con on the Russians.

Arturas was conning me but, more important, he was also conning Volchek. I had sensed the tension between the two of them, and I'd watched Arturas nursing that facial scar.

Volchek stood over me and said, "Five minutes to trial, Mr. Flynn. I hope the money was worth it, for your sake. If Tony Geraldo says anything that implicates me in Mario's murder, I'll have Arturas call his girlfriend, and your daughter can blame you as she entertains my men."

"Tony will keep his mouth shut," I said.

Arturas lifted the suit jacket from the back of the chair.

"Put this on. We will plant the bomb during the lunch adjournment," he said.

Again I felt the weight of the device on my back and the cold dread of having such a lethal thing close to my skin. With the FBI readying their warrant for my apartment, I knew I probably wouldn't make it to the lunch adjournment.

If I was right and Arturas was running some kind of con on his boss, I still had no clue about his ultimate aim. I remained convinced that my answers lay in the false bottom of that suitcase. I needed to take a look inside without Arturas seeing me, and I had no plan on how to do it.

"For you," said Arturas, handing something to Volchek, who examined it before slipping it into his pocket. Arturas had just given Volchek a detonator.

One of the fakes.

CHAPTER FIFTY-ONE

Apart from the fresh shirt and tie, I wore the same clothes as yesterday, and that slight change was probably what I would normally have done anyway. My usual practice for the second day of a trial would be to wear the same suit, but I would put on a fresh shirt and a different tie. Day three of a trial, and I could wear a different suit. Then a different suit again on day seven, but never more than three different suits for any trial unless we were going over a month—then five suits, but that was my absolute limit. I had around fifteen very good suits in my apartment. I could wear a different suit every day if I wanted, and I used to do that regularly. Then the jury noticed me doing it, and then I noticed the jury noticing me. That was bad.

When juries whispered about my suits, that meant they weren't listening to the evidence. They were thinking how nice it must be to wear a different suit to work every day, how much those suits cost, how much I was getting paid to do this, and that guilty men would pay anything to stay out of jail. A trial lawyer can dance through the evidence and entertain the jury and still get his client convicted in a heartbeat for any number of reasons. Even the best trial lawyer can be undone by a really good suit. If I showed up to trial in Armani, my client might as well just fire me and call the public defender.

My normal court attire was a plain tan suit, alternated with a dark navy suit. Clear changes and changes back again, so the jury doesn't start thinking about my bank account, but still thinks I'm a regular guy, clean and professional and trustworthy.

The jury waited patiently for the judge. Pike had told the clerk to bring them in and that she would be right out. The jury were silent. Most had their heads bowed, and one or two occasionally glanced my way. I couldn't see Arnold in the court that morning. He probably told Miriam that he'd been made by the defense, that he had been compromised.

None of the jury looked at Miriam. I'd burned her pretty bad yesterday. Even so, she still had plenty of time to recover. Trials ebb and flow, rise and fall. You can be almost home one minute and guilty as sin the next. That's the way the evidence goes: direct examination, cross-examination, argument, and counterargument. Most lawyers would spend days cross-examining witnesses if they could get away with it. Poking through every little detail and nuance of the evidence and aggressively putting minor inconsistencies to the witness as if they'd just admitted to being behind the grassy knoll when JFK bought the big ticket. As far as I was concerned, that was all wrong. The longer the battle of words went on, the longer it looked like the witness was winning.

The trick was to be quick and devastating and therefore memorable.

With the trial bundles spread out on my desk, I suddenly realized that I'd forgotten something. A pen. I patted my pockets. I tut-tutted and told Volchek that I must have lost my pen somewhere and needed to borrow one from the clerk. He nodded. Jean gave me a spare pen and a cute smile on the side.

I had a possible four witnesses to spar with today. I had to cut that down. Kennedy would get that damn warrant signed, and God knows what Arturas planted in my apartment. Probably something bad, something that linked me to his plan, something that would put me away for the rest of my life.

"All rise!"

Everyone stood, and I turned as I heard Arturas swearing loudly. He ended a call on his cell phone, whispered something to Volchek, and left the courtroom with Gregor, leaving Volchek sitting beside me at the defense table and Victor sitting behind us, babysitting. I didn't know what had happened. I hoped it was because they couldn't get in touch with

Alvin, who had probably woken up and in all likelihood remained safely cuffed to the radiator. My gut told me something different; it told me Arturas had tried to contact Elanya and couldn't get through. If he checked on the apartment in Severn Towers, which was close by, and found them dead and Amy missing, then it would all be over. Arturas would run and hide before taking his revenge on my family. I couldn't think about that now. Amy was safely tucked up in a Mafia stronghold with at least one law-enforcement agency outside watching the place, so at least she was safe, for now.

I turned back to the judge's bench, fully expecting to see Harry sitting beside Judge Pike. He wasn't there. I needed Harry here, in case I ran into problems.

Miriam rose to her feet. She'd been careful not to say a word to me today. No note, no smile, and to give her a little more edge, her skirt looked to be even shorter than the little number she'd worn yesterday.

"The state calls Tony Geraldo."

A mistake. Miriam didn't know it yet. She was trying to court sympathy for the victim, but she was doing it too early. The girl's evidence would have been better coming first. Nikki Blundell puts Volchek in an argument with the victim a day before he's murdered. Nikki didn't hear the argument. She just saw the scuffle. So the jury will ask themselves, what was this argument all about? Then Miriam calls Tony to explain it all. It creates a relationship with the jury. Let them put two and two together. Juries love that.

I looked around the courtroom and spotted Tony sauntering up to the witness stand. From the smug look on Tony's face, I guessed why Miriam was calling him first. She must have realized Tony wasn't going to cooperate, and Miriam had shifted into damage-limitation mode: Get off to a bad start now, get it over with, and finish strong.

Volchek watched Tony intently. He probably wondered what he'd bought with his four million dollars. He held the detonator in his hand. I could see it, inexpertly hidden in his palm. The real detonator remained safely with me.

Tony's shiny silver suit was really something to behold. Paired with comfortable cream shoes, a jet-black silk shirt, and white tie—Tony looked like a low-rent pimp. The jury would be unlikely to give him their sympathy.

Tony's shoes sent loud, metallic clacks bouncing off the walls with every overconfident step.

He stood in the witness box and the clerk, Jean, approached him. Jean's face took on a look of disgust when she saw him chewing gum. She held out a napkin in front of his mouth. Tony's jaw worked noisily. Jean took the oath seriously, dead seriously. Helpfully, Tony spat the gum into the napkin.

"You can keep that, sweetheart," he said.

He managed to read the oath on the card with one hand on the Bible and then sat down before the judge gave him permission to do so.

"Mr. Geraldo," Miriam began, "would you please explain to the jury your relationship with the victim in this case, Mario Geraldo."

Silence.

"Mr. Geraldo?" asked Miriam.

No response. Tony just sat there. The jury seemed to lean forward.

I kept my head down. I could feel Miriam's eyes boring into me like twin lasers.

"Mr. Geraldo, please state your date of birth for the record," she said.

I couldn't help but hang my head even lower as I heard the reply: the prearranged response that I'd written for Tony in Jimmy's restaurant, the response that Tony had learned by heart.

"I refuse to answer the question on the grounds that I may incriminate myself."

The jury looked at Miriam. Then they looked at me. Miriam shifted her weight onto one hip, her mouth slightly ajar. She appeared hurt and ready to deal out a reprisal the size of Hiroshima. A jury can always tell when something goes wrong, and when something goes this wrong, it's as plain as watching a subway car derail right in front of you and just as messy.

"May I remind you, Mr. Geraldo, that you've signed an immunity agreement with my office? If you breach that agreement by refusing to testify here today, you will go to jail."

Tony said nothing. In fact, he made a mistake. He started to smile.

Miriam's face flushed, and momentarily she became lost for words. She was about to say something when she caught her tongue just in time. The judge helped her out.

"Ms. Sullivan, you may wish to make an application to treat this witness as hostile, but before you do so, may I suggest we take five minutes for you to consider that course of action?"

And with that, Judge Pike left the courtroom.

I stood up and sat on the edge of the defense table, my arms crossed, awaiting the inevitable tirade from Miriam. I didn't have to wait long.

"You bastard, Eddie. Are you even aware of what you're doing? Interfering with a state's witness? Are you crazy?"

"No. I'm his lawyer. I happen to represent Tony Geraldo in relation to those drug charges. All I can say is that I got very recent instructions."

"How recent?"

"I spoke to him this morning."

"Well, I hope he fires you and gets a better lawyer, because he's going down for possession with intent to supply, trafficking, distributing, and whatever else I can think up. You know the way this works just as well as I do; it's a two-way street, Eddie—no evidence, no deal. Why don't you tell him that?"

"Whoa, hang on. Can I see his agreement?"

Miriam looked as if I'd just propositioned her. Before she could bite my head off, one of her clerks put a copy of the agreement into my hand. I knew the agreement by heart. It was the state's standard immunity deal, and in the right lawyer's hands, it could develop holes. Lots of real big holes.

"This is your standard immunity agreement. It states that in exchange for giving evidence at this trial, my client will not face any charges. It does not detail what evidence he has to give. Nor should it. Coaching a witness will get you disbarred," I said.

At the phrase "coaching," her eyes widened. Lawyers can prep witnesses for trial but what is absolutely off-limits is agreeing to precisely what answers the witness will give in evidence. The evidence can't come from the lawyer.

"You think *I'm* coaching a witness? Where did he get that little Fifth Amendment sound bite from, Eddie? Did you tell him to say that? And you're going to lecture me about coaching a witness? He won't get away with this, and you won't either."

"He will. You know he will. No judge will allow anyone in the United States to stand trial because they exercised a constitutional right. The right against self-incrimination is fundamental and inalienable. It doesn't matter that he may be breaching a contract by exercising that constitutional right. The Constitution supersedes all agreements or subordinate legislation. And I wouldn't call him as a hostile witness if I were you. He won't say a thing, and it will only damage your case further. The jury will think you're scrambling for scraps of evidence because your case is so weak. Just move on. You got played by the Mafia. So what? It happens to the best of us. Call your next witness, Miriam."

You don't get to be in Miriam's position without being smart, tough, and ruthless. She knew Tony Geraldo was a lost cause, but she wasn't going to let me off easy.

"What was all that about yesterday? You talking about a bomb?" she said, folding her arms.

"Your jury consultant is a lowlife. Either he made it up, or he misread me or took whatever I said out of context. You can't rely on him. Why'd you hire a guy like Arnold, anyway? I always thought you played it straight."

"I didn't know he lip-read juries. I just knew he got results. He's like you, Eddie. You don't care how you get your result. You just want to win. I think you did talk about a bomb. Not a real one. An imaginary one. I think you were playing for a mistrial."

"Bullshit. I'm just doing my job."

Miriam grabbed my arm as I turned to leave.

"You're the lowlife, Eddie. That's your job, representing scum like that," she said, nodding to Tony.

The last of the jury filed out of court, and Tony stood up in the witness box.

"Hey, lady, don't be talkin' about me like I'm some kind of criminal. I'm a good Catholic," he said.

Miriam gave Tony one of her vicious looks.

"Leave it, Tony. Don't get on your high horse about this. After all, you are a criminal. Otherwise you wouldn't be in this mess. What does the Bible say about that?" I said.

Tony grabbed the Bible and sprang out of the witness box. The security guards rushed forward, but I held up a hand and shook my head at them, letting them know it was all right. Tony thrust the Bible into my arms and said, "*You* should read the good book once in a while, Mr. Flynn. You might learn somethin'."

Tony resumed his seat, and I returned to the defense table and put the Bible down in front of me. Just as we'd arranged in Jimmy's earlier that day, Tony was giving me a little religion. Volchek seemed amused at Tony's outburst. I sighed heavily and remained standing, angled to my left so my back was to Volchek. Opening the case files, I removed the medical examiner's report on Mario from the file and placed it on top of the Bible with both hands. With the Bible shielded from view by the document, my right little finger dipped beneath it and flicked through the good book until I found something lodged between the pages. I slid it out with two fingers and sandwiched it in between the front cover of the Bible and the last page of the medical examiner's report. When I'd lifted the report, I'd made sure to put my fingers beneath it, so I could lift the envelope. I put the report, with envelope hidden beneath it, on the table and handed the Bible back to the clerk.

It was called a beggar's lift. The absolute perfectionists of the art mostly lived in Barcelona, the hustlers' capital of the world. I'd seen the lift done myself in that great city when Christine and I had traveled there with Amy for a few days' vacation. We sat outside a café, enjoying the sun, and I'd noticed a homeless guy wandering around with a laminated card around the same size as a magazine. He approached the middle-aged British couple at the table next to us. The husband was being a real dick to his wife, telling her she looked fat in her summer dress. It couldn't have happened to a nicer guy, really. The homeless guy placed the laminated card on the table and left it there while he clasped his hands in prayer and said, "Please read. Please read. I have no English." The British guy read the card. No doubt it was an elaborate sob story about the guy's family, and at the very end it would ask the reader to give the man bearing the card some money. The British guy read the card, then waved him away and said, "No, no, no. Get out of here, you dirty little man." The dirty little man then thanked the British guy and lifted his laminated card off the table and used the card to hide the lift. Along with the card, the hustler took the Brit's cell phone and wallet from thc table, having placed the card deliberately on top of those items in the first place to disguise the move.

The same guy approached our table, and I whipped out some cash before he could put the card on top of Christine's purse. I winked at him. He took the money and winked back. I wasn't a hustler then, but I still admired talent when I saw it.

Miriam hunched over her desk while I flipped through my case file and removed all of the crime-scene photos. Swiftly, I flicked through the medical examiner's report so that the folded pages hid the envelope from everyone's view. I continued to hide the envelope with the report while my fingers worked underneath the pages—opening the envelope and setting the photographs among the crime-scene photos. I put the report aside and looked at the mass of photos on my table. A casual glance would not be enough to discern which photographs didn't belong in the pile. Volchek paid no attention to me. Just in case he chanced a look, I piled the photos together and held them close to my face.

These were the photographs that started this whole mess; they got Mario killed. Two photographs. The first showed Volchek sitting down to dinner with Arturas and a third man. The photo was taken in a dark restaurant, probably the Sirocco Club. Volchek must've seen Mario taking the shot and immediately threatened him. That's what the nightclub dancer Nikki Blundell had seen.

The third man in the photograph wore a navy suit and a white shirt. He had neat red hair, a thin, well-kept mustache, and a wide smile—Tom Levine. Volchek got papped having dinner with an FBI agent. Mario must have known Levine. I remembered Tony telling me in the restaurant that morning that Mario got busted by the feds and did five years in Rikers for it. Either he met Levine then or, more likely still, Levine was the agent who busted him. Volchek must have spent a lot of time and money buying Levine, and he wouldn't want such a valuable asset exposed by an idiot like Mario. There was no doubt about it—anyone who tries to blackmail the Russian mob has to be an idiot.

The second photo was taken at a different location. A parking lot at night. I saw Arturas, Levine, and three other men. Initially, I didn't recognize them. Then I turned around, and I saw the same three men sitting in court. One was Japanese—the Yakuza. The other two were representatives of the cartels. The same men who had stood and applauded Volchek as he walked into the courtroom yesterday morning. Jimmy had told me Volchek hadn't played well with others, that he had resisted making deals with other criminal organizations, that this resistance was costing him his business. Levine must have facilitated the meeting between Arturas and the three gang leaders. For what purpose, I didn't yet know, but I was sure that this photo was part of the reason behind Arturas running a con on his boss.

I could have kissed Tony. The photograph of Levine and Volchek together would seal the persuader on Kennedy and maybe save my life. I looked around the court and saw Kennedy sitting a few seats behind Miriam. I didn't see Levine or Coulson beside him. That would make things easier for me, but I still had to find a way to talk to him alone and in private.

My time was running out. I needed to make a move. I would have preferred to get a look in the suitcase before speaking to Kennedy, but there was no time to lose.

Victor saw me looking at the suitcase. If I could have gotten a glance into it at that moment, I felt sure that I would find all the answers. At that time, it was still too risky: too many people around and Victor would not easily let me get near the damn thing.

My watch read 10:05 a.m. Two hours until the warrant application. I turned and looked at Kennedy. He was checking his watch. I had a terrible sinking feeling that Kennedy might be lying. That AUSA Gimenez might be sitting down with Judge Potter right now. If that was the case, I had no more than an hour or so before they broke down my door. I thought it was more and more likely that the Russians had planted something in my apartment, something the FBI could use to nail me to the wall for trying to blow up Little Benny. I prayed I was wrong. Wrong about Kennedy, wrong about the Russians. Somewhere, on some deep level, I knew that at least one of those suspicions would be true.

CHAPTER FIFTY-TWO

Judge Pike and the jury came back into court. Miriam dismissed Tony Geraldo. Still no sign of Harry. I had no questions for Tony, and he walked confidently from the witness box like he was Frank Sinatra.

"The people call Officer Raphael Martinez," said Miriam.

Miriam would be back on strong ground with Martinez. No over-elaboration or theorizing in his statement. He just recounted the facts. I suppose in this case he didn't need to get creative. He'd caught Benny red-handed in the dead guy's apartment, and Benny gave up the head of the Russian mob for the murder.

Martinez was a handsome Hispanic male in his late thirties, dressed in a well-fitting suit. He moved confidently but without swagger to the witness box. The file of papers in his arms was feathered with Post-it notes to mark important documents and to show the jury that he was well prepared. He held his head up and looked the jury members in the eye. Martinez had nothing to be afraid of.

"Officer Martinez, would you tell the members of the jury your rank and experience on the job?"

Not good again from Miriam, two questions at once. She was better than that. I thought that her nerves were affecting her. Lesser advocates might have thrown in the towel by then, but Miriam came back strong. Within ten minutes, she broke into a good flow, and Martinez rattled through Benny's confession and plea bargain in under thirty minutes.

Solid.

As she got her last answer, she turned away from the witness and walked toward me on her way back to the prosecution table.

She smiled as she said, "Your witness."

If I tried to shake Martinez, I'd lose. Sometimes there are witnesses who cannot be broken, and Martinez certainly belonged in that category. I decided to keep it brief and question him on topics that Miriam hadn't touched upon in her direct examination.

"Officer Martinez, please open the bundle and look at folder three, tab nine, page two," I said. In cross-examination there is no "would you?" or "can you?" Everything, absolutely everything, should be a statement, not a question. They say good lawyers never ask a question unless they already know the answer. This is true, but it's not because lawyers have any greater knowledge than anyone else. It's because we give you the answer we want in the question.

Martinez found the page, which he'd marked with one of his yellow Post-its.

"Officer, this is a photograph of a picture frame, found smashed in the apartment?"

"Yes."

I turned to the jury and smiled, deeply satisfied with the answer, and I paused briefly before turning to the witness again.

"The description below the photograph states 'broken photo frame,' but it does not tell us how many photographs were in the frame, does it?"

His eyes narrowed. He seemed slightly puzzled. "No, it doesn't."

Beaming a satisfied and knowing grin, I turned again to the jury and repeated Martinez's answer slowly and joyfully, "No, it doesn't," holding it before the jury like a prize won in hard-fought battle. The jury nodded. They weren't sure what I'd won yet, but they seemed intrigued. Miriam didn't react. She froze in a look approaching boredom, like any good attorney should when they think their opponent has just landed a blow. Best to look unconcerned and hope the jury follows your lead. In truth, those questions weren't for the jury's benefit—they were for Kennedy: I wanted him thinking about that photo frame.

"Can I have a second to consult with my client, Your Honor?"

"Yes, Mr. Flynn."

I leaned over and whispered to Volchek. "What did you have for breakfast?" I said.

"Your favorite, pancakes. Why?"

"Just playing a game with the DA, letting her think I'm hatching a master plan and generally making her nervous. But there is something I need to know. I think you're close to an acquittal and you won't have to use the bomb. What I need to know is what Little Benny will say to the jury. The one thing the DA doesn't have is motive. My guess is Little Benny provides the motive. So I need to know, why did you order the hit on Mario Geraldo? What was hidden in the photo frame that you wanted so badly?"

Arturas wasn't there to advise him and Victor didn't appear to be too quick on the uptake.

"Mr. Flynn, do you have any other questions?" asked the judge, but I pretended I hadn't heard.

"Come on. Give me the shot. I can destroy Little Benny, but I can't do it if I don't know what he'll say in the witness box. What was in the photo frame?"

Running his hands over this thighs and smoothing his pants, Volchek considered my question again.

"Mario took a picture of me with someone. Someone that I work with in secret. Someone close to law enforcement. He is my biggest asset. I could not risk losing him. Mario wanted money for the picture. I sent Little Benny to kill him and destroy the evidence."

"How many photographs did he have?"

"One, no copies. That's what Arturas told me. I wanted to deal. Arturas wanted to send a message."

"And Arturas told you it was just the one photograph, the photograph Mario took in the Sirocco Club?"

"Yes," said Volchek, nodding. His eyes were natural, his facial muscles relaxed, his hands open and resting on his lap. He was telling the truth. That was all I needed to know.

Arturas had dealt with Mario because Arturas knew Mario had another photo—of Arturas meeting the cartels and the Yakuza. If Volchek found out that Arturas had met the cartels and the Japanese in secret, then Arturas probably would have found his name on one half of a torn, one-ruble bill. Arturas had kept this meeting secret from Volchek, and Little Benny made sure it stayed secret by killing Mario and destroying the photos.

It was as much as I was likely to get without examining the suitcase.

10:40 a.m.

I couldn't risk taking any more time over this. I had to speak to Kennedy before he got his warrant.

CHAPTER FIFTY-THREE

Mr. Flynn, do you have any further questions for this witness?" said Judge Pike, finishing her sentence with an impatient snap of her teeth.

"Your Honor, may I take just another few minutes with my client?"

"Fifteen-minute recess," said Pike.

A nod of the head as she rose was good enough for me, and I strode quickly to the aisle.

"Bathroom break," I said as I passed Volchek and heard Victor get up noisily and follow me as I headed for the door of the court. My pace slowed as I approached Kennedy. I could hear the deep, resonant footsteps of Victor behind me, getting closer as I moved purposefully toward the fed.

Five feet to Kennedy's seat.

I quickened my pace, putting distance between me and Victor, and locked my eyes on the FBI agent. Kennedy saw me staring at him and started to rise. I grabbed his tie in my left hand, pulled him to his feet, and came close, nose to nose, chest to chest, and my hand slipped unseen into his jacket.

Before Victor got to me, I had time to mouth a short sentence, just two words.

"Trust me."

Kennedy pushed me away like I was crazy. I kicked open the court doors, marched through the crowd in the hall, and locked myself in the disabled bathroom. After ten seconds, I heard a knock on the door and a deep, Slavic voice.

"Don't go nowhere, lawyer. I'm waiting." Victor, standing guard outside. I could hear the background noise build up in the hall as the courtroom emptied for a break. Reaching into my pocket, I took out Kennedy's cell phone and dialed the number for my secure cell. After four rings, Kennedy answered.

"What the hell is this?" he said.

"This is Eddie Flynn. I have your phone. You probably guessed that already. No doubt you recognized your number on the caller ID. The phone you're holding is mine. Sorry I couldn't take your card this morning. I needed to call you and I didn't have your number, so I had to switch phones. Thing is, I've been kidnapped by the Russian mob and I need your help. Your friend Tom Levine is working for them. They've kidnapped my daughter, and I've got their bomb. Looks like you're about to have a very bad day."

CHAPTER FIFTY-FOUR

I held the phone tight to my ear and whispered as loudly as I dared. "My best guess is that Arturas is planning to take over the Bratva. He's setting up his boss, but I can't figure out how he's going to do it."

"You've lost your mind, Mr. Flynn," said Kennedy simply.

"Maybe, but I'm right about this. Mario Geraldo got killed because he saw Tom Levine having dinner with Volchek and he photographed them. Benny never told you why he killed Mario. It was because Mario was trying to blackmail Volchek with the photos. Plus, Arturas was meeting other gang leaders behind Volchek's back. You don't get in bed with the competition unless you're either going to jump ship or hijack the ship you're already on. You've got the photo of Levine; it's in your right-hand jacket pocket."

This was my play. I was gambling everything on Kennedy believing me and arresting the Russians, but I didn't dare tell him everything. The bomb in my jacket, the vans downstairs, there was nothing that linked them to the Bratva. My fingerprints would be on the vans and the bomb. I needed to be sure Kennedy believed me before I told him everything. I waited for a few seconds.

"You got it?"

"This doesn't prove a thing."

My back hit the bathroom wall, and I slid down the tiles. A hollow feeling in my chest spread into my throat.

"Wh-what?"

"Not that it should concern you, but Agent Levine worked undercover for a couple of years. His mission was to infiltrate the mob. I wouldn't be surprised if he'd had more than one dinner with Volchek."

"But I found an FBI card in Gregor's wallet. It had a number on the back written in pen; it's Levine's number. If he was undercover a couple years ago, then at some stage he flipped to the other side. He's working for the Russian mob. I couldn't tell you any of this earlier because he was listening and he would report straight back to Volchek."

"Tom Levine is a decorated agent. I'd need more proof than that. I have to say, Mr. Flynn, your story is a little crazy. We know you've just returned to practice after a stint in rehab. You feeling okay?"

I rubbed my face and thought hard.

"Take a look in the same pocket as the one you found my phone in. You'll find a flashlight. Only it's not really a flashlight; it's a black light. Volchek gave me a million bucks to bribe Tony Geraldo. I marked the money I got from the Russians. Check out Victor's right hand. You'll see the chemical mark. It matches a million dollars in cash that's being held by a friend and that chemical signature takes it right back to the Bratva. I'm in the bathroom opposite the court. Victor's waiting outside. Check out his hand and I'll call you back."

"Just so you know, we got our hearing with Potter bumped up the line. Gimenez is waiting outside Potters' chambers. The hearing shouldn't take too long. All being well, we'll have agents in your apartment within an hour."

I smacked the back of my head off the tiles.

"You didn't get bumped. The hearing was always going to be at eleven. You just didn't want to give me a heads-up."

Kennedy disconnected.

He'd played me, for the second time. First with the consent form that guaranteed he'd get the warrant and then with the timing of the warrant hearing. But more important, Kennedy hadn't bought my story. I thought again about telling him to search the basement lot for the vans and decided it was too risky; with nothing to link the vans to the Bratva, that could backfire on me big-time. I called Harry, but he didn't answer; maybe he saw the call and didn't answer because he didn't recognize the number.

Kennedy's phone vibrated. The caller display read Andy Coulson, the other FBI agent that I'd met that morning.

"Yeah," I said, doing my best impersonation of a straight-laced Kennedy.

"We got a situation—a shooting," said Coulson.

"Where?" I said, trying to sound concerned. I knew it was only a matter of time before the FBI got involved with the pile of Russian bodies that Anthony and the Lizard had left in the wake of Amy's rescue.

"Little Italy. ATF are asking for our assistance."

I dropped the phone and then quickly picked it up.

"You there, boss?" said Coulson.

"Yeah, I'm here. Where in Little Italy?"

"You don't sound right. Reception must not be too good here. Anyway, it was Jimmy Fellini's place on Mulberry. We got seven dead. It happened about twenty minutes ago. You think it might be related to the hit on Volchek's crew this morning? I think we could have a link. It would take some serious muscle to shoot up Jimmy the Hat's restaurant. I think it's a Russian reprisal for the Severn Towers thing this morning. If we're not careful, we could have a gang war here."

I muffled a scream, forcing my fist into my mouth as my body froze in shock.

"You there, Bill?"

A question became lodged in my brain and burned like a bullet ripping through my skull. I gripped the phone with both hands and opened my mouth to speak, but no words came. If I didn't ask the question, my head would tear itself apart, but I knew if I got the answer I was dreading, I would die.

"Is . . . is . . . ?"

"You're breaking up, boss."

I thumped my head into the wall and spat it out.

"Is a little . . . a little blond girl one of the dead?"

"I've got an e-mail from the ATF on my phone here. Let me check."

Victor knocked on the door of the bathroom, and I flushed the toilet. My hand began bleeding from my nails burying into my palm.

"No. I got nothing on a little girl. I'm told two guys on the door, a waitress, and three made guys. Anthony Fellini was one of 'em. Apparently, a couple of guys walked in with machine guns and left through a secret tunnel in the back. I'll look into it and let you know."

Coulson hung up, and I dialed Jimmy's cell.

He answered immediately, and I could hear the roar of a car engine and car horns in the background. Jimmy was on the move.

"Jimmy . . . it's Eddie . . . The goddamn Russians hit your place. Anthony is dead. I think they've got Amy."

"I know. I heard. The Lizard and I were hiding the money you gave us when I got the call. Sit tight—this ain't over yet. If they wanted to kill her, they'd have shot her and left her in the restaurant. She's alive. I'm sure of it. They've taken her. The Lizard and I are on our way to you now. I'm handling this personally. Anthony was a good kid. My sister's gonna kill herself when she finds out. Eddie, there's no way anybody can think they can walk into my place, take down my guys, and leave. I have to be seen to be taking care of this, you understand. Those bastards are dead."

"Jimmy, you can't start a war. They've got Amy."

"I can't let this go. We're going to wait outside the courthouse. Soon as we see Volchek and his crew, we're gonna hit 'em."

He hung up.

I ran to the sink and splashed cold water over my face and head. Arturas must have gone to the apartment to check on Amy. It wouldn't have taken a genius to figure out who double-crossed him and where they'd taken Amy. I'd been stupid. I shouldn't have let Anthony take Amy back to the restaurant. At the same time, I never expected Arturas to declare all-out war on Jimmy. That kind of action forced people's hands. Unless Jimmy took these guys down hard, every two-bit pimp in the district would think that Jimmy was ripe for the taking.

Kennedy's cell rang again. It was the number of my disposable cell on caller ID.

"I've seen the mark on Victor's hand. Wasn't easy. He almost spotted the flashlight. I still don't think it proves anything. I called my office and had an agent call your wife. I don't know what kind of phone you've given me, but my office had a hell of a job calling me back. Anyway, your wife says your daughter is on a school field trip in Long Island. She hasn't reported your daughter missing and neither have you. Don't lie to me. I know you want help, but you have to start telling me the truth. We've got a file on you. We know your history; you used to be some kind of a hustler, but you can't hustle me. Help me. Tell me the truth."

I breathed out and spoke slowly and softly.

"Kennedy, I told you the truth. If you don't believe me, then you can go to hell. I'm going to finish this my way."

CHAPTER FIFTY-FIVE

Volchek turned to face me as I came back into court. I resumed my seat and felt him lean forward to catch my ear.

"After you finish with the cop, it's the dancer next, yes?" he said.

"Yeah. They'll keep Benny till last."

"After the dancer, you have to think about planting that jacket. I don't mind, of course, if you want to keep it on and stand beside Benny when I blow you up. That's up to you," said Volchek. Turning around to face him, I saw the detonator in his hand.

"Where are the rest of your men?" I said.

"Checking on your daughter. Don't forget what you're here to do, Mr. Flynn. I can't take any chances. You've done well, but I can't let this go to a jury. We'll plant the bomb during the lunch break."

Turning away from Volchek, I shut my eyes and thought through everything again. The soft whistling from Jean's pen swimming through my fingers seemed to drown out the noise from the crowd. I'd blown it with Kennedy. Harry wasn't here. I didn't have anything solid to link the Russians to Amy's kidnapping, the bomb in my jacket, or the vans. Not that I could risk raising a bomb scare anyway. Court security would evacuate the building and Volchek would run. No. If I let the cops know about either of the bombs, Amy was as good as dead.

Only one option left.

I signaled Pike's clerk.

"Jean, I need a favor. Tell Her Honor something has come up and I need an extra ten minutes with my client. No more."

"It's five after eleven, Eddie, and she wants this case moving today. If she comes back into court and you're not here, she'll fine you fifty dollars for every minute you're late. I saw her do that two weeks ago to poor old Mr. Langtree. You know he's got prostate issues. His sister told me—"

"Sorry, Jean. I have to go consult with my client. I'll be quick. Just stall her if you can."

Volchek looked puzzled.

"I thought of something, but we can't talk here. Let's find a conference booth in the hall," I said.

"What is it?"

"I told you. Not here. They got eyes and ears. Trust me. It's worth it," I said as I packed the files into the case and started for the door, wheeling the Samsonite behind me.

"Leave the files here," said Victor.

I didn't answer him. Instead I turned to make sure Volchek followed me. After a second, he got up, buttoned his suit jacket, and strolled out with me. Victor began to protest again, but Volchek silenced him.

The sign on the closest conference room read ENGAGED.

Without knocking, I opened the door and hefted the case into the corner of the room. A young lawyer and his client were talking, papers spread out on the desk.

"Sorry. I need this room."

"What the hell is this? I'm taking instructions here. You can't jus—"

"Get out now or you'll get hurt."

The young lawyer rose; he was fit, aggressive, and unwilling to have an older lawyer make a show of him in front of his client.

"What? You gonna hurt me?" he said.

"Ordinarily, yeah, but not today. If you don't leave right now, *he'll* hurt you," I said, pointing to the figure of Volchek, framed in the doorway.

The young lawyer's client noticed the head of the Russian mob, grabbed his lawyer, and dragged him out, leaving behind their papers and the lawyer's briefcase. Victor put one foot into the booth. I pushed the door against it.

"Just me and the client, blondie."

Victor pushed back.

"Make sure we are not disturbed," said Volchek.

Reluctantly, Victor exited and closed the door. A heavy insulated material lined the walls to make the room a little more soundproof. All the conference rooms had the same setup because what was discussed in those rooms was confidential and privileged between an attorney and his client. As long as we didn't shout, Victor wouldn't be able to hear the conversation on the other side of the heavy door.

Volchek sat, laced his fingers across his stomach, and lazily turned his attention toward me. Placing my hands on the back of the chair, I leaned over Volchek and kept my voice low.

"What I'm about to tell you will come as a shock, so don't call out; it's important that this meeting is just you and me. Cards on the table, Olek; I tried to double-cross you. I failed. Right now, none of that matters, because I'm the only man who can keep you alive."

CHAPTER FIFTY-SIX

Volchek placed his hands flat on the table, ready to spring at me. "You know what happens to those who double-cross—"

"I said I failed. Some of Jimmy's guys found Amy and took her, and yes, they killed whoever was in that apartment. You'd do the same if it were your daughter. Arturas has just busted into Jimmy's restaurant; he's killed some of Jimmy's family and taken Amy back. But things have moved on. It's not about that anymore. Look, you've got bigger problems than me," I said, tossing Volchek the photograph that Mario took of Arturas in the parking lot.

He got halfway to his feet, saw the photo, and sat back down. A vein stood out on his neck, and a low hiss escaped from his teeth.

"This is a copy of one of the photos that Little Benny burned after he killed Mario. I got a copy from Tony. You don't need me to tell you what's in that picture. That's your boy Arturas meeting with your competition. The guys in that photo are the same men who applauded you yesterday when you came into court. A few minutes ago, I asked you how many photographs Mario was using to blackmail you. You said 'one.' So I figure you didn't know this photo existed. My guess is that this is the real reason that Arturas wanted Mario dead. It *was* Arturas who suggested you take out Mario, wasn't it?"

For a moment his eyes met mine. He nodded and returned his stare to the photograph. A trembling began at the corner of his mouth before his lips drew tight.

"Arturas had been planning to join up with the competition long before you had Mario murdered. You were told that Mario wanted money for the photo of you and your FBI informant, and I know it could hurt you to lose such a valuable asset. But killing Mario because he threatened an FBI source doesn't warrant starting a war with the Italian Mafia. I didn't think it merited the risk, and my guess is that you didn't think so either. Arturas persuaded you to order the hit. He needed someone he could trust to kill Mario and destroy *both* photographs. That's why he told you to use Little Benny. Arturas trusted Benny to kill Mario and clean up his mess. Then Benny got caught. Now Arturas has something else planned, and I have a feeling that whatever is in this suitcase is going to tell us exactly what's going on."

He crumpled the photo in his fist. His arm shook, but I couldn't tell if it was from the effort or from suppressed rage.

"What? What suitcase?" he said.

"This one," I said, placing the case on the desk. "Last night I saw two vans drive into the basement parking lot of this courthouse. They were driven by your men, and each van is filled with explosives."

Volchek's shoulders slumped, his mouth opened, and his anger seemed to dissipate in shock. "I don't believe you," he said.

"Arturas watched the vans drive in, and I saw Gregor put a heavy suitcase, exactly the same as this one, into the passenger seat of one of the vans. I checked that case this morning and found it empty. It wasn't empty last night. That got me thinking why Arturas would have two identical suitcases. I think the case I saw this morning is the one that Arturas used to carry the case files yesterday, and the case that they brought in last night is actually this one. I saw it lying open in the office upstairs. This case has a false bottom."

Flicking open the case, I removed the evidence files and placed them on the floor. I dug my fingers around the false base and found the seam: Velcro for quick release. I pulled the lid.

"You don't need to take my word for any of this. Come take a look for yourself," I said.

I wasn't sure what I would find hidden in the case. Something important, something that was key to Arturas's plans. Whatever my imagination might have envisioned, it was nowhere close to what I actually found.

CHAPTER FIFTY-SEVEN

Inside the hidden compartment of the case I saw two neatly folded piles of coveralls. They were gray, heavy-duty coveralls. They had a harness of some kind, like a safety rig, built into them at the waist. A thin but strong cable came from the belt of the coveralls, and at the end of the line, I found a snap clip. It looked as though the coveralls were made for rappelling. The first uniform was size 5XL, the second XXXL, the third a size large, and the last was a small; I could tell by the labels in the collar.

Beneath the coveralls I found four compact automatic rifles. They looked like MP5s. The weapons were ideal for short-range combat, and up close they could shred a four-hundred-pound man in seconds. The magazines were taped to the barrel of each gun with a single piece of duct tape. The last item in the bag confused me. It appeared to be a remote control for a model airplane. I guessed it to be a mixture of steel and plastic, about a foot square. It had a telescopic aerial, two controller sticks, and two buttons—one green, one red. I placed the control back in the case underneath the weapons.

Volchek had moved around the table to stand behind me so that he could see inside the hidden compartment.

"You didn't know about any of this, right?"

His puzzled expression gave me my answer.

"What is this?" said Volchek, throwing a hand at the guns and outfits.

"This is proof that Arturas has been bullshitting both of us. He told us that I was the only man who could smuggle a bomb into the courtroom. But he could've gotten the bomb in on his own, anytime he liked."

Shaking his head, Volchek moved his lips silently; it seemed as though this was too much for him to take in. He had built his life around the loyalty of his men. Indeed, his very existence depended on utter obedience, honor, and allegiance. He had seen other Bratva destroyed through petty jealousies and he'd taken steps to make sure he had total control over his men. Now those lifelong foundations were crumbling away.

Standing back, I looked Volchek over.

"You're probably around the same size as me. You think you could fit into this?" I said, holding up the large-sized coverall.

"No," said Volchek.

Both of us were at least thirty pounds heavier than Arturas.

"I'd say this was Arturas's size. The big sizes are for Gregor and Victor, the little one . . ."

"Benny," said Volchek.

With that one word from Volchek, it felt as though a key had just slotted into place. All of the questions, all of the inconsistencies in the case, and all the moves Arturas had made melted into one irrefutable thought: Killing Little Benny had never been part of the plan.

"Arturas is going to bust Little Benny out of custody. That's what he's been planning all along. Think about it. Little Benny could've given up the whole damn Bratva and walked into the witness protection program. He didn't; he fingered you for Mario's murder and nothing else. That's because he was hoping Arturas would take over your operation. Arturas couldn't kill you after Benny got arrested because he needed you. He needed you to show up for this trial so the prosecutor would put Benny on the stand. Remember what you said to me yesterday morning? *Even my contacts can't locate Little Benny.* Arturas couldn't spring Benny out of custody before now because he couldn't find him; even your FBI man, Levine, didn't know where Benny was being hidden. Arturas persuaded you to come to the trial and kill Benny with a bomb that he made me smuggle into court. This whole thing is his plan, after all, but it's just to get you here, in trial, so Benny can be produced from his hiding place. If

Arturas didn't have a plan to take out Benny, you would never have come to court—you would've taken off. When Benny gets on the stand, Arturas is going to kill you, shoot up the whole courtroom, grab Benny, and run."

"No. That doesn't make sense. How could he escape?"

"He's going to blow the whole building. That's what the vans are for. He wants everyone to believe he died in the explosion, along with Benny, Gregor, and Victor. I don't know exactly how he's going to do that. The coveralls must be disguises of some kind. But that's the only way it could work. The FBI doesn't have manhunts for dead men."

"That's crazy," said Volchek, taking a step back, his eyes moving around the room.

I tensed, and Volchek could see it.

The sudden realization that everything he knew or believed in was slowly unraveling set him on edge, made him dangerous.

He lunged toward me, but I was ready.

CHAPTER FIFTY-EIGHT

My foot caught him in the chest and punched him backward, sending him crashing into the padded wall. In one fluid motion, I grabbed one of the MP5s, twisted the magazine clear of the tape, slotted it home, cocked the weapon, and pointed it at Volchek.

He put his hands up.

Two knocks on the door, and we could hear Victor calling out in Russian. I guessed he heard some of the commotion and wanted to know if everything was all right.

"Tell him everything's fine. In *English*."

Volchek thought about it and finally called out, "Leave us. Everything is fine."

We both waited for a time, neither one of us moving. Volchek's eyes never left the gun.

"I could kill you right now, wait outside for Arturas, take him somewhere quiet, and have Jimmy's man torture him until he tells me where my daughter is. But I'm not going to do that. I'm not going to kill anyone if I don't have to. Arturas has set me up pretty good. The FBI are on their way to my apartment, and I think Arturas has planted something there to blame this whole thing on me. So we're going to make a new deal. You're going to find out where Amy is, and you're going to release her to a friend of mine. We're going to do this now."

Volchek shook his head.

"You can't go anywhere, Flynn. There are cops and guards all over this building. I think you're still trying to double-cross me."

"What are you, stupid? If you still don't believe me, take out the detonator Arturas gave you."

Slowly, he reached into his coat pocket and drew out the device.

"Light it up."

"What? If the bomb in your jacket goes off now, in here, we'll both be killed."

"Just arm it. Do it."

He hit the button to arm the bomb on my back. Nothing happened: no vibration, no light on the detonator. Shifting his gaze from the MP5, Volchek began examining the detonator while rubbing his brow and muttering in Russian.

"Toss it over," I said.

I caught it one-handed, kept the gun pointed at Volchek's chest, and slammed the detonator into the edge of the desk. A soft crack came from the plastic breaking, the sound eaten up by the padding on the walls.

Tossing the empty halves of plastic onto the table, I watched Volchek's expression change from confusion to realization. It wasn't just the detonator that fell apart. Volchek's whole world just got busted wide open.

Sinking to his knees, he put both hands over his head. Fingers raking his hair, he swore.

"I told you. You're being set up. The way I see it, Arturas is ready to kill both of us to rescue Benny. He couldn't risk giving you the real detonator, just in case you set off the bomb and killed Little Benny. That's the proof right there, in front you. He lied to you. He lied to me. What I can't figure out is why. Why would Arturas take such a risk for one man?"

A deep bellow of laughter escaped from Volchek before he quickly shut it off with clenched teeth. He looked at me like I was stupid.

"Why do you think I cut Arturas when Little Benny betrayed me?" he said, raking his cheek forcefully to mirror the scar on Arturas's face.

"Arturas had to take responsibility for his little *brat*," said Volchek, spitting that last word out like it disgusted him.

That word again, brat, only this time it made sense. I'd overheard Arturas saying "*moy brat*" in a conversation about Benny. If Bratva meant *brotherhood*, brat meant . . .

"Brother. They're brothers," I said.

Volchek forced a fake smile and held out his hands, as if it were all too simple. Taking a second to appraise him, I decided Volchek finally saw the truth.

"Arturas persuaded you not to run, to come to this trial so he could kill you and spring his brother. You want to let him get away with that?"

"No. But I can't trust you."

"You're going to have to trust me. Let Amy go, and I'll get you out of this."

"By going to the police or FBI? No."

"We can't do that. Kennedy doesn't believe me. And you can't rely on a single word Arturas told you. I bet there's no plane waiting for you. You're in as much trouble as I am. You can't run anywhere, not with Arturas setting you up and not with a murder trial hanging over your head. We're in this together, Volchek. There's no other play here. We have to set up Arturas so he takes the fall for all of this. Let Amy go, and I'll help you."

He bit his thumb for a second and pushed himself to his feet. He was no longer questioning the situation. He had moved beyond that. Now he was thinking of a way out. He adjusted his pants and sat down.

"I cannot let her go. Not until I know I can trust you."

I lowered the gun and thought things through.

"There's nothing I can say to make you trust me. I certainly don't trust you. Right now we have a common enemy, and that's all we've got. Show me some faith. Bring her to me. I need to know that she's still alive. I've got somebody who will take her somewhere safe."

Slowly, Volchek shook his head.

"No. You get me off this murder. Then I'll release her."

"There's no time."

"Then there's no deal."

It didn't matter that I was holding the gun, didn't matter that I was the only one who could save Volchek from his own crew. He still held my daughter, so he had all the cards.

And he knew it.

"Are you sure you have someone in your outfit you can still trust?"

"Yes. My driver, Uri. He's my nephew. He would rather die than betray me. He is blood. And Arturas has kept him away from the trial; he arranged for another driver for me last week. Arturas will have brought your daughter to my office. It's close by. There's nowhere else safe within driving distance. Uri will be there. He is the only one I can trust now. I don't know who else Arturas has corrupted—probably everyone—but he would not even try to turn Uri against me. Flynn, killing your daughter does not benefit me anymore, not if we have a new scapegoat. Get me off this murder, and you will have your daughter. I give you my word."

This maniac was my last hope. Amy's last hope.

I had nothing else.

Pulling the clip clear of the rifle, I looked on the floor at the open briefcase left behind by the young lawyer, smiled as an idea formed, and said, "Okay. We don't have much time. I'll get the prosecution case thrown out. You get me Amy; then we'll both get Arturas. This is how it'll work . . ."

CHAPTER FIFTY-NINE

The wheels at the bottom of the case rattled as I jogged back to the defense table. Unpacking the files, I heard a commotion at the door—Arturas calling Volchek back out of the courtroom; the scarred man had just returned. They stood at the entrance, whispering. Volchek became aggressive.

Jean tapped her watch at me and mouthed, *Sorry.* She must've spoken to the judge and got a frosty reaction to my plea for more time with my client. Judge Pike was about to make her entrance and call back the jury. The witness, Officer Martinez, remained seated in the witness box.

I got up and walked toward the arguing Russians.

"Where is she?" said Volchek.

Arturas whispered his response.

"I want to speak to her now. The lawyer can get me off. I want him motivated. Get her into the car with Uri and get her on the phone, now," said Volchek.

"He tried to screw us, Olek. We can't—"

"Do it now, or I leave for the plane."

Volchek was playing his part. Arturas must've told him about the hit on the penthouse at Severn Towers and his retaliation: shooting up Jimmy's restaurant and recapturing Amy. Arturas couldn't afford to let Volchek run; he needed to see his brother on the stand or everything he'd planned fell to pieces.

From his coat, Arturas removed his phone, dialed, gave the phone to Volchek, and both men stepped outside into the hall. I followed and kept an eye on Victor, who was looking at me suspiciously. The giant, Gregor, took a seat in the courtroom.

I joined Volchek and Arturas in a quiet corner of the hall.

"Uri, this is Olek. Take the little girl—just you, no one else—and bring her to the court. Use the Mercedes. Text me when you get outside. I want you to wait. I will give you instructions when you get here. Put her on the phone . . ." He spoke in English, for my benefit, as we'd agreed.

A hard punch to my ribs doubled me over. It was fast, discreet. The hall was virtually empty. Everyone was in the court, waiting for the trial to restart. Arturas's face was a mask of hate. He tried for another punch, but I caught his fist.

"Even if your daughter lives, you will die today. I promise you that," said Arturas.

I said nothing. He wrenched his fist clear, straightened his coat, and spat on the floor.

Volchek pressed speaker.

Amy couldn't talk. All I heard were her terrible, uncontrollable cries. My stomach felt as though it were trying to climb out of my body, and I could taste bile in my mouth. In the background, I could hear Uri trying to calm her down. Amy screamed. Arturas wore the same sickening smile that I'd first seen the morning before. I tried to focus on Volchek, on Amy, on anything other than ripping out Arturas's throat.

"Is she hurt?" I asked.

Before Volchek could answer, Uri said, "No. She just cry. I bring her candy?" Uri sounded as if he was a little slow.

"Yes. Get her candy. Calm her, Uri. Go now."

Without Arturas seeing it, Volchek gave me a slight nod. He wanted me to see him playing his part.

I returned the nod. Time for me to hold up my end of the bargain.

CHAPTER SIXTY

Volchek had already taken his seat at the defense table, and as I was about to join him, Arturas pulled me to one side and we walked about halfway up the aisle.

His cold, low voice still sent a chill over my skin.

"You think you know what you're doing with your little lawyer tricks? You might fool Olek, but you don't fool me. You can't win this case. You know *nothing*. The bomb on your back isn't the only bomb in this building. There are two devices in the basement. They are very large. If you want your daughter alive, you get Little Benny on the stand fast. Not a word to Olek, or we kill her right now."

My immediate thought was that Levine had tipped off Arturas about the warrant on my apartment. Whatever Arturas planted there wasn't meant to be found until the smoke and the rubble had cleared. Arturas didn't want me arrested until this was all over. Everyone was working to the FBI's timetable now.

11:20 a.m.

Forty minutes to get Benny on the stand and get Volchek a result.

"All rise! This adjourned court now stands open!"

The quickest judge in the building ran her little legs through the door and sat down. I knew in all likelihood I didn't have forty minutes. Kennedy's men could be in my apartment at any moment. I had to believe that there was time. There just had to be.

I adjusted my watch to countdown to noon.

"You'll need this," said Arturas, shoving something hard into my stomach. My hands clasped the object before it could fall. I knew what it was without even looking at it. The pen that Amy had given me, the same pen I'd given to Jimmy so that he could show Amy that he was a friend. It felt wet, and when I looked, I saw drying blood on the cap.

Before I could ask, Arturas muttered, "It's not her blood, lawyer. She was holding it when I shot the man next to her. Get Benny up, quickly."

"If you're quite finished, Counselor?" said Judge Pike as Arturas returned to his seat.

"We'll deal with your tardiness at the end of the trial. So, now that you've had your little break, Mr. Flynn, do you have any further questions for this witness?"

Volchek nodded.

I pushed the warrant and the vans from my mind. None of that mattered. I needed to get Volchek a result, for Amy. I was about to play the justice game for my daughter's life.

"Just a few questions, Your Honor," I said.

Martinez smiled. He'd expected to be done by now.

"Officer Martinez, you had overall responsibility for the investigation of Mr. Geraldo's murder, yes?"

"Yes."

"Isn't it correct that the witness, Witness X, is the man who shot and killed Mr. Geraldo?"

"Correct, but he says he did it under orders from your client."

"And he was found by police officers in the deceased's apartment with the murder weapon and he subsequently confessed to killing Mr. Geraldo?"

"Yes."

"I appreciate you're not a lawyer, but you've investigated a number of homicides and seen plenty of murder trials. If a suspect was found in an apartment with the deceased and the murder weapon at his feet, in this case an *actual* smoking gun, he wouldn't have much of a defense, now, would he?"

Martinez forced back a smile and said, "He might if you're defending him, Mr. Flynn."

The jury sniggered. They liked the cop. I had to go lightly.

"Given your experience with murder trials, a man in that position might do or say anything to get a lighter sentence."

"It's possible."

"And there was no forensic evidence found at the crime scene that in any way linked this murder to the defendant?"

"No. Just the one-ruble bill found in the possession of Witness X."

"The defendant's fingerprints were not on that bill, correct?"

"The only discernible fingerprints came from Witness X and the custody officer who booked him in. All other fingerprints were obscured by the prints of those individuals."

"I'm sorry, Officer Martinez. You actually mean, 'No. The defendant's fingerprints were not found on the one-ruble bill.' Isn't that right?"

"The defendant's fingerprints were not found."

"Officer, the NYPD have secured convictions in the past with partial palm prints. Isn't that correct?"

"I believe so."

"The defendant's palm prints were not found on the bill."

"No, they were not."

"So there's no forensic evidence to suggest that Olek Volchek even touched this bill?"

Martinez looked at Miriam. She couldn't give him any help.

"That's correct."

"No further questions."

By no means a killer cross. Even so, I'd accomplished all that I could. Given an hour or so, I might've done better, but I didn't have time.

"No redirect," said Miriam.

I whispered to Volchek, "What type of Mercedes is Uri driving?"

"White, S-Class."

The cop thanked the judge and stood to vacate the witness box. At moments like this, when one witness is excused and another is called, the judge, the lawyers, the crowd, take it as a little break—like a new batter stepping up to home plate. Arturas sat behind me and to my right. I leaned left, palmed Kennedy's cell, and typed a text message to Jimmy: *I made a deal with Volchek. Amy will be in a white Merc, S-Class, parked somewhere around the court building. Don't make a move until I say so. But be ready to take her on my signal.*

CHAPTER SIXTY-ONE

Ms. Sullivan, are we to have your next witness?" said Judge Pike.

"Yes, Your Honor. The people call Nikki Blundell."

A beautiful young woman with pale skin got up from the public seats and began making her way to the stand. She wore long, flowing black slacks and a cream blouse, her auburn hair tied up in a bun. Tall and athletic, she moved quickly and gracefully. Miriam would likely take thirty minutes with her. I ran to Miriam just as the nightclub dancer opened the half door to the witness stand.

"Why don't we cut to the chase? Forget about the dancer. Just call Witness X, and let's get this over with."

"She's next on my list, Eddie. You'll have to wait for my star man."

"Lead her evidence. I won't object. Just get things moving," I said.

Ordinarily, the prosecution can't ask their witnesses any leading questions. I needed things to move fast, and Miriam would gladly take the opportunity to lead the witness through her best points, making sure Nikki hit all the right notes.

While I stood beside Miriam, I felt Kennedy's cell phone vibrate. With my back to Arturas, I checked the messages—a reply from Jimmy. *I'll be waiting. I'm sending the Lizard to watch your back.*

While the nightclub dancer took the oath, I tapped out a discreet reply. *There is a gun in a trash can near the basement elevators.*

Miriam got straight to it.

"Ms. Blundell, you're a dancer at the Sirocco Club on 12th Street?"

"Yes."

Nikki Blundell appeared elegant and spoke without much of an accent. I thought that Miriam must have spent a good deal of time picking out clothes for this witness to make her look professional and not at all like a typical nightclub dancer.

"And what do you do when you're not working at the Sirocco Club?"

"I'm a law student at Columbia."

I'd been expecting Nikki Blundell to be a pretty, if slightly trashy young girl I could handle easily. No way was I expecting this; Nikki Blundell suddenly became the kind of semi-professional witness that jurors love.

"You've worked at the Sirocco Club for two years now?"

"That's correct."

"Seems a little unusual—law student and erotic dancer?"

The crowd liked that one. The jury looked a little embarrassed, but they smiled and drew closer to hear the answer.

"Well, I'm a pole dancer, and the style is more exotic than erotic, actually. It's tasteful." She turned to the jury for the last part of her answer. "Actually, I learned how to pole dance at a night class in the community hall next door to my church. A lot of girls do it these days for fitness. It's a really good workout, and the tips are fantastic. I'm paying my own way through law school. I couldn't make that kind of money waiting tables. My dad—he's the pastor of the church—well, he's okay with it, so I figure, why not?"

The jury exchanged nods with one another. Even some of the ladies wearing crucifixes smiled and shrugged their shoulders. Any mileage I could've gained out of Nikki Blundell's line of work just went south, permanently.

"Ms. Blundell, I'm going to refer you back to the night in question, around two years ago, April fourth. You were working in the club that night and you saw something?"

"Yeah. I'd just finished my routine, and I saw a camera flash from the crowd. That got my attention. Customers aren't allowed to take pictures in the club—manager's rules. So the flash was a big deal, and I wanted to see who had taken the picture."

"And what did you see?"

"Oh, I saw the defendant, that man over there." She pointed to Volchek. "I saw him clearly. He got into a fight with another guy—the guy who must have taken the picture. There was a lot of pushing and shoving; then they separated."

"How certain are you that one of the men you saw was the defendant?"

Nikki looked at the jury, nodded her head, and said, "I'd swear my life on it. It was one hundred percent the defendant. He started the fight. It looked as though he wanted to kill the other guy. It was him, no doubt about it."

A great answer, and Miriam paused, letting the jury chew on it for a second or two. Some of the jurors exchanged glances with one another. Nikki was proving to be a big hit with the jury.

"How far away were you from the defendant and the other man?"

"I'd say around seventy feet."

"When you saw the fight, did you recognize the man with the camera?"

I underlined the word "camera" in my notes. It gave me an idea on how to handle Little Benny and buy me a little alone time with Volchek.

"Not at that time, but about a week later, I saw his picture in the paper. The article said his name was Mario Geraldo and that he'd been murdered the day after I saw him being attacked in the club. I felt just awful, so I called the police."

"You subsequently attended the police precinct and you were shown some photographs of individuals who may or may not have been the man you saw attacking Mario Geraldo that night. Do you remember?"

"Yeah. I went through a bunch of them until I saw the picture of the man who had attacked the victim."

Miriam held up a photograph of Volchek. NYPD carry photos of every suspected gang leader in the city.

"And was this the photograph that you picked out?"

"Yes. That's the man who attacked the guy with the camera."

"Let the record show that the witness identified a photograph of the defendant, Olek Volchek."

Another pause for effect.

"Ms. Blundell, the defendant might make the case that this was a crowded nightclub. How is it that you saw this happen so clearly?"

"Because I was on stage, so I had a bird's-eye view of the whole club. In fact, I had the best view in the whole place. I had, like, an elevated position."

"Ms. Blundell, you say this fight occurred on the night of April fourth, just twenty-four hours before Mario Geraldo, the victim in this case, was murdered. What makes you so sure what you saw actually happened on that particular date?"

"Oh, that's easy. It was my grandma's birthday the next day. I remember going home after my shift and staying up till five a.m. baking her birthday cake."

Miriam turned away from the witness, winked at me, then took her seat with the rest of the prosecution team. I checked over my notes.

"She's damn good," said Volchek.

"She's toast in twelve questions," I said.

CHAPTER SIXTY-TWO

"Ms. Blundell, how much did you have to drink that night of April fourth?"

I wanted to get the hard question out of the way first.

She leaned toward the jury with her answer, as if it were a private matter, just between them.

"The manager brings a bottle of champagne to the dressing room, for all the girls, before we go on stage. So I had maybe one glass?"

"You said you were perhaps seventy feet away from the two men you saw fighting; could you have been eighty, ninety, a hundred feet away?"

"No, not as far as that. I'd say eighty feet maximum."

"The Sirocco Club would be like most other nightclubs in that part of town—bright and well lit?"

She laughed, covered her mouth with her hand, and batted her eyelashes at the jury.

"No. Of course not. It was dark."

"But you were well lit. You're one of their big stars; you would have maybe two or three spotlights on you?"

"Four, actually. No, wait—yeah, I think it's four."

"And the Sirocco holds how many people? Two, three thousand?"

"April fourth was a Friday night, so the club would've been full. Yeah. I'd say a couple thousand easy, but I saw what I saw. Like I said, it was the camera flash that drew my attention. I saw that man, the defendant, attacking Mr. Geraldo. I saw him clearly."

She'd been well schooled to hammer home her identification of the defendant at every available opportunity.

"So let me get this straight; you've consumed alcohol, you're presumably pretty tired because you've just finished your routine, you have four big, bright spotlights shining directly into your face, and eighty feet away, in the dark, in the middle of a couple thousand people, you're able to see the defendant clearly?"

Nikki Blundell uncrossed her legs, crossed them again, blinked rapidly for a few seconds, looked at the jury, and said, "Yes."

A couple of the jurors sat back and folded their arms; they were beginning to question their first impressions of Nikki Blundell.

"You didn't think too much about this fight at the time; it was only after you read the article in the paper that ran a picture of Mr. Geraldo that you contacted the police. That was your evidence, correct?"

"That's correct."

"This article?" I said, holding up a copy of the *New York Times* article that I'd read the night before in one of the files. The page was folded in half, and I let the witness and the jury see the masthead, the picture of Mario, and the headline. MOB LINK TO MURDER.

"Yes. That's the article."

"You said in your direct examination that at the precinct you picked out a photo of the defendant and identified him as the man who had a fight with the victim, but you had no other reason to pick him out other than your memory of what you saw on April fourth at the club, right?"

"Right."

"You had never seen a photograph of the defendant before?"

"No. Of course not. I'd never seen a photograph of him before."

I flipped the newspaper, letting the witness and the jury see the photo below the fold: the photograph of Volchek coming out of the courthouse, having been arraigned for the murder.

"Let the record show that the article the witness accepts that she read before contacting the police carries a photograph of the defendant, Olek Volchek," I said, careful not to actually ask the witness about this directly and give her a chance to explain herself.

Holding a photo taken at the crime scene in my hand, I asked, "When you saw the defendant in the huge crowd, in the dark, eighty feet away, with four spotlights aimed at your face, did he have a beard, like he has today, or was he clean shaven?"

My dad's old trick again. She saw the back of the photo in my hand and bit her lip. For all she knew, I had CCTV images of Volchek leaving the club that same night. She didn't know if he was clean shaven or not, and who could blame her? Details like that escape most eyewitnesses, even honest ones. She had to be careful, as I'd already caught her out with the newspaper article.

"I don't know. I was too far away."

I bent over and made a note of the answer on my legal pad, repeating it loudly and slowly, for the jury's benefit, as I wrote it down. "*I—don't—know—I—was—too—far—away.* Just one more question, Ms. Blundell. After you finish law school, will you be applying for a position at the district attorney's office?"

"I haven't thought about that," she said.

Even if that were true, it wouldn't stop the jury thinking about it.

"Thank you, Ms. Blundell."

Some members of the jury looked sternly at Miriam, like she'd just wasted their time.

"Redirect?" said Judge Pike.

Miriam shook her head. As Nikki left the witness box, she gave Miriam a half smile. The prosecutor didn't return it.

"Your Honor, we call Witness X," said Miriam.

CHAPTER SIXTY-THREE

The court guard opened the side door on the right-hand wall, about six feet behind the witness stand. A security guard wearing a black flat cap waited outside the door. He came in, followed by a man in a good-looking suit. The guard unlocked the handcuffs and took them from the wrists of the witness.

Volchek held the detonator in his hand, making sure Arturas saw it there. Witness X was a small, well-presented man. As he came forward onto the witness stand, I took a long look at him, at his eyes and his mouth. I recognized that face. Although smaller and younger than Arturas, he bore his brother's harsh features. I looked over my shoulder and saw Arturas smiling at his little brother. The smile was different from the cold grin that Arturas usually wore. I got the sense that it was a knowing smile.

Benny was in on the plan.

The court clerk offered the witness a choice: to swear an oath on the Bible or to affirm. Benny chose the Bible, took it in his right hand, and began reading from the card. Benny finished the oath and sat down with Her Honor's permission.

I checked my watch: twenty minutes till noon.

If I let Miriam take Little Benny through his direct examination, my time would run out before I'd even asked a question. I'd had a couple of ideas on how to handle this problem, but that one little word—"camera"—in Nikki Blundell's direct examination had given me the best idea.

All I needed was for Miriam to give me a way in. If I was lucky, she might give me a chance with her first question, her settler. Then she would do the rest of the work for me.

Miriam stood and asked her first question, an innocuous hello-and-welcome-to-the-trial kind of question. I held my breath as she put down her notes, looked at the witness, and popped it right out.

"Is it okay if I call you Mr. X?"

I got to my feet fast, my hand in the air. "Objection, Your Honor."

Miriam recoiled in confusion and then quickly replaced that with anger. Her voice took on a thick staccato rhythm, and each syllable made her loathing for me abundantly clear.

"Your Honor, I have until now put up with Mr. Flynn's behavior, but this is inexcusable. He can't possibly object to me asking that question."

Judge Pike, who until that outburst from the prosecutor looked at me like I'd just pissed on the floor, suddenly flashed a silent rebuke at Miriam by tipping her glasses to the end of her nose and gazing over the rims at her, as if to say, *I handle the assholes in this court, thank you, Ms. Sullivan.*

"Mr. Flynn, what're you doing? You can't object to that question. Overruled. Please sit down and keep quiet unless you have a valid objection," said Judge Pike.

I wasn't finished.

"Your Honor, I can object to this question, and if Your Honor will permit me, I would like to explain why." I needed a little time to let the judge understand. Before she could object again, I went straight into it.

"Your Honor, a man or woman, in a United States court, has the right to know and face their accuser. This is enshrined in the Sixth Amendment. I have a motion for the court in respect of this issue."

A look of sheer incredulity spread over Gabriella Pike's face. She turned to Miriam as if asking for help, for somebody to have a little bit of common sense.

"I cannot understand why Mr. Flynn is only bringing this up now, Your Honor. This witness has been on the list for months. Mr. Flynn had ample time for legal argument on objection. I invite Your Honor to dismiss this motion."

She was getting better, "inviting" instead of "demanding."

"I think, Mr. Flynn, that you should've raised this point earlier. But, as you have raised the point at this crucial stage, I shall have to rise and let my clerk find the relevant case law. I'll sit again in five minutes. The jury will not be required to listen to this legal argument. We'll send for the jury when we're ready to resume the evidence. I presume, Ms. Sullivan, considering the heart of this issue is whether or not Witness X will be able to maintain his anonymity, that you wish Mr. Flynn's motion to be heard *in camera*?"

"I do, Your Honor," said Miriam.

They had to deal with this *in camera*. This old legal term means that the court sits in private, without a jury and without the public.

The judge rose and said, "Clear the court," then made her way to her chambers.

I heard Volchek laughing behind me.

"I knew you had something," said Volchek.

The court officer ushered everyone out of the courtroom except the lawyers and the defendant.

Arturas lifted the suitcase.

"Hey. I'll need the files," I said.

He hesitated and then began walking away with the case.

"Arturas, wait. He said he needed them," said Volchek.

As far as Arturas was aware, neither Volchek nor I had any clue what the suitcase really contained. He tapped his finger on his watch as he stared at me before dropping the case and leaving the courtroom.

This short adjournment cut into my time with Benny, but I needed one more try with Volchek.

When I was sure that we were alone and out of earshot of the prosecution, I placed Kennedy's cell phone on the table. I'd told Volchek I would get us some alone time to set up the exchange. Secretly, I'd hoped he would have seen enough already to let Amy go.

"I got my shot at Little Benny. Let's do this now. Call your guy and tell him to release Amy."

"No. We stick to the plan. I need the decision first. We set up the exchange now, like we agreed."

He dialed and waited on an answer. I did the same.

Jimmy picked up first.

"It's me. You see the car?"

"Got it. It's about thirty feet away from me. The driver is on the street, leaning against the rear door of the car. You can't trust Volchek. He'll screw you and kill Amy," said Jimmy.

Cupping my hand and keeping my voice low, I said, "I don't think so. Right now I'm the only one he can really trust. I'm gonna save his ass, so he needs me. But if it all goes to shit, I need you to do whatever it takes . . . Amy is . . ."

"You don't need to say it. I might be able to take her now. Wait. The driver's answering his cell," said Jimmy.

Volchek began his conversation in Russian.

"English," I told him.

"Uri, wait until I give you signal. It will be a call or a text. Either you let the girl go, or . . . well, you know what to do," said Volchek.

"Eddie, the driver's carrying. He just flashed me a pistol from his coat pocket. There's no way I can get to her in time. He's standing right beside the door. If Amy's in the back, he'll only need a second," said Jimmy.

"Wait for the exchange. I'll call you. If I don't call . . . If something happens to me, promise me you'll get her out. Tell her . . . tell her Daddy's so sorry. Tell her I love . . ."

My throat gave up, strangled with the thought of losing my daughter.

"She knows. I'll get to her. Good luck, bub. The Lizard is on his way to you."

The chambers door opened; Judge Pike appeared.

Volchek and I hung up our calls and put the phones away.

As soon as I put the phone in my pocket, I felt it vibrate. Pike stared at me. I couldn't check the message. Not yet.

CHAPTER SIXTY-FOUR

"What is your motion, Mr. Flynn?" asked the judge.

"Your Honor, no doubt you've read the People v. Stannard and the related authorities." This case law set out what the DA had to prove in order to keep the identity of a witness a secret. If you were a criminal attorney with a half-decent practice then you would have come up against this problem at least once. I'd done two cases where this had been an issue before. Both were buy-and-busts: An undercover police officer poses as a buyer for drugs; the buy is recorded, and when the matter comes to court, the undercover cop usually keeps his or her identity hidden and they're identified in court only by their shield number.

"My client's defense is prejudiced by this witness remaining anonymous; it adversely affects our ability to conduct an effective defense. Your Honor, I request permission to cross-examine the witness on the issue. I will not seek to reveal his identity. I only wish to test the strength of his evidence on why he feels his life is in danger. If you rule that evidence is insufficient, then there is no need for his identity to be protected and he should be named."

"That's agreeable. We can do a quick direct examination," said Miriam, "on the condition that the jury get to hear that evidence."

Miriam was coming back at me strong and smart. She wanted me to give Little Benny hell in front of the jury so that they would feel sympathy for him and begin to think that I was a real hard-ass.

"Agreed," I said. I needed Benny on the stand as soon as possible.

"Fine. Let's have the witness and the jury back. If the jury is to hear this, then is there really any objection to the court proceeding in public?"

Miriam and I shook our heads.

"I'll rise until the jury is reseated," said Pike and went back into chambers. That bought me some time. The court security guard disappeared through a side door to collect Witness X.

The court officer opened the doors and the gallery filled up again. Arturas, Victor, and Gregor came back into court. As Arturas made for his seat, he punched out commands on his cell phone, held the phone to his ear for a few seconds, then, with a *tut*, he brought the phone before his eyes again and repeated the process. When he reached the top row of seats, he put his phone away in case the judge saw it. Before sitting down, he looked longingly at the courtroom doors. He sat and folded his arms. I thought he was trying to reach someone on the phone, someone he was expecting through those doors any second. Whoever he was expecting hadn't shown up.

I felt Kennedy's phone vibrate again. Arturas had taken a seat closer to me. I couldn't take the phone out of my pocket and check without Arturas catching me. I whispered loud enough for Volchek and Arturas to hear me, "I have to talk to the prosecutor, see if there are any judgments she wants to refer to."

Volchek considered it for all of a second and said, "Fine."

Miriam scowled at me as I approached her table. I remained standing, leaning over the desk, shuffling papers. I put my back to Volchek. The phone stopped vibrating.

"You want to take a look at this," I said to Miriam as I took her copy of the crime-scene photos.

"What? You going to show me a photograph that isn't there . . . No. Show me why the jury should give a shit about a missing photo," she said.

"Come here," I said, and she got up and stood to my left, giving me good cover from the Russians. As I chatted a little with her about the broken photo frame, I could feel Kennedy's phone vibrating again. Two short bursts of vibration, then nothing. He must have been receiving a mixture of calls and texts.

I slipped the phone out once I got Miriam to look again at the photos.

Kennedy's cell phone registered two new texts and four missed calls.

I looked at the missed calls. The first two were from somebody called "Ferrar," and then two from "Weinstein," and I guessed they were agents. I checked the texts.

First text was five minutes ago from Ferrar. *We're at the lawyer's apartment. Are we still good? We're going in 60 seconds unless you say otherwise.*

I opened the last text, sent two minutes ago. I'd underestimated Arturas, badly. *Found a suicide note from Eddie Flynn. He's going to blow up the whole building. We found a shipping manifest for the* Sacha *and a schematic of the courthouse. Get him and search the building.*

The phone vibrated in my hand— Ferrar calling again. Miriam was too busy with the pictures to notice. She hadn't seen anything. I glanced over her shoulder. Kennedy sat four rows back. He sat alone. No other agents around, but of course, they couldn't reach Kennedy because I had his phone. I played the likely scenario in my head. Both Ferrar and Weinstein would be hauling ass from my apartment to this spot. I estimated it would take a half hour, forty minutes tops. I figured if Ferrar couldn't raise Kennedy, he would try calling some of the other agents.

The double doors swung open with force, and Agent Coulson made his way to Kennedy's seat. Coulson whispered something to his boss. Kennedy stood and started moving toward me. I stepped away from Miriam and stood in the center of the courtroom. Lawyers call it the "well." Drawing his weapon as he advanced, he shouted, "Freeze, Flynn. You're under arrest."

I'd blown it.

CHAPTER SIXTY-FIVE

Volchek spotted Kennedy making a move toward me, and his right thumb slipped over his cell phone.

For once I could think of nothing to say.

Kennedy stopped in front of me, the barrel of his Glock aimed at my head. Coulson had also drawn his gun, but he stayed back and covered his boss.

"You've got the wrong man," I said to Kennedy as I held my hands up.

"On the ground slowly, facedown," said Kennedy.

"He's my lawyer. This is harassment," said Volchek.

Keeping my hands high, I went down on one knee, then two; then I put my hands on the floor and went down. The marble floor felt cold on my cheek. Spreading my hands out in a crucifix position, I heard my pulse thumping in my ears.

My hands were pulled behind my back and cuffed. A strong arm hauled me to my feet.

"What the hell are you doing?" said Miriam. "I warned you not to fall for his crap. Can't you see Eddie's hustling you? He wants to be arrested. He's playing for a mistrial. Take the damn cuffs off before the jury gets back."

The agent ignored Miriam.

I managed a whisper to Kennedy. "Trust me. Don't do this. They've got my daughter. Arturas is going to spring his brother. He's got automatic weapons in that suitcase."

Kennedy took a step forward so that he could see over the heads of the people in the gallery. The suitcase stood open, with a file sitting on top of the false bottom.

"You mean that empty suitcase? Too late, Flynn. We found your suicide note in your apartment, along with the manifest for the *Sacha* and the plans for the courthouse. It's all over."

At that moment, all I could do was pray that Jimmy would get Amy, that somehow he could get to her and take her home to her mom. I hadn't prayed in a long time. My hands clasped together, and I asked God to help Jimmy save my daughter. The pain in my limbs fired up and my body felt heavy, slow, the exhaustion finally kicking in as the last reserves of adrenaline trickled away in my failure.

Kennedy began to lead me from the court, but he hadn't realized he'd inadvertently created a small riot up ahead as reporters fought to get out of the courtroom so they could take a picture of me in cuffs.

A voice from behind me stopped Kennedy dead.

"Officer! You there! Turn around. Goddamn it!"

I knew the voice.

Kennedy and I both turned and looked back. Judge Pike stood in front of her chair, and Senior Judge Harry Ford stood beside her. His sixty-some years seemed to fall away. He no longer looked like an old judge. His back was straight and his chin proud.

"Who are you?" said Harry, rooting Kennedy to the floor with the power of his stare.

"I'm Special Agent William Kennedy, and I'm bringing this suspect in for questioning," he said, about to turn again and leave.

"*Special Agent* Kennedy, you set one foot out that door with that man and you will be *Mr.* Kennedy within the hour. Turn around, take off those handcuffs, and sit your ass down," said Harry, more like the captain from Nam than the judge. Kennedy did stop, and he did turn, but he didn't take off the handcuffs.

"Guard," called Harry to the security guard who had just returned to court with Benny, "if Special Agent Kennedy does not release Mr. Flynn, then you are to arrest that agent. If he resists, shoot him," thundered Harry.

Beginning to protest now, Kennedy addressed the court. "This man is a . . ." he began—a major mistake.

"If those cuffs are not off in five seconds, you will spend a long time in the cells of this courthouse," said Harry.

I saw Kennedy's eyes moving quickly between me and Harry. A silence like no other I'd ever heard seemed to grip the courtroom. I could hear Kennedy's breathing becoming heavier. I heard the guard move forward and draw his gun. Whatever magnetic power emanated from Harry was clearly finding its way to the security guard, who pointed his gun at Kennedy like he meant it. He leaned close so no one could hear him but me.

"You gonna blow up this place, Eddie? End it all?" said Kennedy.

"I've been set up. I'm going to do whatever it takes to save my daughter."

"Where's the bomb?"

"I told you, Levine is dirty."

I couldn't tell him about the vans in the basement. If I did, Kennedy would clear the building and I needed a little more time. Just a little more time.

"I don't believe you. Levine is a decorated agent. Security are searching this whole building right now. I don't trust you, not one bit."

"Kennedy, let him go," said Miriam.

"I can't, and by the way, this is a federal matter. You've got no jurisdiction here, Ms. Sullivan," he said.

"You can let him go and you will. You're in a courtroom governed by state law, and you're about to hand the head of the Russian Mafia a mistrial. If his lawyer is arrested, the trial collapses and he walks out of here. This is what Eddie wants. Can't you see that?"

I sensed hesitation. Kennedy's eyes began darting around the floor as his head worked overtime.

"Time's up," said Harry.

"I need a little more time, please. Stay here. Watch. It should prove interesting. I'm not going anywhere. In my left-hand jacket pocket you'll find a business card. Look at it."

With my back to Arturas, he wouldn't see Kennedy taking the card. The FBI agent turned the card over in his fingers.

"That's the FBI card I told you about. You're Levine's senior officer. You read his logs. Tell me that's not his handwriting."

Holding the thing in his hand had given Kennedy pause. I should've given it to him earlier. His expression softened; the lines on his forehead disappeared. With his mouth slightly ajar, I could smell the morning coffee on his breath. He recognized the handwriting.

"That card came from Gregor's wallet. Look. You're searching the building, fine. Give me the time while you're searching. Give me thirty minutes. If you still don't believe me in half an hour, you can arrest my corpse."

Harry had enough. "Agent Kennedy, your five seconds are up already."

I heard screams from the crowd, followed by people climbing over the seats behind us to get out of the firing line as the security guard advanced on Kennedy.

Miriam had her cell phone in her hand.

"I'm calling the city field office. Your director will want to know why one of his agents just messed up the biggest mob trial in fifteen years."

Kennedy hesitated. Head down. Fingernails working swiftly on his thumb, tearing the skin, drawing blood.

"What did you tell me this morning, Agent Kennedy? Do you remember? You told me Eddie Flynn used to be a con artist. He's conning *you,* Kennedy. He wants to get arrested and blow this trial. The longer this process takes, the harder it is to keep the witness safe from his old boss. Come on. Think! You're not going to blow my career case for this. No way," said Miriam.

A heavy breath and his head came up.

"You got twenty minutes, Flynn. I'm watching. You make a move? You die first," said Kennedy as he took off the cuffs, nodded to the judge, and walked back to his seat, keeping me in view the whole time.

The guard put away his gun. Harry and Gabriella looked at each other and sat down.

"Agent Kennedy, I am the law in this court. Don't forget it," said Harry.

I took my seat at the defense table. The noise from the crowd sounded more like an audience at a heavyweight title fight than a murder trial. Volchek grabbed my arm and pulled me close.

"What the hell was that?" said Volchek.

"It was luck. Sheer, dumb luck."

Judge Pike seemed ready to get the trial moving again. She considered herself a modernist reformer when it came to judicial office, and she refused to have a hammer and gavel in her courtroom. She banged the flat of her hand against the mahogany desk in front of her and then shouted for quiet.

"Judge Ford will be observing the remainder of this trial," she said. "I'm glad to have him here, considering the behavior of certain members of this court."

Judge Pike clicked the top of her pen into action and rested the point against her notepad, ready to hear from the witness. The last of the jury members filed in, and Little Benny regained his seat in the witness box. Miriam would ask only a few questions on the threat to Benny's life, and then I'd have him.

Kennedy never took his eyes from me.

Rising to her feet and adjusting her jacket, Miriam got herself comfortable and began her short direct examination.

"Mr. X, how did you become a witness in this case?"

Benny appeared surprised by the question, but he answered quickly, usually a good indicator of an honest response.

"I was caught at the scene of a murder by police."

"Whose murder?"

"Mario Geraldo."

"And who murdered Mr. Geraldo?"

A pause. Benny wiped his mouth.

"I did," he said, matter-of-factly, as if telling someone the capital of Australia.

"You did?" asked Miriam. The witness had omitted a little piece of evidence, and she was giving him another shot. I should have objected, but I didn't.

"Yes. Olek Volchek sent me a message. The victim's name on half of a one-ruble note. I had the other half. It is old Russian code for a hit."

I got to my feet to object. I needed Miriam to hurry so I could get to Benny.

"Your Honor, this is not going anywhere near the issues."

"Is it leading there?" said Judge Pike.

"Yes, Your Honor. Just getting there now," replied Miriam. "After you were arrested for this murder, what happened?" she asked.

"I made a deal. I tell police who ordered the hit, I get discount on my sentence."

"Have you been in prison all this time?"

"No. Once I made my deal, I went into FBI protection."

"Why did the FBI put you in protective custody?"

Damn. Had to object again. "Objection. The witness doesn't know the FBI's motives."

Judge Pike made a circular motion with her pen to Miriam, telling her to rewind and rephrase.

"Why do you think that you're in protective custody rather than in jail serving your sentence?"

Benny didn't say anything. He looked at Miriam, then the judge, and then his eyes came to rest on Volchek. A look of purest hatred.

"It is simple," he began. "Olek asks other people to kill for him. He would have me killed if I was in prison. The FBI protects me from Volchek's word because that is all it takes from him—one word and you're dead. He knew I was testifying against him and he wants me dead."

Miriam knew it wasn't going to get much better, and she bowed out. "No further questions."

The judge looked at me, waiting for my cross-examination. Court security, the FBI, and probably the NYPD were tearing the building apart right at that moment, searching for anything that might look like an explosive device. With a window broken in each van, the search team would definitely find the bombs this time. It would be only a matter of time. Maybe minutes. The crowd was silent, waiting for the murderer to be tested by the defense.

"I have just a few questions," I said. I stood eighteen feet from Benny, outside the kill zone. The lead in my limbs faded away as my heart rate went up.

Everything that had happened in the last day and a half all came down to these final minutes, these final answers. I thought of my father and felt the cold touch of his medal against my skin.

"How might Mr. Volchek kill you?" I asked.

This seemed to amuse Benny. He laughed and looked around the courtroom, shifted in his seat, and wiped his face a few times.

"The man you represent does not care how he kills."

"How do you know that?" I asked.

"I know—I work for him for twenty years. He wants somebody dead, they're dead. Doesn't matter how."

"So give me an example."

Benny wasn't laughing now.

"Well, Mario Geraldo—Volchek sends me the other half of my ruble with Mario's name on it. So I shoot Mario. He did not say shoot him, stab him, drown him. His name on the ruble means he must die."

"I just wanted a few other examples, say, the last three people he had killed. How did they die?"

"How should I know that?"

"You say you fear for your life; you say my client is a killer. Tell me about it. Tell me how he kills."

"I told you—he writes down their names . . ."

"So tell me the names of the last three people he killed."

I saw a flash of anger on Benny's face, there and gone in a second. I needed to build that anger in Benny. Amy's life depended on it.

"Tell me!"

Little Benny leaned forward, clenched his fists. "I do not tell. I tell only this murder."

"You made a deal and you got twelve years to serve. Yet you could have told the DA and the FBI a lot more. You didn't. Is that because you're still loyal to someone in the organization? Or is there more to this?"

Shifting in his seat, Little Benny pulled at his shirt collar, which must have suddenly felt tight around his throat. He ran his fingers around his neck before reaching for a glass of water.

"I don't know what the hell you're talking about," he said.

"Oh, you *do* know, Mr. X. You were caught red-handed at the scene of a murder. You made a deal. You gave the FBI my client, Olek Volchek, for this murder, correct?"

"Correct."

"But here you are today, under threat of death apparently, and you won't give any evidence about any other murders this man has either committed personally or had carried out upon his instruction. You didn't tell the police or the FBI about any other murders, and you've not done so today, correct?"

"Correct."

"You did not tell the FBI about my client's alleged drug empire?"

Volchek didn't react. I'd already told him where I was going with this.

"Your client doesn't face any drug offense charges, Mr. Flynn, but you're stipulating that your client has a drug empire?" asked Judge Pike.

"No, Your Honor. The prosecution has alleged that my client runs the Russian Mafia. It's safe to assume they don't sell cookies door to door."

Miriam had opened the case to the jury by alleging that Volchek was the head of the Russian mob. I hadn't objected at the time, but that part of her opening wasn't at the forefront of my mind; no, it was something else she had told the jury that gave me a shot. A long shot.

"Mr. X, you did not tell the FBI about my client's alleged drug empire, correct?"

The whole plan could come crashing down around me if the alarm went off now. I pushed Benny, trying to build a repetitive rhythm with the "correct" answers, bouncing my case off him like a ball, getting him riled up so that he answered in anger, without thinking.

"Correct . . . I—"

I cut him off. "That's right. You did not tell the FBI about my client's alleged drug operation, and you didn't tell the FBI about my client's alleged prostitution rings, correct?"

"Correct." The answer came in fast, even before the lightning-quick Pike asked if I was stipulating for the record that my client runs the best little whorehouse in Little Odessa. Moving around the defense table, I fixed Benny with a stare. He looked away.

"And you didn't tell the FBI about my client's alleged money-laundering operations, correct?" I said as I slowly walked toward Benny, cutting down the distance between us, building the confrontation, stepping into the kill zone.

"Correct," he said, his eyes skirting around the room.

Moving closer, we locked eyes. Benny leaned forward, a scowl on his face.

"You didn't tell the FBI about my client's alleged people-trafficking network, correct?"

"Correct."

Three feet between us. Benny visibly tensed the closer I got to him, as if he was getting ready to leap over the rail of the witness stand and choke me to death.

"You didn't tell the FBI about my client's alleged illegal arms dealing, correct?"

"Correct."

"You didn't tell them about these operations because if the defendant was running a criminal organization, the FBI would close it down and . . ."

Gripping the rail of the witness stand, I pulled myself up close to Little Benny, so I could get right into his face when I blew his dirty secret wide open.

"Then there would be no business for you and your brother to take over after this trial is finished, correct?"

"Correct."

As soon as he said it, he came to and shook his head. Pike dropped her pen. Harry let out a gasp.

"No. I mean, I don't know what you mean, you lawyer prick!" said Benny.

I whispered to him, "Volchek knows the truth," and he stood. I turned and put my back to the gallery. Benny pushed me away, but just before he grabbed my shoulders, my hands reached out to him, fast, soft. I stumbled backward but managed to keep my balance.

The guard put a hand on Benny, forcing him down into his seat. Pike started to bawl at Little Benny for getting physical with me. Miriam began protesting that I was intimidating her witness. But I held up a hand, stopping both of them. Before I wound up the cross-examination, I chanced a glance at Kennedy; he was paying close attention.

"My fault. I apologize. I have one last question. You've been in police and FBI protective custody since you got arrested. You've never been in public lockup. So when did you get word that the defendant put out a contract on your life?"

He hesitated. The question was strange to him. He knew, as a lifelong member of the Bratva, what would happen to him if he ever betrayed his boss.

"I didn't get word," said Benny, still a look of confusion on his face.

"So you never received a death threat?"

The question hung in the air. Benny sat back, snorted, and shook his head like I was the idiot.

"No. I did not receive a death threat. That is not his way. We know what will happen if we betray the *pakhan*—the penalty is death."

"Who else has the defendant ordered to be killed for betraying him?"

"I cannot say," said Benny.

That was it.

The key to the whole damn thing.

"Your Honor, in light of the witness's last answer, I have to stop the trial," I said.

The crowds gathered in the gallery instantly began to murmur, whisper, and protest. I heard the rear doors of the courtroom closing and Agent Levine working his way along a busy row of people, making for an empty seat on the right. Before he sat down, he nodded in the direction of Arturas, who sat only a few feet from me. It was a quick signal; a nanosecond and you would've missed it.

Kennedy missed it.

Arturas shifted in his seat, putting his back to the judge, and I saw him make a call. I couldn't hear the conversation, but the numbers he'd dialed were clear on the digital screen of his iPhone.

He was calling 911.

CHAPTER SIXTY-SIX

Pike ordered the jury out. Like most juries, they were getting used to regular interruptions in proceedings. While we waited for the jury to move out, I thought about Arturas making that 911 call. My guess was that Arturas just tipped off the cops that there was a bomb in the building, and I would've bet that he'd given them the precise location of each van and how much explosive they contained. Emergency Services deal with tons of hoax calls every day. It wouldn't take long for a flag to go up and the dots to be connected; the head of the Russian mob on trial for murder, the FBI protecting an important witness, the warrant out on my apartment, the explosives stolen from the *Sacha*. My best estimate gave me three, maybe four minutes before court security started evacuating the building. Arturas could've made that call earlier, but he'd waited until Levine gave him that nod. There could be only one thing behind that signal; Levine must've started the timer on the bombs in the basement. The next part of the plan relied on the NYPD being on the ball and calling for the emergency evacuation of the building. When the evacuation call went up and all hell broke loose, it would provide the perfect distraction for Arturas and his men to dive into the case, break out the automatics, and bust Benny free.

Judge Pike cleared her throat—no doubt readying herself to deal with yet another unnecessary interruption from the defense.

She took off her glasses slowly, put them on top of her notes, and folded her hands beneath her chin. As the last of the jury filed out, I winked at Volchek. He put his phone on the table, ready to use it.

"Mr. Flynn, I want you to be very clear about what you're asking. I suspect that you have a motion to nullify the anonymity of Witness X?"

"I'm not arguing that motion. The issue here is not anonymity; the issue is mistrial," I said.

Pike's eyebrows shot up. I slipped Kennedy's phone into my hand, ready to call Jimmy. The crowd picked up the scent of drama, and the hushed murmur began to grow into a choir of excited voices. Miriam sat forward, ready to fight back, and both judges exchanged concerned glances.

"You're going to argue a motion to declare a mistrial?" said Judge Pike.

"No, Your Honor." I turned to Miriam. "The prosecution is going to do that for me."

Miriam got up, her face a mixture of astonishment and disgust. Her neck had instantly turned red, and she was so pissed off she threw her pen into the air and let it bounce onto the floor.

"Your Honor," I began, "you just heard the testimony from Witness X—his sworn evidence is that he hasn't received a single death threat. Not one. The jury have been misled by the prosecution." I picked up my notes. "In her opening statement, Ms. Sullivan told the jury that my client was the head of the Russian mob and that her witness had been threatened. She said, and I quote, 'This man is living under a death threat.' It's here in my notes. I underlined it—twice. If the jury believed that Witness X was under a death threat because he was a witness for the prosecution in a trial where the defendant is alleged to be the head of the Russian Mafia, then the clear implication is that my client threatened him. We know now there has been no such threat, from my client or anyone else. I asked the witness directly if he received a death threat, and he said 'no.' The problem is that the prosecutor told the jury something very different, something that wasn't true."

I heard a loud thump as Miriam punched her desk. "Your Honor, the witness will state that he was part of a vast criminal organization, that he was a hit man for the Russian mob. It's abundantly clear what happens to snitches in such organizations."

"No, Your Honor, it is not. The witness has not given any evidence about this alleged organization. I made sure to cover that in my cross, and I gave him every opportunity to spell it out—drugs, prostitution, money laundering, murders. The witness told us nothing. He refused to give any evidence regarding the organization. There is no evidence before the jury of a death threat, and the witness denies receiving one. The prosecution has misled the jury and the court. Your Honor, we don't make the case that the DA's office deliberately misled the jury, but the misrepresentation by the prosecutor clearly prejudices the jury against my client." I turned to Miriam. "We're sure it was an innocent misrepresentation, and if the prosecution does the right thing and requests a mistrial, then I will encourage my client not to make a complaint of prosecutorial misconduct."

Miriam kicked her chair out of the way and stormed toward me, ignoring the judge's plea for her to remain seated. She knew I was right, and it was killing her. As a seasoned prosecutor, she knew Pike wouldn't risk letting the case go to verdict with a slam-dunk appeal point waiting in the wings.

"You bastard. What're you doing?" she said.

"I'm doing this for you, Miriam. You're going to lose this case. Pull the trial. Get a different handwriting expert and start over. I could've asked for the mistrial. But if you do it, you can sell it any way you want, make it look like the smart move because your expert got blown away."

She shook her head. "You're finished, Eddie. I'm going to make sure your client goes down next time. I hope you enjoy this because you're officially on the DA's shit list for life."

If this played right, I didn't want to have to answer questions about why I got my client a mistrial. By having the prosecution argue the motion, I'd created a little distance between me and the storm of violence to come.

Miriam adjusted her blouse, and without another word, she returned to her desk and began to address the court through clenched teeth. "Your Honor, in light of Mr. Flynn's point, I have no alternative but to ask the court to declare a mistrial."

She sat down heavily and folded her arms.

Benny sat pensively in the witness box, his fingers drumming on the rail. Arturas shifted forward on the bench, ready to dive into the suitcase.

Tilting his phone toward me, Volchek let me see the text message he'd typed. *Let her go.*

"Send it," I said as I called Jimmy, shielding the phone from view beneath the desk, waiting to see the indicator that my call had been connected. No one was looking at me—all eyes were on the judge.

Judge Pike closed her eyes for a moment and rocked back on her chair, oblivious to the reality that the life of my ten-year-old daughter rested on her decision.

Sighing heavily, she said, "I don't feel I have any other choice. Let's have the jury back, please, and I'll discharge them. I declare a mistrial," she said and began whispering with Harry.

The crowd boomed.

Volchek pressed the send button.

Jimmy answered my call. "Jimmy, he's letting her out. Go get her."

"I'm going for it . . ."

"Jimmy, wait until he sees the text . . ."

We got disconnected. I instantly hit redial. Pike was too embroiled with Harry to notice what I was doing. Not that it mattered to her. As far as she was concerned, the trial just died, so they were off the record.

The jury began filing back into court just as the room filled with the roar of an alarm.

The rear doors banged open, and a security guard rushed into the courtroom, shouting to be heard over the alarm. "We have to evacuate now. Bomb squad's orders."

The guard bent over and coughed before being swept up by the crowd. The screaming began, and the public gallery emptied in panic. People pushed and hit their way past one another, each person fighting for the doors. Miriam's team left their files and ran. Miriam didn't move. She was rooted to the spot, her eyes on me, her mouth open and her expression a mixture of horror and shock. One of her paralegals ran back, grabbed her arm, and dragged her toward the exit.

Kennedy sprinted to the panting guard, trying to reach him, but he was already leading the first wave of reporters into the hall.

Arturas dove into the suitcase.

This was the perfect distraction for the Russians. The whole building just got dumped into chaos, people climbing over one another to get out. I watched Harry shepherd Judge Pike through the door to her chambers.

Amid the panic, Volchek made his play; he climbed onto his seat, pointed at Little Benny, and screamed, "He's got the detonator. It's in his pocket!"

For a second, the screaming intensified. The rhythm of the alarm seemed to slow to a heartbeat, and all eyes turned to Little Benny. Arturas lifted his head from the suitcase and looked at his brother in amazement.

Benny shook his head and patted his pockets. The guard escorting him drew his gun and aimed it at Little Benny. Drawing his own weapon on Benny, Kennedy began shouting instructions. "Lie down! Down on the floor!"

Little Benny stood openmouthed, confused, as he patted his pockets and then, in his left-hand jacket pocket, he felt something that shouldn't have been there. As his hand stopped on the unfamiliar bulge, his expression turned to fear and he began to tremble. With one hand held up in surrender, he could not resist checking what was in his pocket, and as he drew out the fake detonator, his eyes found me and he made the connection. He held the fake detonator that Volchek had given to me in the conference booth, the same detonator that I'd broken open in that room and then sealed back together with a sliver of duct tape from the MP5's magazine, the same detonator that I'd planted on Benny when he'd pushed me from the witness box only moments ago.

Benny's surprise and sudden realization froze his body like a liquid nitrogen shower. The immediate, visceral beat of the alarm seemed to quicken again in that moment of shock and fatal hesitation. Volchek knew law-enforcement protocols as well as I did—when a suspect holds a detonator in his hand, you take that man down with immediate lethal force.

Kennedy opened fire, the guard a half second later, and Little Benny died with his eyes wide and confused.

Any chance of Volchek being retried for murder died along with Witness X. It was as good as an acquittal, and the only deal that I could've made with Volchek in return for my daughter's life. I heard a guttural roar from behind me. I didn't need to turn to know that it came from Arturas.

I spun around in time to see Volchek running for the door. Halfway up the aisle, he stopped and watched the remaining Russians pull on their coveralls and grab the MP5s from the case. Arturas was too busy with the large RC unit that I'd seen in the case. He had switched it on, hit a few controls, then dumped the remote control on the ground. Volchek wasn't about to wait around. He had his victory. He turned and fled. When Arturas stood to look for Volchek, the head of the Bratva was already gone.

CHAPTER SIXTY-SEVEN

Guns!" I cried and dove for cover behind the defense table. I leaned out a little, just enough to see that Gregor and Victor were wearing their coveralls and staring at the empty rifle magazines. The ammunition for each assault weapon lay underneath papers in the young lawyer's briefcase, which he'd abandoned in the conference room. Volchek and I had shredded each bullet from each and every magazine before repacking the case.

"Drop your weapons and get on the ground," shouted Kennedy, who'd seen the Russians trying to gear up. Agent Coulson joined him, his Glock trained on Gregor and Victor. There were no fresh cries from the crowd; the last of them had already fled through the doors.

The guard who had been security for Benny moved toward the Russians, his weapon extended.

My heart hammered in my chest as I tried calling Jimmy. He didn't pick up. I lifted my head, but I was too late to shout a warning.

"Don't move," said Levine.

He stood behind Kennedy and Coulson, his gun tracking both men. Kennedy and the younger agent froze. Shaking his head, Kennedy closed his eyes, lowered his head, and swore.

"Put the gun down or they're dead," cried Levine, shouting over the alarm at the security guard, who could barely hold his gun he was breathing so hard, terrified and full of adrenaline at having fired his weapon moments ago and killed for the first time.

"Levine, don't do this," said Kennedy, lowering his pistol.

"I'd prefer not to have to pull the trigger, Bill. I just hit start on two devices in the basement, and in twelve minutes this building will be rubble. If a rescue team ever does find your body, I'd prefer it didn't have bullet wounds. Drop your guns and tell the guard to do the same."

The FBI men slowly lowered their weapons to the floor. Dropping the useless MP5, Gregor marched over to the security guard and snapped the Beretta from his hand.

Footsteps beside me. I heard the metallic rattle from the harness around his waist—Arturas.

He picked me up by my collar and threw me down in front of the judge's bench.

"On your knees, hands behind your back," said Levine, and both Kennedy and Coulson obliged.

"You believe me now, asshole?" I said, but Kennedy couldn't meet my gaze. His eyes were locked on his weapon, sitting two feet from him on the marble floor.

Arturas backed away from me and pulled the detonator from his left pocket.

"You piece of shit. You made a deal with Olek. Don't worry. We'll find him. You're going to die today, lawyer. That's the price you pay."

He backed off farther, out of the kill zone.

For a few moments, everything seemed to happen in slow motion. My body felt electrified, hypervigilant, alert, and yet my movements were slow; my head pounded along with the rhythm of the alarm.

Gregor tucked the young security guard's gun into his belt, then casually broke the kid's neck with his huge hands.

The dirty fed, Levine, slammed the butt of his gun into Coulson's head and watched with some amusement as his partner keeled over.

Victor picked up Coulson's weapon and walked slowly toward the doors, making sure the room was clean.

That mortuary smile appeared on Arturas's lips as he watched me crawl farther and farther away from him.

He hit the detonator for the bomb that I'd carried on my back for a day and a half. Nothing happened.

That second of hesitation broke his smile. He hit the detonator again. The detonator that Harry had picked up last night.

Nothing.

"Kill them all," he said.

Instead of bringing the Beretta down on Kennedy's skull, Levine swept the weapon down and fired two rounds into his boss before taking aim at my chest.

I closed my eyes and saw my daughter lying in the grass in Prospect Park on a warm summer's day.

A shot.

I felt no pain, no warmth, no cold, nothing.

I opened my eyes and saw Levine standing still, the gun falling from his hands as a red mist evaporated beside his head. He fell forward, bullet wound in his neck, and behind him I saw the Lizard.

Instantly, the Russians ducked for cover.

At the back of the courtroom, the Lizard took aim at Victor with the Beretta that I'd left in the basement trash can. The blond giant didn't react quickly enough. His shots were wild, and the Lizard was deadly accurate.

The window behind me exploded. Shards of mahogany leaped from the prosecution table, three feet away, and I realized Gregor was unloading the security guard's gun in my direction. Scrambling to my feet, I turned and ran. Another shot hit the prosecution table, sending dust and splinters into my face.

There was no cover.

Nowhere to go.

I heard another gun kicking back, but I didn't dare stop.

My jacket got whipped around from a bullet tearing through the lining. The window was coming up fast. I sprinted the last five feet to the broken fourteenth-floor window and leaped through the last shards of glass only to be engulfed in cold New York air.

As I watched the breadth of the whole city come up beneath me, I prayed that I was one smart son of a bitch.

CHAPTER SIXTY-EIGHT

I screamed.

Some of the remaining shards of glass that clung to the frame cracked and splintered from the gunshots before they were swallowed by the endless sky.

And I fell.

For a moment all I could see was the top of the building and clear blue sky above as I dropped backward, my ass hurtling toward the concrete a quarter mile below. It seemed a lifetime that I fell, but it was probably two, maybe three seconds before my left shoulder exploded with pain as I hit the stage and my head smacked against the steel floor. White droplets of light seemed to appear and pop in front of my eyes.

The hanging scaffolding that held me had been specially constructed for the exterior refurb of the courthouse. It was one of the longest in the city, forty feet long and six feet wide. The steel cables that anchored the stage to the roof were as thick as my wrist and ran all the way to the ground. I'd remembered seeing the workmen on this stage before I'd entered the court yesterday and again this morning. I'd also remembered the coveralls with the built-in harnesses and the large remote control hidden in the Samsonite.

This was the Russians' escape route. While the NYPD cordoned off the courthouse and the street on the west side entrance, the Russians planned to quietly slip down the east side of the building on the steel stage in their rigger outfits, step into a car, and go, without anyone realizing they'd ever left the building. The cops and the feds would believe them dead, buried under the building when it blew. They would run and hide and take over Volchek's operation from afar. And no one would come looking for them.

The gunshots from the courtroom stopped.

I got up tentatively. The fall had caused the stage to shudder, and it began rocking gently. Holding the safety rail on either side, I got to my feet. The controls for the stage were locked, a key needed to operate the system. The stage wouldn't move. I'd guessed that the radio control that Arturas had briefly operated in court controlled the stage remotely.

I heard a shot blow out the window behind me; one of the four arched sandglass windows that had been in the courthouse from day one. I walked along the full length of the platform toward the broken window. A figure appeared on the window ledge.

He was breathing heavily as he threw a chair behind him. The same chair that he'd used to break the window. His robes were white with plaster dust. He coughed and almost fell.

It was Harry. He'd come back for me.

CHAPTER SIXTY-NINE

Careful," I said.

Harry wobbled and then gripped the ornamental masonry as the height hit him. I stepped onto the rails of the stage to boost myself onto the ledge. The gunfire in the courtroom started up anew.

The stage shook and juddered as Arturas landed on the steel platform at the opposite end. Arturas had leaped from the same window that I'd come through. He snapped his lifeline onto the platform's safety rail. The line extended from the waist and bolted on to a thick leather three-way harness sewn into the coveralls. Kneeling down, he put the remote control for the stage on the floor, slid back his false heel, and removed his knife.

"Take my hand, Eddie," said Harry.

"Lawyer," cried Arturas.

He smiled just like he had the day before, when we'd first met in the bathroom of Ted's Diner. That jagged scar that seemed to reach for his upturned mouth took on a pinkish hue in the cold air. He looked different, no longer the coolheaded killer. His eyes held a pain and longing for revenge. My head still rang from the fall. Blood trickled down my neck from a head wound, and I thought my shoulder and back would be bruised for a month.

"It's over, lawyer," said Arturas.

I backed away quickly as far as I could go, Harry's outstretched hand just within touching distance. Arturas stood maybe twenty feet away.

"I bet those coveralls are real heavy."

Arturas didn't acknowledge me. He began to move forward.

"I bet those suits are so heavy you wouldn't notice a couple of extra pounds."

He froze and slowly dipped his head.

His hands moved over his chest, his back, and then stopped when they reached the large pocket on his right thigh. Both Volchek and I had figured the large-sized suit for Arturas. I'd hidden the bomb in those coveralls as soon as I'd made the deal with Volchek.

I took the real detonator from my pants pocket, held it up for him to see, and said, "Smile at this, asshole." I grasped Harry's hand, leaped for the window ledge, and hit the detonator.

The ex–army captain pulled me up just as the stage fell. The blast cut Arturas in half, blew the shit out of the control panel, and then the stage bucked and shot toward the ground. As I got my knee onto the ledge and pulled myself to safety, I heard the groan of tumbling steel as it accelerated toward the empty pavement below. *Thank God NYPD evacuated the block,* I thought. The sound of the stage hitting the earth seemed to vibrate into my teeth, a terrible wrenching and crashing as the stage bounced and snapped.

"A little help here?" I turned from the window at the sound of Coulson's voice. He was carrying Kennedy's semiconscious body over his shoulder. Kennedy was breathing, barely, and it looked as though a vest had taken at least one of the shots. Tucking the Beretta into his pants, the Lizard jogged toward us and took the bleeding Kennedy from Coulson. The young agent looked a little unsteady on his feet.

"The big Russian's dead. He was the last," said the Lizard.

"Let's move," said Harry.

Everything had happened so fast, but even so, I guessed that at best we had six, maybe seven minutes to clear the building before the vans blew.

CHAPTER SEVENTY

The elevator plummeted toward the ground floor. We didn't have time to take the stairs.

The alarm seemed to mark the passing of every second with increasing urgency.

Shifting his feet to find a steady base, the Lizard hefted Kennedy so that the injured man's weight spread evenly across his shoulders. I couldn't control my breathing—a mixture of panic and sheer exhaustion. Coulson was still holding his head. Only Harry appeared calm, but I could tell he was really boiling with fear. His eyes never left the floor readout at the top of the control panel.

Harry silently mouthed the passing of every floor.

The alarm continued to thunder.

The seconds rolled away.

"Did Jimmy get her?" I said.

"I don't know," said the Lizard.

I tried calling him again, but there was no signal.

Please tell me you got her. Please . . .

The elevator stopped at the lobby, and we poured out. The entrance doors had been flung open, and I could see the last of the evacuees about two hundred yards away, hurtling toward the police cordon.

Coulson grabbed Harry's arm and yelled, "Run."

The Lizard flew past Harry. And we followed.

As we reached the court steps, we heard a voice booming at us through a megaphone. A cop stood maybe five hundred yards in front of us, his head poking around a blast barrier. We ran, slipping, down the steps. Blood from the dying agent soaked the Lizard's back and his pants, and he began to slide a little from the blood soaking his shoes.

Harry and Coulson went ahead of me, my pace slowing as I tried Jimmy's cell again, letting it ring as I sprinted for the barrier.

My lungs were burning, and even though we were clear of the building, I could still hear the alarm in my head, pounding away time. That relentless beat mixed with the sound of my heels hammering the ground as I ran, and my legs seemed to get slower as time sped up.

I was almost done, my breath gone, my strength gone. My head was screaming with pain. It took all I had to keep my legs moving, arms pumping—mouth open wide but unable to take in enough air.

We were close to the cordon now—fifty yards to go. I could make out some faces in the crowd through the gap in the blast barrier that had opened up to let paramedics through to help us. I searched the faces in the crowd, but I didn't see Amy or Jimmy.

Up ahead, the Lizard dumped Kennedy onto a waiting gurney that had raced toward him.

I redialed.

I was close now.

Coulson, Harry, and the Lizard reached the barrier and ducked behind it.

I was almost there when the call connected and I heard Jimmy's voice. "Eddie I—"

Then the world caved in.

The blast instantly deafened me. Like plunging suddenly into dense water. I had the sensation of being airborne, even though I didn't remember my feet leaving the street. My head hit the pavement, but I didn't register the pain, only the internal hollow sound of flesh and bony skull hitting the paving flags. I felt as though a cloud of foul gas and soil and brick had hit my throat and buried itself in my teeth.

Lying on the ground, I could see a terrifying cloud of black dust now stood where once there was a courthouse. As the building came down, a terrible roar shook the city, and although I couldn't hear anything, I felt that ferocious pounding of tons of crumbling brick. A thick smell of burning metal and old wood choked me, and I was engulfed in dirt, stones, and smoke. Before I passed out, I thought I heard Harry calling me over the screaming and the cacophony of a billion pieces of glass churning through the air.

And I remembered no more.

CHAPTER SEVENTY-ONE

I felt something warm and wet on my mouth. My lips were dry and the kiss was soothing.

With effort, I cracked open an eye and saw Christine's face, inches above my own.

It took me a second to realize I was in a hospital bed.

My wife pulled away from me. Her eyes were tinged with red, her face dirty with tears. She covered her mouth as more tears came, her fingers trembling. As she cried, she lashed out, slapping me in the chest and arms. I raised my hands gently, and she stopped and broke down, sobbing as she stepped away from me and shook her head.

When Christine stepped away, I saw a small figure behind her, someone asleep in the visitor's chair in my room. I'd never seen midafternoon sun as beautiful as it was that day as it played upon my daughter's hair. I stared at her for a long time, not knowing if the light came from the sun or from my daughter. She wore her little jacket that was more pins and badges than denim, a Springsteen T-shirt underneath, green jeans, and her oversized boots.

She looked so peaceful.

"You son of a bitch," said Christine softly, not wishing to wake our daughter. "She's so lucky. She could've been killed. You put her life in danger—you and that firm."

"I would never put her at risk. She's the most important—"

"But you *did*. When I think about what they could've done to her."

"Chrissie, I love you, and I love Amy."

"That's not enough, Eddie. Your life, your clients—it's too dangerous. I won't take that risk. It's not fair to Amy."

She stood silently, shaking her head.

"They weren't my clients . . ."

"I don't care. They took our little girl. And I'll never forgive you."

I couldn't answer her.

"I have to go tell someone you're awake."

She looked at our daughter, still asleep in the chair.

"She's exhausted. We're both tired, Eddie. You might as well wake her up. She's been waiting. I'll get the nurse."

Christine wiped away her tears with a tissue, turned, and left. I felt as though she was leaving more than just the room. She was turning her back on our marriage, permanently.

"Amy," I called.

She woke and ran to me. I held her as I had never held her before. I kissed her hair and together we cried. The pain in my back, my shoulder, didn't stop me from getting up and checking Amy, making sure she was all right—no bruises, no cuts, no scrapes. She didn't let me look at her for long. Her little arms grabbed my neck, and she held me as tightly as she could, enveloping me in her wonderful scent—a mixture of hair spray, pencils, denim, and bubble gum.

"I got you. I got you . . ." I repeated.

Eventually, she let me go, sat down on the bed beside me, and held my hand.

"Daddy, this might sound a little weird, but I want to get you a new pen," she said.

Taking her again in my arms, I told her that the pen didn't matter. I didn't care what inscription she put on a pen—that I was an asshole sometimes, but that I loved her completely and I didn't want to let her go. Ever.

I told her she didn't need to worry anymore.

I would make sure she was safe.

That night, I slept without the usual dreams of Hanna Tublowski tied to Berkley's bed. I was able to sleep that night without seeing her for the first time since I'd found her.

Within a week, I felt well enough to speak to Kennedy properly. He was in the room next to me, damaged and slowed way the hell down for a long time, but fixable and alive. Considering all that had happened, I'd come out of it pretty well; I had a bad concussion, four busted ribs, and some cuts and deep bruises. I told Kennedy my story but not all of it. Harry backed me up, like he always did. Kennedy apologized a lot and even helped out when the feds came from his office to interview me. Jimmy turned over the spray-coded million through his lawyer, keeping two mil for himself and one for me.

Harry came and secretly plied me with alcohol, which I drank without another thought, and we played cards in the evenings. But mostly, I had the best thing in the world.

I had my kid.

Couple of days later, Harry arrived to pick me up from New York Downtown Hospital and take me back to my apartment. He'd changed the locks and tidied the place for me. He carried my bag as I stepped carefully along the sidewalk toward his beat-up convertible. Just as Harry unlocked the car, I heard a horn. Across the street I saw a white limo. Olek Volchek stood at the passenger door, beckoning me over.

"Eddie, don't do it," said Harry.

My ribs sent a shot of hot pain into my body as I skipped through the traffic to the other side of the street.

"What do you want?" I said.

Volchek put his hands up and said, "I just wanted to know what you told the FBI."

"Don't worry. I told them Arturas planned the whole thing, that you were just as much a victim as me. You're clean. As much as I would've liked to send you down, I'm not stupid. I know that if I tell the FBI everything, you'll let them know about me arranging the hit on Severn Towers."

He smiled—only for a second.

"Good. I'm glad we understand each other. Don't ever cross me again.

We're about even. I say we leave it at that. Remember, I know where your daughter lives."

Another man, probably Russian, wearing black jeans and a black leather coat, got out of the driver's seat, walked around the limo, and opened the passenger door for Volchek. The driver was big, ugly, with a boxer's nose and small, black eyes. He looked at me like a Doberman looks at a burglar's ass. This guy was clearly employed to do a hell of a lot more than drive. Volchek was rebuilding the Bratva. Having this guy open the door for him was all about displaying his newfound strength, letting me know he was still in charge.

I took one step away, stopped, spun around, and called out, "Hey, one more thing . . ."

Volchek had one foot in the limo, and he half turned toward me, his driver still holding the open door.

Ignoring the pain that hit me with every breath, I got my balance and kicked the driver in the shin as hard as I could, sending him onto one knee. As I brought my foot down, I adjusted my stance, locked my hip, and threw a right hook. The punch sent Volchek's head clean through the passenger window. Grabbing the open door, I slammed it into the driver's punch-drunk face.

The boss of what was once the Bratva lay on the wet asphalt, tiny cubes of glass covering his torso, his hands raised to protect himself.

"That was for Amy, Jack, and his sister. You don't need to worry about the FBI. You need to worry about Jimmy the Hat. He still wants blood for his nephew. If I were you, I'd take myself and my big monkey here and get on a plane. And just so you know—we're nowhere close to even. My daughter has more security now than the mayor. Jimmy and I made sure of that. There are people watching her constantly, so you don't scare me anymore, asshole. If I ever see you again, or if one of your soldiers comes anywhere near me or my family, I will watch you die, slowly."

Cars and taxis skidded to a halt as I crossed the street to Harry's car. The judge rubbed his head and looked at me disdainfully, and when he spoke, his voice was soft and leaden with disappointment.

"That was stupid," said Harry.

And like most things he said, he was right.

CHAPTER SEVENTY-TWO

I'd been out of the hospital a month. Amy was beginning to readjust. She was still fearful and wouldn't go out on her own, but she was slowly coming around. Hopefully, she would go back to school soon. Jimmy's guys still watched over her and Christine, and no one had heard anything from Volchek since I'd laid him out on William Street. Amy and I talked on the phone every night at eight, but Christine refused to speak to me. I couldn't blame her. She also refused to let Amy out of her sight, so I got fewer visits—one every two weeks, for two hours, in my former family home.

Parking my secondhand Mustang on the corner, I got out and removed the leather duffel from the passenger seat.

The little house in front of me was a run-down two-story in a particularly poor part of the Bronx. The windowsills had all but rotted away, and even from the outside, I could smell the damp of the interior. I'd driven past that house many times. On each occasion, I'd lacked the courage to stop the car.

Not today.

Five past seven in the morning. The street was quiet.

I put the duffel down on the front step and rang the doorbell.

Footsteps in the hall.

I heard the rattle of door locks and security chains behind me as I opened the door of my Mustang and got in. I drove off as Hanna Tublowski opened her front door. She picked up the duffel and the letter that I'd placed on top of it.

I didn't want forgiveness. I didn't want her to tell me that it wasn't my fault.

I knew what I had done; I knew that I would never make that mistake again; I knew that there were bad people in this world and that as long as I played my part in the justice game and I remembered who I really was, those people wouldn't get a second chance to harm anyone else.

In my rearview mirror, I saw Hanna Tublowski drop the letter and open the bag, spilling some of her nine hundred thousand dollars onto the pavement. She looked up at my car as I turned the corner.

I put the Mustang in third and hit the gas.

ACKNOWLEDGMENTS

Without the passion, knowledge, and skill of my agent, Euan Thorneycroft of AM Heath, this book would not exist. He has been an editor, a mentor, and a friend. I would like to thank everyone at AM Heath for working so tirelessly to turn me into a published author. In particular, my thanks go to Jennifer, Helene, Pippa, and Vickie.

My thanks go to my criminally talented editor at Orion Books, Jemima Forrester, for all her hard work, keen insights, and abundant enthusiasm. Orion has been a joy to work with and my thanks and praise go to Graeme Williams, Angela McMahon, and the whole Orion team. Very special thanks go to Jon Wood, who is something of a hustler himself, at least on the pool table.

I would also like to thank Christine Kopprasch and Amy Einhorn, for giving Eddie Flynn a home in the U.S., for their skill and vision, and for their passionate advocacy for this book. Eddie could learn a thing or two from Christine and Amy. And a huge thank-you to everyone at Flatiron Books for their dedication and hard work. My thanks also go to George Lucas of Inkwell Management.

I'm very lucky to be represented and published by such good people.

To all my family, friends, fellow writers, and beta readers, especially Simon Thompson, Ace, McKee and John "the debacle" Mackell, thank you for your encouragement—it really meant a lot to me.

My biggest thank-you has to go to my amazing wife, Tracy, for putting up with me, believing in me, and for every little thing that she does for me and the kids, every single day.

ABOUT THE AUTHOR

Steve Cavanagh is a leading civil rights lawyer from Belfast, Northern Ireland. *The Defense*, his debut novel, was nominated for the British Crime Writers' Association Ian Fleming Steel Dagger Award for Thriller of the Year. In 2010, Steve represented a factory worker who suffered racial discrimination in the workplace and won the largest award of damages in Northern Ireland's legal history. He continues to write and practice law. He is married and has two young children.